# A MASTERY OF MONSTERS

# ALSO BY LISELLE SAMBURY

*Blood Like Magic*
*Blood Like Fate*
*Delicious Monsters*
*Tender Beasts*

# A Mastery of Monsters

## Liselle Sambury

Margaret K. McElderry Books

New York   Amsterdam/Antwerp   London
Toronto   Sydney/Melbourne   New Delhi

MARGARET K. McELDERRY BOOKS
An imprint of Simon & Schuster Children's Publishing Division
1230 Avenue of the Americas, New York, New York 10020
For more than 100 years, Simon & Schuster has championed authors and the stories
they create. By respecting the copyright of an author's intellectual property, you enable
Simon & Schuster and the author to continue publishing exceptional books for years to come.
We thank you for supporting the author's copyright by purchasing an authorized edition of
this book.
No amount of this book may be reproduced or stored in any format, nor may it be
uploaded to any website, database, language-learning model, or other repository, retrieval, or
artificial intelligence system without express permission. All rights reserved. Inquiries may
be directed to Simon & Schuster, 1230 Avenue of the Americas, New York, NY 10020
or permissions@simonandschuster.com.
This book is a work of fiction. Any references to historical events, real people, or real places
are used fictitiously. Other names, characters, places, and events are products of the author's
imagination, and any resemblance to actual events or places or persons, living or dead, is
entirely coincidental.
Text © 2025 by Liselle Sambury
Jacket illustration © 2025 by Tom Roberts
Map illustration © 2025 by Chris Brackley
Jacket design by Greg Stadnyk
All rights reserved, including the right of reproduction in whole or in part in any form.
MARGARET K. McELDERRY BOOKS is a trademark of Simon & Schuster, LLC.
For information about special discounts for bulk purchases, please contact Simon & Schuster
Special Sales at 1-866-506-1949 or business@simonandschuster.com.
Simon & Schuster strongly believes in freedom of expression and stands against censorship in
all its forms. For more information, visit BooksBelong.com.
The Simon & Schuster Speakers Bureau can bring authors to your live event. For more
information or to book an event, contact the Simon & Schuster Speakers Bureau at
1-866-248-3049 or visit our website at www.simonspeakers.com.
Interior design by Irene Metaxatos
The text for this book was set in LTC Metropolitan Pro.
Manufactured in the United States of America
First Edition
10 9 8 7 6 5 4 3 2 1
Library of Congress Cataloging-in-Publication Data
Names: Sambury, Liselle, author.
Title: A mastery of monsters / Liselle Sambury.
Description: First edition. | New York : Margaret K. McElderry Books, 2025. | Audience
term: Teenagers | Audience: Ages 14 up. | Audience: Grades 10–12. | Summary: While
investigating her brother's mysterious disappearance, eighteen-year-old August teams up with a
shapeshifting boy to infiltrate a secret society of monsters and those who control them.
Identifiers: LCCN 2024013680 (print) | LCCN 2024013681 (ebook) |
ISBN 9781665957366 (hardcover) | ISBN 9781665957380 (ebook)
Subjects: CYAC: Missing persons—Fiction. | Siblings—Fiction. | Secret societies—Fiction. |
Shapeshifting—Fiction. | Fantasy. | LCGFT: Fantasy fiction. | Novels.
Classification: LCC PZ7.1.S2545 Mas 2025 (print) | LCC PZ7.1.S2545 (ebook) | DDC [Fic]—dc23
LC record available at https://lccn.loc.gov/2024013680
LC ebook record available at https://lccn.loc.gov/2024013681

FOR THE OVERACHIEVERS
who thought you needed to have
everything figured out at eighteen.
You don't. You're allowed to
stumble, and crash, and burn. You're
allowed to still be figuring it out.
You're enough just as you are.

# AUTHOR'S NOTE & CONTENT WARNING

While this is a work of fiction, some of the topics discussed do exist in our real world. I've compiled a list of content warnings to help those who may need them. I've done my best to address everything here, but I keep an updated list on my website in case I am later informed of triggers that I may have missed. Please visit that site for the most updated information.

Death of a parent, death of a teenage child, fatphobia, mentions of disordered eating (restriction), dismemberment, drug and alcohol use, violence/gore, and a mention of suicide.

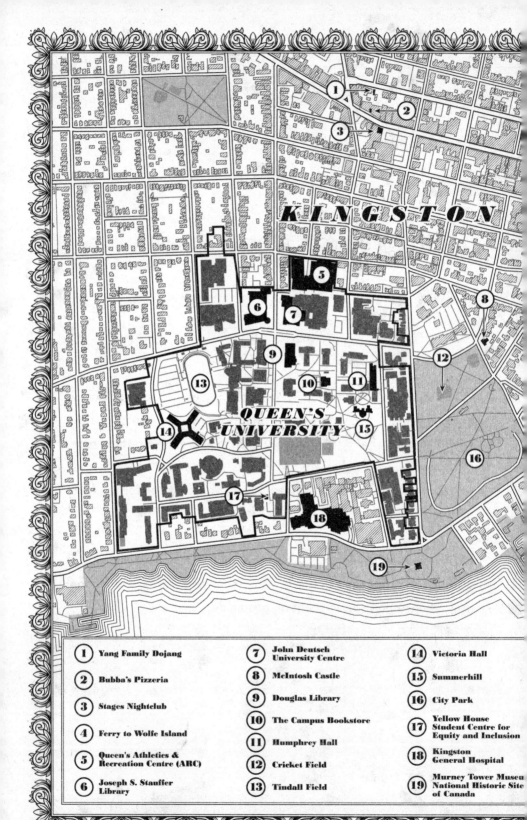

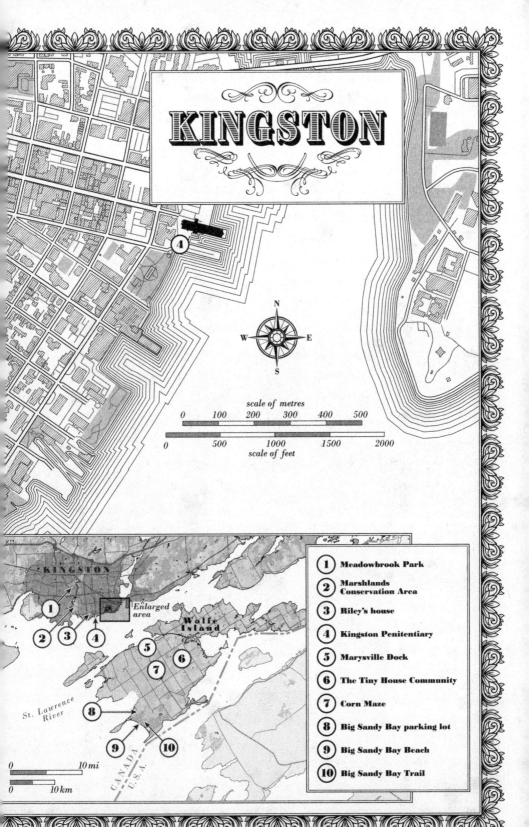

# PROLOGUE

Sammie should have realized she was too drunk three drinks ago. She stumbled behind her friends as they wound around bodies to the exit. Sweat slicked and slouched, mascara smudged. They hadn't chosen Stages because it was the best club downtown—it was probably closer to being the worst—but it'd had the shortest line to get in. The strobing lights flashed in hot pinks, electric blues, and neon greens, illuminating the galaxy glitter she'd spread on her face earlier. Only, she kept forgetting she'd put it on and had rubbed off a lot. She swayed as she walked, the motion gentle and soothing, like being rocked to sleep. It didn't fit with the stench of body odor and sour bite of spilled beer.

She pulled her phone out of her purse and opened the top message thread. Her own blue wall of text stared back at her. She flushed. The club was too hot, she told herself, unable to look away from her screen. She and Riley weren't the same. She knew that. Sammie didn't have this grand legacy, and she wasn't trying to prove anything to anyone. She wasn't a Historic. She just wanted to have fun. That was the point of university, wasn't it? You were supposed to party.

"Come on!" A hand gripped hers, and she jumped, dropping her phone. It clattered on the tile with a crack.

She closed her eyes and groaned. Once she managed to peel them open, she picked up the phone and stared at the shattered screen. A few swipes confirmed that at least it was still functional. Her friend kept apologizing to her and promising to replace it. She wouldn't. They were both broke. Sammie would just have to put clear tape on it and then beg her parents for a new one when she went home for reading week. More likely they would say she should replace it herself. Ask where all that money went. She stayed in Kingston over the summer specifically to work. Riley was meant to line something up for her. Instead, Sammie was left on read, unemployed, and burning through her student loan.

She trudged forward and pushed the door of the club open. Outside, people were leaning against the side of the purple building and spilling into the Metro grocery store parking lot. The summer air was cool, but she was still too hot. She walked through a cloud of weed and vapor smoke, batting it away with her hands and fluffing her curls. They were crunchy as fuck. Too heavy handed with product, Riley always told her.

Across the street, the black sign with the Bubba's logo gleamed. If Riley were here, they would have gone inside and split a poutine. Extra curds, extra gravy. Plus, two Cokes. Not Zero or Diet because they were supposed to be having fun. They would have made their way back to campus, arms entwined, on the edge of too full, snickering over some shit they were watching on Sammie's phone. Then fall asleep on

Riley's bed when they were supposed to be watching a movie.

She turned away.

"You should call Walkhome," her friend said. The same one who'd made her drop her phone. "We're gonna split an Uber."

Sammie scowled. She wasn't about to wait twenty minutes for the volunteers at Walkhome to reach her from their on-campus hub. None of her friends lived her way, but she would be fine. She waved off the pleas of the girls to find someone to go with her. When their Uber came, they gave up and got in. Riley would have added Sammie to the route, making sure she got dropped off first, even if that meant going in a different direction.

The shouts and gleeful screams from people on the street rattled in her skull. Sweat cooled on her arms and she shivered. She cut through the Burger King drive-thru and headed down Division Street. She'd promised to stay close to campus where there were lots of people around. She searched her purse for her vape pen, tried to click it on, and found that it was dead.

There was a laugh from across the road, and she followed the sound to a group she recognized from the Black student society. She searched among them for Riley, trying to spot her passion twists without any luck. When they looked over, Sammie ducked her head.

She didn't need them. Didn't need their obsession with Black excellence and their judging stares and their bullshit.

Didn't need Riley, either.

Sammie's foot hit grass, and she stopped, blinking. She'd already made it through campus without noticing and had started to cut across the open field by Biosciences to the park.

She was supposed to meet her secret admirer here hours ago.

She'd had to google "City Park" because she didn't realize that was what it was called. Not that she'd planned to come.

The only sounds were the leaves of trees and shrubs rustling in the wind. That and the rhythmic flapping of tent plastic from the few that had been set up all summer. Sometimes into winter, too. This close to the lake, the breeze was cooler. She let the chill roll over and caress her shoulders. If you accepted the cold, it wasn't as bad.

She stumbled forward, attempting to stand tall and walk in a mostly straight line. The swaying wasn't like being rocked anymore, more like being shoved from the side over and over, even after you'd begged to be left alone. There was one other person in the park, bathed in the shadow of a tree. Not smoking or playing on their phone or anything. Just leaning against the bark, a hood pulled over their head, hands in their pockets.

The person jerked to the side as if they'd been yanked by some invisible force. Sammie slowed to a stop, leg muscles tensed as though she were bracing for a fall.

The stranger hunched over, and their body began to get larger. Shooting both up and sideways at the same time.

Sammie swallowed, inching her phone out of her purse. Eyes darting between the person in front of her and the screen as she typed. She hit send right as she took a step away. Her heel caught in a crack in the sidewalk, and she went down. She cried out—from the pain or the shock of what she was seeing, she wasn't sure. She scrambled backward on her ass as the person became more wrong. There was no humanness to their shape anymore. There was only this grotesque *thing*, its mouth open to show pointed teeth the same iridescent white as the glowing moon in the sky.

Even in the dark, she knew that it was looking right at her.

Sammie's head spun as she struggled to get up, kicking off her heels and running through the grass in bare feet, taking no notice of the sharp sticks and rocks that stuck her. Everything kept tilting on its axis. She thought she was getting close to the edge of the park when the thing appeared there.

She whimpered and fled in the opposite direction. This park, there was something in this park that could help her. Her phone! Where was her phone? She must have dropped it, and she didn't exactly have time to make a call. *Focus.* She just needed to remember where the hiding place was. *Fuck! Where was it?* Tears leapt to her eyes. Had Riley seen her text? She couldn't still be ignoring her, not now. Riley would have known where to look. Riley would have remembered. Riley would have just fucking waited for Walkhome.

She kept searching, and the thing continued to circle her. It moved so quietly. She couldn't track it with her eyes. But it wasn't attacking. Her head was pounding, and she kept trying to search for the right spot. If she could find it, she would be fine. Everything would be okay.

Sammie fell to her knees in the grass, panting. Her face was soaked with sweat, glitter and makeup sliding down, a galaxy collapsing on her brown skin. She peered at the shadow looming in front of her, choking on her sobs. "What do you want from me?!"

The beast didn't answer.

She couldn't keep searching. She had to run.

Sammie made another desperate attempt to escape, this time darting toward the open field, not caring that it wasn't in the direction of home. She just needed to get away. She managed to make it across the baseball diamond, and when her feet touched the sidewalk, she smiled.

She had only a moment of relief before the pain began.

She had screamed at concerts, as she was reunited with friends, when her dad surprised her with a new phone before her first year. But she had never before screamed like this.

The sound burst from her lips, long and hoarse. Tearing at her throat, mixed with a whimper. It was strained and soft. Too soft for the violence of it. It was her best effort.

And no one heard it.

She fell face-first with claws raking down the back of her body. The monster ripped open her party dress, shredding fabric and flesh, and stained both with blood.

In her mind, she wasn't there. Wasn't lying on the dirty concrete, bleeding out.

She was in Bubba's, gravy on her lips, laughing at something Riley had said.

# CHAPTER ONE

Drunk girls are the best.

I grin at the one next to me, who winds her elbow around mine and shouts about what sort of guy she wants to marry and why he's very different from who she's going home with tonight. The other girls are discussing what drinks they're going to get and what club they want to go to after this one. They offer me hits off their vapes, and we make a joke of blowing the vapor in each other's faces. When asked my name, I tell them August, and they laugh because that's the month it is. I act like I lied and tell them the name on my ID instead. After five minutes together, we're besties.

When we get to the front of the line, we show our IDs together. All nineteen. Legal. The girls make high-pitched pleas to skip cover, and the bouncer rolls his eyes and waves us in for free.

Inside, Stages is packed wall-to-wall with people jumping and dancing to the blaring music from the DJ, screaming over each other to be heard. It's busy for a Friday night in the summer. Usually it's slower around this time since the students aren't back yet. But I guess this DJ is popular enough to draw a crowd. The tiled floor is sticky under my feet, and the crowd smells like too many combinations of perfume, cologne, and body spray, coalescing into one sharp, stinging scent that I can't describe as anything other than "strong."

I tell the girls that I think I saw someone I know. They head to the bar, and I wait in a corner and scroll on my phone for a few minutes. By the time they have their drinks, they've forgotten me. That's the best part about friendships with drunk girls—they're short-lived. I head by myself to the bar, where I'm asked for my ID again, which I flash. And it passes because it *is* real. It's just not mine.

Another great thing about drunk girls is that they lose their IDs all the time. And no bartender is going to look too long with a throng of people pushing and shoving, trying to get served. It's a Black girl on the card, and I'm Black too; good enough.

My phone vibrates, and I fish it out of my jeans pocket. The screen lights up with Bailey's name. I ignore the call and check a text from Jules. He's sent me some cheesy video of a dog using a voice command system to swear at its owners. This loser. He's wanted a dog forever, but we moved too much so our parents always said no. And now he's in the dorms and still can't have one. So he's pining over other people's pets. I send back a video I watched on the walk over that's not dog related because I wouldn't be caught dead unironically sending that shit.

I accept the doubles of vodka-cran from the bartender, balancing the four plastic cups by squishing them together and holding the outsides between my fingers. I bring them to one of the small stand-up tables, where I down them all, one after the other, as fast as I can. I know it's going to be a good night because I can taste the liquor. I order one more round before I finally go out onto the dance floor.

I don't recognize the song, but it doesn't matter. I can dance to anything. I just close my eyes and move. My braids sway and brush against my shoulders and back. I'm getting used to the changes in my body, bigger hips and butt, and folds of skin that weren't there before. When I open my eyes, I spot a guy wearing the Queen's standard club uniform of a hoodie and jeans watching me. It's the sort of attention I always get when I dance. I was sure that wouldn't be a thing anymore now that I look different. There were a lot of things I was convinced I would lose that never went away. Not for that reason, anyway. I close my eyes again.

Time slips and curls around me. Dancing for myself means that no one else matters. It's like being in my bedroom when I was ten, music blasting, hairbrush in hand, feeling like a rock star. Nothing in the world could deny me that truth in that moment. I could be anything and anyone. I wasn't pretending. I just *was*.

I could do this for hours.

And I do.

I'm downing another round when the bartender makes last call, and everyone surges to the bar. I've already got the spins. But I'm still pressing the plastic cup to my lips and slurping the drink down. I stopped tasting the vodka a while ago. I fumble with my phone and there are dozens of messages now. Not just Bailey. Jules, too. I finally notice the time at the top: 1:45 a.m.

*Fuck.* I missed the last ferry to the island.

I tip the rest of my drink into my mouth and stare at the other three I ordered. In the crowd, I spot the girls from the line. They aren't bothering with trying to get to the bar and are lounging against the railings that line the upper level. But they look over when I call them, squinting as they try to place me.

I remind them of my fake name and recognition spreads across their faces. I say, "My friends had to leave so I have extras. Do you guys want them?" My voice is slow. It's like everything I say is coming out on a delay.

The girls share a moment of hesitation. I get it. I'm technically a stranger. But they must decide I'm trustworthy enough because they accept the drinks and continue our conversation from the line like no time has passed. I start to move away from the table when one of them grabs me. "Do you have someone to walk home with?"

"I'm fine. My brother lives on campus." Jules isn't expecting me, but he'd never turn me away. He'll make his "serious face," which has never been that serious with me, and fold anyway. He always folds. Unlike Mom, who's an iron wall. Sometimes Dad can be won over. Not anymore, though. He's reached his limit with me.

The girl bites her lip. "Shit. We're north of Princess." I vaguely understand that she's talking about Princess Street, the main road that goes through downtown. Most students live south of it, closer to campus. "You're a student, right? I can call Walkhome."

"I'm not a student," I snap. I don't mean to, but I do. I do a lot of things that I don't mean to now. Everything used to be reined in so tight, but not anymore.

I can't tell if she's too drunk to notice my tone or if she doesn't care. "This girl went missing like a week ago walking home. You shouldn't go alone."

"I'll call a friend outside."

I don't think she believes me, but she lets me go. I leave the club and start walking, trying to find my way back to campus. The streets are filled with people milling around in groups, making their own way home, their loud conversations and shouts filling the air.

I'm unsteady on my feet, but I'm wearing my Docs, so it's better than if I were in heels. I like to think that Mom would prefer it. She always asked where I was going dressed like I was grown when I wore heels and tight dresses to parties with my friends.

Now Mom is gone. Has been for almost nine months. And I don't have friends anymore.

I look around, trying to remember where Jules's dorm is. Queen's University looks like someone took a chunk of Victorian England and dropped it in the middle of a town in southern Ontario. There are cobblestone streets and ivy crawling up brick buildings. It has winding paths through campus lined with trees and carefully manicured shrubs. But there are enough modern touches to remind you of where and when you are. Still, it's hard for it to not feel like its own world apart from the rest of Kingston. Especially with so many of its buildings clustered in one place.

And unfortunately for me, I've found myself on the outside of that cluster. I'm at the edge of campus next to a park. It's basically abandoned. There are tents set up, but even those are quiet.

I yank my phone out of my pocket and search for a bench. I find one and drop onto it, resting my head on my knees and squeezing my eyes shut. Even with them closed, the world is still spinning. I force them open and send a text to Jules asking where his dorm is. I want to lie down. And throw up. Actually, I can do that last bit right now.

There's a crunch behind me. Feet on grass. I don't bother looking back. It's a park. I doubt I'm the only person here.

"Hey, you doing all right?" I turn toward the edge of campus,

A MASTERY OF MONSTERS

and a group of three guys are ambling toward me. But not from behind where I heard the sound. They're the same white guy in different fonts. All wear jeans and hoodies. Do these guys never look at each other and think they should maybe diversify their wardrobe?

"Fuck off," I say.

The guy who spoke reels back. "Wow, okay, chill. We're trying to be nice, right?" He nudges his buddies.

"She's not worth it," one of them says, without bothering to lower his voice.

I stand to leave and sway in place. Their ringleader grins at me. His hoodie is navy blue with QUEEN'S embroidered across the chest. "Why not? She looks like she'd be down to f—"

I'm not thinking about it. Not really. I reach under my shirt to the belt at my waist, pull the knife there from its holster, and throw.

Mom would say, "Don't give yourself time to doubt what you're doing. If you have to spend time on anything, use it to make sure your aim is good."

And then I would hit the bullseye. Because I was the perfect daughter until I wasn't.

The guy screams as the blade clips his ear and embeds itself in the tree behind him. "What the fuck?! You bitch!"

I'm still drunk, but the experience sobers up his friends, who start pulling him away. Though he's fighting them.

I reach behind me again. "I have more."

I don't. But they don't know that.

The ringleader spits at me, the saliva falling short and leaving drool on this chin. He and his friends flee to campus, and I lean forward and puke like I've been wanting to, tasting cranberry on my lips. I spit for good measure. Mine comes out of my mouth properly because I'm not an amateur.

That sound again. Footsteps on grass, but not from the direction the guys went.

I shuffle back to avoid my puddle of sick and look around the park. There's an empty children's playground, tents, and trees, spaced out enough that you can see most of the area from wherever you stand. It's how I spot the person hunched against the shadow of a tree, their head bowed. Slowly, they look up at me, a black bandanna wrapped around the lower half of their face. In the dark, it's too hard to see their features, but there's no mistaking the careful way they close one eye, lowering the lid with perfect precision, and then open it.

A wink . . . as if the two of us are sharing a private joke.

"There she is!" a voice shouts, and I jerk toward the sound. The guys from before are coming back, and this time they're followed by a man in a bright yellow vest that says CAMPUS SECURITY.

That is less than ideal.

I sprint across the park to the baseball diamond, trying to put as much space as possible between us, then dart toward the residential area, spying a house whose white barn-style doors are cracked open. I take the opportunity, slipping between them and ducking into the small garden area, shutting the doors behind me. The walls around it are stone, so I can't see what's happening, but hopefully that also means they can't see me.

I turn around, meaning to try to sneak out via another entrance, but the motion throws me off balance, and I vomit again.

"You're trespassing. We have you on the cameras." I jerk my head toward the boy leaning against the side of the house. He stands with

A MASTERY OF MONSTERS

his hands tucked into the pockets of what I think are actual silk pajamas. His skin is a smooth and rich brown, and he towers over me, his curls short and lined up with a fade that looks fresh. Meticulous, even. The guy's built like a football player—stocky in the arms and thick in the chest and stomach. Perched on his nose are a pair of oversized circular glasses. His whole look is manicured. Like even in the middle of the night, he's considered his whole ensemble.

The worst part is that it's working for him. He's like a hot librarian jock hybrid.

And I just threw up in front of him.

In a bid to leave with whatever dignity I have left, I return to the barn doors, peeking through them. The guys and security have disappeared as far as I can see. My phone vibrates, and I fumble to get it out of my pocket. Jules sent me a pin. I open it and realize I'm on the other side of campus from where he is.

I push against the gate.

"Did you seriously come in here, casually expel the contents of your stomach, and now you're leaving without saying anything?" He waves at the cranberry-colored puddle soaking into the spaces between the patio stones.

I shrug. "Sorry?"

He rolls his eyes, then glances over my shoulder. "You shouldn't throw knives at people."

"You shouldn't throw knives at people," I repeat in a mocking voice. His jaw drops. "Obviously! It's too late now. How did you even see that?"

He points at the cameras mounted on the side of the house. "We have monitoring. They saw you and sent me outside in case you proceeded toward the property. Also, why are you acting like you couldn't have just *not* thrown a sharp projectile at someone?"

I thought security cameras could only see things at short range. What sort of high-tech 50x zoom shit does this guy have? Fucking rich people. "Are you going to report me or something?"

He just stares for a moment. Finally, he shakes his head. "I would suggest avoiding the park."

"Planning to." If security decides to come back, that's where they'll go, and so that's the last place I want to be.

"Be careful," he adds as he turns back to the house.

"You can keep your concern." I leave, letting the white barn doors slam shut behind me.

# CHAPTER TWO

The correct dorm is Victoria Hall. It's a massive gray six-story structure that's not anywhere near as picturesque as the buildings along University Avenue. There's a boxiness to it, and from the front viewpoint, the left and right sides slant inward at a diagonal. Since it's summer, the place is deserted. The only people still here are students like Jules who stay over the break. I avoid the main entrance, instead going to the one at the side per Jules's text instructions.

I wait, leaning against the wall under the overhang until the door is shoved open.

Jules scowls at me. "You're drunk."

"Surprise!" I say, throwing my hands in the air.

When my brother frowns, his already angular jaw becomes sharper, and the narrowing of his eyes has a strong effect with his thick brows. He's always had the look of a strict military leader. But he's as soft as the molten core of a chocolate lava cake and somehow sweeter in disposition. In comparison, I'm more like a cake left too long in the oven, obviously a failure but kept on the counter for a while because it hurts to throw away something you've worked that hard on. Every once in a while you take a taste, and the dry, rough texture reminds you not to try that again.

Jules ushers me inside, and we walk to the elevator, where he makes a point of crossing his arms and sighing. He's doing that thing where he presses his lips together so hard that they ripple, like crumpled paper.

Mom has the same look when she gets mad. I only made her look at me like that once.

The last night I saw her.

On Jules, the expression doesn't have any threat behind it. He's more putting on a show than anything, so I know he's displeased. He got the same things from our parents that I did: Dad's obsession with academic performance, and Mom's vague expectation that we be "better" in a way that wasn't understandable but something you still wanted to achieve.

We never asked that of each other. It was an unspoken rule of our upbringing. We didn't need to be perfect when it was just us. We could be whatever we wanted. We'd complain about the classes we hated that we took anyway because they were the "right" ones, or we'd skip Mom's extracurricular training exercises and go waste time at the mall.

And the additional rule that Jules followed was that if I messed up, he covered for me.

I glance at him out of the corner of my eye and then away.

Throwing up twice made me feel better, but it hasn't gotten rid of the spins, and now the taste of vomit clings to my mouth.

We get out of the elevator, and I follow Jules down a series of corridors until we reach a hallway that splits in two, one set of rooms in one hall, and another set in the second one. Jules goes to the left. We pass a common room, where a few girls are sitting on a couch that looks like it was brought in from someone's front lawn.

The atmosphere of the whole space is like being in an apartment building that hasn't been renovated in years but has high rent because it's in a nice area.

We stop at room 416, which Jules unlocks to let me inside.

"Bathroom?" I ask.

"Across the hall. Hold on." He goes into the room and rummages in a drawer before handing over a new toothbrush and an unopened box of mini toothpaste. Overly responsible, as always. "Wait. Pajamas." He digs around in his closet and tosses me one of his T-shirts and a pair of shorts.

I go to the bathroom and brush my teeth, wash off as much makeup as I can, and change. I come into the room and kick off my Docs and dump my clothes by the door. Jules's bed is raised so he can store things underneath, so I have to basically climb onto it and scramble to the side closest to the wall, cocooning myself in the sheets. Meanwhile, he stays standing, arms still crossed over his chest.

"You couldn't have texted Bailey back?" he asks.

Here we go.

He doesn't give me a chance to hop in. "She was worried. And I called her once you texted me, by the way. In case you cared."

"She's not my mom," I mumble.

Mom is gone. And the thing is, when you've been missing for almost a year, people assume you're dead. I don't want to be one of

18     LISELLE SAMBURY

them. I refuse. But I also can't keep looking. Can't keep pasting up posters and shouting on socials. Begging people to share and repost. I want Mom to be a scar. Something I carry with me and always remember, with the hopes of it healing well enough to barely notice it one day. Instead, she's a scab. And every time I try to find her and fail, I rip the dry crusted skin away, exposing the pink injured bits underneath, and have to wait again for it to start healing. But it never finishes. Because the instant a bit of it forms, it's torn away again.

"No, she's not Mom, she's our aunt, and you live with her, and she cares about you."

"We hadn't spent more than a weekend together until this summer." Me and Jules were born in Kingston, but our family left when I was four and he was five to accommodate Mom's job in consulting. I never understood what the work was, just that it required us to change apartments frequently enough that we didn't often see anyone else in the family. Including Dad's little sister.

"I'm not trying to guilt you," Jules adds. "I'm just saying."

And I know he is. Unlike our parents, Jules has never decided who I should be and then shoved that image onto me. He's the only person who's ever pushed me to do what I want. Be who I am. Not only when it's just us. All the time, with everyone. And I never listened to him. Because I wanted to do everything our parents wanted. My friends wanted. And in the end, it didn't even matter. Everyone ended up disappointed, so why bother? If anything, speeding up the process would have saved us a lot of time. Bailey will figure that out eventually. And then she'll leave too.

Jules leans against his desk. "Do you really want to spend every weekend coming to the city to blow your paycheck clubbing? Not

A MASTERY OF MONSTERS

to mention that you're only seventeen. You're two years too early for that."

"Hardly."

I have a late birthday, just like him despite my summer month name. I'm basically eighteen.

I close my eyes and pretend to sleep, facing the painted brick wall. I didn't ask Dad to drag me from Toronto and dump me on Bailey. Jules was lucky since he escaped to campus. And of course, Dad is too busy working at the college. I don't know what he thought ditching me was going to do. Everyone is doing their own thing, so I'm doing mine.

Jules says, "Can you at least not wander around at two in the morning? It's not exactly safe behavior."

"Sorry I tried to exist as a girl and didn't have someone around to protect me because I'm so weak and vulnerable."

I don't open my eyes to see Jules's expression, but I can picture it. His mouth opening and closing, the furrow of the brow, maybe even an eye roll. "It would be unsafe for *anyone* who was alone! What if something happened to you?"

"It didn't." Nothing I couldn't handle, anyway.

"I get not wanting to just do what Mom and Dad want. I'm legit happy you're finding your own way. But does that have to mean throwing away everything that you worked hard for? I know they pushed it, but I genuinely thought you wanted to go to Queen's."

I shrug.

"Is any of this making you happy?"

I open my eyes, and turn to face him, grinning. "Don't I look happy?"

He shakes his head. "Be serious."

I spent my whole life trying to live up to what they wanted. I studied hard for things I didn't care about. I kept up an active social life with "friends" who didn't know me. I recorded and tracked everything I put in my mouth and ate things I didn't like so I would look the way people wanted me to look. I hadn't enjoyed any of it. I hadn't been happy.

But I didn't want to ruin the delicate ecosystem of our lives.

And none of it mattered in the end.

Because the one time I tried to do something for me, Mom had given me that *look*. Like she didn't know me. And then she left and never came back. A lifetime of being perfect undone because of one disappointment.

There's no point to it. To any of it.

I don't know why Jules doesn't realize that. He's kept it all up and what does he have to show for it? He's got the job of looking after first years in the dorm while the second years like him become legal and party even harder than they did last year. "Why didn't you move off campus with your friends?" I ask, turning the spotlight on him. "Don't all the second years do that?"

"I wanted to stay on campus."

It's then that I notice my brother's room, which I haven't seen since I last visited a couple of weeks ago. He's usually so neat, but now there's all this random shit shoved under his desk, and papers sticking out of his drawers, and a laundry heap exploding from underneath the bed. "Why?"

"Stop trying to deflect. We're talking about your life. I'm trying to help. Just like Bailey, and like Dad, whose calls and texts I know you've been actively ignoring."

"What's he going to do? Kick me out of the house?" I pause and pretend to be shocked. "Oh right, he basically already did that."

Jules rubs at his face. "I know he isn't perfect—"

"Understatement."

"But he and Bailey are all we have now. If you don't want him in your life, cool. But if this is an attempt to push him away because you're struggling like you tried to do to me, then why not stop? If alienating yourself from him isn't what you want, why are you trying to make it happen? I don't want you to live your life so afraid of losing people that you never let anyone get close again."

"You're here, aren't you?"

"Is just me enough?"

"It's not that serious," I say.

Jules sighs. "Where were you tonight, anyway?"

"Stages."

He makes a face. "No, when you got lost. You said you were in a park. Which one?"

"How am I supposed to know? It's a park."

"And nothing happened, right? You didn't see anything strange?"

"Some pervert winked at me."

"August."

"Nothing happened!"

Jules lets it drop. He moves to the door and flicks off the lights. "I'm gonna sleep in the common room so you can have the bed. Come get me if you need anything."

I grunt, and he leaves.

The spins die down enough that I can sleep.

In the middle of the night, I wake up to search for water and, of course, Jules has a bunch of bottles in his mini fridge. I chug one. Then I go through his desk drawers until I find it. Our special pen.

I rip a piece of paper out from his printer and write, *Sorry*. The ink fades in seconds.

Mom gave us each a pen. She's always liked this sort of shit. Magic tricks. Little mysteries wrapped in pageantry and secrets. She'd leaned close and whispered how it worked. How the words disappeared on their own and how to make them come back. Me and Jules oohed and aahed. We loved learning with her.

If only she'd shared the secret of her own disappearing act.

I stumble into the ARC the next day at eight a.m. The Queen's Athletics and Recreation Centre building is huge, with modern glass balconies and cafeteria-style seating. It holds not only a giant athletics center but also a pharmacy, small grocery store, and a Queen's owned and operated coffee shop in addition to the franchised fast-food places.

When I walk in, I send a dog video to Jules in case he doesn't find my note.

I drag myself through the employee entrance for Tim Hortons and duck into the utility room to take out a fresh uniform— unflattering black pants paired with an equally unflattering gray-and-red polo. They're supposed to be for new hires only, but I wasn't going all the way back to the island to get mine.

I grab a hairnet and put it on the bun that I twirled my braids into that morning. Then I strap on a visor, which I often try to "forget," but my manager is strict about us wearing them. Speaking of, she comes around the corner and spots me right after I sneak out of the utility closet, giving me a quick once over.

She must not notice that I took a new uniform because she just says, "Bagel bar for you."

If I had the energy, I would cheer. Working bagel bar means I'll be facing away from the customers, mindlessly making sandwiches, wraps, and yes, bagels. Instead of working cash or having to stand in the front and run coffees. I drank a bunch of water and took some of Jules's Advil before I left, but I still have the edge of a headache. Dealing with the general public would make it worse.

Thankfully, Saturdays tend to be slower, especially in summer. I work silently for the first couple of hours before more staff come in, including Cam and Janey, the two other Black girls who work on the weekends. They stand in the doorway to the work area, laughing with each other before Janey goes on cash and Cam joins me on the bagel bar. I focus on my work.

I need money to go out, that's all. No point in socializing.

I used to have an allowance, but Dad stopped that. He claims it's because he doesn't have the extra money, and maybe he doesn't, but it feels like a punishment.

He didn't so much as make a Facebook post when Mom disappeared. Just sat at home, waiting for the police to do something. And the day before he dropped me off with Bailey, he was on the phone to someone. Talking about Mom.

Only, he didn't say she was missing.

He said that she left.

In one way, I understand why he would think that. My parents had what I assumed was a normal relationship. They weren't particularly affectionate, but they'd settled into that sort of family tie where I couldn't imagine them ever splitting up. Divorce was something couples did when they had problems. And Mom and Dad never had any. Dad moved when Mom said we had to, and he didn't even seem bitter about it. He always made it out like this big new adventure, even though it meant he had to start over at another college and further decrease any chance he had of getting tenure. I assumed that meant he loved her more. If anyone was going to leave, it would be her, not him.

But in another way, in the most prominent way, I can't understand how he thinks that could be real. That she'd left without intending to come back. She must have planned to come back. There was a reason she hadn't. And none of us knew what it was, but that didn't mean it didn't exist.

When the authorities decided they couldn't help anymore, Dad accepted it without complaint.

And that's the man whose calls I should be answering? Who's supposedly trying to help me?

Help me do what? At least when I gave up looking, I owned it. I didn't change the narrative to suit me.

Dad can keep hoping, but the old August is gone, and she isn't coming back.

# CHAPTER THREE

I toss my hairnet in the garbage as I walk out of the employee entrance after my shift. My phone vibrates, and I tuck myself into a corner to check it. Meanwhile, Cam and Janey come out from behind me, laughing at something on Cam's phone, their heads pressed together. The center is busier now that it's a more reasonable hour to be awake, and students filter in and out with backpacks or lounge at the tables. As my coworkers reach the exit, they're stopped by another Black girl. She's giving them some sort of pamphlet as she tosses her waist-length passion twists over her shoulder. The girl has this almost obnoxious modern hippie look—gold septum ring, a shirt with an ungodly amount of tassels, and a half dozen rings on her fingers.

I look at my phone again. Texts from Bailey asking if I'm coming home for dinner, which I guess I will be. And one from Jules telling me to text Bailey back. I send her a simple *yes*. I'll go to the island . . . eventually. Midway through my shift, I realized that I didn't have my knife anymore. It took a bit of piecing together of my memories to figure out where it could be. I know I went the wrong way and had been in a park. I threw my knife at someone, which wasn't great, but it happened, and then I ran away.

I pull my hair out of its bun, shaking the braids out. The knife had better be where I left it. I head toward the exit. By then, Cam and Janey are gone, but the girl handing out pamphlets is still there.

She shoves one at me. "Hi! I'm letting folks know that the Queen's Black Student Society is accepting new members." My eyes are drawn to one of her many necklaces. It stands out because it doesn't have pendants or charms like the others, and the chain links are larger than I would expect given her style. Every other piece of jewelry around it is small and delicate.

I switch my gaze to the sheet of paper. Why is she advertising a club in the summer instead of waiting until fall when all the freshmen will be here? "I'm not a student."

"Too bad," the girl says, actually looking upset. Then she glances over my shoulder and frowns. "Do you know that guy?"

"What?" I turn around but can't see anyone I recognize. "Probably not. Like I said, I don't go here."

She nods, her eyes narrowed. "Okay . . ."

"Right . . ." I walk out of the building, shaking off the interaction. Campus isn't busy, but it isn't empty either. Classes are still held during the summer, and there are always enough students around. I go left since I remember that the park is around this end of campus.

It looks different during the day. For one, there are a lot more people. The tents still seem unoccupied, but there are couples walking their dogs, students heading to campus, and some kid on the

A MASTERY OF MONSTERS

baseball pitch throwing a ball around with his dad. Still, I know this is the right place.

I examine the trees, looking for my knife. The more I search without finding it, the faster I walk, and the tighter my jaw clenches.

"Look who it is," says a voice behind me. I turn to see a group of three guys. They look a couple of years older than me. Not first year students. Maybe second or third? "Told you she'd come back to the scene of the crime."

I ignore them and continue my search.

"This bitch," one mutters.

I freeze. I try to remember what happened last night. I threw the knife at someone . . . fuck. I look back at the guys, and a twinge of familiarity strikes me. That girl had thought someone was looking at me in the ARC. It could have been this guy and his friends.

"Can I help you?" It comes out sharp with attitude, the way I want it to.

The main guy gestures to his left ear, which is wrapped with gauze. "Yeah, how about you fucking pay for this?"

"We have free health care."

"You got jokes, eh?" He advances toward me with his friends.

I look around the park, but people are purposely veering around us.

I swallow and plant my feet. I need knives. Without them, I'm going to get the shit kicked out of me. My eyes dart between the trees, searching for the one with my blade. I've often thought about carrying the whole set on a chest holster, but it's risky enough to have one concealed on me as a Black person. Never mind a dozen.

"Is something wrong?" I turn, and there's a Black boy approaching

28                                    LISELLE SAMBURY

us. He's tall and thick. I look over to the three guys, who stiffen as he approaches. They're skinny, and the tallest one isn't much bigger than me.

It's good the boy is built like that because nothing else about him is intimidating. He wears tan slacks and a burgundy polo with a dark brown sweater-vest overtop. It's *summer*. Who wears a sweater-vest in summer?

The guys look at him and then at me. I grin. "Not so eager now that the odds are more even, are you?" I reach behind me, knowing full well there's nothing there, and the guys flinch.

"Forget it," the leader says, and they walk away from me and the boy toward campus.

My shoulders drop, and I let out a slow breath. I look around the space again. The knife. I go back to searching, and a laugh sounds behind me.

"Oh, thanks, I guess." I throw to the boy over my shoulder. That's clearly what he wants. He's shockingly cute given the way he dresses, but digging for a thank-you for being decent? Big ick.

He says, "The words I was looking for were 'Sorry I threw up and then ran away without offering to help clean.'"

"Uh, I doubt that. You're a literal stranger."

His mouth drops open. "You seriously don't remember?" He points toward the baseball diamond. "I live over there on the corner across from the courthouse. White fence leading into the patio area. Brick house with green trim. Any of this ringing a bell?"

I squint at him, trying to place his face or remember any of those details, and shrug. "Nope."

He sighs and rummages around in his pocket, pulling out a knife. *My* knife.

A MASTERY OF MONSTERS

"That's mine." I stalk toward him and reach for it, but he pulls it out of my grasp, holding it high above his head.

"I'll be straightforward because I do try to be a gentleman when I can."

I fake gag. "Oh my God, did you really just say that?"

He continues as if I haven't spoken. "I need to ask you some questions, and I'm not giving this back until you answer them. It's in your best interest to cooperate. Let's start with a name. You are . . . ?"

I drop my arm and take in his wire-rimmed glasses and leather loafers. This dude dresses like a seventy-year-old man while looking like the sort of football player whose only job is to tackle people. Which is enough to intimidate those other guys, but I'm built different.

My phone dings with an alarm. It shouts, *MUST LEAVE FOR FERRY NOW*. "Shit," I mutter. "Give it to me. I'm going to miss my ferry."

"Ferries come every hour. Also, in case you didn't catch that earlier, I was asking for your name."

"I want to take the ferry that comes *this* hour."

"A woman of mystery, are we? Wonderful. Well, I haven't been to the island in a while. I'll come with, and you can answer my questions."

I don't want to entertain this guy. But I also want my knife, and I'm not naive enough to think I could take it from him otherwise. Also, my headache has come back, and Bailey is supposed to pick me up from the dock. If I'm late, she'll tell Jules, and I'll get yet another lecture about how poorly I treat our aunt.

I sigh, and the boy grins.

I refuse to say anything on our walk to the bus stop, nor on the actual bus ride, and then again nothing as we wait to board the ferry.

Meanwhile, Virgil—his name, which he helpfully supplied—has no problem filling the quiet with talking. Dude even has an old man name to go with his aesthetic. And his last name is apparently Hawthorne, which only adds to it. When I ran away last night, he went and got my knife, since he saw me throw it on the security cameras. I thought icing him out would make him give the knife back to me, but it hasn't.

I drop onto one of the seats on top of the ferry. Most of the space on the vessel is taken up by cars and trucks as people from Wolfe Island head home after a day of working on the mainland. It's only twenty minutes, so it's convenient. It's free, too. It just sucks when you miss the last one and get stuck in Kingston.

Virgil is in the middle of droning on about how much he enjoys the breeze off the lake when I finally say, "What do you want from me?"

He smiles. His teeth are unnaturally white. Like he grew up wanting to be in a Crest commercial. Judging by his attire, I don't think it's entirely outside of the realm of possibility. "A name would be great."

"August Black. Make a joke, and the first thing I'll do when I get my knife back is throw it at you."

"I can assure you that I'm not pedestrian enough to mock someone's name. Nice to meet you. That wasn't so bad, was it?"

"Get on with it."

"I'm curious about how you accurately threw a small knife when you were so drunk that you literally forgot about meeting me, and how you managed to put enough force into it to embed it in a tree." His expression loses the easy mirth it had before. "It's not exactly the work of a beginner."

"I have practice." I shrug. "Aren't you glad you came all this way for that?"

"Remains to be seen. You practice throwing knives?"

I slouch in my seat and stare out at the water. From here I can see not only Kingston but some of the Thousand Islands. In the distance, the largest of the islands, Wolfe Island, is marked by the dozens of tall white wind turbines on the land.

I glance at Virgil's pocket, where the knife is hidden. The first time Mom put a knife in my hand, I stared at her in wonder. Jules already had his, something that I spent months being jealous of. And here was mine, finally. She wrapped her fingers around the hilt and turned me toward a tree in our yard. She'd painted a series of circles on it for a makeshift target. "The trick to this is a sharp knife and accuracy." I nodded like I understood what she meant. I thought I had. I let it fly for the first time. It hit the tree and fell to the ground. But it hit within the smallest circle. Mom beamed at me, an unrestrained sort of pride. The kind that said I was the daughter she'd wished for. I would have done anything to make her look at me like that again.

I still felt that way, even on the night when I'd had enough. She'd gotten so intense about drills suddenly. Wanting me to keep going through them past dinner. I was exhausted, and all I wanted was to escape to Rachel's place and hang out with my friends. It was the last party of the year. Once December hit, I would be busy studying for exams. This was my one chance to relax before the pressure of acing all my midterms hit. Mom wasn't having it. She kept pushing for more. You grind a knife too hard past the point of sharpening, and you ruin the blade. I'd let her go too far for years. I was already dull and worn.

I insisted that I was going to go out. That was when she gave me that look.

Jules got on Mom for getting on me, and I left while they were still arguing, walking the forty minutes to Rachel's place on foot. I did everything Mom asked of me, and the one time I wanted something for myself, it was unacceptable.

So that night when she called, I didn't answer the phone. And come morning, she was gone.

The last and only time I had disappointed her. Nothing I'd done before mattered. All the times I had met her expectations and been that good girl were washed away in a single moment.

I narrow my eyes at Virgil. "Why does it matter to you if I can throw a knife? You want to start a darts league?"

"I'm looking for someone capable with a certain set of skills."

I laugh. He doesn't.

"I'm not the one." I don't care what this guy wants from me. I'm here to make money and spend it drinking and dancing until I physically can't anymore. Soon, Dad will stop trying to call. Bailey will wear out at some point. Jules will be here, but school will start, and he'll get busy. He'll have less time to be worried, and barriers to my lifestyle will drop to none.

The ferry docks, and I say, "Maybe don't make a habit of following girls home."

"Oh, I'm not done yet."

"Really? Because I am. Give me my knife." I hold out my hand as people walk past us to exit the ferry.

Virgil stands and follows them, forcing me to trail after him, gritting my teeth the whole time.

The dock at Wolfe Island lets you out into Marysville, a quaint

A MASTERY OF MONSTERS

section of the island with a general store, a few restaurants, and a museum. Some of the houses and businesses are painted in bright pastel colors, adding to the sweet small-town charm. It's easy for tourists to get out on foot and explore the instant they step off the ferry. Or to rent bikes and spend the day cycling along the island trails. As me and Virgil exit, there is, as usual, a line of new cars waiting to get onto the ferry as the old ones go past.

I can always spot Bailey's car waiting for me. It isn't hard because it's an offensively bright yellow Honda Civic. This woman paid money to get that wrap on it. But it isn't there when we walk out.

Instead, a red Ford F-150 truck comes around the corner with Bailey in the passenger seat and Izzy behind the wheel. Izzy's long dark hair is tied up in a ponytail while Bailey rocks her usual fro. I can see dandelions peeking out from it. Jesus, she's cheesy. Mia, Izzy's fifteen-year-old daughter, is in the back, eyes glued to her phone screen.

"Your mom?" Virgil asks, nodding toward them.

I scowl. "Aunt. She's like thirty; how would she be my mom?"

"Some people have kids young, and I don't know how old she is."

"Here's a tip," I say, looking at him sideways. "Does your mom look like that?"

"My mom's dead."

Great. Awesome.

He continues, "Both my parents died when I was little. I don't know what they would have looked like older."

I turn away because I don't want to apologize.

I walk toward the truck, and Bailey says, "We're gonna do a barbecue at Big Sandy Bay." She looks over my shoulder at Virgil. "Does your friend want to come?"

"We could use the help carrying everything," Izzy adds. I don't know much about the woman except that in 2020, she started the tiny house village on the island where Bailey lives, and she's Mohawk. Which is positive, at least. If it were run by a white guy, it would 100 percent be a cult, and Bailey honestly seems susceptible. Technically, Izzy's husband, Jacques, is white, but he pretty much defers to her for everything, plus he collects comic books and plays the harmonica. Nothing about that screams cult leader material. The Levesques overall seem like decent people.

I motion at Virgil with my hand. There's no way he wants to get looped into a barbecue. I try to keep my wrist low because I don't want Bailey to see the knife exchange.

Virgil says, "I would love to help! I haven't had barbecue in forever."

"Really?" I shove the words out of my clenched teeth.

Virgil grins. "*Really.*"

And so I get in the back seat with the boy who's extorting me.

A MASTERY OF MONSTERS

# CHAPTER FOUR

Big Sandy Bay is part provincial park and part beach. Though I would ideally not even be here, I understand why they wanted the help carrying everything. It's a fifteen- to twenty-minute walk through trees on a dirt path to get from the parking lot to the actual beach. Bailey, Izzy, and Mia will go ahead of us with the lighter items to get the food started. Jacques is already at the beach setting up the grill and chairs. Meanwhile, me and Virgil will bring up the rear with the heavier coolers of drinks and ice.

Mia slides next to me, tucking her dark hair behind her ears. She's pretty in a way that's powerful. Like she could get anyone to do anything for her. Big brown doe eyes, long lashes, thick shiny hair, and warm brown skin. "He's cute," she whispers.

"I am *not* interested," I say, as if I hadn't made the same observation earlier.

She tilts her head to the side. "Then why are you on a date?"

"We're not on a—" I pause and lower my voice, attempting calm. "Not a date."

"If you say so," she singsongs, collecting a cooler from her mom.

My aunt's eyes linger on me as she leaves with Izzy and Mia, and I look away. I'm not in the mood for a conversation and she isn't good with confrontation. Guess that runs in Dad's family.

They hadn't packed the drinks with the bags of ice yet, so that becomes Virgil's and my job. By the time we finish cutting open the bags, distributing the pop between the coolers, and locking up the truck, my aunt and the Levesque mother-daughter duo are way ahead of us.

The open path narrows as we walk it, the trees becoming denser, crowding in on the sky and cloaking the area in much-appreciated shade. Unfortunately, it does nothing to help the humidity. The air is so heavy that I feel like I could stick out my tongue and lap up the moisture. I swat at the mosquitos and gnats buzzing around my face.

"So," Virgil says, as he pulls the cooler without any physical effort. "Where does one learn knife throwing?"

I don't want to play his game, but this is getting old. All being stubborn got me was him following me here. "It's circus arts stuff. My mom did it when she was younger, so she taught me and my brother a bunch of it."

"Circus arts . . . Can you clarify what that entails?"

"We learned knife throwing and combat, slacklining, gymnastics, swordplay, sometimes magic tricks, that sort of thing. I'm not, like, an expert in anything, but I'm pretty good at it all. It was just for fun." That's how Mom sold it. An enjoyable set of hobbies. Though sometimes she was so serious about it, like we were going to compete, but she never signed us up for anything. She demanded perfection in everything. Even our casual pastime.

Virgil stops on the path. "I'm sorry, circus arts, like Cirque du Soleil, right? Since when does that include knife combat and swordplay? Even being generous and assuming some kind of movie circus with sad elephants and lions, that's far-fetched."

"It's *artistic* combat and swordplay." I wave my arms around. "Like, you make it pretty and stuff."

"And what exactly makes it pretty?"

"The way you move, I guess."

His eyes soften, like he's speaking to a small child. "Oh my God, you're *naive*."

"Fuck off." I restart walking and leave him standing there. I know it's weird. It was why I never mentioned it to my so-called friends, who already thought my mom was strange. One was even convinced that Mom had, like, stalked him. Or was checking up on him or something. They're full of shit. It just took me longer than it should have to realize.

"Sorry," he says, catching up with me. "You have to admit it's a unique set of skills to share with children. What else did she teach you?"

"Basic survival skills, which is responsible parenting, by the way."

"Of course. I wouldn't know because my parents are dead."

Fuck, I'd already forgotten.

Virgil opens his mouth, then stops. He stares at the trees like he's looking for something. His lips flatten into a line. "Get off the path."

"What?"

The trees shake across from us. Rattling from the trunks to the top branches, and expanding outward, like something is pushing them. Bending the bark to its will.

He yanks both his and my cooler off the path into the trees. Then he lays down on his stomach and motions for me to do the same.

I don't move. "What are you doing?"

A low growl sounds near us. I jerk my head around. Someone's dog? I'm about to search through the trees for it when Virgil pulls my foot out from under me. I shoot toward the ground but catch myself in time, getting my hands out in a bent position and landing softly.

I kick him in the face for good measure.

He grunts, and when I look back, he's brought his hands up just in time to block the blow. I scowl. He grins. "Great reflexes," he says.

The second growl comes, and this time, I do see something.

And it isn't a dog.

It lopes forward on two furred legs, at least six feet tall, its arms tucked up to its chest. Its eyes are huge and bulging from a thin face with giant ears. It looks like a horror movie version of the Easter Bunny. The proportions are twisted and odd, and when its mouth opens, the signature buck teeth I'd expect of a rabbit have sharpened points.

I blink like the more I do it, the more likely it is that this thing will disappear.

A fine tremble rushes across my body, stamping its little feet and ripping up goose pimples.

Its ears twitch, and it turns to where we lie. Virgil swears, muttering for me to stay down and not move. But he's too late. I'm already standing.

A MASTERY OF MONSTERS

If Virgil expects me to be a good girl and listen to him, he'll have to get used to being disappointed.

The thing's lips stretch into a perfect arched smile. It's a sight I don't expect I'll ever forget.

It charges at us.

Virgil shoves me out of the way, and I tuck and roll, scrambling to get my bearings. "Give me the knife!" I shout at him.

"Run away!" he shouts back.

The thing charges at me again, hopping over Virgil like he's not even there. But in what feels like an instant, Virgil is back in front. Fast. Too fast. The monster head butts him, and he flies into a tree with a grunt. It tilts its head, regarding me.

I rush to Virgil and tug my knife out of his pocket.

Groggy, he mutters, "*Run.*"

"You're barely conscious, so you kind of need me, and also, there's no point in running." It only took two attacks for me to realize that this thing wants me. I raise the knife in my trembling hand. I'm trying to think of everything Mom taught me. Attempting to anticipate its movements, its plan. But it's a fucking deranged animal. I don't even know if it has one.

But if it wants me dead, why would it wait until I've recovered to attack? Why not go for the kill?

I don't have time to guess its motives.

I throw the knife, aiming for those big brown eyes. The thing attempts to dodge, but it goes the way I expected. To the right. There's no space for it to go left. And I threw the knife just off course enough for it to sink into its eye.

The beast screeches and bats at the blade. It falls out, and I dart forward to retrieve it, skirting between the thing's muscular legs.

Which I realize is not the greatest idea when one of those legs shoots backward at me.

Somehow, Virgil is in front of me, and he takes the brunt of the kick, digging his heels into the ground and managing to stay upright. How is he so fucking fast?!

The mutilated rabbit snarls at us and then pauses, freezing, its ears perked. Then, as quickly as it came, it darts away into the trees.

I'm panting and gasping for air as if I weren't breathing at all before. Like this is my first time trying it out.

Virgil whirls on me. "What is wrong with you?! What would possess you to do that? I said to run!"

"If I'd run, it would have chased me."

"And I would have stopped it!"

"Would you? Because you kind of seemed like you needed my help. We had a better chance of survival working together."

"You could have gotten yourself killed! Do you not have any impulse control?"

I do. I just choose to ignore it. "And if I'd left, *you* would have gotten *yourself* killed."

Virgil stares at me, open-mouthed.

I ask, "What was that thing?" *And what are you?* Is a question I decide to hold back. Priorities.

He shakes his head, then retrieves both coolers and brings them back onto the path, dragging them toward the beach.

I follow him because what else am I supposed to do? When we reach the edge of the tree line, he drops the loads. "You have your knife. I'm leaving."

"I thought you needed my skills?"

"I do, but I don't need what comes with it. I need someone

with focus and drive, who isn't going to jump into danger for the sake of it."

"Me jumping into danger saved you, if you didn't notice. Where's my thank-you?"

He turns away. "Thanks, and goodbye."

I step forward. "Wait! You're not going to tell me what that was? What if it comes back? It was targeting me."

"I'm going to deal with it. You'll be fine."

I scoff. Yeah, because that vague proclamation fixes everything.

But Virgil's apparently done listening to me, because he doesn't stop walking.

I caress the knife in my hand, looking at the steel handle with Mom's initials engraved in it. I don't need him. I defended myself well enough. Even gone, Mom's still protecting me.

When I go to the barbecue, I help with the cooking and brush off the questions about my "friend."

I keep an eye on the tree line and make sure my hands are hidden as much as possible so no one can see that they're still shaking.

The next day, a girl on Jules's floor finds his door unlocked with a note in his room saying he's decided to leave. Leave Queen's. Leave Kingston.

And apparently, leave me.

Me and Bailey are suffocating each other. Her house isn't helping. It's tiny on purpose. She had it built to be two hundred square feet. A hundred on the main floor that houses the kitchen, a micro-sized bathroom, and the small living area, and then another hundred in the two loft areas—one which makes up my bedroom and the other hers. Except it's all open. The only interior door is to the bathroom. As I sit in my "room," I can see her across the house in her own, typing something on her laptop. We say nothing to each other.

It's been like this since Jules went missing last Sunday.

I could go outside. The tiny house community is on a few acres of land. But I don't want to be outside right now. Not alone. The landscape is pretty much flat farmland as far as you can see, not many places for the spawn of Satan rabbit to hide, but still. I keep looking over my shoulder for it, but it hasn't appeared again.

So now I have to be here with Bailey.

I stare at my phone again. I've been doing it a lot in the last week. I look at the text that I sent to Jules about a weird animal coming after me. I didn't know how else to word it without seeming completely unhinged. Part of me hoped he would text back knowing about some random animal species that I didn't. Or suggest I hallucinated the whole thing, which I could get behind with some encouragement.

But he hadn't responded.

He'd left.

I grip the phone in my hand and think about throwing it over the ledge of the loft. It's tempting, but Dad wouldn't get me a new one. Instead, I reach for the letter I found in Jules's stuff. The university packed up everything he had, and me and Bailey went and got it. I tore through it all, looking for any sort of clue, and this is the only one I have.

Something from these people called the society for something-something, a long name that I've never heard of and couldn't find on Google, saying they can help Jules with his "current circumstances." It was sent in February. He never mentioned anything like

A MASTERY OF MONSTERS 43

this to me. And if it was junk mail, why would he keep it?

I set the letter on my bed, and when I look up, Bailey is staring at me. She gives me a small smile. I look down.

I sigh when I hear the creaking sound of her moving. She walks from her loft to mine, pausing to sit on the top step leading into my area.

"Hey," she says, playing with the rings on her fingers. "You don't have work today? I thought you always do Saturday mornings."

"No." I do. I just decided not to go when I woke up.

"Heard from Jules?"

"No." I bite the inside of my cheek.

"I'm sure he'll—"

"He wouldn't have done this. He wouldn't have left without telling me. He wouldn't not text me. He wouldn't drop out of school."

He wouldn't do what Mom had already done to us.

Not to me.

I yank the note out of my pocket. The tiny piece of paper that the police didn't even bother to take because it meant there was no case. After all, it's his handwriting. Even I can see that.

It's bullshit. Even when I'd tried to shove him away, Jules had stayed when no one else would.

Bailey makes this pathetic sad face at me. "August—"

"Can you drop me at the dock?"

"... Yeah. Okay."

On our way to the car, Mia comes out of her house dressed in a pair of shorts and a T-shirt, her long woven purse around her shoulder and a hockey stick in her hand. Given the lack of ice currently, I assume it's for indoor hockey. "Are you going to the dock?" she asks.

"Yup," Bailey says. "You want a ride?"

"Please!"

I groan.

Bailey side-eyes me. "Be nice."

I don't have any issue with Mia. She's fine, as far as fifteen-year-olds go, but I want to sit in the car in silence. Now she and Bailey will talk the whole time.

Which is exactly what happens. I let Mia have shotgun, and for the whole ten-minute drive, they talk about her intramural floor hockey league—she'll switch to ice hockey in the winter—and some dinner thing that she wants to plan. I tune out and lay my head against the window, then practically sprint out of the car when we stop.

"August!" Bailey calls.

I force myself to turn around.

"If you want to talk, I'm here. I know we haven't gotten to spend a lot of time together, but I'm always available. I can do things other than give you rides."

Dad said something similar before. Jules, too. "I'm fine."

I leave and stand in line for the ferry, arms crossed and foot tapping. I don't have a plan. But at least partying in Kingston will distract me for a while. If I play my cards right, I can probably crash a pregame, too.

Mia says, "She's trying to help."

"Yeah, I know." I light up the joint I stole from Bailey. She thinks she's slick with where she hides them.

Mia eyes me. "Did you steal that?"

"No, it's mine."

"You definitely stole it."

I pull the note out of my pocket and look at it again. I took the letter too, but it's more confusing. This, at least this is Jules's words.

A MASTERY OF MONSTERS

45

*I need to get away for a while. I'm fine. Don't look for me.*
*—Jules*

I hold my lighter to the note, smiling as the flames eat the paper. Until I notice the words appearing on the other side.

The joint falls out of my mouth, and I drop the lighter as I scramble to stop the fire. Of course! Of fucking course! The invisible ink. I flip the paper over, and a new message appears, written in small, cramped letters.

*I know this won't make any sense to you, but I am serious when I say this: Monsters are real. Monsters are real, and dangerous, and they are here. From that text you sent me, you've already seen one. I wish I could tell you to run, but unfortunately, they might follow. Instead, use everything Mom taught us to keep yourself safe. Bailey and Dad, too. Don't do anything that might put you in danger. Stay away from the parks and forests, anywhere with tree cover and no people, especially at night. And if you hear growling or snarling, RUN. Someone's already been hurt, and I don't want you to be next.*

*Don't search for me. The best way for you to stay safe is to stay away.*
*—Jules*

Monsters, plural. As in, there are more things than the cursed Easter Bunny running around?! I swallow and lick my lips. And Jules knew about it. He disappeared the same day that monster had come after me. Maybe even because I'd texted him about it. And I was right, it had been coming after me specifically, but why? And why did it leave without finishing the job?

*The best way for you to stay safe is to stay away.*

If everything was fine, he wouldn't have left in the middle of the night without even saying goodbye. He wouldn't warn me away from trying to find him. He would have had time to explain what's going on.

"What's up with the paper?" Mia attempts to peer over my shoulder, and I crush the note in my fist.

"Shut up. I'm trying to remember something."

"So fucking rude."

*Someone's already been hurt, and I don't want you to be next.*

The last time I went out, what did that girl say about me walking home? Some other girl had gone missing. Yes! Like, the week before or something. I shove the crumpled note into my pocket and yank out my phone, Googling until I find her.

*Nineteen-year-old Queen's second year student Samantha George went missing in early August and was last seen near City Park.*

I look up which park that is on Google Maps. It's the same one I walked through. Where that dude winked at me. But there wasn't any monster there.

Or there wasn't any when *I* was there. But Jules . . . He wanted to know where I was that night. He was worried.

Worried about monsters.

And I recently met someone who knew exactly what that thing at Big Sandy Bay was.

The ferry's bell tolls as it pulls up to the dock.

Suddenly, I have a new destination in mind.

# CHAPTER FIVE

Unsurprisingly, I didn't get a good look at Virgil's house when I was drunk, and even if I had, I wouldn't have remembered. But he did a thorough enough job of describing it when I was sober that I was able to find it. It's a literal castle in miniature form. The house has an immaculate yard with bright green hedges, neatly trimmed trees, and a paved walkway up to the front door. And the main front section looks like a chess piece. A rook. But if it was covered in thick green ivy and tacked onto an already existing house. It's like a quaint cottage mixed with a medieval castle. And it feels on-brand that Virgil lives in a place like this.

I go to the front door, which has an intricate metal design over the wood and a brass knocker that I lift and bang down because when else will I have a chance to use one?

Shortly after, the door opens, and an East Asian–looking girl appears. Her black hair is loosely tied back from her face with a white ribbon, and she wears a cream blouse with the sleeves pushed to her elbows and tweed pants. It's a similar aesthetic to what Virgil rocks. "Yes?" she asks.

"Um . . . I'm looking for Virgil . . . ?"

She studies me for a moment, and then a grin breaks out on her lips. "Oh, you're *August*." I scowl. There's something teasing to the way she says my name, but I don't know her like that. And it makes me wonder what she knows about me. "Come in!" She waves me inside, and I step over the threshold. "Shoes off, please. Slippers over there."

The entryway is a small octagonal room with yellow patterned wallpaper that looks decades old, and the space is decorated with antique furniture and accents. I take off my shoes as instructed and set them next to three other pairs. I pick the black cloud slides.

As I'm putting them on, I notice the brown ones the girl is wearing and that her left foot is made out of something other than skin and bone—rubber, maybe. I look away so I won't be the asshole who stares like I've never seen a disabled person before.

She smiles as I straighten. "Welcome to McIntosh Castle. I'm Corey."

"August," I say. "But you already know that."

"I was hoping I would get to meet you." She tilts her head and regards me. "He said he told you to run, and you didn't."

I stiffen. He told her about that thing we fought. "I don't like to back down."

"Good. That's what he needs. The worst possible partner would be someone who encouraged this self-sacrificial thing he insists on."

My brow raises. "Partner?"

Corey moves on like I haven't said anything. "I have a patron to deal with right now, so you can follow me into the sitting room, and I'll fetch Virgil."

I trail after her into the hallway. We pass several rooms on the main floor, many of which are devoted to books. Some have tables inside while others more prominently feature winged armchairs and fireplaces. We go into one of those rooms, where a white man is sitting with a cup of tea. He looks like he could be in his mid-forties, with curly, gray-flecked brown hair that goes to his shoulders, a mostly trimmed beard and mustache combo, and tortoiseshell glasses. I notice he's wearing a Hawaiian shirt and try to keep the judgment off my face. He seems like the sort of guy who strikes up conversations with strangers in grocery stores.

"Sorry, Bernie," Corey says. "I'll get the books now." Of course, a dude who wears shirts like that would prefer to be called Bernie instead of Bernard. She turns to me. "And I'll grab Virgil for you."

I sit next to the man and pull out my phone so I'll have something to stare at. I know Mom would think it was rude, but she isn't here to stop me. The couch is stiff like no one was ever supposed to sit on it, and I shift, trying to get comfortable.

Despite my conversation avoidance tactic, Bernie asks, "New student?"

"Uh, no, I don't go to Queen's."

"Ah." He nods to himself. "I used to teach there. I'm on a sabbatical now. Health reasons. They have wonderful libraries, but I love coming to borrow from this collection. It's special."

"Right . . ." I glance at the doorway, willing Virgil to show up so I can stop being engaged in small talk.

"If you don't go to Queen's, does your family live here?"

"My dad teaches at St. Lawrence." I know he would rather work at the university, but the college had openings and Queen's didn't. "My mom is missing." I always add this now. I don't want people thinking that Dad raised me by himself or that I have some terrible relationship with my mom. That I'm not mentioning her because of something she did. Though, she did leave. And we did fight before that. But if she'd come back like she was supposed to . . . I guess I don't know. What would have happened? Would I have stayed the old August, or would the new version, the one who disappointed her, have appeared anyway?

Bernie's smile slips off his face. "I know what that's like. Family is the most important thing, don't you think?"

"And here we are," Corey says, coming back into the room with a stack of three books. She sets them down on the table and then stamps and signs some slips of paper about an inch bigger than a bookmark before offering them to Bernie to sign. She's missing the pinky and middle fingers on her left hand, though her movements are precise and practiced, like she's used to managing without. She tucks the papers into the books and hands them to him. "Due in three weeks."

"Thank you." Bernie takes his books and stands. "Nice to meet you," he says to me.

I nod without saying anything.

As he goes to leave, Virgil comes into the room. He beams at the man. "Bernie! Glad I caught you before you left."

They hug, clapping each other on the back. Virgil is so much larger than the other man that the guy gets knocked forward. Bernie says, "I'm sorry I can't stay, but I'm sure I'll be back soon enough. I don't suppose I can expect you in one of this year's candidate pairings?"

Virgil's beaming smile sags. "I'm working on it."

Bernie's head dips. "You deserve to be a part of it. Don't ever let them make you feel otherwise. You're a bright and capable young man." His voice gets heavy, as if he's struggling to get the words out. "I see so much of Davy in you. You have all the potential in the world. Should you compete, I hope you'll have a better result than he did."

The corner of Virgil's lip twitches. "Thank you."

Bernie claps a hand on Virgil's shoulder as he strains to keep a smile on his face. Then Bernie says goodbye to us all and leaves.

Virgil sighs as the sound of the front door shutting reaches us.

"Wow, it's almost as if you didn't enjoy being compared to his dead son," Corey muses as she sinks onto the couch next to me.

"Technically missing," Virgil says.

Corey gives him a look. "If he were alive, there would be—" She cuts herself off, looking at me. "Well, we'd know if he were still living, wouldn't we? I wish he were, for Bernie's sake, but he's not."

"I know."

I guess that explains Bernie's reaction to me talking about my missing mom. He has a son, missing and presumed dead. And like with Mom, no one believes his son is still alive. Great, now I share a common tragedy with a guy who wears Hawaiian shirts.

Virgil bites his lip. "He should have taken more time off. Davy hasn't even been gone a year yet."

Corey shrugs. "He wants to keep busy, I'm sure."

I frown. Bernie told me he was on sabbatical. That's basically the definition of taking time off.

"Bernie used to tutor Virgil," Corey says to me. "Both of us, actually. Him and Dr. Liu, who's usually the librarian here, though he's on sabbatical until the new year." She leans toward me. "But enough about us. You live on the island, right? How is it? Are you going to Queen's in the fall? How—"

"I was thinking this would be a private conversation," Virgil cuts in, leaning against the doorframe.

Corey pouts, turning to him with wide eyes. "But—"

"I'm immune to the pout."

She drops the expression. "It was worth a try." She turns to me. "Well, I'm sure we'll have lots of time to get to know each other."

"Presumptuous," Virgil mutters.

"Is it?" The corner of her mouth lifts up. "I guess we'll see." She pats my leg and leaves the room.

And then it's just the two of us. He meets my eyes. "Corey is the interim librarian here. Though I guess she's technically in training."

"Are you a librarian too?" He definitely looks the part with his round glasses and the blazer he's casually wearing inside his own house.

"More of a ward of the library. I'm not interested in the job or research like Corey, more of a fiction guy. Dr. Liu was kind enough to let me live here when I had nowhere else to go. And when I . . . Well, there was an issue with my attending schools, and that's when Bernie volunteered to tutor me, so I did my schooling at McIntosh Castle. Corey joined eventually. I've called this place my home for a long time."

The fact that he was homeschooled explains a lot. Both he and Corey exist on some separate plane, from their clothing to the formal way they speak.

He crosses his arms over his chest. "The question now is what you're doing here."

A MASTERY OF MONSTERS

I straighten. "The same day we were attacked by that thing at Big Sandy Bay, my brother disappeared. Or left, technically."

Virgil raises an eyebrow.

"I get it. Sometimes people go missing or take off or whatever. My mom has been MIA for a long time now. But this is different. I think he's in trouble, and I need to find him. He left a note. . . . He said that monsters are real." I look at Virgil expectantly.

He clears his throat. "You think I might know something? About the monster or your brother?"

"Yes . . . I mean, both, or one or the other. Do you?"

"I might."

Fuck this guy. "Okay . . ."

"It was quiet the night we met, except for when you were at the park practicing your knife throwing." I roll my eyes, and he carries on. "A couple of weeks ago, our cameras caught a glimpse of what seemed to be someone running from something monster-like. It was too far to confirm any details, but we suspected there might have been an attack, which is why we increased our monitoring capabilities. It's not impossible that one was there when you were. Maybe the same one that targeted you at Big Sandy Bay."

It's like Jules's note. He said someone had already been hurt and now Virgil is basically saying the same thing. So a monster maybe targeted us both, but I got away and she didn't. I shake my head. "Nothing was in the park when I was there. That thing we saw was huge. I would have noticed it."

"It's not always in that obvious of a form."

"What does that mean?! What are these things?" Virgil twitched as I spoke but didn't interrupt. "How many deranged Easter Bunnies are running around? Why aren't more people seeing them?"

54                                                                    LISELLE SAMBURY

Virgil pushes off the doorway and settles on the couch in front of me. "As far as we know, monsters like the one in Big Sandy Bay have existed for at least one hundred and sixty-four years. And their existence has been carefully concealed and controlled for just as long. It's not a well-oiled machine, but it is efficient when you consider the amount of money and influence it takes to keep monsters under wraps. Though it helps that most people don't want to believe these sorts of things live among them."

I can get behind that. I already wish I'd never encountered that thing.

He continues, "They don't represent a large portion of the population, but they do exist, and the numbers increase year over year, which is also monitored and dealt with. If it makes you feel better, the ones that might run wild, killing and maiming, are kept under lock and key."

"Excuse me? You mean whoever has been managing this for one hundred and sixty-four years is just keeping these monsters around? Why wouldn't they kill them? The fact that we got attacked proves their system is shit."

Again, he reacts in an odd way, his shoulders hunching and mouth pursing. "You think the monster we encountered had something to do with your brother's disappearance just because everything happened on the same day? Bit of a shaky theory."

Okay, so he's going to selectively answer questions, apparently. I pull the letter out of my pocket and hand it to him. "There was also this. I don't know if it means anything."

Virgil narrows his eyes at the envelope and then opens it, scanning the contents. He licks his lips. "Where did you get this?"

"It was in my brother's things."

A MASTERY OF MONSTERS

"Not so shaky a theory after all," he mutters, handing it back to me.

"You know it?" I lean forward. "You've seen this?"

"I have." I wait for him to expand but he doesn't.

"And . . . ?"

"Let's wait until we reach an agreement to discuss the letter more. But I can say that yes, it is related to all this. We reported the initial incident of that possible monster attack we saw on the cameras that I mentioned. It seemed to happen near the cricket field. But—"

"Where?"

"The cricket field," he repeats. "By City Park, there's a field."

"I thought it was a baseball field."

"It's technically both, but I always call it—never mind, it doesn't matter. We were told that it would be handled, but it wasn't, hence the additional monitoring on our part. Mind you, something is perhaps being hidden from us."

"Hidden by who? These people who deal with the monsters? Is that who sent this letter?"

Virgil shakes his head. "What matters for your purposes is that I'm of a low rank currently, so we don't have all the information we need. However, I still have access to enough knowledge to be helpful to you."

"But?" I ask, sensing it's coming.

"*But* I need a favor in return." He jerks his head toward the door. "You may have heard Bernie mention me pairing up with someone. There's a competition starting soon, and I'm looking for a partner with sufficient combat abilities."

Is that why he was following me around the other day? "I thought you said I was too impulsive."

"You are." His smile is tight. "I've been exploring other options since, and the skill level is . . . disappointing. I've seen you fight. You're rough around the edges but honestly better than the limited selection I have access to. And here, we find ourselves in need of each other. I need you for the competition, and you need me for information to find your brother. In addition to that, winning will grant you access to, let's say, an exclusive club which will have even more information. The one-hundred-and-sixty-four-year-old one I mentioned earlier. And lucky you, there's more than one winner. Good odds."

"Why do I feel like this competition thing is something hard?" But he has me. For one, he knows about that creature. With anyone else I would have the hurdle of getting them to believe me. And for another, he's right here. Time wouldn't be wasted. Jules may have left voluntarily, or he may have been taken and only had enough time to get me that message. Either way, he's in trouble. He needs me.

Virgil swallows. "Because it is. Sometimes people get hurt, and sometimes people die. There's no point in sugarcoating it. But you have the skills needed to succeed thanks to your not strictly circus arts training. You help me win, and after, you'll have access to everything."

I can't tell if he's trying to scare me to see how serious I am, or if he's being honest about the risk of dying. "Convenient that I only get what I want after you do."

He grins. "Can't have you quitting on me. Maybe I'll be more generous once I see some commitment. You may be rash, but you care enough about your brother to come here. That's called focus. It seems you can do it when you try. That's all I'm asking of you."

It's annoying, but it's a legitimate precaution. After all, if I find Jules early, I'm not sticking around to uphold my end of the

A MASTERY OF MONSTERS

bargain. In fact, that's the goal. "And if I say yes, what happens next?"

Virgil stands. "Next, I call a friend."

I need him. But he also needs me. Mutually assured success . . . or destruction.

I meet his eyes. "Then call them."

# CHAPTER SIX

ailey's house is practically made of windows. There are two huge ones on either side of the living area, small ones lining the bedrooms, including two skylights in each loft, and another long, wide window in the kitchen. She doesn't own curtains because it would destroy the natural view, she said. And she refuses to turn on any overhead lights unless absolutely necessary, choosing instead to use multiple candles. As eight o'clock hits and the sun goes down, I stay bathed in darkness in my room and watch Bailey doing her regular routine of candle lighting.

My phone vibrates, and I glance at it before swapping out my ratty at-home sweatshirt for a T-shirt and pulling on a pair of bike shorts. I leave my loft, making my way down the stairs to the front door.

Bailey pauses, a lit match between her fingers. "Going out again?" Her voice is unnaturally high-pitched. I guess because she's worried about where I'm headed. I came back from Virgil's place hours ago, and she picked me up at the dock. I spent the rest of the time scouring the internet for anything more about that Samantha girl without any luck. The only thing I found were pleas from her family for her to be found, and that she was part of the Queen's Black Student Society.

The fire on the match is getting closer to the tips of Bailey's fingers.

I say, "I'm staying on the island. I'll be back soon." I don't give her time to answer, just open the door and leave.

The tiny house community paths are marked by solar-powered lights stuck in the ground so that you don't get disoriented at night. It's a big property, and there are about a dozen homes on it, spread out in a semicircle.

As has become my habit, I scan the area as I walk. Checking for massive rabbit ears. At night, I lie in bed thinking about Jules resting between those folded arms, the claws digging into his skin.

I don't know if he found my note. If he knew I was sorry. Not for the new me. Just, I guess, for blowing off the fact that he was trying to care about me. It always felt like me and Jules were on the same page. We were our own island against the world. Now I'm finding out he had a boat all along, and he's left me here, supposedly for my own safety. Once upon a time, I would have stayed put like I was told.

I follow the long path down to the road, where a white Toyota RAV4 is waiting. Virgil's in the driver's seat, and Corey's on the passenger side.

When I get into the back, she beams at me. "Nice to see you again!"

"I didn't need you to come," Virgil says to her.

"But what would you do without my moral support?" Corey says, pressing a hand to her chest.

He rolls his eyes.

"I thought we were meeting someone," I say.

Virgil says, "We are. She's already there, so I'm borrowing her car."

Down the path, Bailey is standing outside the house in her shorts, watching us. I hunch, lowering myself in the seat. I don't want her to see me with the same boy twice and start asking uncomfortable questions. I'm lucky Mia isn't here. At least Corey is a good buffer. It would be worse if Virgil came by himself to pick me up.

I stare at the fields out the window as we drive. Farm after farm after farm. Giant swaths of green land and wind turbines. They're still now—white towers with frozen blades.

Corey is surprisingly quiet during the journey. I was sure she'd pick back up with a barrage of questions. Instead, she and Virgil share wordless glances, having a silent conversation.

It's the sort of thing me and Jules would do all the time. That intuitive understanding of another person that comes with knowing each other well. My brother could communicate several things to me with a slight widening of his eyes and tilt of his head. And I could do the same to him.

And yet he'd kept something from me. Whatever he was involved in that led to his disappearance. I pull up the hem of my bike shorts, then smooth them back down, over and over.

Finally, Virgil turns down a road that's more a collection of dirt and rocks and brings us to an area surrounded by trees. I have my knife back, so if this goes sideways somehow, at least I'll be prepared. We get out of the car and walk a ways down until we reach a small clearing. There are two people waiting for us—a Black girl about my age and a boy who seems a couple years younger.

The girl looks me up and down as we get close. Her eyes are lined with black wings, lips painted a deep mauve, and her curls are cut in a tapered style, short and shaved on the sides and back, with long, defined ringlets at the front. She gives me the vibes of a girl who has no problem with looking like she tries hard. She does, and she does it better than you ever could.

She's committed to stoicism, but the boy grins and waves. He's wearing glasses that remind me of Virgil's. His hair is also shaved at the sides, but his curls are shaped up tall and undefined. It's a strangely retro style to see on a kid.

"August, this is Margot," Virgil says, tossing the keys to the girl. "And her brother, Isaac."

"Hey," I say, stopping before them.

Margot stares down her nose at me, and I meet her gaze head on. I'm comfortable with the whole "top bitch" thing. I spent most of my time in high school following around that sort of girl and being the best friend she stepped on. I smoothed things over when she was shitty to people, and I ignored it when that attitude turned on me. It's a thin veneer for deep insecurity at the end of the day.

Though as I look back at Margot, I don't get that feeling. She's not playing at tough to hide insecurities. This is just how she is. I find myself turning away to Virgil.

"Well," he says to her, rocking back on his heels. "You wanted to meet up."

Margot crosses her arms over her chest. "Do you understand what it is that Virgil's asking you to do?"

I say, "We're teaming up for this competition."

She scoffs. "So no, not at all."

"He told you more than that," Corey says, eyes wide. She turns to Virgil. "You told her more than that, right?"

He shifts in place. "That's the whole point of coming and talking to Margot, so she can learn more."

"She's not one of the candidates Henry suggested," Margot says.

"He said I could pick someone else if I wanted. I believe she's the most suitable."

This guy basically told me that I was his last resort, but now he's talking me up to this girl.

"Yes, they are somewhat disappointing, aren't they? But we did know you'd have slim pickings. It remains to be seen if she's any better."

"At the risk of seeming rude," I say, though I couldn't care less, "what exactly do you have to do with all this?"

"This competition, as Virgil is *loosely* describing it, is an initiation process that takes skilled students from our society and attempts to mold them into masters of their craft. And what Virgil is skirting around is what we're seeking mastery of."

"Okay . . ." I glance sidelong at Virgil, who widens his eyes at Margot, trying to nonverbally communicate something to her, but it doesn't work the way it does with Corey. Mostly because Margot purposely looks away from him. "What are you seeking mastery of?"

Margot's lips pull into a full smile. "I'll demonstrate for you right now."

"Margot," Virgil says, his voice strained. And for some reason, he looks at her little brother, who begins to unbutton his shirt.

My face flushes, and I step back. "Whoa, is this a sex thing?"

"No," Isaac says, clearly offended, as he toes off his sneakers. "I'm here with my sister. Jesus."

I ask Virgil, "What is this, then?"

But he isn't paying attention to me, he's still talking to Margot. "You said that you and Isaac were just going to talk with her about the bonding and then discuss training. You didn't mention this."

"Slipped my mind," she says, rolling her neck back.

"Maybe we can ease into this using some other method?" Corey asks, stepping next to Virgil. "Is this really the ideal way to do it?"

"It's my way."

"Please," Virgil says. "She's my best option."

Margot looks down her nose at him the same way she did to me. "Your situation won't change because of what I do here tonight. She's either capable or incapable, and better you find that out with me right here, right now, than drag our names through the mud and have me waste time training her. You risk embarrassing Henry with your choice and damaging his position, which affects all of us."

Virgil grits his teeth so hard it's like he's gnashing them, and they almost seem . . . longer somehow.

"I can put you down like a toddler for nap time," Margot says. "Don't test me."

He gets a hold of himself, ceasing any mouth movements. His eyes dart to mine and then away as he wrings his hands. To me he says, "Please try not to freak out. It's safe. It's not like at Big Sandy Bay."

I glance from him to Margot. "What does that mean?"

"Ready?" she asks, turning to her brother. He stands in nothing but his boxer shorts.

He nods. "Ready."

"It'll be okay," Corey says to Virgil, who's treading a perfect circle in the ground with his pacing. She doesn't look so good either.

He shakes his head. "You should go wait in the car."

I expect Corey to refuse, but she swallows and throws a wounded look at me before retreating the way we came.

"Okay, for real, what's going on?" I ask Margot.

"You'll see," she says.

I stare at Margot and then Isaac, who stand still until we hear the sound of a car door shutting. Then Isaac bends forward, and his spine, already bony, begins to push and shove against his skin, becoming larger and larger until it bursts from his back. A noise leaves my mouth, but I can't process it. His skin keeps splitting from his neck to his tailbone, blood spurting from the wounds, and fur expands out from them. It's brown, wiry, and thick. His body folds in on itself, almost turning inside out, and what's being birthed from beneath it keeps growing.

He makes small gasping noises as his limbs stretch, claws grow onto the ends of massive paws, and rippling muscle covered in fur emerges, wet and slick with blood. And he . . . *it* is getting bigger, and taller, and by the time the head appears, I've somehow backed up to the tree line, because I'm clinging to the trunk, my nails digging into the bark.

And then it's finished, and the creature that looks back at me is the sort of doglike beast I would expect to guard the gates of hell. Its mouth is so filled with razor-sharp teeth that they're protruding from its wet lips, drool dripping down and sizzling where it lands in the grass, scorching the earth. This is the kind of dog that barks and snaps at you from behind a fence with a sign warning you away, the sort that you know would tear you apart if it ever got near you.

But worse because it has the height and size to crush me under a single paw.

"August," Virgil whispers.

I turn and sprint through the trees.

What the fuck is happening right now? I joined up with Virgil to help me figure out how this monster stuff is involved with what happened to Jules, and now this kid literally transformed into that thing. . . . I don't know what to do anymore. But now I know what Virgil meant when he said the monster might have been in a "different form" when I was in City Park. The thing that tried to kill me could be standing right beside me in human skin and I wouldn't even know.

My head is too heavy for the rest of my body, like I'm drunk again, making me stumble across the dirt trail that I can barely see in the dark. I have no plan or sense of direction. The only thing I want to do is get as far away as possible from that thing and just think for a minute.

I trip over a root, slamming into the ground and gasping. I push myself onto all fours and stay there, panting and trembling. I need to move, but my body has seized up.

"August."

I whip my head to the side, where Virgil is standing in the trees. I hadn't even heard him. Hadn't noticed he was following. "What is this? What are you?" He was so fast. Way too fast with that rabbit at Big Sandy Bay. And the way his teeth seemed to grow longer as he got frustrated with Margot. I think back to how he'd reacted when I asked why they don't kill monsters instead of locking them up. He'd been weirdly upset. . . .

Because he's *one of them*.

Virgil swallows. "Our society works in the pursuit of the mastery of monsters. Some of us are born like this, and others are made. Everyone has a unique shape, but they're all . . . well, they're all monstrous. We appear human, but at a certain point we become unable to retain that form. When that time comes, we must find a partner to bond with. That bond allows us to control ourselves in monster form and shift between the two forms at will. We call these partners Masters."

"Slavery, much?" I spit.

The corner of his lip twitches. "It's academic. And the first Master was a Black man, if that helps make the distinction clearer for you. Everyone belonging to the society is a student. Bachelor and Master are ranks. Ranks that must be earned through initiation. The competition. You have to win the right to bond."

"The competition where people *die*. Doing what? Fighting monsters?"

He winces. "Technically, yes, at least in the latter stages. I know this is not a small ask." He runs his hand through his curls. "My parents, they weren't great. The people who will agree to partner with me are . . . well, kind of the bottom of the barrel. But *you*, you can fight. And you're not affiliated with the society and therefore might give me a chance."

"What did your parents do?"

"They attempted to kill the leader of our organization, murdering a couple dozen people in the process," he says, biting his lip. "Obviously didn't gain them a lot of fans."

Okay, some light mass murder. Making Virgil the son of mass murderers.

He comes closer, slowly, as if he expects me to bolt again. I'm

A MASTERY OF MONSTERS

considering it. I'm so fucking in over my head right now. He squats down in front of me. Reaching out, he pulls my hand into his own, enveloping my fingers between his, and looks into my eyes, his face only inches from mine.

"I need you, August," he breathes. "That thing you saw, it's still Isaac in there. He maintains control because of his bond with Margot. But without it . . . we become wild. Mindless. A beast who doesn't know how to do anything but maim and kill. Those things, they get put underground, imprisoned within themselves. Fodder for the front lines. You heard Bernie mention his son. . . . His son was a monster too, and he and his partner lost last year, so he ran away to escape that exact fate. But if we run, they chase us down and either take us back or kill us. There is no escaping this. Either you win this competition, or I lose. And losing means my only existence would be to wait to be useful or die, and even if I can be used, it will only be to fight until I die. But if a monster is paired with a Master, we become a protector. A real soldier worth something. We're allowed to have a life." His eyes shine with unshed tears, but he doesn't turn away to hide the emotion. He keeps his gaze on me.

He's like Isaac. Just like I guessed. Inside of Virgil, there's a thing like that. Fur and sharp claws and teeth.

*A monster.* Just like Jules warned me about.

I don't understand any of this soldier shit, but I get that he needs me to avoid becoming a wild monster locked up by this society they keep talking about. Needs me to fight things that could kill me.

"I promise you," he says, voice cracking. "I promise you that if you win, if you become a Master and partner with me, I will do everything within my power to help find your brother. And it could never be a lie because I will need you, *forever*. But you have to save me, and to do that, you have to succeed. You have to work hard. And you have to be able to face monsters."

His hands have started to tremble. There's tension throughout his entire body. He should be the one with the power, and yet here he is, begging.

He wasn't trying to scare me before. This is serious. I could get hurt. I could die.

*The best way for you to stay safe is to stay away.*

Jules is all I have left. He could be in real danger. I could lose him, permanently.

This is the one time that Jules has seriously asked me to do something. He wants me to stay away. He wants me to not get involved.

Some part of me wants it too. To go out and get drunk and dance and forget about living in a world with monsters. To forget this boy holding my hands and staring at me, pleading for my help.

But I can't lose Jules.

This time, I'll have to disappoint him, too.

"I'm no one's hero," I tell Virgil.

"You are to me." The worst part of him saying it is that I know he isn't lying.

I pull my hands away, and he lets me go, his eyes dropping to the ground.

When I stand, he stays on his knees. "This isn't a rescue mission," I say. "This is an exchange."

Virgil's head whips up. "Is that a yes?"

"It's a 'fine.'"

His lips peel into a smile, and I turn away, crossing my arms over my chest, my face hot. I couldn't care less about Virgil and what he wants me to do. But I need him as much as he needs me. He hadn't

A MASTERY OF MONSTERS

just known about that thing we saw at Big Sandy Bay. He was intimately familiar with it. This is bigger than I thought. Something is going on, and if I have any chance of finding out what it is, it's going to come from associating with these people.

I don't like the idea of a long game, but I need to get in the game somehow. Even if I'm starting to wonder how equipped I am to play.

I walk back to the clearing with Virgil beside me.

When we get there, Margot is next to it—not *it*, her *brother*. He's calm. As if he's a tame puppy instead of a vicious beast.

I force myself to stare into his wide, dark eyes, and somehow, I can see him. He's in there. They're Isaac's eyes. He's not just a monster. It's not that simple anymore.

I turn to Virgil. "What's next?"

He laughs, tears pricking at the corners of his eyes from the force of it. I ignore the way it makes my lips pull into a smile.

Margot is more reserved. "Welcome to the Society for the Pursuit of the Fundamentals of Learning. You are now a student." Then she mutters under her breath. "May you not come to regret it."

My limbs go stiff.

It's the exact name of the organization that sent Jules that letter. No wonder Virgil recognized it. I whip toward him. "The letter my brother—"

"I know," Virgil says. "We keep track of everyone we send an invite to, and everyone involved in the society, even at the student level. I checked, and his name isn't there. I don't know how he got that letter, but it didn't come through the official channels. I also checked out that monster from Big Sandy Bay, ran its description through our public database. There's no monster like that registered either."

"What does that mean?!"

Margot says, "It means finding your brother is going to be more complicated than you think. I suggest you take this candidacy seriously, because our help depends on your performance."

I can do that. Play by their rules. Do this competition.

And the second I find Jules, I'm ditching this monster cult.

# CHAPTER SEVEN

I groan when Mia weaves her way around the other passengers on the ferry to sit next to me. I'm used to traveling to Kingston early in the morning because of my Tim Hortons shifts, but that was on weekends. On a weekday, this is one of the busiest times to get on, and I was lucky to find a place to sit, much less one alone. I tug the open flaps of my zip-up hoodie closer to my body. Even in summer, the morning breeze on the ferry can get cold.

"I'm so happy to see you too," Mia chimes, propping her hockey stick between her knees.

"You practice this early?"

"Sometimes." A sly grin slides onto her lips. "Going to see your special friend? I saw that he came by last weekend."

I don't have the energy to dig into how she even saw Virgil. After I got over the whole Isaac-can-turn-into-a-monster-and-I-guess-Virgil-can-too thing, they drove me home. I've cemented myself into the plan to enter this competition, or at least, to make them think that's what I'm doing. Really, I'll use whatever resources of theirs I can to find Jules as soon as possible. But for now, I'm playing along. Which is why I'm going to meet them on campus and get introduced to some guy.

"I have work," I say.

"Bullshit."

"Do you want something from me?"

Mia's face lights up, and she tosses her shiny ponytail over her shoulder. "Now that you mention it . . ."

"What?"

"I'm trying to arrange a community dinner, and I need some help with cleaning up that old barn. You know the one, right? It's behind our—"

"Pass."

This girl actually stomps her feet. I can't with her. "Just help me!"

I smile. "No."

She slides closer to me on the bench and says, "I've noticed you practicing your knife throwing. Some of those blades are awfully dull. I think if you could sharpen them yourself, you would. Meaning you can't. I could help."

How does this girl notice absolutely everything I do? Though she's right. Mom used to sharpen our knives for us. And of course, Jules learned how to do it and sharpened mine for me. Besides that, it's not like I have a whetstone lying around. "Why do you know how to sharpen knives?"

Mia leans back on the bench, steepling her fingers. "Every year I carve a knife from stone and sharpen it, leaving it in the shadow of the moon to grow fruitful with energy."

A MASTERY OF MONSTERS

"Really?"

She rolls her eyes. "No. Wow, you'll believe anything. My dad is a massive nerd with a giant fantasy sword collection, and they sometimes require sharpening."

"Maybe I'll ask Jacques then."

"And open yourself up to the trap of having to spend hours listening to him tell you about his collection? Plus, then he'll always ask you about knife throwing whenever he sees you. Is that what you want? To be my dad's knife bestie?"

She has a fair point. I gnaw on my lip. "My knives work fine."

"You would seriously rather have them be dull than help me?"

"Why do you even want to do this dinner thing?"

"We're a tiny house *community*. You do know what community means, right? We should be spending time together and helping each other."

"We already do that. People bug me all the time about joining them gardening and shit."

"No," Mia says. "*My mom* asks you to join her in the garden. She asks if you want to come over for dinner. She asks if you want to do things. Just her. And you always say no! Bailey's the only one who ever does stuff with us."

"You can't force people into being a community."

"Urg! You sound like my parents." Mia sighs. "Why would you want to be on your own? There are people who live on the same land you do who you could get to know. And you'd rather, what? Ignore everyone forever? Be alone? You don't think that's sad?"

"I'm not helping."

"Fine! I'll do it myself." She shoves a pair of earbuds in and plays her music so loud that I can hear it.

I put in my own earbuds and close my eyes, trying not to think about Mia saying, *"You don't think that's sad?"*

Humphrey Hall is a gray brick building near the park I'm starting to feel too familiar with. Virgil and Margot meet me at a side door, and we enter the building. Instead of walking to wherever this guy's office is, they stand right inside the door.

"Are we going or what?" I ask.

Margot says, "We want to brief you before you go in. You'll be meeting Henry. He's the Master who nominated me for the candidacy last year, which means he cannot nominate you this year, but he can find someone who can. Without the nomination, you don't even get to participate."

"The candidacy being this competition thing?"

"Yes. Henry is also an important person to have on your side. It's crucial that you make a good impression."

I figured as much. I remember them mentioning this Henry guy when I first met Margot. About how he'd found other candidates for Virgil to partner with but apparently they hadn't been any good. I don't know how great this guy could be considering that, but whatever, I'll make nice with him. "Okay, let's go." I move forward, eager to get this over with.

Virgil steps in front of me. "You do get how important this is, right? Henry has the power to help us. The Doctorate is the head of the entire organization—like, the whole thing, all of Canada and beyond. And the sixth Doctorate, our current leader, raised Henry alongside his youngest son, Adam, when Henry's family died. And Henry himself is a direct descendant of the first Master. He's a big deal. And we're lucky he's already on our side. He wants us to win."

I feel a headache coming on from trying to understand all this stuff. But the Doctorate is their leader . . . meaning the guy Virgil's parents tried to kill. "Why is the Doctorate so important? Like, do you guys vote him in or is this a cult-y dictatorship thing?"

Margot massages her temple. "Doctorates, who all come from the same bloodline, are born with the ability to control any monster without bonding. Even monsters who are already bonded. Usually, there's only one in every generation, though as you'll come to see, the current generation is a little different. All three of our Doctorate's sons have inherited the ability, though I suppose only one of them will get the official title."

"Why don't Doctorates all have, like, a bunch of kids if their special power is so important?"

"Because, like I said, traditionally only one child has inherited the ability even if they have multiple children, and it creates succession issues that we'll now have to deal with, which is why the original Doctorate said they should only have one child and—" She cuts herself off. "That doesn't even matter right now. What matters is that when the apocalypse comes, the Doctorate will be paramount in our ability to win. All the monsters locked up underground will be released into their control to fight."

I remember what Virgil said about becoming fodder for the front lines. Is this what he meant? "To fight . . . the *apocalypse*?" I cannot control the skepticism on my face.

"No," Margot says, narrowing her eyes. "To fight what comes along with the apocalypse. We'll get into that later. Right now, you need to focus on impressing Henry."

"Okay . . ." I'm perfectly fine with not having to hear about whatever wild end-of-the-world shit they've been brainwashed into believing. "I get it. Henry's very powerful and very important. I'll behave."

Virgil and Margot share a glance but finally start moving through the halls until we reach an office with a plaque on the door that reads, HENRY SCOTT, PH.D. PSYCHOLOGY.

Looks like Mr. Fancy has a fancy degree to go with all his clout and tragic backstory.

"The door is open," Margot says, waving at me to go inside. "He said he'll be along shortly."

I expect the two of them to follow, but they stay in the hall.

The office is decorated in dark, moody tones—the colors of avocado skins and autumn leaves. Large enough to fit both a desk area and a small sitting room with a real goddamn fireplace. This guy must have tenure or something to have a space this nice. The walls are covered with wallpaper that has delicate vines wrapping around each other and cupping open pomegranates, whose juice spills onto the leaves. The two side walls are lined with bookcases that reach the ceiling, the shelves stained umber and filled with books. And not just the old-looking decorative kind that I'm convinced no one reads— this has a bunch of memoirs, historical texts, and self-help books. I didn't realize that actual psychologists read those.

I sit in a chair with wooden arms and a velvet cushion in front of a massive desk, also wood. The items on top of it are an assortment of aesthetic knickknacks. And the guy's computer is a giant iMac. It's jarring, with its sleek silver surfaces surrounded by the gloomy antique decor. Like he should have covered it up with a box or stashed it underneath the desk. It doesn't belong among the wood polish scent and literal cloves in a bowl that's probably hand carved.

I pick at my nails and don't bother stopping when the door

opens behind me. I wait until the man makes his way fully around the desk and sits.

He looks like a guy who should have glasses. His shoulder-length locs are pulled into a ponytail and his hairline is neatly lined up. Glasses would really complete the professor look.

He adjusts the neck of his cardigan and pulls out a leather-bound notebook, unwrapping the cord around it and opening to a new page, where he writes my full name.

It's almost like we're in a session. Not that I've ever been in one. Considering my life, maybe I should have. But even if I was amenable to spilling my guts to a stranger, which I'm not, I don't think we'd have the money for it.

"Presumably you know who I am," Henry says.

"Henry."

"Dr. Scott or Professor Scott to you. I haven't given you license to address me that casually."

I bite the inside of my cheek.

He stares at me for a moment and then writes something down on the page. He's pulled it closer to him, so I can't see what he noted. "You've agreed to partner with Virgil for the candidacy. Do you understand what that means?"

"I'm going to compete to become a Master. When I do that, I'll be able to help control Virgil when he's in monster form."

"I see, so you don't understand."

Great, an asshole. "Enlighten me, then."

He narrows his eyes. "You're rude."

I reel back with a laugh. "*I'm* rude?" I get that I'm supposed to impress this guy or whatever, but they could have warned me how shitty he'd be.

"You do not understand the seriousness of what you are committing to, and you'd better start understanding right now before you ruin that boy's life. Virgil deserves more than he's been given. He deserves more than *you*. But unfortunately, you are who he has chosen, and so I hope your will to find your brother is strong enough to make up for it." My eyes widen. "Yes, Virgil has told me about your deal. I agree that you should keep this particular motivation concealed, but I need to know about it because I am the one who must now put my reputation on the line to pitch a girl who I don't think is worthy of being a candidate in order to give him this chance to save his life."

This man decided to hate me the second he walked in the door. I thought everything was fine after last week. I came back to face Isaac, didn't I? But apparently both Margot and Virgil talked shit about me. I can't see any other reason for him to be treating me like this.

"Well," Henry says, leaning his chin against his hand. "What will you tell people when they ask why you've decided to compete?"

"Why don't you tell me, since I'm so useless?"

"The Learners' Society has a long history, Ms. Black. The candidacy itself is a tradition that has been carried out annually for over a century. Candidates come from families who have been students of its teachings for generations, some even descended from Masters. You are nothing and no one to them. These people are then nominated for the honor of just being considered as candidates by Masters like me who stake our personal reputations on our picks. Trust me when I say that it is not easy to advance in this society without pedigree. All of us do this because we understand there is a threat in the shadows. We train because we believe in protecting the students who commit themselves to this cause. And looking for your missing brother is not good enough. Nor can I tell you what to believe."

"So, I should be doing it to save everyone from this apocalypse thing?" I haven't stopped picking at my nails. There are bits of black polish collecting on my jean shorts.

"I would recommend that you change your tone and take the apocalypse seriously. The candidacy was created to prepare for it specifically. It is not a joke. It would be a tragedy for you to only consider its reality when everyone you know and love is suddenly transformed into a snarling beast with the will to do only one thing: *kill*. You should feel fortunate to get to join the society and have a chance to become a Master, which is the only thing that will protect you from suffering the same fate. And when that time comes, you will be expected to fight and die to guard the Doctorate, the only person on the *planet* with the power to turn the tide in humanity's favor. If you don't have it in you to be noble, come up with a better reason for competing."

I curl my hands into fists. I don't bother correcting him with my newfound knowledge that there are technically four people on the planet with the Doctorate's ability, not one. I'm busy thinking about the idea that this supposed apocalypse is apparently everyone in the world, except for Masters and the Doctorate, turning into monsters. It sounds unhinged, but then again, so does the existence of monsters, period. Still, it's a wild escalation. I guess I shouldn't be surprised that the cultlike secret society believes in an end of the world that, of course, can only be combatted by their leader and higher-ups. This shit is textbook. I don't care what Henry says. Unless I literally see random people becoming monsters, I'm not buying it.

"Fine, I'm doing it for Virgil, then." I grin at him. "You're all so in love with him, so why not me too?"

Henry closes the journal. "Intimate relationships between partnered monsters and Masters are forbidden."

"I'm heartbroken."

"You're insufferable." He points at the door. "Get out."

I fly out of the room, as glad to go as Henry is to have me out. Margot pushes off from the wall with a frown as I leave the office and Virgil's eyes dart from me to the door. I don't stop as I walk down the hallway, trying to find my way out of the building.

Margot calls after me to ask what happened, but I'm too far ahead to bother answering.

Virgil, however, puts in the work to catch up to me. "What did you say to him?!"

"He's an asshole," I hiss.

"He's not a sunshine-and-daisies guy, but his entire family was massacred in a random monster attack, so yeah, sometimes those people are grumpy."

I stop and turn to him. "Tough titties. Everyone has a sob story. He was shitty to me, and so I was shitty back. I don't know what else to say to you."

"We told you it was important to impress him!"

I keep heading to the exit, and Virgil doesn't follow this time. Which is just as well, because I don't have anything to say to him.

It's done. There's no way Henry will find someone to nominate me now.

I've fucked up before we even started.

A MASTERY OF MONSTERS

# CHAPTER EIGHT

On Monday, I follow Virgil, Margot, and Corey into Summerhill with my eyes down and my hands stuck in the pockets of my skirt. Margot told me to dress up, so I dug the skirt and a sleeveless mock neck out. I refuse to part with my Docs, but I think they're formal enough. They're black.

Margot fiddles with her phone while Virgil ignores me. Corey explains that Summerhill is the oldest building on campus. It was previously used as a private home and looks like it, with its two stories and its porch lined with perfect white fencing. In the mid-1800s, Summerhill was the entire university, though that changed as the school grew. Part of it is designated as the principal's residence, but Corey says it's uncommon these days to use it like that. But since the last few principals have been society members, they often use the accommodations as lodgings for visiting Masters. It's also regularly used for Learners' gatherings and sometimes for their weekly lectures.

The latter I've been told I should go to, though it's not mandatory, meaning I'm definitely not going. Tonight's lecture has been swapped for this nomination ceremony.

We join the queue of people filing into the building, some of them murmuring about what else might be discussed. Almost no one ever says the full society title that Margot shared that day on the island. It does suffer the sort of wordiness that people enjoyed in the 1800s. Corey told me that their founder, Dr. Edward Weiss—actually a doctor, Queen's School of Medicine class of 1865—made the name purposely vague to assist in its secrecy. I think he was probably just shit at naming things. But I'm slowly getting used to the terminology. What I'm less clear on is how this nomination is going to work, since I pissed Henry off. Aka, the reason why Virgil isn't talking to me.

We enter a large room with high ceilings and a stage set up at the front. It's plain, featuring a podium and a projection screen. The rest of the space is set up like a banquet hall. There are multiple circular tables with white tablecloths and antique chairs, pitchers of water and tea at each one. And whoever designed the house was not shy about either wood paneling or chandeliers.

A lot more of the tables than I expect are already occupied. We manage to grab one in the middle. As I look around the room, I'm struck, once again, by the diversity of the people. I mean, I'd thought a secret society of people "Mastering monsters" had to be a bunch of white guys. Virgil said it was academic, but "Master" as a title in the context of what is probably a cult doesn't sit right with me.

"Can I ask you something potentially offensive?" I say to Corey.

Virgil snorts. "Wow, you ask permission for that now?"

"Shoot." Corey turns to me with a smile, unaffected by her friend's fury. Though her gaze keeps darting around the room periodically.

I say, "There's, like . . . not as many white people as I expected."

Corey laughs and then claps her hand over her mouth to stifle the giggle as people look over at us. Some of them curl their lips. There are more than a few attendees peering at our table with barely concealed disgust.

I concentrate on Corey, who says, "The society prizes diversity. Our founder's father gambled away much of their fortune, so he grew up poor. He was working in the Kingston Penitentiary when he discovered who we call 'Patient Zero,' the first monster. Though he was different from modern monsters, mostly human-looking. He'd bitten a bunch of people who Dr. Weiss then sought out and with whom he formed the society with the goal of understanding and eventually curing monstrosity. Most of them were people of color, as the white victims were more dismissive of Dr. Weiss because of his class. He hadn't yet become a doctor at that time. Dr. Weiss held those victims who helped him form the society in high regard and wanted to be sure that they continued to be represented in the organization. He even encouraged his children to have kids with people of other races and to be accepting of other types of marginalized people. We, as a society, are above those sorts of divisions. We're inclusive. And you can tell by looking at us."

"Oh." I didn't expect a full historical explanation. Though I doubt they're truly above it all, like Corey says. I'll believe it when I see it. "Wait, so the first monster was Patient Zero. Does that mean being a monster is like a virus? Is that what you're trying to cure?"

"It's a mutation." Corey glances at Virgil as she says it, but he's staring at his phone. "It's fascinating. The abilities of the Doctorate are also a mutation. It's kind of a one in a million circumstance, that Dr. Weiss and Patient Zero found each other. Two people with unique mutations that complement one another. It's how Dr. Weiss discovered the bonding process between Master and monster in the first place. He found that he had an unnatural calming effect on Patient Zero that no one else did, and the same with his victims."

"It's genetic? That's why the Doctorate's descendants have the same ability or mutation or whatever? And why monsters are born?"

"Yes, exactly. But not every child with a parent who has the mutation develops it. And in both cases, the mutation takes some time to be expressed or activated. Monsters born with the mutation don't transform for a while."

"What activates it?"

"Time, the serum, or the bite. We don't know the particulars of how much time it needs to activate. We thought maybe puberty for a while, but the results were inconclusive. However, there are signs of turning, and so we use those symptoms to attempt to predict activation. Things like increased aggression and partial transformations. The serum was invented by the Doctorate. It's what allows monsters and Masters to bond. And the bite both immediately causes the development of the mutation and activates it. That's why those people turn right away."

"Wait, but you said that Patient Zero was different and that his victims joined up with the society before Weiss even discovered bonding via this serum thing. How is that possible if they were in monster form?"

"Dr. Weiss," Virgil corrects, setting down his phone. "They were different, like Patient Zero, a sort of blend of human and monster. They could pass for human but not enough. They were ostracized and imprisoned or sent to asylums. But the bonding permanently changed the monster mutation, leading to the monsters we know today, who are either fully human-looking or fully monstrous. It was a relief for the victims because they could lead normal lives in control of themselves."

They gained what Virgil wants so badly for himself. He ducks his head, staring at his phone again, even though he's not using it. I look around and, once again, people are gazing at our table with narrowed eyes. I glance at Virgil. Is that the reason he keeps looking down? "Second potentially offensive question?" I ask.

"Go for it," Corey says.

"Do people like . . . hate you guys, or . . . ?"

Virgil stiffens next to me.

Corey plays with the teacup in front of her. "I was the youngest candidate in a century. You're supposed to be at least eighteen, but I got special permission to participate at fifteen and failed. A lot of people were invested in my success, and it . . . caused issues, basically."

"Henry nominated me last year when I was a freshman," Margot says. "Which pissed people off because I was an outsider, like you. I grew up with my grandma, who, when Isaac started showing signs of turning, let me know exactly what was happening. She sent us here, where we were lucky to have Henry take us in. Obviously, I was going to do everything to try to fight for the Master title to help Isaac, but my parents had left the society a long time ago, so we were seen as both outsiders and traitors. And then I won the title, which pissed them off more."

I turn to Virgil. "What about you? Is it your parents?"

"My parents," he repeats, rubbing his face. "Some of the people they hurt are in this room. Or they're the relatives or friends of those they killed."

"Basically, this is the public enemy number one table."

"Pretty much." Corey takes a long sip of her tea.

"Or almost, anyway," I amend as a South Asian—looking man in a black suit and tie, enters the room and immediately makes his way over to our table. "He seems like he's a fan."

"Why is he coming over?" Virgil whispers to Corey.

"No idea," she says.

He arrives at our table with a big smile on his face. "Margot! Just the girl I was looking for."

"Nice to see you. Where's your better half?"

"He's at home with the kids. We prefer to attend the monthly children's lectures with them. They don't quite have the attention span for the general weekly ones yet. But I didn't want to miss the nominations, so I'm flying solo." He spots me then. "There's a new face." He holds out his hand, which I shake. "I'm Corris. I semiregularly participate in the candidacy as a Master. Meaning it's my job to challenge candidates in tests."

Margot waves to me. "This is August. She's pairing with Virgil." At that, Corris glances at the boy in question with a nod. "Corris neglects to mention that he's never had a candidate get past him. Best to avoid him in the competition."

He laughs. "Yes, yes, perhaps. It's lovely to meet you, August." I don't know what else to do other than press my lips into some approximation of a smile. Corris leans toward Margot. "I was hoping to pester Henry, actually. I heard a rumor someone very interesting has shown up today and wondered if he'd seen her."

"He isn't here yet. He likes to come just before six o'clock for lectures."

"Right. I assume to avoid any pestering."

Margot doesn't deny it. "Who are you looking for?"

Corris is about to answer when he pauses, his face lighting up. "Well, never mind, there she is, as I live and breathe. Natalie Soer."

Corey chokes on her tea, and Virgil just about breaks his neck looking around. Only Margot maintains her cool.

"Who's Natalie Soer?" I ask.

"At your four o'clock, Black woman, great hair," Margot says.

I spot her toward the back of the room having a tense conversation with an older white guy with a gray-flecked ginger beard. The two walk as they talk. The man keeps looking away, his brow furrowed, like he would very much like to shake her off.

Corris is delighted. "And she's arguing with Garrett. My, this is heating up to be one hell of a nomination ceremony."

"They don't usually come to these things," Corey supplies for me. "Natalie is part of a society faction that . . . well, they're not supposed to exist. None of the factions are. But the Pro-Libs especially. Cyrus broke them up years ago when Natalie and Garrett led the Wilds rebellion. Garrett was the one who switched to peace talks, so they don't get along. His family are direct descendants of Patient Zero."

I massage my temple. "Why is this organization so complicated?"

"Too much history and too much politics," Corris says. "Well, I guess I found her without Henry's help."

Margot purses her lips. "You don't mind being seen with her? People will talk."

"Oh, darling, people always talk about me." Corris flashes her a wide grin and then takes off, walking in the direction of Natalie, who's broken away from her heated conversation. Not by choice, either. Garrett stalked off, and she didn't follow. Corris makes a big show of greeting her, which causes multiple heads to turn as they embrace and then settle at a table together.

"That woman's shit doesn't stink," Margot mutters. "Henry says it's her greatest talent. She somehow manages to surround herself with powerful people despite her own infamy."

"Because she leads this Pro-Lib thing?" I ask.

"First rule of factions, do not publicly speak about them. It's fine with us, but don't with anyone outside of this group, *especially* the Pro-Libs. They're pro-monster in the wrong way. Trust me."

"Will do." I don't know who I would even encounter to speak about it, anyway.

Virgil eyes Natalie and Corris. "Why is she here, do you think? And Garrett, too."

"Gives me a bad feeling," Corey says.

Virgil's knee is bouncing so violently beside me that I'm starting to develop an involved fantasy of driving my knife into his leg so he'll stop. "You good?" I ask him.

He responds by glaring at me.

"It'll be fine," Corey says to him. "I'm sure Henry found someone to nominate her."

"Really? You're sure?"

"If he hadn't been such a dick to me, I wouldn't have been a dick back," I say.

"It's called holding your tongue! I don't know why you're incapable of doing that."

The thing is, I'm quite accomplished at keeping words in. I did it for years. I didn't protest when Mom once again declared that we would be moving. I didn't correct my "friends" when they said I didn't sound or act Black. I didn't disagree when people suggested that I needed to watch my eating. And even better, I encouraged it. I tried to get the family excited about once again being uprooted from a new place. I laughed with my "friends" and agreed that I was an Oreo, like I was happy to be compared to a cookie. And I meticulously recorded everything I ate and stopped when I hit my calories for the day, even if I was still hungry. Congratulated myself when I ate less than the minimum. So I am more than capable of holding my tongue.

Margot straightens as Henry enters the room. He goes to the front, where a seat is conveniently empty at a table. Like it was reserved for him.

"See? That's the shit I'm talking about," I say. "He couldn't even say hi to us? Maybe reassure Virgil a little so he can calm the fuck down?"

"There is a reason for everything that Henry does," Margot says. "It's not for you to question."

I slouch, crossing my arms. "Why can't you nominate me? You're a Master."

She shakes her head. "I don't have the full Master title yet, which you need to nominate. And Virgil can't afford to wait. He's already showing signs of turning. It has to be now."

Virgil's leg bouncing increases.

"Stop it," Margot snaps.

Corey says, "It's anxiety. Leave him alone."

"I meant stop freaking out. Don't bother having faith in August at this point. Have faith in Henry's desire to help you."

Virgil's knee comes to a standstill. I can't feel bad for him or myself. It's too late now. Either Henry came through or he didn't.

Everyone's heads swivel to the stage as three men walk onto it.

Corey says, "That's Adam, James, and Carrigan Shaw. Their father, Cyrus, is the Doctorate." One is a light-skinned Black man with warm eyes who looks Henry's age, wearing a loose, billowing dress shirt and pants. The second is an older East Asian—looking man who's decked out in a full suit. And finally, the last man, dark curls falling into his eyes, has deep bronze skin, looks South Asian, and is dressed almost absurdly casually in a black hoodie and cargo pants. He gives me big middle child energy. "Some students think the fact that they all inherited the Doctorate abilities means the apocalypse is imminent."

Margot's left eye twitches. I assumed she believed this apocalypse bullshit as much as the others, but she didn't grow up in the society like Corey and Virgil. She speaks like she believes it, but that doesn't mean she actually does.

I glance at Corey. "What do you think?"

She frowns. "I wonder if the mutation is changing for some reason. For example, born monsters become more powerful with every generation. That's why we have legacy monster families. I've always been curious whether that would start happening to the Doctorates."

I look back at the stage, eyeing the men there. "Is Cyrus a person of color or . . . ?"

"He's white-passing," Margot says. "Meredith Grant, the fifth Doctorate and his mother, was multi-racial, and his father was Korean. Cyrus, on the other hand, never married. His sons are technically half-brothers. They all had different mothers, though who they are is a mystery. You'll find that our Doctorate is more eclectic than those who came before him."

Eclectic is an interesting way to put it. Sounds more like a man with commitment issues. I guess they took their founder's encouragement to heart. In practice, it's kind of weird to think of them seeking out people of color for partners. It's the sort of thing that sounds good until you think about it for a bit. "And where's Cyrus?"

"Sick," Virgil says. "He hasn't been out in public for a while."

I lean my head against my hand. "Could it be one of them, the Doctorate or his sons, controlling our favorite homicidal Easter Bunny? They'd have the power to have reports ignored too." It's clear to me that the monster at Big Sandy Bay was acting consciously. It wasn't attacking like a wild animal. There was intent.

Corey shakes her head. "Why? The only person more powerful than them is their father, and it's not like attacking you or kidnapping your brother would change that."

Fair, even I can admit that. The continuing problem is motive. Why would that monster attack me? And has it really backed off? Did Jules leaving do something to make it stop? Or was the point always to get to Jules, and I was just a means to that end? Which opens up a whole new host of questions about Jules and his connection to that monster.

Virgil stares at the stage. "First Natalie and Garrett show up, and now Carrigan, who hasn't been to so much as a lecture in years, is here too? What's going on?"

"I guess we're about to find out," Margot says.

The clock above the stage strikes six, and James walks toward the mic.

# CHAPTER NINE

James Shaw seems no different than any other man on the street. He's got the look of a friend's dad. Soft around the middle and stern in the face. Just a man. But when he raises his hands, the entire room falls silent. The level of obedience is oppressive. It's a hand on the back of your head, shoving you to the ground, and you on your knees, glad of it.

And this man isn't even the actual Doctorate.

"Welcome, students," he says. "I am honored to learn with you."

"And us with you," the crowd intones as one.

If that's not some cult shit, then I don't know what is.

James goes on to talk about the number of new students, who he points out in the crowd, and encourages them to spread the truth to new trusted Learners. He notes the importance of sticking close to those in the community and avoiding excess involvement in the affairs of the unenlightened. He speaks about people outside of the society like they're a separate species, and no one bats an eye. I can't tell if everyone is buying this, or if they're just going along with it to take advantage of the power and opportunities supposedly associated with this organization. I've yet to see any of this promised opulence, but there wouldn't be all this politicking if there weren't money on the line. Weiss may have grown up poor, but at some point that must have changed. His society became profitable and powerful.

James steps back, and Adam comes forward. His voice is lighter and less severe than his brother's, and he wears several overlapping cord necklaces. "I'm excited to share the details of this year's Bachelor candidacy with you. First, many thanks to our professors who will be running the competition, to our Masters who have arrived today in advance of their judging and participation duties, and to the students who assist in keeping this process running smoothly."

*Get on with it already.* Isn't the announcement of nominations the whole reason this meeting is happening?

He turns to Carrigan, and I wait for the third brother to come forward and say something. Instead, he raises a single eyebrow.

Adam sighs and turns back to the mic. "I suppose I will lead the nominations for candidates. If you have a student to nominate, please stand."

Virgil's eyes dart around the room, examining the people getting up from their chairs, I assume searching for whoever he thinks might nominate me.

In the crowd, I spot Natalie looking at me. But in a blink, her gaze is elsewhere. Fast enough to make me question if she really was watching me. She doesn't stand and neither does Corris beside her.

Adam points to a Master and asks to hear the woman's nomination. She names Violet Sharma, a South Asian—looking girl with dark hair and equally dark eye makeup and lipstick. The crowd claps, Adam wishes her luck, and both the nominator and nominee sit down.

It continues on like that. Adam points to a Master and hears their nomination, and more and more of them sit down. James is rapt with attention during the ceremony, while their brother Carrigan scrolls on his phone the whole time.

When one boy's name is called, Caden Mosser, Virgil sucks in a breath beside me. I look at him, and he shakes his head. There doesn't seem to be anything special about the kid. He's white with brown hair cropped neatly, dressed in a button-down shirt and pants. He looks like the guy in class who raises his hand to ask a question and makes a devil's advocate statement instead.

As the nominations continue, my own knee starts bouncing, and I do nothing to stop it. I lick my lips and try not to think of Jules, who it is becoming increasingly obvious I've already failed. Fuck. I didn't think things would go wrong so quickly. I should have sucked it up and groveled to Henry like I was supposed to. Like the old August would have.

The final Master names his candidate, and it isn't me.

When they both sit down, the sound echoes in my ears, even though I know it was only a slight swish of fabric.

Beside me, Virgil sits ramrod straight. I think if I touched him, he would fall over.

I make the mistake of looking around and see smirks directed toward us. Toward *him*.

I swallow and bow my head. I'm thinking of Mom. Of what she said that day, the last time I saw her.

*"You need to learn to take things seriously and be responsible! You can see your friends any day of the week. That's a privilege! I'm trying to teach*

*you a skill. I cannot believe you would be this ungrateful. This flippant. Do you think success is something that gets handed to you? Do you?!"*

"I'm still grateful," Virgil mumbles, and I start, choking on nothing. "You tried. I asked, and you tried. And I'll always appreciate that."

My bottom lip trembles, and I suck it into my mouth to hide it. I can't listen to this. I can't listen to him try to act like he isn't disappointed. Like he isn't furious at me. If he could, he would say the same things she did. He's thinking them. He must be. *Ungrateful. Flippant. Irresponsible.*

"The final nomination shall be made by me."

I'm so caught in my thoughts that I almost miss Adam's words. My neck snaps up. And I'm not the only one. Everyone was already listening, but this level of attention is sharper. The air in the room is humid and stifling. So thick that I'm struggling to breathe.

Adam says, "I would like to nominate August Black."

He . . . Did he just . . . ?

"Stand," Margot hisses, and I shoot to my feet.

I lock eyes with Adam, this man who's clearly important and yet a complete stranger to me. "I wish you luck," he says with a smile.

His brothers, on the other hand, look less than delighted. James's lips are pressed together in clear disapproval. And Carrigan has finally decided to look away from his phone to stare at me through the curtain of his curly bangs. Like he's trying to figure out what possessed his brother to nominate me.

There's clapping, but it's choppy and scattered, like people can't decide if they should be doing it or not. Margot tugs the hem of my skirt. I sit, smacking onto my chair hard enough to actually create an echo in the room.

I look at Virgil, who stares back with wide eyes.

Somehow . . . we've done it. Or, no, Henry did it. At the front of the room, he's focused on the stage, not looking back once. When I shift my attention to the platform, Carrigan is still staring. Though he returns to scrolling on his phone when I meet his eyes.

James steps forward again and clears his throat. "Finally, we have a grave announcement for you all. I admit that I'd hoped to open the meeting with this, but the Doctorate insisted that no part of the candidacy be interrupted for his sake." If the crowd was rapt before, now they're ravenous. They lean forward in their seats, licking and biting lips, nails digging into thighs. They hang on James's words, ready to rip into what's said next. "Our father, the sixth Doctorate, Cyrus Shaw, has passed."

The room explodes into chaos. People burst into literal tears, crying out. Some fall to the floor sobbing. The whole room becomes a bleeding wound of weeping and screams.

"What the fuck?" I whisper.

Nothing could have prepared me for the sheer devoutness of these people. No wonder they believe in this apocalypse. They seem like they would believe anything the Doctorate told them. How did a group of people trying to cure a dangerous mutation become this?

James lets the people mourn, though he doesn't cry himself. His face remains stoic, but there's a sort of irritation to his expression. It's the way the creases at the corners of his eyes crinkle and narrow. I notice Carrigan studying his brother.

"Silence," Adam commands, raising his hands, and all at once, the crowd collects themselves. For some people, this means physically clasping their hands over their mouths.

James continues, "As you may be aware, our father has three

A MASTERY OF MONSTERS

living sons—myself, Adam, and Carrigan—who have inherited the Doctorate's gift. It was our father's wish that the choice for who among us shall lead you next be decided . . . democratically."

"Holy shit," Virgil breathes.

"Is it not usually democratic?" I whisper to him.

"We've never had multiple options for a Doctorate, period," Virgil says. "Either they've only had one child per the rules of succession that Dr. Weiss set, or if they ended up with two, only one inherited the ability. We'd assumed that Cyrus would just appoint one of his sons."

James says, "Everyone shall have the right to vote, from students, to monsters, to Bachelors and Masters. We will reconvene for the vote at the end of the fall term before the Bachelor candidacy initiation. Please be intimate in your grief and lean on your peers for support. As in everything, there is a learning in this."

"There is a learning in all," everyone says back. And it's worse now, with most of the crowd overcome with tears and snotty noses.

But all I can think is that I got the nomination. And not because of me, I know, but because of Virgil. Because of these people around him willing to bet on me because he picked me.

I don't care how I did it. All that matters is that I'm one step closer to finding Jules.

# CHAPTER TEN

Sweat pours down my forehead into my eyes as I pump my legs harder and faster to the sound of the whistle blows. I sprint across the field, the sun punishing on my back, and as the whistle sounds twice, I spin on my heel and run in the other direction. It blows again, and I run, again and again, until I trip over my feet and land flat on the grass. We've been going like this for half an hour already. And I only got nominated yesterday.

I'm wheezing. Actually wheezing.

My knife holsters, which Margot insisted that I wear every time we train, are digging into my thighs even set on the largest notch. Before we moved, I threw away all the clothes I had that didn't fit. I was never going to be the old August again, and that extended to my body. This is me now, in every way. But I hadn't thought about my holsters. I need a new set.

Corey squats in front of me and holds out a water bottle, which I take from her. "Thanks," I gasp.

Margot spits the whistle out of her mouth. "Did I say it was time for a water break?"

"But she fell down," Corey says. "And she seems thirsty."

My trainer rolls her eyes.

"Let's just take the break." Virgil sticks his hands into the pockets of tweed shorts that expose the massive muscles of his calves. Shorts that he's tucked his maroon polo shirt into without an ounce of shame.

I shake my head. "Where are you buying your clothes?"

"At stores? Like everyone else?" He gestures to his body. "The quality that I assume you're noticing actually comes from the tailoring. Good tail—"

"No, stop, I don't really care." I push myself up, gulping down more water.

When the three of them showed up, I thought they'd decided to train on Wolfe Island for my convenience, only to have Margot clarify that she wanted to train here so no one in the society could see how shitty I am.

"Is this preliminary test just running drills?" I ask.

"No," Margot sneers. "That was your warm-up."

I close my eyes and try to take a deep breath. My usual form of physical activity is drunken dancing. It's fun. Throwing knives is fun too. Running is something I did because I hated myself.

"Get up," Margot says.

I open my eyes and glare at her.

"Maybe a longer break than that," Virgil says, stepping between us. "We can use the time to explain the process more."

I refuse to be grateful to him, because his deal is why I'm suffering like this in the first place, but at least I feel like Virgil is on my

100                                           LISELLE SAMBURY

side. Corey, too. Margot low-key seems like she wishes she could train anyone but me.

"Whatever. Call me when you're ready." Margot stalks away from us, disappearing into the trees that surround the massive flat field we've been training in.

I unstrap the holsters, freeing my squished thighs, and toss them to the side.

"Prelims do actually involve a beep test, though," Corey says with a grimace. "And rope climbing."

I flop back on the grass. "Great. It's gym class."

"Just that one part," Virgil says, sitting next to me. "Everything will be split into three sections. Physical endurance, societal knowledge, and monster affinity. You need to get through prelims first, then there will be three training sessions you need to do well in so you can be nominated by the professors to go into the finals, which is three tests with eliminations. The top five scorers will be allowed to participate in the initiation for the possibility to become Bachelors."

The information is dizzying and confirms that everyone was right—Virgil hadn't explained very much. Though knowing the details wouldn't have made a difference. I was all in for Jules's sake. "I thought I was becoming a Master."

"Not quite." Corey settles on the grass between us, so the three of us are in a circle. "Once you've gone through the initiation, which is the bonding process, you'll have made the connection to allow Virgil to maintain control. At the ceremony after initiation, you're officially given the title of Bachelor. You don't get a Master title until you've competed in the Monster's Ball. Then you're a Master-in-training like Margot, and once you've defended your title in a second round of the Monster's Ball, that's when you become a full-fledged

Master. And after five years, you're considered senior."

"Is this Monster's Ball another competition where I could die?"

"Yes," Corey and Virgil say at the same time.

I groan. "Why do you have so many of them?"

Virgil says, "Monsters have to be pushed in order to evolve and become stronger. That requires life-threatening circumstances. The entire point is to train so we're powerful enough to help in the apocalypse. For that, we have to be better than just any wild monster. And we have to be better as a pair."

"And what are all these Masters doing while we wait for the end of the world?"

"Some teach like Henry. They usually have a day job, but they're also expected to do missions," Corey says. "Masters who are done with the competitions are dispatched to help deal with bitten monsters who have to be corralled after transformation, or born monsters who turn before they're bonded, or monsters whose partner dies abruptly and need to be controlled, Wilds who act out, and—"

I lift my hands up to stop her. "So, out-of-control monsters?"

"Yes . . ." Corey bites her lip. "Though some also take on private security contracts, which is technically allowed."

I snort. Wow, so people *are* making money off this. I can't fault the opportunists. It's not that different from what I'm doing.

Corey says, "Either way, even Bachelor rank is a status boost, so you'll have the clout to find information about your brother."

"It's just easier to say Master than to explain the full thing," Virgil adds.

"Okay, and once I'm a Bachelor or whatever, I control you and stop you from killing people and stuff? That's what the bonding does?"

He winces. "That's . . . simplified. It's passive. The bonding itself will allow me to maintain control. You don't actually need to *do* anything."

"What does the bonding entail, then, if initiation is just the bonding? You guys are talking about it like it's another trial or something."

He hesitates, and I look at Corey. She looks at Virgil, who stares back, more of that silent communication passing between them. She says to him, "Probably best to share the details now rather than later."

Because that's not ominous at all.

Virgil swallows. "The initiation is the final stage of the candidacy. We'll each be given the serum. It was developed by Dr. Weiss three years after forming the society. It forces monsters to transform, and it's also what allows us to bond through flesh exchange."

I remember Corey discussing the serum as one of the methods that activates the monster mutation, but she failed to mention that last bit. "Flesh exchange," I repeat.

"Yes . . . Usually, chunks of skin or toes or fingers. You'll probably notice that most Bachelors and Masters have scars. That's often why."

I force myself not to look at Corey's hands. *Fingers* . . . She said she participated in the candidacy once. "I thought Weiss was trying to make a cure, not force monsters to transform."

"*Dr.* Weiss," Virgil corrects once again. *For fuck's sake.* "And he was. The serum was supposed to be a cure. Instead, it transformed the Patient Zero victims into the sort of monsters we know today. But it also allowed for the bonding and became more of a temporary solution. It changed the monster mutation, and in ordinary humans, it created a new mutation that's similar to the Doctorate ability. The serum formula is kept secret, but we do know that something of the Doctorate's body goes into it. That's why Masters are able to develop some of a Doctorate's power, at least enough to control one monster. A lot of this stuff doesn't follow the known rules of science, which is exactly why finding a cure has been so hard. But basically, something about the complementary mutations allows for the bond."

"Humans gain some monster abilities, and monsters gain human control," Corey says.

"Monster abilities? Like what?" At no point before had they mentioned that I might change too. "Like, horns or something?"

Virgil scrubs at his face. "No, like, increased speed, endurance, and other abilities unique to that monster. And even those require additional training to master. For now, you only need to focus on getting to the initiation and successfully bonding."

"But when you take the serum, you'll turn into monster form right away, won't you? How are we supposed to do the flesh exchange and this bonding while you're like that?"

"That's the challenge of initiation."

"Amazing," I say with a laugh. "I guess that's the deadly part of this whole thing?" He nods, and the water I chugged swirls in my stomach. If I get to the end of this competition, I have to lose a part of my body *and* avoid being murdered by a monster.

This is why I need to find Jules before it gets that far. Sure, fancy monster superpowers sound cool, but at what cost? With any luck, I won't have to do any of that shit. I avoid looking at Virgil as if he can read my thoughts from my expression. It sucks for him, but I don't owe him anything. When the time comes, I'll act like I failed to perform at a task. It's me. He's already primed for disappointment. I'll just be fulfilling his expectations.

I ask, "If the bond is passive, does that mean our deranged rabbit friend is acting on its own? Meaning that even if a Master is connected to the monster, they might not know it came after me?"

Virgil shakes his head. "It's unlikely. This is a partnership. The Master would be aware of what the monster was doing. Letting the monster act like that would mean cosigning it."

"Unless the Master is scared of the monster coming at them or something. I imagine the bond dissolves if the Master dies, but they could still be hurt and threatened, right?"

"It's not possible. The bond is passive but it *can* be active. Masters can exert conscious control over their partner when they're in monster form. They can only do it in that state, not when their partner is in human form, but still. That's why it's important to pick your partner carefully. So you don't end up with someone who would do that to you. In a normal partnership, the bonding would passively allow me to maintain control, and we would work together as a team."

"That's kind of fucked up. There's no recourse for the monster." It adds a potential new spin on the Easter Bunny from hell. Maybe it was forced. Then again, I'm not warm to giving it the benefit of the doubt. It did try to kill me, after all.

"They can report the Master while in human form," Virgil says.

"Though punishment for that isn't well enforced," Corey says, pulling a blade of grass from the ground. "And the punishment would be that the tie between the monster and the Master is severed by the Doctorate, leaving them partnerless. They'd be sent underground. So how likely are they to report?"

"It's not supposed to happen," Virgil says. "Also, most monster forms are huge. To keep them in that state to exert control, you'd need to have a good place to hide them. It's not feasible. Eventually, the Master would need to sleep. Controlling a monster like that is something they have to actively do. It couldn't happen while they're sleeping, so the monster could transform back into a human and be free."

"Free to lose their partner and become a mindless monster again like Corey said?" I add. "Or otherwise keep quiet and never transform again? How would that fly if they got sent on missions?"

Virgil stands. "It's not relevant to us. And you should get up. I know Margot can be . . ."

"A bitch?" I supply.

He sighs. "That's ruder than I would have put it."

"Intense?" Corey suggests.

"Yes, that, but she means well. It's just a lot of pressure for all of us. Adam is a Doctorate candidate in a voting situation now. Your performance reflects on him and on Henry. Henry will blame Margot if you're not properly trained, and his status helps her take care of her brother."

Everyone in this society is so obsessed with their reputation. Minus Margot, I guess, who cares more about her brother. Something that's at least relatable.

"Besides," Virgil says. "We want to get in as much training as possible before the school year starts."

"Yeah, I guess she'll be busy with classes," I say.

"You will too."

I laugh. "No, I won't. I finished high school. I'm done."

Virgil and Corey exchange a look.

My eyes dart between them. "What the fuck was that?"

Virgil says, "To confirm . . . would you . . . for some reason, be opposed to going to one of Canada's most prestigious universities? Queen's, for example? Also, why?"

I jerk to my feet. "I'm not going."

"You have to go," Margot says from behind us, returning from between the trees. "It's compulsory. You cannot even participate in the candidacy unless you're enrolled in a university. Corey only could at fifteen because her grades were ridiculous, and she was already being educated by the society, and even then, strings had to be pulled. And you have an acceptance to Queen's on file with a nonresponse, so Henry facilitated things. You start in the fall. Do not be late enrolling in your courses, and do not fall into academic probation. Both will result in disqualification."

The ground seems to shift beneath me. Rippling and roiling, doing its best to toss me off my feet. "Is there anything else I should know before we get started, since there's apparently a bunch you guys decided not to share?"

Virgil keeps giving me this wide-eyed, open-mouthed stare. This boy truly cannot comprehend why I wouldn't want to go to this school.

Going to Queen's was the plan from *before*. Now not only do I have to attend, but I also have to do well enough not to flunk out. All while participating in this physically demanding competition that will require me to learn about this cult, and somehow in there, I'm supposed to find time to figure out what happened to Jules in order to avoid actually having to compete in anything that might unalive me.

"Let's just run the drills," I say, tossing the water bottle onto the grass and standing.

Margot picks up a discarded holster and pulls out a knife,

A MASTERY OF MONSTERS                                         107

running her thumb along the edge of one, then another, and another. "These are dull."

"Wow, it's like you're Sherlock Holmes or something." The look she throws me actually makes me step back. "I know they're dull. Do you have a sharpening person?"

She speaks slowly. "You don't know . . . how to sharpen your own knives?"

"I do," I say quickly, although I can feel my cheeks get hot. "Just wondered if you had a designated person. But I can do it."

"Good. Sharpen them for the next session. You should be practicing regularly. We need to build up a strong base, and then Corey and I can help with more specialized combat training. I do still get paid a TA fee for your training if you do nothing, but I would appreciate if you did well. For Henry's—"

"Yes, I get it. Everyone's reputation or whatever."

"No," she says, pointing a finger at me. "You don't get it. You have no idea what you've stumbled into, and neither did we, because none of us predicted Cyrus dying and an election both happening this year. Now these cute factions everyone has been sitting in have become relevant. The Progressives are the only ones who want to give my brother even the tiniest scrap of rights within this society, and for that to happen, Adam needs to win. And believe it or not, if you fuck up, it's going to make him look like his judgment is flawed. Or maybe it won't, but we can't gamble here. You will go to classes, you will do well, and you will finish this candidacy with some kind of respectable standard. Ideally, you will win so Virgil can live as something other than a rabid beast."

The box is closing around me. All I want to do is rip and tear and scream until I'm out, and then run as far away as possible. I don't need this shit. More rules and expectations. I'm done with that. I've been done for nine fucking months.

It was one thing to do what my parents wanted because I didn't know any better. But at least this time, there's a goal. I'm not just doing this for the sake of it. I'm doing it for *Jules*. It has to be worth it.

# CHAPTER ELEVEN

That Saturday, I drop my bag on the floor and look around the small space that I'll be living in for as long as it takes me to find Jules. The society prefers that I stay on campus, and so Henry is not only covering my tuition for the year but also my room in Victoria Hall. The same dorm Jules was in. Though I'm on the fifth floor in the B wing.

The halls are crowded with parents and students carrying suitcases and bloated garbage bags filled with clothes. Lots of tear-filled hugging and goodbyes. Or otherwise, loud shouts and laughs.

Dad used to talk about this moment all the time. Moving me into the Queen's dorms. He was in peak form when we dropped Jules off last year. He and Mom both wore their old tricolor rugby shirts, and he talked about the places they used to hang out on campus. He wanted to make sure that I was paying attention since I would be here next year. Then he lectured Jules about balancing his schoolwork with fun—good friends will always be there, but you can destroy your GPA for all four years with a single full credit course.

We took a bunch of pictures in front of the buildings. The perfect family being perfect. That was us, always. There are these memories, family vacations and Christmas dinners and movie nights where, in the moment, I thought I was happy. Maybe I was. But only because I was being who they wanted me to be.

I was jealous when we moved Jules into Vic Hall because he was already here, and I would have to wait until next year. I wanted that warm glow of our parents' beaming smiles and tight, generous hugs.

Now that expression on Dad's face is the last thing I want to see. How happy he'd be to see me back on the road he's spent my whole life steering me on. He's called multiple times today and sent a text about how proud he is, and how he's busy with his start of the school year prep, but he'd like to drop by.

I have no intention of responding.

I'm grateful when me and Corey arrive at the quiet of my room at 506. Virgil had to go get some paperwork set up with Henry, who is apparently his legal guardian. I said I could move in alone, but Corey insisted that would be depressing and she should come.

The room is big enough for a single bed featuring a bare mattress pushed against the right wall and a desk on the opposite wall that has a flat laminate wood tone with shelving overtop. There's a window overlooking a parking lot, and the walls are painted brick and cool to the touch. Finally, near the door there's a set of drawers and a narrow closet in the same laminate tone as the desk. It's basically the exact reverse of Jules's room.

Corey bustles in with a giant bedding set that she told me was my housewarming gift. I'm glad, honestly, because I hadn't even thought about getting one. Without her, I would be sleeping on a naked mattress.

"I also put a topper in. You gotta separate yourself as much as possible from their mattress." She strolls around the room and brushes aside the curtains to peer down at the parking lot. "Not much of a view, but at least you're central. Can you believe we're first years? And a little birdie named Henry told me he can even get us into the same frosh group. It's like a dream!"

I stare around the room. "Dream? Nightmare? Same difference."

She sits in the desk chair, crossing one leg over the other. Today she has a skirt on. Her prosthetic leg starts just below her left knee.

I groan as I sit on the bed. My entire body has been sore ever since Margot started her training, which consists of constant horrible drills and her getting pissed at me for not having sharpened my knives yet. Even though they work perfectly fine as is! I've also been forced to go running every morning by myself, which is especially grueling.

Corey makes a face, looking from me to the bed. "Separation from the mattress . . ."

"I'm wearing shorts!"

"Still . . ." She eyes the bed like she expects a torrent of bugs to erupt from it.

I drop my head back against the brick.

Corey shifts on the chair. "Can I ask you something personal?"

"Shoot."

"Why didn't you confirm your acceptance?"

"Because I didn't want to." It's an honest answer. But it's also a lot more complicated than that. "Can I ask *you* something personal?"

"Sure."

"The society is a cult, right?"

She laughs. "Wow, I do like you."

"I mean . . . you believe in an apocalypse. That's kind of cult-y." Not to mention those reactions to Cyrus's death. It made me feel like I was living on a separate plane of existence.

"I know what it sounds like, but the apocalypse is real. Tracking monster births was simple at first. We watched bloodlines via born or bitten monsters. We also prevented a lot of bites when we started imprisoning out-of-control monsters. However, Dr. Weiss predicted that one of the early signs of the apocalypse would be spontaneously born monsters. No bloodline and no bite. Just appearing. And that's been on an upward trend for a while. And those monsters turn faster too." She swallows. "There's an eight-year-old girl who turned. Spontaneous. No one in her family was ever a monster. She was having an argument with her mom, and then . . ." Corey shakes her head. "She tore them apart."

I flex my hands, the palms feeling hot suddenly.

"The full apocalypse will see people spontaneously developing the mutation and having it activated instantly. Like the effects of a bite without an actual bite. It's never happened before, but Dr. Weiss felt that the spontaneous births, which already existed, were the closest step toward that. I know it sounds silly. I do think we should consider rebranding since 'apocalypse' is, like, very dramatic. But it's real. We have the data to prove it. There's a feeling that the serum can help protect people from turning when the time comes, but we don't know for sure." She licks her lips. "I think most of us just hope it won't happen in our time."

"You and me both." I can't imagine the sort of carnage that would bring. A big part of me still wants to deny it, but a couple

A MASTERY OF MONSTERS

of weeks ago, I would have denied the existence of monsters, too. Ignorance isn't my friend right now. Even if I don't buy into the apocalypse thing, clearly, the spontaneous monster births make things more dangerous for everyone. If the society couldn't keep up anymore it'd be bad. "But it's not just the apocalypse that's giving cult. There are other things too."

Corey nods. "Honestly, I understand that impression. Especially with the way people responded to the Doctorate's death, but cults are controlling and abusive. The society helps people."

I cross my arms. "Interesting, because I have this vague memory of being forced to attend a school I didn't want to attend."

She opens her mouth and then shuts it, thinking for a moment. "The society is an organization, and it's integrated into the country's academic systems. Beyond Canada too, though they organize their chapters a little differently. But overall, it's a means of protection for you. Our students are embedded at every level. This is how Bachelors and Masters like Margot can automatically get TA positions that fund living. Or how payment can be provided for extracurriculars like the training of a candidate. And I know you didn't want to go here, but you being a candidate is also the only reason that Virgil can attend."

"What does that mean?"

She shifts in place. "Monsters . . . because of volatility, are not allowed to attend any post-secondaries unless they're paired with a candidate, Bachelor, or Master. They have special society-created monster schools for compulsory education like elementary and high school. To keep them apart from the general population and decrease possible exposure. But none of the ones in the city would take Virgil. Bernie offering to tutor him and Dr. Liu agreeing to have him live at

McIntosh Castle is the only reason he got a base education. And he still wouldn't have even gotten that far without Henry vouching for him and becoming his guardian. Of course, Virgil wanted to go to Queen's, but without you, he couldn't."

"How is this supposed to be convincing me that this isn't an oppressive cult?"

Corey smiles without mirth. "I'm trying to show you that the society is an imperfect organization. No different from the university itself or the government. But it helps people. We have a lot in place for that. My parents came in as students and within a couple of years were given the rent-to-own condo that I grew up in. Only possible because the society owns the building. Many students experience that. It's just that for people like Virgil . . . it's flawed. That's why the Progressive faction exists. So those sorts of rules can be amended or abolished. The faction has existed on and off throughout the society's history, like the others, but this is the closest we've come to making big changes. And we now have a democratic process to achieve that. It's not perfect, but cults don't hold elections."

She's got me there. And I guess I know now why Virgil was so desperate to find someone. It's not just about the monster thing, it's also about what he is or isn't allowed to do. It's like he said that first day on the island. With a partner, he can have a life.

Or, at least, he can until I find Jules and leave.

I swallow and wipe my palms on my shorts.

Corey leans back in the chair. "Dr. Weiss said that everyone has two shadows. The physical projection you see on the ground and the inner projection of your monster. We all swap shadows with the monster sometimes. It's a grave mistake to assume that only the monsters you can see require mastery. For each and every one of us,

A MASTERY OF MONSTERS

in the absence of control, our monsters can destroy one another as surely as claws and fangs."

I don't ask Corey if maybe some monsters need to be set free. If sometimes, destruction is better than the stifling feeling of being controlled by someone else. Of having everything you do decided for you. Isn't breaking free of that worth a little damage? Instead, I say, "Wow, all that wisdom, and he still couldn't realize that shadow metaphors are both cringey and overdone."

She laughs. "It is kind of cheesy, isn't it? But I believe that it's true. I also believe that what the Progressives could do, what Adam Shaw could do, is have more people acknowledge that truth. In the early days, 'monster' wasn't even a designation. There were just Masters and their partners. The title was a subversion of servitude, celebrating the mastery of a monster by *both* parties, an equal partnership. One day, I hope people will remember that was the original teaching of Dr. Weiss. But first, we'll focus on helping Virgil."

I know Corey believes what she's saying, and there is something beautiful about the way this society was supposed to be. But at the same time, why not call both people in the partnership Masters if it's so equal? Why give one a title and the other nothing? "And what makes Virgil so special? Why are all these people so invested in helping him?"

"Because we like him."

My jaw drops a bit. "That's it?"

Corey shrugs. "Henry knew his parents, so that contributes. And I think Dr. Liu would help anyone who needed it and loved books. But for me and Bernie, that's it." She grips the edge of the desk chair. "I came to McIntosh Castle after I failed the initiation. My partner and I . . . It didn't go well. I lost some bits and pieces." She lifts her prosthetic leg with a wry smile, and then lets it drop back to the floor. "Everyone was disappointed. My parents. All the people rooting for me. The Master who nominated me won't even look at me anymore. I wanted to escape, and Dr. Liu was the only one willing to help. I wasn't . . . I wasn't very nice to Virgil, not at first. Wouldn't speak to or interact with him in any way. I pretended he didn't exist. Honestly, I was afraid of him. I was afraid of all monsters. . . . Still am."

I think back to when Margot had Isaac transform. That was the reason Corey went to sit in the car. She couldn't bring herself to be that close to a monster in that form.

"But Virgil was always kind to me," she says. "He has spent his entire life being treated like scum, and he's still *him*. He's better than who he should be. I guess it's hard not to want to protect someone like that. And so I have no choice but to believe in you, for his sake. You have the potential to achieve Bachelor. I'll help with societal knowledge and some of the physical training along with Margot, and Virgil can handle monster affinity."

"Why would I be able to do this if you couldn't after training for it your whole life?" I ask, gaze on the ground. And what would she think if she knew my real plans?

Corey regards me for a moment before she answers. "People act like this competition is only about skill or knowledge, but when you've been through it, you know that the most important part is the relationship between you and your partner. Mine and I . . .Well, I was born to fight for him. Literally." She licks her lips. "My parents were invited into the society in the first place because their bloodline was traced back. There was a possibility of my mom having a monster child. We have testing for the mutation, but only for postnatal,

A MASTERY OF MONSTERS                                                117

so they couldn't know ahead of time. When my brother was born, his test came back positive. He had the mutation. So they started trying for another baby. One who could partner with him. It's rare for two monsters to be born in a row, after all. The odds were good. From the moment I came into the world, I had a specific purpose. I was here to fight for my brother's humanity. I know you have a different relationship with your brother, so perhaps you can't imagine what it might be like to grow up knowing you only exist because he does."

But Corey failed. So then . . . what happened to her brother? Did they imprison him, or did he try to run away like Bernie's son and get taken out? Until this moment, I hadn't even known she had a brother. Not that it feels anywhere near the right time to ask. "I'm sorry," I say, because it seems like the only appropriate response.

She flattens her lips into a tight smile. "You aren't the one who should be apologizing. What I'm saying is, I know you don't see eye-to-eye, but you and Virgil are a good pair. He doesn't view himself as human, and I know that, strictly speaking, his isn't, but he's so willing to compromise himself for other people, maybe to prove that he *is* human. Honestly, you're kind of giving him a taste of his own medicine. After all, you're risking your life for someone else too, aren't you?"

I swallow. "You guys said that the chances of dying are low."

"But not zero. And no one gets out of the candidacy unscathed." She grips her left hand into a fist. The one with the missing fingers. "You are actively putting yourself in danger. And I kind of feel like you like it that way. I see that in you because I've seen it in Virgil. You two are more alike than you think, and that's why you'll work well together. Instinctively, you understand each other."

"Work well together? All we've done so far is piss each other off."

She grins. "You don't know Virgil like I do. He doesn't go out of his way to follow girls he doesn't know to learn more about them. He doesn't push against Henry, which rejecting his candidates and choosing you definitely counts as. Virgil has spent most of his life passively accepting his circumstances. But you, you make him fight. So yes, I do think you two have the potential to do well together."

I don't know what to say to that. Virgil is wound so tight, and I let everything go a while ago. It's hard to think of us being similar in any way, but I can't dispute what Corey said either. And this is a competition. We'll need to fight to win, and if that's what I bring out in him, our chances are better. I'm willing to do whatever it takes to help Jules, even knowing that this is the last thing he would want me to be involved in.

Corey stands. "Now, let's make this bed so you can stop sitting on it. It's giving me the ick."

# CHAPTER TWELVE

The weekend passes in a blur of frosh activities that Corey forces me to attend, including painting what looked like an auto worker's uniform, getting shaving cream in my hair, and learning a choreographed dance that we have to perform at random intervals. All of which is supposedly fun. While still doing grueling training sessions with Margot alongside my daily morning run. By the time the first day of class rolls around on Tuesday, I'm almost glad. Almost.

I'm late for my first, second, and third classes of the day. Unlike in high school, where I kept perfect attendance. Here, I'm in lecture halls that can easily hold hundreds of students, so walking in late doesn't carry the same weight. I sit in the back with my laptop, staring as they go through the syllabus while people beside me watch videos or play on their phones.

Under Henry's strong suggestion, which I received via Margot, I decided to be a psychology major. I hoped this was so he could affect my grades to make sure I didn't fail, but Margot assured me it was to make it easier for him to find me tutors or potentially get me a paid TA position in the future. I wondered if it was another way for him to keep me under his thumb and make sure I wasn't endangering his reputation.

It doesn't matter. All I have to do is study well enough to pass, and psychology is at least straightforward. You memorize facts, and you spit them out. I can do that. It's the same with the society basics that Corey has gone over with me, dates and names. Everything else she said that I needed to know, I'd already learned conversationally via her, Margot, or Virgil.

It's not like the old August was going to study anything she wanted to either. Mom wanted a doctor and Dad a professor, and she won, so I was looking down the barrel of maybe a decade of school and intense competition. If anything, Henry's forced major is kinder. And as a first year, the only requirement for the major is to take PSYC100. The rest can be electives. I could take classes I'm interested in. Instead, I sign up for the courses that seem the easiest to pass.

Actually being engaged in my studies would make me try to do well instead of coasting. Study harder. Excel, even. And one day I would turn around and find myself staring into the mirror at the old August. Doing what Mom and Dad wanted again. Being a "perfect" student. And then, how long until everything else reverted too? Back to trying to impress the "perfect" people who were supposed to be my friends. Back to chasing the "perfect" body.

It was better to avoid it completely. After all, I'm not supposed to be here in the first place. All this is temporary. And it's not like I had any idea of what I'd prefer to do instead. I never thought about it because it was never an option.

When my final class ends, I leave Humphrey Hall with the other rush of students. It's technically September, but the weather is still operating on summer heat as if fall is more a dream than a reality. The sun beats down on me, and I shield my eyes with my hands because I refuse to be like the rest of the freshmen, who are either wearing designer shades or the free ones that dozens of brands threw at us during the first week in a desperate attempt to entice new customers.

All I want to do is go back to my room and sleep.

Instead, I hike my bag onto my shoulder and head toward the bookstore. I'm still not used to navigating campus, and after ten minutes of being confused, I give up and use Google Maps. I pass by Summerhill, my eyes lingering on the building. In a little over a month, I'll be called back there to find out if I made the first cut after training. Though I won't even get to the training phase if I can't pass the preliminaries today.

Why would they make it the first day of class? It's like they're trying to overwhelm us.

I walk through one of the back alleyways, following my phone's instructions. Though alleyway isn't quite the right word. Between a lot of the buildings are these separate paths and roads, some of them large enough to fit multiple car lanes, and others only big enough for a footpath.

I spend five minutes walking around the same gray stone building before I realize that the entrance to the bookstore is inexplicably not at the actual front of the building facing the main street but at the back that faces nothing. Which I guess is why the map wanted me to go the back way.

The store is packed full of students with textbooks in their arms and others looking at the shelves and racks of Queen's branded merchandise—hoodies, sweaters, mugs, key chains, and more. I'm about to turn when I see a familiar white girl.

Rachel notices me at the same moment that I notice her. If it were just the two of us, we could have moved on. But unfortunately, her mom is with her. I'm not even surprised that Ms. Hanes overstayed past move-in day when normal parents know to go home and instead planted herself like a fungus all the way to the first day of class.

"August?! Is that you?" she exclaims, coming toward me.

Rachel is forced to follow. She's ditched her signature high ponytail for a bob that is maybe an attempt at a wolf cut. She manages a tight smile. I don't bother.

Her mom is oblivious. She's a Queen's alum, wearing a faded leather jacket with her graduation year stitched on her arm. My parents hadn't gotten the jackets because they were too expensive. "I almost didn't recognize you!" she says. "You look so different."

"Yeah. I'm fat now."

The smile slides off her face, and the corners of her mouth hang limp.

I grin in response. To her, fat is a bad word. For me, I've stated a fact, one that she was already dancing around with her "you look so different" comment. No one but me has the right to make fun little observations about my body, but everyone else is so eager to do it.

"I thought you weren't going to Queen's anymore?" Rachel asks, sparing her mom any further struggle.

"I changed my mind."

This is the girl I used to spend all my time with. Countless days at her house and school and choir, which she forced me to join over dance. We stayed put in Toronto the longest of all Mom's job-related

A MASTERY OF MONSTERS

moves, and so even though me and Rachel had only known each other since tenth grade, she was my oldest friend. We were going to be roommates at Queen's.

Then Mom disappeared, and I became less interested in the upkeep of being friends with Rachel. I didn't stop myself from saying the "wrong" things. I didn't dress or do my hair the way I was supposed to anymore. And she tried to help me, of course she did. Suggested that I stop being "weird" and made comments about what I was choosing to eat for lunch—like, didn't I want to try this new workout routine with her? Just to tone up before first year. And eventually she stopped inviting me over, or meeting me after classes, or sitting with me at lunch.

When the deadline for roommate sign-ups came and I told her I wasn't going to Queen's anymore, the relief on her face was palpable. That is, until I said I'd be moving to Kingston, so we'd probably see each other. She promised we'd still text and that we'd meet for coffee once she got on campus.

Neither of those things ever happened.

Ms. Hanes recovers enough to say, "Well, I guess you girls will see each other around, then."

"We won't." It's the quiet part out loud, which makes both Rachel and her mom shift their gazes around the space. Like something will jump out and save them from the conversation.

My former bestie tugs on her mom's sleeve. "Let's check out the hoodies."

Ms. Hanes gives me a small wave and pained smile as she and her daughter retreat. They don't even wait to get out of earshot before Rachel says, "Why would you go up to her? We haven't talked in months."

Her mom starts to say something about grief and kindness, which I take as my cue to go into the basement, whose bookshelves are organized by subject. I do my best to push the entire interaction out of my mind.

I walk to the psychology section and fumble with my phone, trying to find the books I'm supposed to get. Henry via Margot gave me a credit card to use for them and other school supplies, noting that statements would be checked, and it would be taken away if abused. This would have been my wet dream early last year. Going to Queen's with everything paid for and involved with a group that held real-life influence, even if they were also cultlike. Not because I wanted those things but because it was what I knew everyone would want for me. What they would be impressed by.

Jules should be here, and I shouldn't.

"And here I thought you weren't a student," says a feminine voice. I turn to a girl who I vaguely recognize. She has her hair styled in passion twists piled on top of her head and she has a gold nose ring. She catches me trying to place her and says, "I'm Riley. Part of the Queen's Black Student Society. You work at the Tim's in the ARC, right? But I distinctly remember you saying that you didn't go here."

Right. Her. "Well, now I do." I don't owe this random girl updates on my life.

She smiles and hands me a flyer. "Great. Well, we're having a freshman mixer soon, and we'd love for you to come. There will be food and drinks, nonalcoholic obviously. You can meet some people and get to know what we're about."

I take the flyer in the hopes that maybe this will get her to leave me alone.

"Psychology, that's what you're majoring in?" she asks.

A MASTERY OF MONSTERS

For fuck's sake, now it's a conversation? "Look," I say. "I'm trying to get my books and get out of here. I don't want to meet people. I don't want to go to events. I want to get my degree and get out."

Ever since they decided Mom was dead, it's like the tightly screwed lid I kept on my life has flown off. And I can't find it anywhere. Everything just spews out. All the messy shit that I would have kept hidden, now open and exposed.

Riley grins. "Wow, all business, eh?"

"No," I say with a smirk, pointing up at the sign. "Psychology."

"You're not cute," she says, her expression sobering.

I jerk my head back, my mouth ajar.

But then she smiles again. "I don't know where you come from or whatever, but there are going to be some things that only other Black people are going to get. We are trying to form a community within this place where you can feel safe to be yourself. We hang out, we support each other, and we make our voices heard when the school inevitably does some racist shit. All I'm asking is that you come for one mixer and see how you feel."

"You're persistent."

"I have to be, because a lot of kids here are from places that messed up how they experience their own Blackness. And not having support will make it worse. They don't realize they need this." Riley watches me roll my eyes at her, unfazed. "I hope to see you there. And at the very least, if you come, I'll stop bothering you."

"That is tempting."

"Oh, I know." She turns and walks upstairs.

Most of the students in the bookstore are shopping in groups, but she was alone. Plus, she didn't even grab any books. Did she . . .

did she see me and come in here just for that? Okay, she's persistent, but that would be too much. That's literal stalking.

I finish collecting my books and go upstairs to the checkout, where I give the cashier the credit card. It's black with both mine and the university's name on it. As the woman at the counter puts the books in the canvas tote for me, she whispers, "Good luck in prelims today."

I stare at her. She calls the next person in line, and I don't have time to wait around. Corey was right about the society students being inserted around campus. I have no idea who that woman is, but she definitely knows me.

Hefting the heavy tote onto the shoulder not occupied by my backpack, I walk up University Avenue toward the ARC. The one building that I know the location of. Though when I enter, I make sure not to look in the direction of the Tim Hortons. I never went back, but also never quit, so I assume I was fired.

I drag myself up the giant set of stairs to the second floor, only realizing halfway that I could have taken the elevator. There was a time when I refused to take an elevator for anything less than four floors, no matter what. Because I thought that was the clincher on whether or not I hit my goal weight for the week. "Every little bit counts," I used to whisper to myself.

When I reach the top of the steps, I have a thin sheen of sweat on my forehead. I know it's because I'm carrying new textbooks plus everything in my bag. I wish I could not think about people watching me, but I can't yet. It's funny how it literally doesn't matter what you do when you're fat, people will find a way to judge you. The same people who would be pleased to see me taking the stairs are also judging me for sweating while doing it. When I was thin, I could do

A MASTERY OF MONSTERS

whatever I wanted. Instead, I took the stairs and still found a way to hate myself.

Corey waves at me from a table where she, Margot, and Virgil sit. I fall into a seat next to them, and Corey hands me a smoothie. "I didn't know what you would like, and I know some people hate banana, so I got you peach mango."

"Thanks." I would never say it aloud, because I couldn't handle being that cringey, but Corey might be an angel.

"She agonized over that choice for fifteen minutes," Virgil says, staring at the drink.

Corey flushes and glares at him. "You didn't have to tell her that."

"She'll appreciate it more."

"I won't," I add. Now Virgil is narrowing his eyes at me. "It was a joke!"

"Oh, you got jokes now?"

"Focus, children," Margot says. "The preliminaries are happening inside the athletics section of the building. The first will be the societal knowledge test, which you have studied for?" This with a pointed look at me.

"Obviously." It's ridiculous the sort of stuff they want me to remember. The names of all six Doctorates and when they graduated to the title, and who their children were, and who they married, and what contributions to the society they made, and so on.

Margot continues, "Then we'll have monster affinity. Virgil will come in for that one. And then the physical endurance test. Make sure you conserve your ener—"

"Wait, what am I doing for monster affinity? That's the one thing we haven't been over."

128    LISELLE SAMBURY

"We don't need to go over it."

"Um . . . I think we do?"

"No, we don't. Because you're not afraid of him."

Me and Virgil lock eyes then and look away just as fast. I say, "That . . . that can't be the test, just not being afraid of him?"

"You'd be surprised," Margot says under her breath.

Virgil stares at the tabletop.

The one thing I've learned more than anything in studying the society is that monsters ain't shit. They have all these tenets about the importance of keeping them contained and preparing for this inevitable apocalypse, and still, monsters are footnotes in their own story. The histories are of the first Masters and their achievements. Not of the monsters they were paired with. Or if they are, it's very much like, *Phillip was exceptional at handling the unusual underwater traits of his unnamed monster partner.*

"You'll do great," Corey says to me before turning to Virgil. "This is what we've been waiting for, for years now. You're entering the candidacy with a capable partner. Remember what Bernie and Dr. Liu and Henry have always said."

"The hardest part of the process is finding the right partner." Virgil looks at me as he says it.

His gaze is like shackles on my wrists. It's Dad staring at me as he drops me off at school the morning of an important exam. It's Mom pointing at the target as she puts a knife in my hand.

I look away as a chime goes off in the building. Virgil, Corey, and Margot's heads perk up, though everyone else either looks around in confusion or ignores it.

I know what it means without needing to be told.

It's time.

# CHAPTER THIRTEEN

Sometimes you think everyone's looking at you and it's just paranoia, but in this case, I *know* everyone is looking at me.

I walk into a dance studio. The walls are lined with mirrors and ballet bars, and the floors are a shiny pale wood. The room is filled with rows of about thirty evenly spaced desks and chairs. On each lies a single slim piece of paper and a mechanical pencil. As eyes follow me, I make my way to the back of the room and slump into my chair.

As a first for the day, I'm on time because Virgil and the others made sure of it. I slouch in my seat and play with the pencil, twirling it between my fingers.

A boy two rows ahead of me twists back in his chair. "I have a question for you." It's the guy who Virgil had that weird response to being nominated. Caden.

I meet his eyes but say nothing.

He continues like I told him to go on. "I've never seen you once. Not at a lecture or gathering."

"More of a statement than a question."

"Why do you think you deserve to be here?"

"I was nominated."

The girl beside me laughs. She's the one who was nominated first, Violet. Her brown skin is dewy, and her eyes and lips are covered in expertly applied black makeup that matches the black outfit she wears. I approve of the color and find her appraising my choice of high-waist wide-leg black jeans with tears I personally made with a box cutter paired with a tight black T-shirt.

"And yet somehow that doesn't seem to be enough," he counters.

"She answered your 'question,' Caden," Violet says, rolling her eyes.

Caden doesn't get to say more because a familiar man walks into the room dressed in a fluorescent-pink-and-green Hawaiian shirt. When Bernie spots me, a smile lights up his face before he looks away. I didn't expect to see him again, especially since he said he doesn't teach anymore, but I guess this is an exception. Now I understand what Virgil meant when he said Bernie should have taken more time off. If his son hasn't even been gone a year, that means he failed in last year's candidacy. The same round Margot was in. And now Bernie is back, smiling at us like he didn't just lose his son in this process.

"Welcome to the societal knowledge portion of the preliminary testing. I'm Professor Mathers. I will be reading the questions aloud, and you will have one minute to select your answer on the sheet in front of you. Do not check or cross it out—fill in the circle as indicated on the sheet. You must achieve a minimum score of fifty percent to be accepted as a candidate. We will begin now."

I scramble to ready myself. *What the fuck?* Corey said I should

A MASTERY OF MONSTERS

have lots of time to go back and check my answers. She made it seem like I was going to get a packet or something like a normal test. Not this reading aloud thing.

For the next hour, we sit in silence with only the sounds of pencils scratching and Bernie reading in monotone. My neck keeps stiffening, making the whole exercise even more uncomfortable than it already is. I try to focus, but the questions aren't quite what we studied. Some of them are straightforward, like "Who was the fourth Doctorate?" But others are things like "According to apocalypse protocol, which quadrant is our safe zone?" and "What was Edward Weiss's philosophy meant to inspire?"

At the end of the session, we're given a couple of extra minutes to consider our answers. It's useless unless you memorized the questions and their order, which I didn't.

Bernie instructs us to remain in our seats while he collects our sheets.

I sigh and tip my head back.

"That bad?" Violet whispers.

"I've done better, and I've done worse."

"Fair. I'm Violet, by the way." She jerks her head to the white boy sitting next to her. His dirty blond hair is carefully styled. He wears square-framed glasses and has a warm smile. "That's Bryce."

"August."

I'm saved from any more socializing when Bernie clears his throat. "Please proceed to the right to the room next door. Your monster affinity test will take place there. If you already have a partner, they'll be waiting. For the majority of you who have not yet declared one, we've provided volunteers."

I scrape my chair back with a slight nod to Violet and Bryce. I don't care about making friends, but I'm not an asshole. She didn't need to help me deal with Caden or bother introducing herself, but she did. I can be nice sometimes.

On my way out, Bernie says, quiet enough so I can hear, "I'm glad to see you. For Virgil's sake."

When I look back at him, he's already turned away to fuss with his bag.

I proceed to the next room, which has the same sort of setup except the desks are pushed together in pairs with chairs at either end so you're facing the person you sit with. And the space is bigger to accommodate twice the number of desks.

There's a bottleneck at the front of the room. The other candidates are gathered at the door. I assume because, like Bernie said, most of them don't already have partners and they're deciding who they want to go with. I squeeze between them and head to Virgil, who is, in classic eager fashion, in the first row.

I sit down in front of him and sigh.

"That doesn't inspire confidence," he says.

"It was different. The test."

"You're not supposed to talk about it yet." He pauses. "Different how?"

I cross my arms. "Am I supposed to talk or not supposed to?"

"We'll discuss it after." His eyes stray to the other candidates, many of whom are still lingering in the doorway, though some have started to fan out to the different volunteers, who comprise most of the monsters in the room. I notice Virgil looking at Caden again.

"What's up with that guy?" I ask. "He's a dick."

A MASTERY OF MONSTERS

Now it's Virgil's turn to sigh. "Keep your voice down. And yeah, I thought he might be. It's not you, it's me."

"What does that mean?"

Virgil picks at a hangnail. "My parents . . . they killed his mom."

"That's not on you."

He stares at me and then becomes reabsorbed in his nails. "Yeah, well."

"It's bullshit, you know that, right? For people to treat you like this because of something your parents did."

"Can we drop it?"

"If you want." I look around the room as more candidates pair off with monsters. It's strange to think of them that way. That these people have the ability to become massive, snarling beasts. "I thought more people would be partnered up."

"Most candidates don't know any monsters personally unless they're related to one. That's why so many pairs are siblings."

"It's concerning that you have mostly sibling pairs but still make rules about monsters and Masters dating."

Virgil splutters so much that a few heads turn our way. He cringes and ducks his head. "How did—who told you that? Corey?"

"Henry."

"*Henry?* Why did that even come up?"

"I was making a point."

Virgil's mouth drops open. "Making *what* point?"

An East Asian–looking woman enters the room, and everyone turns to her. She wears a long black dress that hugs her body like a second skin and nude heels whose red bottoms peek out when she walks. Her hair is dark with a slight wave to it and falls to her shoulders. She's gone for a bold red lip.

She waves at the candidates who still haven't moved from the front of the room. "Take a seat within the minute or I'll fail you right now." Her voice is unexpectedly deep.

The candidates she addresses scramble, rushing to find a seat. And when they finally do, they're either stiff or shifting in place. It's only then that my mind catches up enough to realize that they weren't hesitating in the door because they were indecisive.

They were scared.

"I'm Professor Chen, and I will be conducting your monster affinity preliminary exam. I will also preside over the associated training sessions, final tests, and initiation. Some of you may be familiar with this process, but others will not be, so I'll outline it for you." She leans against the wall. "I will be coming around the room and doing a diagnostic test. The only thing you are required to do is join hands with your partner and match breaths. You must foster a strong empathetic relationship with your partner throughout this process in order to successfully bond during initiation. That is what the sessions will help with, and the tests will judge. However, if you can't even manage this simple exercise, you have no business being in the candidacy." She looks around the room as if waiting for questions but there are none. "Join hands now."

"I thought we only had to do it when you came to us?" Caden asks, and the candidates seated around him nod.

"And I'm telling you that you have to do it now," Professor Chen says. "So do it now."

I reach out, and Virgil takes my hands in his. Technically, we've already done this. When he begged me to do this competition. He was close enough that I could feel a whisper of his breath on my face. I wasn't paying much attention to his hands then, but they're

A MASTERY OF MONSTERS

135

surprisingly rough. I expected soft and supple. After all, the guy literally lives in a library.

Virgil looks away from our hands. "Should be a quick process."

"Nervous to hold hands with a girl?"

He turns back to me. "Don't be a child."

I glance across the room at a candidate who's practically trembling as she holds the hands of another girl as small and slight as she is. "Why are people freaking out so much?"

"You saw Isaac in a controlled environment and state. And we got lucky at Big Sandy Bay. I don't know why it stopped its attack, but even the attack itself was weak. It wasn't trying to kill us."

I raise my brow. "You sure about that?"

"Yes. It got in some good blows, but it could have easily tried to cut or bite us. It had its facilities intact. But real uncontrolled monsters can do terrible damage. Most of the students who come to us come because they've experienced that. It's what allows them to understand the teachings of the society. And the candidates here are the ones motivated enough to become soldiers to fight against those types of monsters in the apocalypse. The only reason you can stand being this close to me is because you don't know any better." His fingers twitch for a moment, like he wants to tear his hands away and then remembers what we're supposed to be doing. "That's why I chose you."

He really believes that. That he's right on the edge of being a vicious murderer and people should act accordingly. It ladders up nicely to that self-sacrificial attitude that Corey mentioned.

"You let me know when I've seen enough monsters to properly deem you dangerous," I say. He opens his mouth to respond, and I interrupt him to note that Professor Chen is coming.

When she reaches us, she sticks something to the inside of my wrist. "Match breaths now. Breath in . . . and out. In . . . and out. Good. Keep going."

Maybe our eyes are supposed to be closed. But me and Virgil end up staring at each other as we follow the directions. There's a tiny crease between his eyebrows as he concentrates, and his glasses are almost unnaturally clean. Not even a finger smudge obscures his dark amber eyes.

When the professor tells us we're done, it's like coming out of a trance. We pull our hands from each other, but that crease of concentration between his eyebrows stays. Before I can think about it, I reach out and press my finger between them. "It's over."

The crease smooths, and Virgil swallows.

I tuck my hands under the table.

After everyone has been monitored, we're told to proceed downstairs to the main gym for the physical exam. Virgil walks me there in silence. It's only at the entrance to the testing space that he finally says, "Good luck."

"Don't need it."

He groans. "Must you be so acidic all the time?"

I grin. "Yes."

Before I leave, he grabs my hand, and I pause. "I believe in you, you know? You've been training hard for this. You'll do great."

"Is the reassurance for me or for you?"

"It's for both of us."

"If you say so."

Virgil finally lets go, and I give him one last look before I enter the gym. I shove my hands into my pockets, still feeling the ghost of his touch.

A MASTERY OF MONSTERS

I will not let the attractive book nerd distract me. I could never live it down if I actually caught feelings for *Virgil*. It's the muscles. The muscles are so confusing. Why are his forearms that big? From moving books?

I enter the gym and head to the changing rooms, where I put on a pair of bike shorts and a looser T-shirt. A lot of the other girls already have branded Queen's athletics gear. I'm glad I don't match them. It was bad enough that Corey bugged me into getting matching Queen's hoodies.

We leave the changing rooms and line up along a wall to stretch. I run through the set that Mom taught me and Jules before we did any sparring. Mom would say it isn't about winning, it's about what I learn along the way. But that doesn't apply to this competition.

The gym is sizable. Definitely bigger than my high school one. There are bleachers lining three sides, and the usual setup with floating basketball nets. Throughout the space, they've got several stations. One of them, unfortunately, features ropes dangling from the ceiling. I'd hoped that Corey not being totally right about the societal knowledge test would mean maybe not everything she mentioned would show up in physical endurance, too, but no luck there.

Caden and his friends break into unnecessarily loud laughter, and I avoid looking at them. The more I stay away from that guy, the better.

A man who I assume is the professor blows a whistle around his neck. He's younger than Bernie or Professor Chen, with umber skin and his hair shaved close to his head. He looks like he might be Latine. He's got the tall-dark-and-handsome thing going for him, but he also looks like a gym bro, which is unfortunate.

"I'm Professor Perez, but you can call me Luis."

Oh God, not a professor who wants you to call them by their first name. Even Bernie had the decency to introduce himself with his last name in this context. I resolve to always call this guy Professor Perez.

He continues, "You'll be five to a station, and we'll rotate through them, with water breaks in between. My associates are handing out your student number, which you will pin on your shirt. These will mark you so they can easily track your times. You must meet the minimum requirements of at least fifty percent of the skills to advance, with the exception of the rope climb. If you cannot reach the top, you'll be cut. I'll call out student numbers and stations. Please proceed to them."

Love that we aren't told what the minimum requirement of the skills is. I am, thankfully, put on the beep test first. It'll exhaust me, but better to get it over with now while I have the most energy.

"Well, you had a good run," Caden says from beside me. "Nominations can only get you so far."

The beeper sounds, and I sprint.

Margot said to conserve my energy.

I don't.

I *can't*.

Not with that fucking kid in my head assuming that of course this would be where I fail.

I lift heavier than I need to at the weights, I jump higher at the box jumps, I row faster at the machines. I give every single station 110 percent, and by the time we get to the final rope climb, I stare up at the thing with spots in my vision, panting and not giving a fuck that I look as exhausted as I feel. It was worth it, because by the second station, Caden didn't have anything to say to me.

A MASTERY OF MONSTERS

I grip the rope between my hands and squeeze my eyes shut as my vision swims.

"Hey . . . you okay?" The voice is disembodied and echoey, like it was shouted into a tunnel. When I look over, it's Bryce, navy blue eyes staring at me from behind his glasses, a frown on his face.

"I'm fine." Sweat slips into my eyes, and I rub them with the hem of my T-shirt, probably flashing my sports bra to everyone.

The whistle blows, and I heft myself onto the rope and tug my body up. My arms tremble, but I keep going. All I need to do is get to the top. That's it. I just need to reach the top. I keep repeating it to myself, closing my eyes in intervals to help with the way the room's spinning.

I spot the red buzzer, reach out, and slap it.

My eyes close, and my lips pull into a goofy grin.

*I did it.*

My grip slackens, and finally I let go, plummeting toward the ground.

# CHAPTER FOURTEEN

Falling several feet to the ground—albeit a cushioned one, thanks to the mats under the ropes—and passing out in public wasn't great, but somehow the look Margot is giving me now is worse. I let her inside my dorm room, and she's closely followed by Virgil and Corey. I collapse on my bed and reapply the ice pack the nurse at the ARC gave me. I fell on my side, thankfully. And no head injury. Just a giant bruise on my left thigh.

"I don't even know what to say to you." Margot shakes her head. "For one, you didn't pace yourself at all. And then you get injured, and when we show up to the nurse's office, you're already gone. No text. No call. Nothing."

Am I getting a lecture from my trainer or from my mom? Finding it hard to spot the difference. Though I never got in trouble with Mom. Not until the end.

I chance a look at Virgil to gauge how much shit I'm in, but his lips are twitching. They keep trying to pull up, and it's like he's forcing them down. Corey, meanwhile, is looking out the window like the parking lot view is Niagara Falls instead of dusty asphalt.

"I passed, didn't I?"

"You passed!" Corey squeals, turning to me with the beaming smile she was trying to hide.

She sobers when Margot cuts a glare at her.

"Yes," Margot says. "By some miracle, you passed. And you're lucky I'm down as your trainer so that I could have access to the scores, since you ran away."

"I came home to rest." Though I also maybe wanted to avoid this situation, which some people might interpret as running away.

Virgil is smiling unrestrained now. It lights up his entire face. He was too in shock at the nominations, I think, but now he's on cloud nine. "I knew you would."

I clear my throat and look away.

I forgot how that feels. When you do something right and people are proud of you.

Corey and Virgil proceed to high five each other and giggle like they're ten years old. It's helpful, actually. I needed that ick to heap onto any weird Virgil feelings. I should burn this moment into my mind.

Margot crosses her arms. "It's a good start, but it's just that, the start. Your monster affinity score is through the roof. I would say it's probably the best in the group. Which I didn't expect after your reaction to Isaac, but there you go. You have the advantage of not only knowing your partner but not being indoctrinated with so much fear-mongering that you fail."

Maybe this competition thing won't be so bad if I did that well without even trying.

Margot continues, "Your societal knowledge score is fucking abysmal, and you just skated by."

"She said the questions were different from what she and Corey worked on," Virgil says.

I relay to them the sorts of things that were asked, as well as the format. As I explain, Margot's hands curl into fists and release at her sides.

"They changed it," Corey says, eyes darting to Margot. "That's different even from yours, and you did it only last year. It's usually simple stuff. Names of the Doctorates, first Masters, basic monster knowledge. You only need like a day to go over it, which is exactly what we did. It's designed to be accessible to newcomers."

No wonder I didn't understand half the things we were asked. "It's not anymore."

"Which is weird because the Scientist faction are the ones who set the format of the candidacy and the test content. They're the only official faction that's supposed to exist." She gestures to me. "More of a department than anything. Carrigan leads it, actually. They focus on education and finding a cure for monstrosity. They don't even have political leanings. There's no reason for them to make the test less accessible. That feels like something Traditionalists would want."

"Traditionalists?" I ask.

Virgil says, "Another unofficial faction. They say they want to adhere to the traditional practices of Dr. Weiss, but really, they want to exclude outsiders and make rules more lenient for Masters. Give them more ways to profit and make money."

"And you guys are with these Progressives who want better conditions for monsters and stuff?" Virgil nods. "And Pro-Libs are the people who love monsters in the wrong way?" Whatever that means. Honestly, I don't really care enough to have that clarified.

"Basically."

"Corey is right," Margot says. "Scientists don't usually make changes like that. Just like Carrigan doesn't usually come to meetings. I don't know why his faction is suddenly switching things up. I'll discuss it with Henry. Thankfully, the training sessions will guide your knowledge from now. The point is to learn, so as long as you put in effort, you'll be fine. It's not as strict as the prelims or the tests. But let's refocus on that physical endurance score."

I swallow.

"Somewhat above average range, somewhat above average score. You could have reserved your strength the way I told you to and gotten middle of the road. But at least now we know that your best effort needs to be better."

"But she did it," Virgil says. "For someone who hasn't been training formally for years like the others, that's fantastic."

My face gets hot, and I shift on the bed. *Remember the embarrassing high five with Corey. Focus on it.* To Margot, I say, "So I need to be way above average to win?"

"Ideally. You need to get into the top five to even get to the initiation. Most people don't manage that being slightly above average." She pauses and a small smile slips out. "But Virgil's right, you did better than expected. That being said, only five people were cut, so we're at twenty-five candidates. I'm going to make a new physical training program for you, and you're going to follow it. The first group training is less than a week away, but it's for monster affinity, which is to your benefit. That gives us more time to build up your physical endurance. And remember that you need the professors to recommend you for the next stage, so you'd better be as pleasant as a fucking peach."

"Aren't I always?"

Margot sighs.

"No advice for the monster training?" I ask. "Or do I just keep not being afraid?"

"What happens in trainings is dependent on the professor," she says. "And unfortunately, Chen is new. Sometimes they take you down to the Penitentiary to try to scare you, and other times they might have a volunteer Master-monster pair come by. Either way, you need to stay calm. So yes, just keep not being afraid."

"What's at the Penitentiary? I thought it closed down years ago. It's a museum now, right?"

Virgil's smile fades. "It's no longer functioning as a public prison, and yes, it's a museum, too, but for us it's more than that. It is and always has been where we keep the monsters."

So that's what they meant when they said the monsters are locked up underground. I'd assumed some sort of holding facility but hadn't imagined they were at a literal *prison*.

But if it's anything like this initial monster affinity test, it should be fine. Now that we know the real parameters of societal knowledge, we can adjust. And after yet another grueling training program, my physical endurance will be better too.

I might actually be able to do this.

Hopefully those aren't famous last words.

McIntosh Castle, it seems, keeps up its devotion to books even in rooms that aren't strictly library-like in nature. Like the kitchen, where Corey is pulling out a bunch of cheeses and cured meats to

A MASTERY OF MONSTERS

make a charcuterie board for us. On top of several single upper cabinets are an array of books. Most of them are cookbooks, but some just seem to be books that mention cuisine or food in some way. The space, like most of the rooms, is wallpapered, this one with a peach-colored scene of people at a beach in the early 1900s. The countertops are placed to accommodate the odd shape of the room, and the white pantry is above an old radiator.

Corey tugs down a book that references different charcuterie arrangements. She goes back to the fridge, and this time I'm at an angle where I can see inside. There are several stacked containers of leftovers, including a larger one of what looks like kimchi soup with chunks of tofu and cabbage. "Who's the cook in the house?" I ask.

She follows my gaze. "Oh . . . my mom drops these off all the time. Virgil and Dr. Liu eat them."

Shit, now I've waded into the family stuff she doesn't like talking about. She shuts the fridge, setting open jam jars on the counter. I walk over and point to the pictures stuck on the fridge door. One is of Corey and Virgil with their arms around each other, smiling in front of a giant red apple with a face painted onto it. "This is cute."

"Bernie took us to see the Big Apple. His wife was craving the pies, so he said we could come for the drive." She points at a few other pictures of her and Virgil poking their heads into those tourist photo op things and making funny faces. "We took these there too."

"Are you and Virgil . . . ?" I don't even know why I'm asking, but I can't pretend I'm not curious. The two of them are attached at the hip, and even though they don't give those vibes, it would make sense.

Corey squints for a moment, then she catches on and laughs.

"Oh! No, no, I'm very gay. Virgil is like . . . Virgil is the brother I chose." She smiles. "It's funny. I've only known him for three years, but we're closer than my real brother and I ever were."

"Is he in the Pen?" I ask, finally saying what I've been wondering since she brought her brother up.

"Yes." She turns back to her ingredients. "We need some nuts. . . . Almonds or pecans?"

"Pecans. It doesn't need to be that fancy." I'm glad she's recovered so quickly from discussing her brother, and I'm happy to change topics.

She stares at me, aghast. "Yes, it does. We're pregaming."

"I don't think you understand what pregaming means," I say.

The door to the kitchen opens, and Virgil comes in with a textbook under his arm. He does a double take when he sees me. I catch the exact moment when he looks at my chest, which is very much on display tonight. Corey insisted that we "pregame" at McIntosh Castle before the mystery frosh concert, so I got ready at my dorm before coming over. I'm in a bralette and a pair of my nicer high-waist black jean shorts over sheer tights, with a red checkered button-down tied around my waist in case I get cold.

"Sorry," he mutters.

"Are you apologizing for looking?"

He throws his hands up. "Because I know you saw that I looked!"

"Did you want a moment alone?" Corey asks, so innocently that for a second, I think she's serious.

"Shouldn't you two be studying or something?" Virgil sets his textbook on the counter. It looks like a collection of short stories and poems. Unsurprisingly, he's majoring in English, while Corey, to my actual surprise, picked history.

A MASTERY OF MONSTERS

Corey gestures at her cutting board. "We're pregaming."

"With . . . charcuterie?"

"We have wine, too!"

I perk up. "We do?" I would prefer shots, but I doubt that's going to happen.

Virgil shakes his head and grabs a slice of salami from Corey's cutting board. She makes a noise in the back of her throat but doesn't stop him, just continues to slice. With her left hand, she stabs some sort of tool into the salami to hold it steady while she slices with her right. I assume it's more secure than holding it with three fingers.

To Virgil, I say, "While you're here, has anyone responded to your report about the monster at Big Sandy Bay?" I still have no idea what direction to go in as far as investigating goes, and part of me hopes the society will magically respond and we'll get more information.

"No." Virgil reaches for another piece of meat, and Corey physically moves the cutting board away. "Which is weird. Like, it attacked us with intent. That makes it even more dangerous."

"Then they're not wild," Corey says. She tugs a massive wooden board out from a cupboard, along with some small white bowls. "Meaning they're working with a Master."

"That's what I think," I say.

Virgil says, "Or they're a Wild."

I frown. "She just said they're not wild."

"No, *a* Wild. It's different. Wilds are monsters who don't need a partner. They can shift at will and mostly retain control while in monstrous form. Not as much as they would in human form or the way they might with a partner, but enough to retain conscious thought."

"Wait," I say. "There are monsters who don't need partners or this whole process? How?"

Corey says, "Dr. Weiss eventually discovered a boy who seemed to be the same as Patient Zero and learned that it was actually his son. A son he'd had before his mutation activated. Even though the boy's mutation was expressed the same way as Patient Zero—the half-human, half-monster form—he maintained his faculties. But he still didn't have a great quality of life because of his appearance, so Dr. Weiss gave him the serum."

"He experimented on him."

"No! They worked together. It was a collaboration." I don't know how much I believe that, but I let Corey continue. "His mutation, like standard monsters, was changed so he had fully human and fully monster forms. Eventually, Dr. Weiss discovered more people like Patient Zero, and he helped them and their families. Only descendants from those families produce Wilds."

"Do you know why? Like, is their mutation different or something?"

Virgil shakes his head. "No. It's the exact same mutation, it's just expressed differently in them for some reason. Like, if they bite someone outside their bloodline, that person becomes a standard monster, not a Wild. It's unique to their families. Dr. Weiss offered them the serum too, which they took. From then on, all their children were born with fully human forms and controllable monster forms. And the Big Sandy Bay monster being a Wild would explain why this might not be on the society's radar or even why they're neglecting to respond to us on it."

"And there was that guy at the nomination who you mentioned led some Wilds rebellion. Gary?"

"Garrett—Garrett Murphy."

"Right! You all said it was strange that he showed up. Could it be connected?"

"I mean, the Murphys are considered the most powerful Wild family, which is why they live in and around the Kingston area, close to the Doctorate. And it's a tenuous relationship at best. If someone was worried about this being the start of another rebellion, I could see why they'd ignore our reports and work it out internally instead."

Corey presses her lips into a line.

"What?" I ask her. "You don't think the Wilds are involved?"

She shrugs. "Could be."

"You think it's bullshit."

She flushes, looking from me to Virgil. "It's just . . . well, it's highly unlikely. For one, Wilds are rare. That means they're easy to monitor and they *are* strictly monitored at that. There are only three Wild families left in the entire *province*. And there hasn't been a new Patient Zero—like person discovered in a century, so no new families are replacing the old ones. The living Wilds all work in society roles as per the truce they brokered because they were getting killed off left and right. Why start a new rebellion now when they have fewer people and less support? Garrett probably showed up because he, like all of us, knew that Cyrus wasn't doing well. Maybe he wants to broker a better deal for the Murphys. That makes sense. But sending a Wild to attack August, who wasn't even part of the society at the time, and potentially steal her brother, who also isn't, how does that connect to his goals? It already makes little sense for even a Master-monster pair. But zero sense for a Wild." Corey pauses, her face becoming even redder. "But, like, you guys could also be right. . . ."

I shake my head. "No, we're not. For all the reasons you said."

Virgil says, "Like I am always telling you, it's okay to say I'm wrong. Or talk back to me or whatever. To anyone, actually." He attempts to steal a piece of cheese.

"Wait until I'm done!" she snaps.

He grins. "See? Just like that."

Corey sighs and starts chopping up a hunk of brie.

"We're definitely looking for a Master-monster pair, then?" I ask. Which helps me basically not at all in figuring out where to investigate from here.

Corey nods. "I would say so. But we're not in a position to be questioning any Masters. Not at our level." She goes to get some more jam from the fridge.

While her back is turned, Virgil makes another attempt at the cheese. "Don't you fucking dare," I say.

The boy actually has the nerve to look betrayed. "We're supposed to be partners," he whispers, pressing a hand to his chest.

A snicker bursts from my lips, and now I'm the one feeling betrayed by my own body.

And the ick of his and Corey's high five moment isn't even working anymore because their friendship is kind of cute. They're just themselves around each other and don't seem to be afraid of calling each other out. I never said shit to Rachel, even when she was out of line. Just another person who I couldn't disappoint. And I was right. Because the second I did, she was gone.

Eventually, Corey finishes her charcuterie board and pours our wine. Unfortunately, she insists upon a single glass per person, which is exhausting. It reminds me of Christmas at home, when Mom would let us each have a glass of champagne.

After our "pregame," we head over to the concert venue,

A MASTERY OF MONSTERS 151

incredibly sober but filled with meat and cheese. Which I guess is a good trade-off.

Though "venue" is generous considering that it's in the Miller Hall parking lot. I've never paid much attention to the building, but I do have a bunch of classes at Humphrey, which is right next to it. They've done a good job transforming the space. There's a huge stage set up as if it belongs there, and we follow the crowd of freshmen trying to find spots to watch. It's a mystery who the performer is, but I've heard a lot of guesses being thrown around, and as I spot the name on the drum kit, I realize that every one of them is wrong.

Lights flash onstage, and the band comes on. The music is so loud that I have no idea what Corey is screaming at me with a beaming smile on her face, so I just smile back and get lost in the sounds. I'm low-key shocked that Virgil, who seems like he might only listen to classical music, actually knows enough songs to sing along, bouncing on his toes and waving his arms around.

I remember what Corey said about him not getting to go to school before. About what it might mean to him to be here now.

I gave up on this dream, but he's just starting to fulfill his.

The lead singer finishes a song and says, "Now, someone told me you guys have a school song. And I kind of need to hear it."

A group in the crowd starts shouting "Ooooooooooooh," and the sound grows louder as more students join in. Everyone's throwing up their right arm, pointer finger to the sky, swinging it around in a circle like a helicopter prepping for flight.

"For fuck's sake," I mutter, and Virgil laughs, though he can't possibly have heard me. Must have read it on my face.

I hold out my arm to drape it across his shoulders, which isn't easy given his height. Corey sneaks over to my left so I can put my arm around her. And both of them put their arms around whatever stranger is next to them.

It's complete chaos because we're so packed together, but we manage it anyway.

Finally, someone starts it. "Oil thigh . . ."

With my arms around Virgil and Corey, we kick up our legs and say a bunch of Scottish Gaelic words none of us understand, becoming half-incoherent as we laugh over the ridiculousness of attempting this in a huge crowd.

I want to hate it.

I really want to hate it.

# CHAPTER FIFTEEN

I stand in front of the door to Henry's office and attempt to compose myself. My first meeting with the guy went terribly, but he did follow through in getting me my nomination. I understand the importance and the necessity of his involvement. He's part of how I can help Jules. The last thing I want to do on Monday during what should be my break between morning classes is be forced to attend his office hours. But Margot was cc'd on the email he sent, so she'll know if I skip it. I have no choice but to suffer through whatever he wants from me. If I'm lucky, I'll still have time to take a nap before monster affinity in the afternoon. Margot's new training program has kept me exhausted all week. I just want to sleep.

I knock on the office door and wait.

When the door swings open, I stumble back, seeing the woman who appears there. She's Black and looks to be in her thirties, Bailey's age, with umber locs that hang to her mid-back and warm golden skin. "Come in. He's on his way from a lecture. I think it ran long."

I'm starting to wonder if him always arriving after his guests is a power move. I enter Henry's office and sit in the same chair I sat in before, in front of his desk. The woman chooses to lean against one of the bookcases. "I'm Laira, by the way, Henry's partner." I glance at her ring finger, and she laughs. "Not that sort of partner."

Right. Obviously. Monster partner. "I'm August."

"I know." Her smile grows wider. "The wild card."

I shrug. "Right place, right time, I guess."

Laira's lip twitches. "I'm not a big believer in coincidences. Most things are by design. It just might take a while to discover that fact."

*What does that mean?* I don't know whose plan I would be a part of. Henry doesn't want me here. Not even Virgil did in the beginning. "So . . . I guess you and Henry have been partners for a long time?" I'm not one for small talk, but I'm curious about who would pair up with the grumpy professor. From what I've gleaned, most candidates compete in their first year. Is she family or a childhood friend or something?

"Not as long as you're imagining." She looks around the room before pointing to a photo. It's on a bookshelf alongside an assortment of frames, featuring a younger Henry and another boy. "That was Henry's first partner. Lewis. He passed away, unfortunately. Very aggressive genetic illness of some sort."

"I thought monsters had, like, I dunno, super health or something."

"We aren't invulnerable. We just tend to be much harder to kill."

"When did you and Henry partner up, then?"

"A few years after he lost Lewis. I was in the candidacy. But my partner was cut in the second test. I was devastated, obviously. Waiting around to be sent to the Pen. You usually have a bit of time

A MASTERY OF MONSTERS

until the signs of turning get severe. Henry approached me. Saved me, really. That's something Henry excels at. Saving people."

I don't like the guy, but I can't disagree. He saved Margot. And he saved Virgil, and me because it was necessary for helping Virgil.

But I didn't realize that Masters could carry on without a partner for a while if they lost them. I thought they'd have to pair up right away. "You went through the initiation with Henry?"

"Fuck no." She laughs. "Thankfully, senior Masters don't have to do the whole initiation thing to bond. I was lucky. Most Masters who've lost their partners pick a monster from the Pen."

"Really?"

She nods. "They can readily observe the forms and potential abilities of those monsters. People don't like to say it out loud, but every Master wants a strong monster. Legacy families especially often take their pick from the Pen if they're senior. After all, the serum can be given at any time, even if the person is already in monster form. And it's controlled. The Doctorate restrains the monster. It's an easier process, honestly."

"That's the vibe I'm getting." It must be nice. And it's one of the few things that's more a benefit to the monster than the Master. To be senior, the Master would have still had to go through the full competition process. But they could pick a monster who'd never been in it.

"If it makes you feel any better, we still had to compete in the Monster's Ball, so I didn't escape all the challenges."

"And if you hadn't passed . . . ?"

Laira shrugs. "To the Pen with me, and Henry would choose again. Of course, he never wanted to lose face like that, so he was very dedicated to our training. That's the benefit of the candidacy.

LISELLE SAMBURY

You take the time to learn to be partners and grow together. You get stronger pairings that way. When you pull a random monster out of the Pen, you make a gamble. And if you lose at the Ball three times, you're done, even if you do it with different monsters. That's how you get Bachelors who never become Masters."

"Well, they don't get the title, but at least they're already partnered."

She shakes her head. "You don't understand. The society doesn't reward failure. Bachelors who never become Masters lose their partners."

The door to the office opens, and Henry bustles in with a leather briefcase. I'm still wrapping my mind around what Laira said. What is the point in being that brutal? Just to make sure they have strong monsters for an apocalypse that may or may not come? The Bachelor doesn't get rewarded, but the monster is the one who suffers. Maybe that's one of the things that will change if Adam wins. Not that it matters to me. I'll be gone as soon as I find Jules. It's not like it'll be relevant. I hunch in the chair.

Henry says, "Apologies for the lateness."

"It's fine," I reply.

"I was glad to meet our newest shit disturber." Laira winks at me. "I like the ones who aren't afraid to rile him up."

Henry scowls. "Of course you do." He comes around to the other side of the desk and opens his briefcase, taking out the same notebook from before. Laira maintains her position. "How was your first week of classes?"

"Uh . . . good." I wasn't expecting him to ask about something that mundane. "It's mostly memorization, so I figure I'll be fine."

He stares at the notebook page. "I noticed you have an eclectic taste in courses. Introduction to Psychology is a given, but your electives . . ."

"They're classes that I think will be personally relevant to my growth at Queen's." As in, they are courses I know I will pass with little effort.

"Like astronomy? Do you actually care about that class?"

I press a hand to my chest. "Of course I do. I'm a Libra rising."

Laira snorts and disguises it, poorly, as a cough.

"That's astrol—you know what? Never mind. Do I think you might get more out of other courses, yes, but it's your choice." Henry closes his notebook, snapping the elastic closure harder than necessary. "You have your first group training this afternoon. Did Margot brief you on it?"

"Yeah, though she said Professor Chen is new and so it's harder to know what she'll do."

"Yes, we'll encounter that difficulty with Perez as well. He's more easygoing, her less so, but you never know. Still, it's best to be vigilant. I hope you'll consider coming to me with any challenges that cannot be handled by Margot. I do, in some cases, have the power to be helpful. We share a goal when it comes to Virgil. Your success is important to me."

All I can do is stare at him.

Is this the same guy I talked to a few weeks ago?

Laira bursts into giggles behind us.

"Something funny?" Henry says with a frown, looking at her and then at me.

I say, "I, uh, I just, our first meeting didn't go that well. I know you didn't want Virgil to pick me. I guess I thought you would be more resistant and not so . . . helpful."

Henry leans back in his chair. "My concern is, and has always been, Virgil's well-being. That was the only thing that I wanted to make sure we were on the same page about. His parents were dear friends of mine, and no matter how they became in the end, I'm invested in bringing up their child right. I want to see him live the life they would have wanted for him. It's in all our best interests to work—"

There's a knock at the door.

Laira and Henry exchange a glance. She goes and opens it.

In the doorway is Adam Shaw. He's dressed casually in a long-sleeved emerald sweatshirt and pair of tan chinos. It's weird because I've only ever seen him on a stage, but this is the man who nominated me.

Henry stands and gives me a sharp look, jerking his chin up. I scramble to my feet.

"No need for that," Adam says. Without a microphone, the soft tone of his voice is more obvious. He comes over to me with his hand outstretched. "So nice to meet you, August."

I shake his hand. It's as soft as his voice. Mostly I'm glad that I don't have to do anything awkward like kiss it. The Doctorate is highly revered, but there apparently haven't ever been Doctorate *candidates* before. I'm not sure what the protocol is.

"I wasn't expecting you," Henry says. "I'm briefing August on some things in regard to the candidacy."

"I know," Adam says with a smile. "I ran into Margot, who said as much, and I thought it would be a great time to introduce myself." His eyes slide to me again. "Welcome to the Learners' Society. And I suppose to Queen's as well. Did your family move you in last week?"

"No, my dad is busy working at St. Lawrence and my mom

has been missing for a bit. Corey helped me get settled. Uh, Corey Yang?"

"Yes, yes, I'm familiar with Ms. Yang. I'm sorry to hear that about your mother. I hope she's found. I lost my mom when I was young to cancer. I know it's not the same, but I wouldn't wish the absence of one's mother on anybody." He does sound sincere. Like, really sympathetic.

"Thanks," I say.

"I'm glad I was able to help you with the nomination. However, it's become a bit of a shit show now, and I'm afraid it might bring you some unwanted attention."

"It's not that bad," Henry says.

"Isn't it? All the vultures have come to roost now that Dad is gone. Carrigan, I assumed, would have the decency to show his face when announcing the death of our father, much as he loathes any public appearance, so he wasn't a surprise. Except he still hasn't left. I thought he would be on the first train back to Toronto, but he's sticking around for some reason." Adam walks to the corner of the room and deposits himself on the chaise longue, leaning into the cushions.

"To campaign?" Henry suggests, which is what I was thinking too.

That makes Adam laugh. "Carrigan takes every opportunity to say how much he does not want the responsibility of being the Doctorate." He waves at us. "Please sit down, you're making me nervous." Me and Henry sit, though Laira stays where she is, and Adam doesn't push it. "No, Carrigan prefers to work in his lair with his test tubes. Which is why his continued presence is concerning. And then Garrett, well, he made sure to accost the three of us at the bottom of the stage and let us know that the Wilds' agreement was with

Cyrus, not us, and now that he's gone, it's null and void. And Natalie picked that exact moment to emerge into the public, and we know Dad made sure to squash her Pro-Lib activities, so this couldn't be anything other than a message to us. Which is just what we need, her stirring people up to create unregistered monster bonds and set them loose. Though we've already increased security on the serum holding tanks. And to round it all out, Carrigan just dropped the recent spontaneous monster birth stats on us."

The Wilds again. I know that I agreed Corey was right, but now that Adam is bringing them up too, I'm wondering if we missed something. Like Corey said, Garrett wants better terms, but instead of negotiating, he's just announced that their deal is off. It's a more aggressive move.

"The Wilds are saying they'll be moving against whoever is elected?" Laira asks.

"No, I think they're only trying to make sure we consider them. In the end, I'm sure they'll sign a new agreement with whoever gives them the best offer."

"Which will be you," Henry says, voice firm. "James will want them as strictly controlled as they have been since the truce. You're the ideal choice, which gives you their vote."

Part of me thinks they may have forgotten I'm in the room. Which is kind of perfect because I'm actually learning shit. If whatever is going on with Jules has anything to do with society politics, these are the people I should be looking at as suspects. I should keep quiet, but I have to ask, "What is this Wilds agreement?"

Henry's eyes widen like he did forget I was here. He waves a hand at Adam. "You don't have to explain—"

"I don't mind," Adam says. "I don't get much opportunity to

A MASTERY OF MONSTERS

teach. The Wilds created a contract with my father to stop the fighting that broke out between them and the society. They agreed to be monitored by the Learners, and they were given jobs and opportunities, including proctoring the Monster's Ball. We also agreed to stop killing them." He utters the last sentence with a frown. "And they would stop attacking us as well. Though I admit that we were killing them in much higher numbers. I assume that in this new agreement, they would like less monitoring and fewer restrictions and duties."

"Duties like proctoring the Monster's Ball?"

"Among other things," Adam mutters.

"The birth rates you mentioned," Henry says. "They're rising?"

"Not just rising, according to Carrigan, but *spiking*."

I clench my hands into fists in my lap. More spontaneously born monsters means we're closer to their so-called apocalypse. I do not want to be put in a position to see if the society is right about the end of the world. Realistically, ignoring a possible apocalypse, more spontaneous monsters also means they'll need more Masters. I know they have their reasons for the candidate process, but they have an increasingly volatile supply and demand issue. There's no way they have infinite space in the Pen. Something will have to give.

Adam shakes his head. "I keep telling my brothers that we need to create a plan. This is the time when we should be working together. Three people with the Doctorate ability. Excluding the time when Dad was alive, it's the most we've ever had at once. That has to be a good omen. Instead, James is saying the fact that his daughter shows signs of having the gift is proof that Carrigan and I should withdraw." He rolls his eyes. "James is determined to be my enemy in this. And Carrigan thinks we should funnel more money into a cure that we have failed to create after over a century of research."

"You're making it too complicated," Henry says. "Beat them, and then you can control what they do."

"I don't want to control them."

"But you will have to."

The two men stare at each other for a long moment. I glance at Laira, who does a slight head shake at me. So I keep quiet until Adam breaks the tension with a smile. "I suppose that's why I have you. You're able to make those hard decisions. You've always been very pragmatic."

"And you've always been overly permissive."

Adam laughs, big and booming. It's on the edge of too much. "Yes. I suppose so." He claps his hands. "Well, I won't take up any more of your time." He rises from the couch. "It was lovely to meet you, August. I wish you the best in the candidacy. Every year it looks so difficult, and of course, I've heard the same from those who participate. Take care of yourself."

"You've never done it?" I ask.

"No, no. Doctorates don't bond. It weakens our wider control abilities. None of us have ever participated." He rocks back on his heels. "We may be the heads of this society, but we've fought significantly less for it. We were just born into the right family with the right power. It's unfortunate, honestly. This election will be the only thing I've worked for in my whole life." He looks to Henry. "And yet my friend, who has toiled harder and had a more difficult life than anyone I've ever known, can never have this title."

A MASTERY OF MONSTERS

Henry holds his face still.

"It doesn't feel fair." Adam gives me a small smile. "You're in the best hands possible with Henry. I hope you know that."

I'm still not a fan of the guy, but with this many people talking him up, it's hard not to be grateful that he's on my side.

Adam leaves, and Henry holds me back for a few minutes to press me on participating more in Intro to Psychology and keeping up with the textbook readings.

When I finally leave the office, Margot is waiting for me in the hall. I raise an eyebrow, but she only turns and walks toward the exit. I fall into step with her. "How was the meeting?" she asks.

"Fine. I met Laira. She's cool. Also, Adam showed up."

"I thought he might. He ran into me on campus and asked about introducing himself to you."

"I didn't think he'd care."

"It's Adam. He's that sort of guy."

"Nice?"

"Very. What did Henry want?"

"Shouldn't you know? Aren't you like his protégé or whatever?"

Margot stops. We're in a different hallway from Henry's office, though it looks the same. Most of the hallways in this building do. "He doesn't always tell me everything. I think he prefers when I find things out. He likes for his mentees to challenge him."

"He asked about my classes and stuff."

Margot nods and walks me the rest of the way out of the building.

"Did you need me for something?" I point in the direction of Vic Hall. "I'm over there."

"Just wanted to see how the meeting went." Without offering a goodbye, Margot heads toward the north end of campus.

I stare after her. Henry is the reason she's part of the society and can protect her brother, but she's almost acting like she doesn't trust him.

Then again, maybe she doesn't trust anyone.

# CHAPTER SIXTEEN

The first group training session happens after classes at the Kingston Penitentiary. The building stretches out in an array of gray brick down the block. It has tall columns and a watchtower in the front with a Canadian flag perched on top. It isn't as grim as I imagined but is still historically maudlin. It feels like a place meant to trap people inside. And monsters, too, apparently. The air is cooler here, closer to the water. I'm glad I wore longer sleeves.

I was emailed instructions about where to go that were adequate at the time but now that I'm here are unhelpful. Instead of going around front, they direct me to walk through the parking lot and head to a not-well-described door. I assume Margot and Corey figured this would be straightforward, which is why they didn't mention it.

"Lost?" Caden asks, sauntering over with the two other boys who follow him around. It's like they watched a bunch of movies from the

'80s on how to be cartoonish bullies. Too pathetic to be intimidating.

I ignore him and stare at my phone, pretending I'm texting someone. Which is when I get an actual text from Bailey asking about how my first week of school went. Caden scoffs, and from the fading sounds of their voices, I assume they're walking away.

Making sure to wait a bit, I follow them, leaving Bailey's message on read.

They enter a side gate, where a man checks our student IDs before letting us go past. And of course, when he gets to me, it takes him forever to find me on the list. Inside, there are no lights, so it's impossible to tell which way Caden went. I try listening, but their footsteps echo too much to figure out a direction.

When I finally get through, I look between the two sets of staircases. The instructions only mentioned *a* staircase, not which one.

"On the right!" Caden calls out, and the boys laugh. The little shit knows I have no idea where I'm supposed to go.

The man who checked our IDs has left, so I can't ask him. I should use the flashlight on my phone to see where Caden and his friends went, or leave and call Margot to make sure, but I don't want to give him the satisfaction.

And I'm sure as shit not going the way he told me to.

I take the left staircase.

The stairs go down seemingly forever. Several times I consider going back up, but I've already committed.

They end at another damp, murky hallway. It's got the stench of a sewer, like a mix of feces and rotting food. I cover my nose with my sleeve and keep walking. The only lights are dim, spread apart, and high in the towering ceiling. Just enough to see that there's a path in front of me, and nothing else.

A MASTERY OF MONSTERS

I must be underground, but the space is bigger than I would expect for it. And the more I walk down the hallway, the farther apart the lights get and the dimmer the space becomes until I'm swallowed by complete darkness.

"Hello?"

I hope for another candidate or Chen, but no sound comes.

I pull my phone out of my pocket, and the screen lights up, illuminating something in one of the cells out of the corner of my field of vision. Something moving. I whip to the side where a giant eye, bloodshot and swiveling, appears, attached to a body with enough fur that I drop my phone. It thumps on the concrete.

"August?"

I scream.

Professor Chen spins me around by my shoulders, and the second cry dies in my throat. She sighs and picks up my phone, hitting the lock button so we're plunged into darkness again. "Come on," she says as she hands it back to me.

I follow her like a lost duckling, clutching my miraculously unbroken phone. She walks up the stairs and stops with a frown. "I did put a sign up to say which way to go. I don't know what happened to it."

*That fucker.*

Chen shakes her head and takes the staircase on the right. At the bottom, the rest of the candidates are gathered in a better lit and less smelly area, including a smirking Caden.

I could kill him. I'm already picturing it in my head. The way I would slide my knife across the skin of his neck. It would be slow. I would take my time.

I force my face to be still and neutral, but his smirk doesn't fade.

"All right," Chen says, standing at the front of the group. She's elected for a pair of shiny leather pants and a fitted black long-sleeved shirt tucked into them. She dresses like she expects to be photographed, and I'm kind, of here for it. "Now that we're all accounted for, we're going to enter some of the holding cells. As you may know, this is where mature monsters without partners are kept for the safety of both the society and the larger population." There's something off about her voice as she says it. Annoyance? Or maybe that's because she had to rescue me? Though she wasn't irked earlier. Honestly, it felt a lot more like pity.

She continues, "Your partners are or will be what we call juvenile monsters. As is the trend, most are born monsters; however, some may be bite victims. All juvenile monsters are unable to assume a monstrous form and will experience several signs of impending maturation, such as intermittent elongated canines and nails, alongside increased strength and speed, and sometimes aggression. They will also, inevitably, reach a peak in which they will transform involuntarily. We call this maturation and it is colloquially referred to as 'turning.' Maturation is often incorrectly linked to age, as many turn between eighteen and twenty-one. But know that monsters can mature at any time. The cause of the activation of the monster mutation has not yet been confirmed. Our only signal is those signs I mentioned. We attempt to partner juvenile monsters before maturation can occur."

It's a more detailed repeat of what Corey told me. Corey also noted that symptoms increase exponentially as monsters come closer to turning. It's why the second his symptoms started to appear, Virgil had to find a partner.

Chen says, "We also separate monsters via stages of monstrosity. Your juveniles are at stage one or two. The first stage is simply knowledge of their existence as monsters. The second is when they show symptoms. Stage three is considered mature and uncontrolled, which are the monsters you will encounter today. The final stage, stage four, is where you want to be, and you will not become a Bachelor unless you reach it. At stage four, monsters can shift at will and maintain control, something that is not possible without a Master partner."

"Except for Wilds," Violet adds.

I say, "Or if they're being controlled by a Doctorate." Look at me, participating. Henry would be proud.

Chen nods. "Yes, and yes. I will also note that at stage four, Bachelors should be passive. The bond allows the monster access to a human level of control in monster form. It is inappropriate for any Bachelor or Master to actively assert their will on their partner outside of emergencies. This is important to keep in mind even now because the point of this process is to strengthen a partnership. No one should go into the candidacy with the mindset that you will be in control of your partner." She waves to the door in front of us. "Your task today will be to retrieve a bell. There is one for each of you. I implore you to remember that your task is to form a strong connection with your partners. You cannot do this if you are distracted by your fear. Remember the words of Dr. Weiss: 'We are one and the same, Master and monster.'"

Someone coughs something that sounds suspiciously like, "monster lover," and there are some accompanying giggles. I notice, not for the first time, that one of Caden's buddies is Black. It's wild that he doesn't see any issue with joining in on monster discrimination when there are still people who think we aren't any better than animals either. The mental gymnastics are astounding.

Our professor is unfazed by the comment. "When you bond, there is a chance that the aggression and wildness of the monster may leak through to you. You shouldn't be controlling your partner, but you do need to control yourself. This exercise is a great place to start." She opens the door. "You have five minutes. Your time starts now."

Candidates rush through the opening, followed almost immediately by screaming.

At the back of the group, I freeze, and the candidates stop pouring through the door.

"Tick tock," Chen says.

Swallowing, I push through the crowd, and on the other side of the door is another large hallway. Well-lit enough to see the monsters in cells on either side. They have red ribbons around their legs with tiny red bells attached. There's only enough room for the monsters to either sit or hunch and not much else. They're all so close to the bars because there isn't anywhere else to go.

The monsters range in size, but each one has either massive teeth, claws, or both. One looks like a crab with too many eyes growing out of multiple parts of its shell, scuttling backward and forward, the bell jingling with its movements. The bars of its cell are thick and spaced far enough apart to stick a human arm through.

"Four minutes," Chen says, coming into the room behind us.

Some of the other candidates still haven't made it inside.

I stare at the crablike monster. It's still scuttling, refusing to stop or stand still. I'm thrown back to that experience with Isaac. I stare into its eyes. And I see it. Just like I could see Isaac. Someone is in there. I mean, of course there is, but these monsters are supposed to be uncontrolled. Stage three.

Except . . . why would the society unleash dangerous monsters

A MASTERY OF MONSTERS                                    171

on a bunch of fresh candidates? Especially without giving us weapons or armor. They can't expect us to just put our hands inside.

I tilt my head at Crabby. Besides shuffling around, it's not doing anything. It's not even remotely hostile.

Drifting over to the bars, I reach my hand through them. The crab stills. I close my fingers around the ribbon, rotating it so that I can get at the knot, which I untie. The bell comes loose into my hand. I stare at the dozen green eyes looking down at me.

The monster doesn't move.

"Three minutes," Chen says. I whip my head toward her.

Caden's fury is palpable. I feel like spite is the only thing that moves him toward one of the cells. His movement spurs on the rest of our peers. Violet comes to the monster in the cell beside the crab, and Bryce goes across the room to a different cell.

When I turn back to the crab, it's still staring at me. *They're* staring at me.

This is what will happen to Virgil without me.

Trapped down here. Alone in a cramped cell. Watching while candidates struggle to force themselves to come near him. Used in a training exercise likely without any consent on his part.

I shake my head.

I just need to find Jules. That's why I'm here. Not to save Virgil. I don't owe him anything. *I don't.*

I repeat it until I believe it.

A hand lands on my shoulder, and I jump.

It's only Professor Chen, holding out a small wicker basket. "For the bell."

I drop mine inside. "How are they like this? They aren't partnered up."

"Think about it. I'm confident you can come up with the answer."

". . . a Doctorate?" I look around.

Chen chuckles and points up. "Two of our candidates are on a higher level of the Pen, facilitating."

"You didn't tell us that."

She grins. "It's not much fun to tell you beforehand. Besides, it's always good to pick out the students observant enough to realize they're being handled with kid gloves."

I match her grin with one of my own. Though it falls away shortly after. "Can't the Doctorate force them all to transform into humans? Masters can do that, right? Then maybe the conditions could be bett—"

"Standard monsters gain the ability to swap between human and monster forms exclusively through bonding. The privilege of swapping forms without is limited to Wilds. If Doctorates could do so, Dr. Weiss would have found a cure right away. He even tried bonding to see if that might help, but it ended up limiting his abilities to one monster instead."

"Yeah, I heard that's why Doctorates don't bond."

"I appreciate you thinking of them—the monsters," Chen says, studying me. "Not many do. I know you're new to the society, but these prejudices run deep. That's why we do these sorts of exercises. It's one of the few cases where things were better back in the day. Dr. Weiss had a different vision for us. He did not imagine a future where monster children would be abandoned by their parents." She pauses to shake her head. "Or worse."

My eyes widen. *What the actual fuck?* "Worse . . . ?"

"We take those sorts of crimes seriously, and they don't happen often anymore. Testing helps, since we can keep an eye on those

A MASTERY OF MONSTERS

children. Still, abandonment isn't uncommon. Either they're afraid of the child or they're afraid for them. This society is built upon the backs of monsters, and unfortunately, you'll come to see that they're the least appreciated. Feared and ostracized with few fighting for their rights."

"Adam is," I say. "And I guess the Pro-Libs."

Chen throws me a sharp look. "I suggest you not say the name of that group in public."

*Oh shit, right.* "What's the big deal about them?"

She looks over at the other students, who are still working on the exercise. "The Pro-Liberation Coalition wish for the complete liberation of monsters. They feel that their existence is natural, and the apocalypse should not be fought. We should embrace it as an evolution of the species. To them, Masters are a stepping stone to help monsters achieve full actualization. They believe that all monsters are actually Wilds and could control themselves if given a chance to develop the ability. Years ago, the Pro-Libs joined with the Wilds to launch a rebellion against the Learners' Master-monster structure. A few decades ago as Traditionalists gained ground, Wilds were forced to bond despite not needing partners. Which both the Pro-Libs and Wilds obviously did not like. In the rebellion, they began to murder Masters, breaking the bond to their monsters to prove the monsters could become self-sufficient."

I lick my lips. Those are the people that Natalie woman led? Given how hated Virgil is for the people his *parents* killed, it's amazing that Natalie can walk around with her head held high. No wonder Margot, Corey, and Virgil were shocked that she was in public and that Corris would be seen with her.

"Did it work?" I ask. "Could the monsters control themselves?"

LISELLE SAMBURY

"No. Many people died. Rates of bitten monsters spiked. When the Wilds were . . . well, when the agreement was signed, the Wilds were made to abide by the terms of the truce, which thankfully, included terms to stop forced bonding. And the Pro-Libs were broken up. Those members of the faction who survived the rebellion were stripped of titles, monster partners, and society-provided jobs and homes. Whatever would make it difficult for them to organize or retain power in the society."

"But not Natalie."

"No. Though many believe she led the movement, there was no physical evidence to prove that she had been involved." Chen gives me a tight smile. "I wish they were right. Self-determination could make a big difference to a lot of monsters. It would negate the need for this." She looks at the crab behind bars. "But it's not reality. And people who don't operate within reality are dangerous." She checks her watch. "It's time." She pats my shoulder. "I look forward to seeing your progress."

The professor walks to the middle of the room, calling time and collecting the retrieved bells. There are about five candidates who didn't manage to get one, and she reassures them that they haven't failed. This is training, after all. They still have time to prove themselves.

I give the crab, huddled in the darkness, one last look before I leave and join the rest of the group.

# CHAPTER SEVENTEEN

I wake up to Bailey calling me. And it's FaceTime. Even better. The dorms outside are noisy with people moving around. Every day here is like living in the world's most chaotic apartment building. I only had one morning class for the whole day and decided to give myself the joy of a nap that's now becoming short-lived. I already ignored Bailey yesterday, and at some point, she'll alert Dad if she fears I've dropped off the face of the Earth.

Or disappeared, like Jules.

I answer without bothering to sit up straight, propping the phone on my nightstand.

"Hey!" She stares around the screen. "How is your room? Do you like it? Do you have a roommate?"

"No, it's a single."

I hadn't explained a lot to her. I just announced that I'd decided to go to Queen's after all. The way her face lit up . . .

"Oh, wow," Bailey says, her eyes going wide.

I know she's wondering how I can afford a single and everything else with just my student loans, since she and Dad think that's how I'm funding my education. That was the original plan. "I need to go meet some friends, so . . ."

"How is everything? Have you heard from Jules at all?"

"No."

Bailey bites her lip. "I wish he would call to let us know he's okay. This isn't like him."

She's right. It isn't.

"Well, I'm always here if you need me. Just a ferry ride away," she says.

"Cool. I gotta go."

"Okay, love you, bye."

I hang up and grip the phone in my hand, squeezing my eyes shut. I don't even know Bailey. But she's the one calling to ask how school is. She's the one texting me to see if I'm enjoying my classes. But Dad was so proud, right? He was going to come by once he was less busy, right?

I don't want him to come, so it's fine.

At least I have some time to breathe for a little bit. I passed yesterday's training with flying colors and have another couple of weeks before the societal knowledge one. Otherwise, I have Margot's horrible running routine plus her grueling sessions, but on the bright side, soon I'll be doing training with Corey, who I know will be a lot less spartan.

I finally have a bit of freedom, and I plan to use it seeing what I can learn about Jules.

With my current knowledge of the Learners, they wouldn't let monsters roam around unchecked. Either (1) this Master that the monster is partnered with is amazing at covering their tracks, or (2) the society is in on this somehow. But why murder and/or kidnap random students? I can guess that maybe the attack on me was a way to get to Jules. But what's the connection between him and Samantha?

I look her up again. It's a useless exercise, since there's never anything new. Except this time, there is.

*The Queen's Black Student Society presents the freshman welcome mixer! Donations will be collected for Samantha George's family to assist in bringing their daughter home.*

I scramble to find the date.

It's tonight.

The Yellow House is actually yellow, though much paler than I imagined. More pastel than sunshine. The small building across from the Adelaide Hall residence looks like something you'd see in the English countryside with quaint rounded windows. The door is painted the same forest green as the first-floor shutters. It reminds me of a less grand version of McIntosh Castle. They have the same aesthetic.

Outside they decorated with balloons and put up a sign that says, QBSS MIXER! It also notes below that this is a safe space for LGBTQIA2S+ folks. I step up to the door, shifting in place.

Probably, I should have a better plan going into this. But I don't. I figure that if I go and take part in enough conversations, I'll learn something about Samantha. Make some sort of connection between her and my brother other than them being Black and Queen's students.

I open the door and enter. I'm low-key shocked that it looks like an actual house inside. There are two couches with colorful slip-covers, a few bookshelves, and a coffee table that's been shoved off to the side. There are only twenty or so people in the room, but it's so tiny that it feels packed.

Obviously, I see Black people on campus, but it's different to walk into a space entirely made up of people who look like me. And it's more than that. There's a curry scent wafting from another room that reminds me of Grandma cooking on Christmas when I was little, before she passed. And music drifting from someone's speakers, soft enough not to interfere with conversation, but loud enough to recognize. It's the sort of song Mom and Dad played in the car, shit that me and Jules made fun of them for because we were like, *What is this?*" Our parents gasping when we didn't recognize the artist. I swallow and shove my hands into my pockets.

"Welcome!" an upperclassman says with a smile, standing behind a desk pushed against the wall. He has a well-kept beard and bright brown eyes. Eager. Like he sits up front in every lecture. He holds out a clipboard to me. "I'm Jackson. I head up our event planning." When he speaks, there's a flash of gold in the back of his mouth—one of his molars is capped in it. It's an odd style choice given his vibe, but it's not my business. "If you put down your name and email, we can get you on the newsletter. This is our first event of the year, but we do a ton. We'll send out emails whenever we have one coming up."

I accept the clipboard and write down my details. I don't want to, but I figure no one will talk to me if I open with "I don't want to be on your email list." I hand it back to him and say, "I also wanted to donate? For, um, Samantha, the girl who's missing."

"I got you, thanks for donating." He reaches for a large jar on the

A MASTERY OF MONSTERS

table that has a photo of the girl. It's the same one they used in the *Queen's Journal* article. She has red, blue, and yellow face paint on and is wearing a tam. We got our own at the end of orientation last week. Corey insisted we take pictures in them, so now I unfortunately have a record of me in the blue beret-looking hat with its striped brim and red pom-pom.

I drop five dollars in the jar and prepare to ask him questions about Samantha when someone says, "You came."

I turn to find myself facing Riley. She's in a black T-shirt dress that looks effortlessly cool and casual on her, accessorizing with her many necklaces, bracelets, and rings.

"You said if I tried this out, you'd leave me alone," I say.

"That's the spirit."

Jackson looks between the two of us. "You know Riley?"

"She's the reason I'm here."

His lips form a tentative smile. "Cool, uh, she's my girlfriend. And our treasurer. Sorry, I missed your name."

"This is August," Riley answers for me, looping her arm in mine. "And I'm borrowing her. See you later."

"Yeah, see you . . ."

His eyes follow us as Riley drags me away, his smile morphing into a frown. "Let me introduce you to some people." She leads me through the other spaces in the house. In the dining room, she presents me to other first years who I assume she hopes I'll be friends with. And then we transition to the kitchen, where I accept a bottle of Ting. I haven't had the pop in years. I twist off the cap and sip from the green glass rim. I eye the plates of curried chicken and rice and peas being dished out. After. I need to focus on getting information.

As we circle back to the living room, I spot Cam and Janey from Tim's. They wave. And I manage a stiff smile. "You know them?" Riley asks.

"We used to work together."

"So, you hung out and stuff?"

"Not what I said."

Riley raises an eyebrow at me. "Okay . . . Hey, actually, I want to show you something." She walks me up to the second floor. It's an open attic with a couple of tables and chairs. It seems to be a flex space, judging by the random assortment of items, including a few teddy bears lined up on the window ledge. It's also apparently off-limits to partygoers, because me and Riley are the only people here.

She sighs as she looks at the file boxes on the tables. "We just bought a house to be the new official club space. Should be ready next semester. We're in the process of moving our files out of the Rideau Building down the street. I forgot they said they'd drop these off for us. Do you mind waiting here? I'm going to see if Jackson can come grab them."

"No, it's cool. I'll wait." I would have texted him, but to each their own, I guess.

As soon as she leaves the room, I make my way to the box of files and set down my Ting bottle. I lift out and flick through the papers and then carefully slot them back where they were. I don't know if there would be anything on Samantha in here, but I may as well take advantage of the opportunity.

What I find is absolutely nothing.

The door opens, and I turn toward it, pretending to look nonchalant.

A MASTERY OF MONSTERS

Riley smiles and pushes the door closed behind her.

I smile back.

She raises her phone and turns the screen toward me, and I watch the playback of a video taken in this room of me riffling through their files. The smile drops off my face but stays on Riley's.

Where the . . . I look at the stuffed animals on the window ledge and then back at her phone, which she's switched to a live feed. I watch myself reach out for one of the bears. I let my hand drop. "Did you seriously nanny cam me?!"

"Yes. And I can see now that it was the right move."

"What's your angle?"

"I could ask you the same thing," she says, her voice cool. "You show up out of nowhere, not on anyone's radar, and then suddenly you're enrolled in a school you said you don't attend, and you're hanging out with people like Margot Bouchard and attending Summerhill meetings."

"So you're straight-up stalking me?"

"I'm observing."

I have to laugh. What a rebrand.

Riley crosses her arms over her chest. "Why don't you tell me what you're looking for, and I'll tell you what I'm looking for?"

"Or you could go first, since I don't owe you shit, but you clearly want something from me."

She narrows her eyes and then exhales slowly, blowing the breath out of her mouth with effort. "Sammie. Samantha. She w—she's— we were in QBSS together."

She doesn't say the letters of the acronym individually and instead says it like it's a word, "Q-biss." "Okay . . ."

"She texted me that night. She was texting me *regularly,* and then she sent one that was very different from the others. She was scared. When I saw it and called at like two in the morning, she didn't answer. I was worried, so I went to her house, and she wasn't there. I traced the path she would have taken to get home from downtown and searched around that area, and you know what I found? Her body. Just lying there, and . . ." She swallows. "I couldn't handle being near her like that, so I walked up the road a few blocks to wait for the police, but she was gone when we got back. Everything was cleaned up. Not even luminol could find traces of her blood. Someone was thorough. Her parents—well, they want to say she's missing until the body is found." Her gaze narrows. "But I know that she was killed."

"I'm sorry, are you accusing me of murdering your friend?"

"No," she grinds out between her teeth. "But I know about McIntosh Castle. The body was close by. They must have seen something. There's no way they didn't. They're tight-lipped because the Learners' Society is always tight-lipped. But now I see you coming in and out. And you don't seem like their type."

Isn't the society supposed to be a secret? "What does that mean, not their type?"

"You aren't properly indoctrinated."

"How do you guess that?"

"Because the society is 'color blind.'" She wraps finger quotes around the word. "None of them would be caught dead at a celebration of Blackness because it's 'exclusionary.' Which means, either you're bad at it, or you're pursuing your own interests. I'd like to know what those are, because if they align with mine, we may be able to help each other."

I bite the inside of my cheek. Okay, so I committed a society faux pas without realizing it. I hope no one saw me come in here. I'm not even going to touch on that color blind philosophy. More importantly, if Riley's looking into Samantha's—or I guess Sammie's—death, then she's already searching within the parameters of the information I'm seeking.

This is the closest I've come to a real lead. "My brother's missing." I avoid thinking about how Sammie is being described as missing even though Riley is saying the girl is dead. It doesn't mean that Jules is too. The same way what the police say doesn't mean Mom's dead.

"And you think this is related to Sammie how?" That bit is harder to explain. "Is it a monster thing?"

My eyes go wide. Apparently not.

She shrugs. "It's not commonly known. Don't freak out. And if it helps you, they know I know. Besides that, Sammie had claw marks down her back. That means a monster killed her. Now confirm, how do you think they're linked?"

"I was attacked by a monster at Big Sandy Bay—"

"And you're alive?" Riley looks me up and down.

"Obviously."

"Okay . . ."

"Anyway, that same day, my brother disappeared but he left me a note saying monsters are real. To stay away from forests or deserted areas, and to run if I spotted one. That someone else had already been hurt. A monster unknown to the society attacked me, has something to do with my brother, and potentially also attacked Sammie. I figured there must be some sort of connection between them."

"Flimsy at best."

"Do you have something better?"

"Not yet, but we do have aligned interests. And you were right. I need you because I need a connection to the society. And I assume you now need me because I knew Sammie. Give me your phone."

I hand it over and let her put her number in. I text her when she gives it back to me, so she'll have mine. "I don't have to actually join up, do I?" I ask.

"QBSS? Oh, no." She laughs. "We don't accept society members. Really, they never join, but if they tried, we wouldn't accept them."

"Because of the monsters?"

"Because we question the morality of people raised in a society that supposedly celebrates diversity but frowns on individuals for expressing any pride or joy associated with their race, culture, or identity. You should question it too."

"Their culture or whatever has nothing to do with me. I'm not joining the cult. I'm just there to find my brother."

"Sure." She waves to the door. "Shall I see you out?"

I follow her downstairs and outside, mourning the curry chicken plate that I didn't get to have, and keeping my head down in case any society people are milling around outside. At least I have a real lead now. I'm not sure if I'm going in the right direction, but it's better than feeling like I'm standing still.

# CHAPTER EIGHTEEN

On Friday, I stumble out of my last class and pause to roll my neck. I have to keep reminding myself that I don't need to excel at school. I'm only trying to avoid academic probation. Still, I find myself falling back into old habits. Today, a girl next to me in psych complimented my notes. I was tempted to burn them.

I start the trudge from Humphrey Hall north to Princess Street, where I told Corey I would meet her, and try to shake the droning voice of my professor out of my head. The guy's lectures are just the textbook readings. There's no point in going. In fact, attending is worse because then I have to listen to people who haven't done the readings ask questions that they would know the answers to if they did the readings. But the instant I skipped a class last week, I got a text from Margot asking if she needed to personally accompany me.

I spot Corey from down the street, typing on her phone with a frown on her face, a gym bag slung over her shoulder.

"What's up?" I ask as I come up next to her.

She glances at me, then back down at the screen. "Nothing. I was trying to find this book. Henry's asked me to look for it. I've been working on it for weeks. I feel like I'm so close." She rubs at her face. "Fuck," she mutters, then flushes. "Sorry, it's fine."

"What's so important about this book?"

"It's Dr. Weiss's journal. Or one of his journals, I should say. He would lend them out to people, and so they got scattered all over the place."

"He would lend out his *journals?*"

Corey tilts her head from side to side. "They're more like his theories and thoughts. The Shaws have the largest collection, but they're missing some. If I could get even one of the lost volumes, it would be huge."

"And it's important that you do it because . . . ?"

"Because then I would—I don't know, I would have done something, you know?" She looks away from her phone at the sidewalk. "I'd be useful."

"And you're not useful now?"

Corey clenches her fingers around her phone. "You don't get it. I failed the Bachelor candidacy. I was lucky that Dr. Liu took me in. I want to be able to help the Progressives. But I'm obviously not going to be a Master. And I'm not a monster. This is the only way I can make a difference. Through Henry. If I can't even do that, then what's the point of me?"

"Um, living your life? Doing whatever you want?"

She shakes her head. "Forget it." She points across the street. "We're gonna head over here." She leads me north of Princess and then turns onto a side street and steps up to the door of a taekwondo

A MASTERY OF MONSTERS

place. Using a key from her bag, she opens the door and lets me in. "The dojang is closed on Fridays, so we should be good."

Inside is a large open space whose floor is covered in giant mats in blue and red. We take off our shoes at the entrance. Corey has to sit on the floor to work her loafer off her prosthetic foot. I guess it's not as easy as just slipping it off. I follow her lead and take my socks off too. The far wall is mostly made up of mirrors, and the left wall has a bunch of equipment.

She brings me to a small room next to the entrance. "Changing rooms are over here." I open my backpack and get my gym clothes out. Meanwhile, she pulls a different prosthesis from her bag. She catches me looking. "This one's for doing athletic stuff that isn't running. It's a little more responsive. A gift from Dr. Liu. I told him I wasn't going to do taekwondo anymore, but he got it for me 'just in case.'" She shakes her head. "And of course, as soon as I could, I started using it."

"Did you think it would be too hard to do taekwondo with your leg, or . . . ?"

"Yes. And it *is* hard. But that's not why I wanted to stop training." She leaves it at that and works on swapping her prosthesis out. I turn away and get changed. She says, "Go ahead and do some warm-ups. I'll come out when I'm done."

I return to the gym area and do some stretches while examining the space. The walls are decorated with framed photos and two giant flags, a Canadian one and a Korean one. And here Riley was talking about the Learners not being able to celebrate their individual cultures. "Is this a society place, or what?" I shout to Corey.

She comes out from the changing room in a T-shirt and shorts, pulling her hair into a ponytail. "It's my family's place. My dad opened this dojang when I was little. He teaches a lot of society students." She holds out a scrunchie to me. I forgot to bring anything to tie my braids up.

"My hair will stretch that thing all the way out."

"It's fine." I take the scrunchie and peer at the photos as I tie my hair. I spot a young Corey, leaping through the air in a kicking stance. I point at it. "You're going to teach me to do that?"

She laughs. "I think that's a bit advanced. You already have a great combat skill base from what you learned from your mom. Margot's going to teach you some boxing. But kicks are kind of my specialty, so she wants you to do those with me. We'll do a taekwondo style more similar to kickboxing so it's easier for you to incorporate what we both teach. Like I said, my dad instructs a lot of society kids. If you don't have a similar capacity, you're going to struggle. Can you do any kicks?"

I nod. Corey collects a foam pad from against the wall and holds it up. I kick out with a roundhouse.

"Good," she says. "Low one. Then higher. Front leg first, and then the back one."

I do as she says. I try not to get thrown back into memories of Mom. She bought a punching bag for us to practice on when I was seven. Me and Jules would take turns kicking and punching it, sometimes having competitions about who could punch or kick the longest, or hardest. Mom would guide us through the motions, commenting. Critiquing, really. Earning a compliment from her was better than getting the first slice of cake at a party. Better than a new bike or shoes. Better than anything.

"Can you do any high kicks?" Corey asks. I kick out with the highest roundhouse I can manage, and she makes a face.

A MASTERY OF MONSTERS

"Wow, that bad?"

"A for effort?"

"Just show me how it's done."

"This is what you want." She sets down the foam pad and then drops into a stance. She shoots her right foot up with a shout, so high that there's a straight line from her left leg to the right. At least, for a moment. Then she wobbles and careens to the side, just managing to hop and keep from falling. "Except, you will keep your balance." She shakes out her left leg. "I'm still working on relearning. Like I said, it's hard."

"I can imagine. You're still a million times better than me."

She grins. "You just need practice. Also, more power." She gestures to the foam pad. "Pick it up." I lift the pad and hold it in front of me. "This is how you're kicking." She kicks out at the mat with a thud. "This is how you need to kick." She kicks the mat so hard that I almost topple over. And she actually falls back.

"Oh, shit! Are you okay?!"

She waves me away. "Like I said, the balance thing is . . ." She sighs. "A lot. I should practice more, honestly. Part of the process. A lot of relearning how to do things." I hold out my hand, she takes it, and I tug her back to her feet. "You get the idea, right?"

I do. That kick felt like it was ten times harder than what I've been doing. I know Corey got all the way to initiation, so she had to be good. I just didn't realize how far apart our skill levels are. She's what I need to get to.

Or no. *No.* She isn't. I'm not planning to stick around that long. Cutting off my fingers and fighting a monster Virgil? No fucking way. I need to focus on making progress with finding Jules and managing this competition day by day. That's all.

Corey runs me through drills that are supposed to help me with my high kicks, which I get to add to my already packed training schedule. She instructs me from the mat with crossed arms and a furrowed brow.

"Strong legs will be important not just for your kicks but for running, too," Corey says. "And you'll need to run in every test there is. But especially during initiation once Virgil transforms. The serum metabolizes faster in a monster's body, so you won't have long to do the flesh exchange."

I don't plan on doing the flesh exchange, period. "Is it possible for someone to get a hold of the serum outside of the competition or a senior Master bonding with a monster? Because, the way I see it, anyone with the serum can bond, right? Could that be why the monster that attacked me isn't registered? Because someone stole serum?"

"Keep your hips aligned." I shift as I'm told. Corey says, "It's not impossible, but it is improbable. I know the competition seems like a lot, but it's necessary. That whole leveling up thing from the pressure of competing is real. If you take the serum without any of that training, it can be difficult for both the monster and Master to adjust. That's why only senior Masters get to bond outside of the competition, because they've already gone through that process. It's one of the reasons why the serum is heavily guarded and protected— you need, like, several security clearances to get access to it."

"But someone *could* have done it, right? What other explanation is there?"

"I mean, if this is a Master with some status and power, they could have bonded with a new monster legitimately and then bribed or coerced someone into keeping their old one on record. Obviously it's not allowed, but after the rebellion, there was a lot of stripping of monsters and new partnerships being made. We've already had some issues with registration because of it that still haven't been fully resolved years later. They could take advantage of that."

"But how would they plan for that? Can Masters just get new partners whenever they want?"

Corey curls her lip. "No. Masters can't swap around as they like and have the Doctorate stripping bonds whenever. But there is a way to break the bond without a Doctorate."

"How—" I cut myself off as I'm asking. Henry's first partner died. That was how he ended up with Laira years later. If a Master killed their old partner, they could legitimately get a new one. It sounds impossible, but Masters can control their partners in monster form. They could have it do anything. "That's fucked up."

"Yeah. But it seems more likely than stealing serum. You have to understand that it's the most protected substance in this society. And if someone did break in, it would be a big deal. We would hear about it."

"How can you stand it? All *this*." The words slip out, as soft as my toes curling into the mat.

Corey stares at the mirror. Not at herself. Just at the glass. "It's all I've ever known. And I believe that it can be better." She pastes on a smile. "Two more drills and then we're done."

Everything I learn about the society makes me more concerned about what Jules had to do with it. And makes it clear why he didn't want me involved. I'm not dealing with someone low level. Whoever is involved in this has some sort of power. And I have no idea why they would be targeting people who have nothing to do with the Learners.

When we finish a few minutes later, as Corey puts away the foam pad, I look at the pictures again. There's one with Corey and her parents, and an older boy too. I assume that's her brother. The one she was born to save, who is now underground.

The door opens, and Corey whips her head toward it.

A woman walks in, and I recognize her from the family photo. Her eyes widen. "Corey?"

"We were just leaving," Corey says, her gaze on the floor.

"You don't have to! You're welcome to practice here whenever you want." She looks at me with a small smile. "August, right? I saw you get nominated. Congratulations. I'm Corey's mom."

"Hello." I glance at Corey, who refuses to look anywhere other than the ground.

Ms. Yang stares at her daughter. "Are you eating well?"

"I'm fine."

Silence stretches. "There may be some leftovers in the fridge? Um, gamjatang, I think," Ms. Yang tries. "Or I was going to drop off some more food at McIntosh Castle this week. Is there anything specific you want? Do you still like—"

"I don't need anything," Corey says. "You can stop doing that. We have food. August and I need to leave." She heads to the changing room, and I'm forced to rush after her as her mom's face falls.

Corey paces the space while I change, shaking her head and muttering to herself, her voice getting louder as she goes. She turns to me, her eyes shining, and says, "I had to crawl to escape. During initiation. I was trying to get part of him for the flesh exchange, and he caught me, and I kicked out and—"

I swallow. I don't know what to do. If I should stop her and tell her she doesn't have to get into it or let her keep talking. In the end, I don't say anything.

A MASTERY OF MONSTERS

"He bit my leg," she says, bottom lip trembling. "Bit straight through flesh and bone. Clean off. I crawled. And the only reason I got away was because he was busy eating it."

Virgil was right. I don't actually know what it's like to have a real encounter with a monster. Not one without any control. I've never experienced anything as horrifying as what Corey did.

She shakes her head. "I hid, and then time ran out. The Doctorate freezes the monsters then, and medics are allowed in. That's the only reason I'm alive. Otherwise, I would have bled to death." She meets my eyes. "When I woke up in the hospital, my parents had the fucking gall to ask if I wanted to visit him in the Pen."

I wince.

"Corey, I'm sorr—"

"If he never existed, neither would I. But sometimes I would imagine what it might be like. If he weren't around and I could be my own person. Now that's my reality. I just want to live like he was never here. I'm sorry that I do. I know it would kill me to see Virgil in the Pen. But I *chose* Virgil. He was never my duty or my burden. My brother is a monster from a nightmare I never want to go back to. That's all he can ever be. Because how am I supposed to live my new life if all I can think about is how our parents ruined everything we could have been from the start? And now he's gone, and we can never be anything else."

Is this why she never talks about her brother? Because she wants to forget him? Better to be afraid of the monster she met in the initiation than to mourn the brother she resented because of how they were raised. How could I judge her for that after everything?

"I'm sorry." She hides her face in her hands. "Please don't tell Virgil I said that. He would be so—"

"I won't."

It would crush him. Corey is his best friend. I know she and her brother never had a great relationship, but the fact is that experiencing him in monster form fundamentally changed how she thinks about him. And that's what she wants. If Virgil knew, he would assume the same thing would happen once she sees his other form. He would understand, I know. He would understand the same way anyone would, given the circumstances. But that wouldn't change the hurt. It wouldn't stop the thought that in his non-human form, she would see him differently.

No longer her best friend or chosen brother, just another ravenous monster in the dark.

Corey mumbles, "Can you please bring my shoes in here so I don't have to sit out there with her to put them on?"

"Yeah, of course."

I walk out to the room where her mom is still waiting. I duck my head and grab both mine and Corey's shoes and socks. I return to the changing room, and Corey sits and gets both her socks and shoes on but doesn't bother changing her clothes or prosthesis. "Let's go." She practically sprints out of the dojang, straight past her mom.

Outside, a man who I clock as her dad comes out of a car. When he sees Corey, he abandons the vehicle, leaving the door wide open to walk over. "Corey? Did you come to practice?"

She freezes, her fists clenched at her sides. "I don't compete anymore. You know that."

"For fun, then? Is this your friend?" He gives me the same smile his wife did. Wobbly at the edges. Like he's barely holding on to it. "August, right? Maybe you could both come for dinner?"

"We have to go." Corey speed walks away, not stopping until

A MASTERY OF MONSTERS

195

we're on the corner of Princess Street and Division. Her parents don't follow us.

"You good?" I ask.

"They just—!" She rips her hair out of its ponytail, letting the strands fall over her face. "They always do that. They don't call or visit or anything. Not even when she drops off the food! She knocks and runs away. Leaves it on the stoop. But then if I show up, suddenly they want to act like everything is fine. If they cared about me, they wouldn't have made me—" She closes her eyes and takes a trembling breath. "This is why I had to go. I . . . I hate the way they look at me."

I think of how Dad looked at me when I said I wasn't going to Queen's. That I wasn't going anywhere. The same look he gave me about a month after Mom disappeared, the first time I came home well after curfew, wasted, and threw up at his feet.

Though I've never seen him stare at me with the sort of desperation in Corey's parents' eyes. But then I think of what she told me. How she was only born to save her brother. I can't imagine the burden of that kind of expectation. Or the fallout of it after she failed to do what they wanted.

"It doesn't matter what they think," I say to Corey.

She shakes her head. "You know that's not true."

This time, I'm the one to let my eyes drop to the sidewalk.

# CHAPTER NINETEEN

A week later, I gather with the rest of the candidates on Monday afternoon. The city finally got the message that it's fall, and the leaves have turned to deep ambers and golden yellows, littering the ground. It's so picturesque with the lake spreading out and meeting the sky, and the historic brick buildings, that it's almost artificial. Like a postcard.

I wait with the other candidates, not speaking to anyone. Caden crosses his arms and says to his friends, "Can't believe they're still letting a Bachelor teach us. Is it that hard to find a competent Master?"

I didn't realize Bernie doesn't have the Master title. Still, Caden is full of shit. Bernie shouldn't need a title to educate. After all, we wouldn't be any higher up in rank at the end of this process. The difference is that Bernie isn't getting any more chances. I assume he's already burned through his and lost his partner. What's worse— failing before you achieve Bachelor, or achieving it and failing after?

When Bernie arrives, it's clear he's fighting the change in season by sticking to his uniform of cargo shorts and a Hawaiian shirt. "Hello, everyone. We're here today at the Murney Tower National Historic Site. It's a nineteenth century defense tower turned museum which still maintains some society role."

A couple people walking near us slow, maybe mistaking us for a tour group. Bernie smiles at them before ushering us toward the entrance. The tower looks like a giant squat cylinder made of bricks and has its own moat, though the dip under the bridge we cross to get inside is empty of any water, holding only grass and weeds.

A single heavy metal door leads into the building. Inside, the space has labeled items and posters on the walls for visitors to read. This level has a built-in brick stove and table for eating alongside a single bed. I assume nonfunctional but needed to set the scene of what living in here would have been like. Some of the other candidates mill around and check out the exhibit.

Bernie stands by the ticket desk beside a large whiteboard and clears his throat. "There will be time for you to explore in a moment." We gather in front of him as he gestures to the board. "There are a number of society connections to be found in the tower. I would like you to locate the relevant items and put the picture together on this board. You may start now."

Great, vague instructions. And from the way the other candidates are looking at each other with furrowed brows, I would say for once, I'm not the only one thinking that. Margot said in her year, Bernie took them to Fort Henry, and they did a historical scavenger hunt, so me and Corey brushed up on my knowledge. This activity seems to be the same format in a different place and with this whiteboard addition.

Caden and his friends head upstairs, which is my cue to go

downstairs. The less I interact with him, the better. I'm sure losing his mom wasn't exactly fun—I have an idea of what that's like—but that doesn't mean I have to be content with being his scapegoat. Especially when I'm two times removed from the actual subjects of his fury.

The stairway leading to the lower level is both narrow and short, and I have to duck to get into the space. It's nowhere near as furnished and nice as the upper room, featuring stone-lined corridors and hefty wooden doors.

I have no idea what I'm looking for, but it has to be at least somewhat obvious, right? And that's just the first hurdle. Then I have to figure out how to make the connections on the whiteboard, whatever that means. Maybe I can hover around with my object until someone mentions it. Though probably Bernie will notice that I'm not actively participating.

I walk into a room with a print of the tower layout on the wall, maybe even the original schematics, encased in glass. I'm staring at it when the door slams shut behind me.

I try to open it, but it won't budge.

*Great. Just fucking great.*

I don't have to guess who did it. It's fine. Bernie will come searching for me at some point. But now my options for finding something are limited. I look over at the barrels and boxes at the end of the room.

At least Caden locked me in the room most likely to have something. I pick through the stuff, most of which won't easily open, until finally, one does. I pull out a laminated photograph and stare at it. It doesn't appear to be part of the exhibit, so I assume this is one of the hidden items.

It's a Black man sitting for a portrait, posed at a writing desk, his short curls neatly parted on the right side. It's in black and white and well preserved. Shit. We didn't study pictures. Margot's scavenger hunt was slips of paper with names.

I attempt to think of the prominent Black men within the Learners' history. Wilden McCray, a businessman in the nineteenth century, was the first Master. And Henry's ancestor. There's also Joseph Lawrence, who worked with Dr. Weiss. But then there's also Robert Sutherland, whose estate saved the university. Corey mentioned that he wasn't part of the society, but he's an important figure, nonetheless. Queen's was in jeopardy of closing, and his money was the only reason it didn't end up folding and becoming some offshoot of the University of Toronto. He's relevant to their history through the school. I wonder if I would have ever learned that if it hadn't been explicitly taught to me for this test. This isn't the sort of school that makes people think of Black history.

Flipping the photo over, I hope for a name, but instead, it notes a date in 1861. Either McCray or Lawrence. I'll figure it out later. For now, I decide to keep searching to see if I can find someone whose face I recognize. Though I'm pretty sure that I've only seen a photo of Dr. Weiss. The man was devoted to growing his mustache.

I turn to an assortment of small black boxes set into the wall and open them. Nothing. I squat and crawl under the shelf. I don't expect to see anything beyond the additional boxes stored there, but when I push them aside, there's a latch.

I shimmy farther underneath and open it, sliding the tiny door aside. It's pitch-black.

Until two orbs glow from within.

I jump, smacking my head on the shelf and groaning. When I look again, it's only darkness.

The door to the room opens. "August?"

Flushing, I slide the latch shut and scramble out from under the shelf.

Bernie looks from me to the space where I was. "Did you find anything?"

"What?" I blurt out. Were those . . . *eyes?* But why would there be eyes down there? Maybe it was lights or something? Like auto ones, and that's why they came on so suddenly?

"For the activity? Did you find something?"

"Oh, yeah!" I hold up the photo. Then I look back at the shelf. "Uh, there's, like, a hole down there." I'm not going to mention the glowing eyes thing at risk of embarrassing myself. I'm now 99 percent sure that wasn't what it was.

Bernie nods. "This is one of the reasons the society used this tower. You saw the underground cells at the penitentiary, right?"

"Yeah."

"There are also connecting tunnels that run through the city. This is one of the places. There are all sorts of secret entrances and paths. Closely monitored by the society, of course. They were made to deal with the apocalypse. So that the monsters can be released to various locations quickly."

"Oh! Okay, cool. I just . . . I thought I saw lights?"

"Yes. They're there to help people navigate, but I admit that the tunnels weren't used as often as expected. As you can see, we haven't had an apocalypse yet. I don't know how many of the lights are even working still."

Old flickering lights. That's what it was. Wow, these people have made me so jumpy. Looking for monsters around every corner.

"Why don't you join the others?" He taps on the door. "I'll leave

A MASTERY OF MONSTERS

this open, shall I? Tends to lock." He shoves a doorstop underneath it and heads back to the main floor. I follow behind him.

Upstairs, the others are crowded around the whiteboard. Bernie excuses himself to gather more candidates, and I stand beside Violet, who's holding on to a black marker while Bryce uses magnets to pin photos to the board.

I make sure my photo is visible while I pretend to study what they have going.

Violet glances at the picture, then me. I widen my eyes slightly, hoping she takes the hint. Then again, she might get it and ignore me anyway. This is a competition, after all.

"Lawrence could fit in with our time line," she says.

The tension seeps out of my shoulders. "You're arranging it by dates?"

"Dates would be too easy," Caden says, sauntering over. "It should be a ranking. Doctorates up top. Then famous Masters." He waves to one of his friends, who has what must be the Wilden McCray photo. "And then disgraced members at the bottom." At that, he meets my eyes.

Maybe even if I find Jules early, I can stay on in the competition until we get to a test where I can beat the shit out of this boy.

"Have you decided what to do?" Bernie asks, coming over to us.

There's a bunch of mumbling, and more candidates join the group. "We're not sure how to organize it," Bryce says, adjusting his glasses. "Some of us think by date, others by ranking, but it could also be by general connections. For example, Dr. Weiss is, in some way, connected to us all. While others, like Lawrence, break off."

I look at the photo in my hands. I thought Caden was just being

202       LISELLE SAMBURY

an asshole to me, but did he mean Lawrence when he was talking about being disgraced? Especially now that Bryce is mentioning something similar.

"Maybe that's the point," I say. "That there are lots of ways you could connect them."

One of Caden's boys snorts, which Caden rewards with a smirk. Jesus, it's like they already took a semester of Bully 101, and we haven't even gotten to reading week yet.

"August has a fair point, as does Bryce." Bernie writes down the words *dates, rankings,* and *general connections.* "How else might we connect them?"

"Factions," Violet suggests. Some of the other candidates bristle. Ah yes, we're supposed to act like those don't exist. Violet immediately gains points with me.

"Good. Anyone else?"

"Legacies and familial ties," Caden says.

"Good, good." Bernie spreads his arms. "The purpose of this exercise is to explore all these connections. However you chose to arrange it would have been correct, as long as you can connect every single photo. So why don't you do that now?"

After a lot of back and forth, the group finally decides to organize based on different sorts of legacies, grouping Dr. Weiss's inner circle together, and then certain families, etc. When it's time for me to place my photo, I decide based on what Caden and Bryce said to put him in the section labeled *expelled,* and no one says anything as I do so. Bernie even nods at my choice.

When the lesson ends and people start to file out, Bernie calls me back.

*Shit. Did I mess up? Why did he nod, then?* I swallow and come back to him, sticking my hands in the pockets of my jeans as we wait for the room to clear.

"Sorry for holding you back," he says. "I wanted to give you some more context. I find this process to be especially hard on new students. You aren't told these stories. Many candidates have been attending weekly lectures their whole lives. It's a little backward, honestly. We always want new students, but these additional levels are harder for them to reach." In a lower voice he says, "Though I suspect some of that is by design."

"By design?"

"Take academia, for example. Do you think the point is to let everyone in? Setting aside the need to charge for tuition and the like, do you believe the goal of this university is to be accessible to everyone who wants to attend?"

"No. I mean, that's why we have grade cutoffs and things like that, right? It's supposed to be elite."

"Exactly." He leans against the ticket desk. "But with the proper connections, even someone unremarkable can have access, can't they? And yet, for everyone else, we act like it's merit. Like they've had to work hard to earn it. Never mind all those who toil and sacrifice and still don't get to partake. So that when you stand on that stage and they give you that diploma, you feel the importance of it. Exclusivity requires scarcity. Whether it's valid or not."

"That's why you all do the nominations, isn't it? I get that the competition is needed for leveling up monsters or whatever, but ideally, anyone who wanted to be a Bachelor or Master could apply. That would be fairer."

Bernie smiles. "You're seeing it now. Yes, there is nothing about this candidacy that is meant to be fair. By design, like I said." He points at me. "You may want to watch your phrasing, though."

I falter. "What?"

"'You all.' 'That's why you all do the nominations,' you said. As if you aren't part of this society now." I splutter, and he holds up his hands. "I won't hold you to it, just something to keep in mind. Now, let's chat about what I held you back for. I gather that you were confused about Lawrence being in the expelled category. For the most part, what we teach is that he simply left four years after the founding of the society, three years after he joined, and a single year after the invention of the serum. However, those in the know understand that he and Dr. Weiss didn't have a clean break. They clashed. According to some of Dr. Weiss's journals, Lawrence didn't think we should have Masters. The idea of bondage of any kind, understandably, upset him. Dr. Weiss wanted bonding to be a temporary solution, and Lawrence wanted to abandon the serum and search for an alternate cure entirely. When Lawrence left, it's rumored that he stole important items from our dear first Doctorate. Special objects as well as the research detailing their functions. Which made Dr. Weiss not his biggest fan."

"Special objects?"

"I hate to use a word like 'magical' because it's so unspecific, but I suppose that may be the easiest way to describe them."

My instinct is to call bullshit. First, I have to believe in monsters, then an apocalypse, and now magic? Nah. The monster thing doesn't follow traditional science, but at least it has some scientific starting point. I can get behind a bit of unexplained science, sure. Even this apocalypse could have some scientific basis. But *magic*? I'll believe that when I see it. "What were the objects?"

"No idea. Lawrence left with them, and that was it. Many years

A MASTERY OF MONSTERS                    205

later he formed his own group devoted to Black activism and philanthropy, and that was it. Dr. Weiss later branded the man a traitor, and that became his legacy."

"I didn't know," I say.

"Don't worry, I won't dock you points. For a newcomer, you did well. And honestly, what I care about is that students learn. It's why my wife and I were put in charge of this historic site." He waves around the room. "Eventually, I'll move on from teaching of any kind, and just do this." He nods almost to himself. "Yes, I think this will be my last year overseeing the candidacy." He smiles, the corners of his lips pinched tight. "Virgil is doing well?"

"Uh, yeah. I think he's anxious, but fine."

"It's good he has you. I dislike politics, society politics even more so, but I hope there is some positive change on the horizon for him. He has so much potential. I would have liked to take him on myself but, unfortunately, I've never been able to move past the Bachelor stage." He plays with the hem of his shirt. "Wasn't much help to my son for the same reason. My father had recommended that I wait before seeking a nomination since we'd had the mutation in our bloodline before. That one day, someone in my family might need me. But I was impatient. I wanted to ascend. To be important in the society right then." The hint of a smile plays on his lips. "I thought I'd proven him wrong when I became a Bachelor, but he was right in the end."

I attempt to arrange my face into something appropriate. Everything in Bernie's body, from his hunched shoulders to his averted eyes, makes it clear that this is the greatest regret of his life. His kid needed him, and he had no way to help. All he could do was watch. Watch his son compete, and struggle, and fail. All because he was impatient for the title.

Bernie says, "He's happier, Virgil. I must assume that is due to you. I cannot take sides, of course, but I am rooting for the two of you. Glory will never be greater than the ability to safeguard the people you treasure. I hope you learn that now instead of later."

I thank Bernie and leave the tower. He stays behind. I get why Virgil and Corey like the guy despite his poor choice in clothing. He cares about the candidates. Chen, too. Even if they realize that the society itself isn't exactly perfect. They're self-aware. They want things to change, and they're in a position to guide the next generation of Masters toward that. It's hard not to root for them at least a little bit. Even if I'm not planning to stay in the Learners' Society.

As I head back to campus, I get a text from Riley that says, *Hello, stranger.*

# CHAPTER TWENTY

The plan was to meet Riley in front of Victoria Hall. The plan did not include Corey and Virgil also being in front of my dorm building. I slow as I approach them. Corey is chatting to Riley at the bottom of the steps while Virgil stands with his hands in his pockets. When they spot me, Corey gives me a wide smile, and Riley throws me a pointed look that I imagine says something like, *What the fuck? Get rid of them.*

It was already hard enough to arrange this around Riley's schedule. It'd been a full week since she sent that initial text. I don't want to postpone things even more when I could make progress in finding Jules.

"Hey . . . ," I say to Corey and Virgil. "I didn't think we were meeting up."

Virgil glances at Riley but doesn't mention her. "Margot wanted us to check in on you. See how you'll be for next week."

The physical endurance group training is next week, and I can't have another fainting spell like last time. This will potentially be the hardest professor to impress. I've also been working my ass off for weeks, so I can do without the micromanagement.

"Can we do it another time? I'm supposed to go to the island since it's Truth and Reconciliation Day. My aunt's community is doing a thing." Which is actually true. The Levesques have organized a charity walk around the island, and I'm supposed to help distribute orange shirts and take donations for residential school survivor funds. Corey and Virgil don't need to know I'm going to that after this Riley thing, not right now.

At the end of last year, Sammie, like a lot of second years, decided to move into a house with her friends. She was the only one of them who stayed through the summer. Riley has been staking out the place since the beginning of the school year, and apparently Mondays are the best time to get inside without anyone noticing.

The letter and note were in Jules's things, so maybe Sammie's stuff will hold some clues too.

"We'll come along to the island," Virgil says with a smile.

"Is that necessary?"

"Yes," he says. "Our track meet is next week. We can't lose any time."

Riley makes an impatient sound in the back of her throat, but I don't know what this girl wants me to do! They aren't going to go away. "Yeah, okay. I just need to do an errand first with my friend."

"We're all going to go together?" Riley asks, her voice high-pitched.

"You have friends?" Virgil says. "Like, other than us?"

"Yes," I snap. "I have *one* other friend. She's right here."

"Good for you." Corey beams, looking proud of me.

And this is how the four of us end up on Wellington Street. Riley leads us to a house that, like many of the houses in Kingston, is made of red brick. It has a tiny front porch that includes a recycling bin filled with beer cans and bottles.

Riley makes a show of acting like she's forgotten her keys and grabs a fake rock that's so out of place on the wooden porch, it's shocking that more people haven't broken into this house. She slides out the key and invites us inside.

The entryway is crowded with sneakers, boots, etc. Virgil starts to take his shoes off, while Corey digs her mini shoehorn out from her purse and looks for a place to sit. Riley says, "Oh, no need. You can keep them on."

"I don't mind," Virgil says, then turns to Corey. "Though it's inconvenient for you to swap shoes, so you don't need to bother if she says it's cool."

"It is . . . but wearing outside shoes in the house . . ." Corey wrinkles her nose. I get it. I'm kind of crawling out of my skin about it too. Mom's in my head shouting, "Shoes off!" But if the actual people who live here come home and notice the addition of shoes—or worse, we need to leave in a hurry—we can't waste time waiting for Corey and Virgil to get theirs on. Corey literally can't rush out unless she goes barefoot. Never mind having to explain to them that, no, Riley does not actually live here.

"It's fine!" Riley insists. "Why don't you guys sit down over here?" She directs them to the living room, where Virgil and Corey get comfortable on the couch—thankfully, with their shoes on.

"Also," I add, "if you see anyone coming, please come get us. It's supposed to be a surprise."

Virgil narrows his eyes. "Your errand is prepping for a surprise party?" He looks around the undecorated house. "Do you have time to do that?"

"Not a surprise party, just a surprise."

"We'll be very incognito," Corey says, and I could hug her. Wonderful, reliable Corey. "And we'll run and get you if we hear anything."

"Perfect, thanks, we'll be upstairs."

Virgil's eyes track up the staircase, and I know from the muttering voices that follow that he's discussing things with Corey.

"Great plan," Riley says as we walk to the landing.

"Yes, well, they weren't going to leave, and I wasn't going to tell them what we were doing. Did you want them to know?"

"Obviously not."

"Well, there you go. And now we have built-in lookouts."

"It's this one," Riley says, pulling open the door to Sammie's room.

I follow her inside. "Why didn't the two of you live together?"

Riley grinds her teeth. "We were supposed to."

"But?"

She shakes her head. "Sammie fucked up, and instead of trying to fix things, she decided she wanted to quit QBSS altogether. I was going to convince her to come back but she was being stubborn about it."

I guess that explains why Riley wasn't out with Sammie that night.

A double bed is pushed against the wall with a faded blue duvet cover and a single pillow. In another corner there's a desk with papers and books stacked on top of it, and a pile of clothes dropped onto an armchair. The walls are decorated with photos and art prints.

It's like no one has touched this room since Sammie was killed.

Riley isn't in any of the displayed pictures. I suspect that whatever went down between her and Sammie was more serious than she's making it out to be.

"Any idea where's best to look?" I ask.

"No."

Helpful. I search the closet while Riley goes through the desk and dresser drawers. There are some clothes and shoes. Bits of jewelry and old returned marked papers. There's a shoebox with pieces of memorabilia from high school. Her old student ID, track and field ribbons, and photos. I stare at a couple of the pictures, and though the girl's hair is in box braids instead of passion twists, I recognize Riley. They went to high school together, but their friendship fizzled out in university.

I get that. People change. I thought I'd be rooming with Rachel in my first year, and making all these new friends from different places, going to parties every week, being a star student.

"Have you seen this before?" Riley asks.

I close the lid of the box and go over to her. "What?"

"You said your brother got a letter. Did it look like this?" She shows me an envelope. It's cream-colored and looks pretty standard. The size of any other piece of letter mail, though it doesn't have a name or address or stamp on it. And I do recognize it.

I wait until she removes the paper inside to say anything. "Yeah. This is the same invite. Or mostly."

Sammie's invite says to meet in City Park on the evening she went missing, months after Jules got his.

And Sammie is dead. But Jules . . . no. He's alive. He has to be.

Riley's eyes light up. "They *are* connected."

The sound of creaking stairs reaches us as Corey calls out, "Someone pulled into the driveway!"

"Fuck," Riley hisses.

I rush into the hall. I hoped maybe we could make a run for the front door, but there are already voices in the entryway. Corey and Virgil stand casually in the hall.

"Get in here!" Riley says to them. "And hide."

Virgil sighs. "Is the surprise thing really that serious?"

"Yes!" me and Riley say at the same time.

He rolls his eyes, but both he and Corey follow us into the room. Riley and Corey are able to fit together in the closet, but me and Virgil are forced to climb under Sammie's bed. I pull the covers down to shield us.

"This is ridiculous." When Virgil speaks, his breath wafts over my face.

There isn't a ton of room underneath since Sammie has a bunch of clothes stored here, and the two of us end up pressed together. And me and Virgil aren't exactly small people. He has to turn sideways, so my side is pressed up against the front of his body.

I was kind of right. His muscles are definitely hard but with a soft outer layer. It's giving cuddly teddy bear who could also pick you up and throw you around.

For fuck's sake, I need to stop.

I attempt to shift to get more comfortable, and Virgil lets out a soft grunt.

"Could you not?" he asks, his voice reverberating with a huskiness that I'm unprepared for.

My entire face goes hot along with other places that I do not want to think about. "Why are you talking like that?"

"Like what?" This time his voice is more normal.

I shift again.

"Stop," he says, and there it is again. That voice. Dropped several octaves and accompanied by a rough throatiness.

"You stop," I say. "Stop doing that voice."

"Stop moving!"

"I'm trying to get comfortable."

"By grinding against me?"

I throw him a horrified look. "I am not *grinding* against you."

"Could have fooled me."

"Shut up," Riley hisses from across the room. "We can both hear you."

Me and Virgil lapse into silence, though I do stop moving. Footsteps come up the stairs, and I hope they won't head for this room. There's literally no reason to. Sammie's missing. Why would they be chilling in her room?

The door opens, and soft feet pad across the hardwood.

A feminine voice says, "I don't think anyone is in here. Maud is probably being paranoid."

"I don't know. True crime fans can be wild, you know? Like what if they were trying to steal her underwear or something?" This second voice also sounds feminine, though higher-pitched.

"That sounds more like a budding serial killer thing to do."

"Whatever," the first person says. "I wish her parents would clear out her room. It's been over a month."

"They're paying her rent, and besides, can you blame them? How would you feel if you came back and your whole room was empty?"

"Sammie isn't coming back." This is said quietly.

"She might . . ."

"Let's go. No one is in here. I told you that motion sensor thing is shit. You can't buy security stuff online for twenty dollars and expect it to work."

"The reviews said it was legit!"

"We're gonna be late for the walk. Let's grab our shirts and go."

We wait through several more door opening and closing noises until finally they go downstairs. And then we wait some more.

"I think they're gone," Riley says.

Me and Virgil shimmy out from under the bed.

"Can we drop this surprise farce now?" Virgil asks, looking between me and Riley. "What is actually going on here, and—" He pauses and squints at the letter still clutched in Riley's hand. "Why do you have that?"

Riley asks, "You recognize it?"

Corey peers over the girl's shoulder. For some reason, Riley swallows and looks away. Maybe worried about catching society cooties. "It's a lecture invite," Corey says. "Um, like, a meeting for our club?" she adds, turning to Riley. "But we don't invite people to parks, and definitely not this late at night."

Virgil meets my eyes, and I know he's thinking about the fact that Jules got one of these too. He reaches for the letter, and Riley holds it away from him. "Do you want to know if it's authentic or not?" he asks. Reluctantly, she hands it over to him. "It's real. It has the seal on it and everything. Why would they send a formal invite like this?"

"Maybe for legitimacy?" Corey says. "Like, if they know they're sending it to people who might know about our, um, club—"

Riley rolls her eyes. "You can cut the subterfuge. I know about the society. I'm the QBSS treasurer. Just come out with it."

To her credit, Corey recovers quickly. "Clearly, they wanted, um"—she checks the name—"Samantha to come. If they sent a random anonymous letter, she may not have bothered. Sending an official society invite, perhaps knowing she would understand the prestige of the society or even want something from them, might tempt her into going."

"Couldn't a good fake do the job?" I ask.

Virgil says, "Maybe, but it would be a risk, and obviously this person didn't want to do anything that might stop her from meeting them."

And Sammie did go. Near City Park is where Riley said she saw her body.

Virgil looks at me. "And what are you doing with the QBSS treasurer?"

I can't think of a single way out of this. I glance at Riley, but she's not offering anything up. "Riley was friends with Sammie, the girl who went missing. Who I think might be connected to my brother. Who I now know *is* connected to Jules because they got this same invite."

"I told you that we would help."

"After the competition. Jules might need me now."

He pinches the bridge of his nose. "And what are you getting out of this?" he asks Riley.

"I'm trying to figure out what happened to my friend. I know you all are involved. It reeks of society bullshit." She snatches the invite from Virgil's fingers. "And now I have more proof that one of your monsters killed her."

"Why would we randomly murder some girl who isn't associated with us?"

"I don't know." Riley throws her hands up. "Revenge, maybe. Ever since our order was founded, you've hated us. Hated that Joseph Lawrence chose to create his own group instead of staying under the thumb of a tyrant pretending to be a messiah. And the only leader you ever had who tried to keep the peace is now six feet under."

Joseph Lawrence. The traitor. QBSS was the Black activism and philanthropy group he started? But that doesn't even make sense. From my Sammie research, the info on their website said their club started in 2011. Lawrence would have been long dead by then. But the society leader who kept the peace must have been Cyrus.

Corey swallows. "I know you have no love for Edward Weiss, but he never pretended to be a god. And Cyrus died *after* Sammie went to that park meeting. The Learners don't engage in targeted attacks."

"What do the Wilds think about that?" Riley asks with a little grin. "Self-sufficient monsters who you slaughtered because they dared to question the status quo when your Masters were desperate to stay in power."

Virgil rubs at his stubble. "It wasn't like that. The Wilds were working with the Pro-Libs to orchestrate a concentrated attack on—you know what? I don't need to explain it to you. It's complicated."

Riley scoffs. "Oh, I'm sure it is. What is it that the Wilds do under that little agreement? Oh yes, they monitor your war games and kill the people you don't like under threat of complete annihilation."

*Excuse me?* No one had ever mentioned the Wilds killing people.

"Wilds aren't used for assassinations. It's a rumor," Virgil says, nostrils flaring. "You don't know anything about us."

"I know quite a bit, actually. And trust me when I say we've tried many more times to be sympathetic to you than you have us. Joseph Lawrence held out so many olive branches to Edward Weiss. But he refused. You didn't want to work in harmony with us. You wanted your monsters in chains and your Masters holding them. Now the Doctorate is dead, and while you squabble in your factions, someone among you has killed one of us, right under your noses."

Virgil throws me an acidic look. "You don't know what you've done, involving her."

"Then tell me," I throw back.

He gnashes his teeth. "This is *messy*. We have an election coming up."

"I can't just wait around doing nothing! Look at that letter. I've only done this one thing with Riley, and we're already making progress."

"By breaking and entering! What if you got caught? Did you know that acquiring a criminal record automatically disqualifies you from the candidacy?" Before I can speak, he cuts me off. "No, you didn't. Because you never think first!" Virgil storms out of the room, and Corey sighs, following after him.

In the doorway, she turns back to Riley. "For what it's worth, I'm sorry about your friend."

Riley bristles.

Corey turns and leaves.

"Those are the people who you're choosing to associate with," Riley says.

"Yeah, and they confirmed that your invite is real. We need them."

Riley crosses her arms over her chest. "I stand by what I said. They're involved somehow. With Sammie. And if I were you, I'd be wondering if they're involved with your brother, too."

I don't say so to Riley, but I already am.

# CHAPTER TWENTY-ONE

Bailey pulls up in her car and grins a little too wide for my taste. "You brought your friend!"

When I finally came out of Sammie's old house, Virgil was waiting for me. For the second time since I've known him, he decided to follow me to the island because we "needed to talk." Instead, he sat on both the bus and ferry ride playing with his phone, not saying a word.

I sit shotgun while Virgil gets in the back, suddenly with a sunny disposition.

"Thanks for having me," he says.

Bailey drives toward the exit of the dock. "No problem. Always happy to have more volunteers." She glances in the rearview. "Do you go to Queen's too?"

"Yup."

"Cool! What are you studying?"

I groan and press my head to the window.

Virgil ignores me. "English. Though I haven't decided on any sort of specialty. I do like some post-modern styles, but I also think contemporary works are exploring a lot of fascinating themes."

For the rest of the drive, I let Bailey and Virgil talk about books they've read recently, and Virgil gives her recommendations for what she should try next. She's beaming the whole time. First, I enroll in a prestigious university, and now I keep bringing around the definition of a "respectable boy." He's exactly who my past self would have wanted. Though, I guess minus entering a deadly competition to help him.

When we arrive, Bailey makes a point of giving Virgil a tour of her house. It takes a short amount of time since you can basically see everything right when you walk in.

Virgil gazes at some of the pictures Bailey has hung up on the fridge. He taps on a photo. I know it's the one of Mom from the position of his hand. I've looked often enough to memorize where it's placed. He frowns.

"What?" I ask.

He shakes his head. "Nothing . . . Just, she looks familiar."

"That's Annie," Bailey says. "August's mom. She did go to Queen's, though that was probably before you were born."

"Yeah, I'm sure I'm mixing her up with someone."

I narrow my eyes at Virgil. Who does he know who looks like Mom? It's not like he's got an extensive social network. And it's not him seeing her in me. I've been told I'm Dad's twin since I was a kid. Jules, too.

There's a knock at the door, and Mia appears. "Ready to help with the shirts?" She pauses when she spots Virgil. "Are you here to help?"

He nods.

"Amazing." She throws a shit eating grin at me that I ignore.

Bailey leaves to help Izzy and Jacques with something, while Mia leads us to a table they've set up closer to the road.

"Here are the different sizes," Mia says, waving to the boxes. "Shirts are twenty dollars for adults, ten dollars for kids. The boxes for kids' sizes are marked too, so make sure you're getting the right ones. All proceeds go to the Indian Residential School Survivors Society, if they ask. If they want to donate more, that's great. Oh! And grab shirts for yourselves, too. Bailey already donated, and it's enough to cover you all."

Me and Virgil outfit ourselves in shirts.

"If anyone has questions about Kanyen'kehá:ka stuff, we printed up some information, and that's in—" Mia stops at the questioning looks on our faces. "That's the word for Mohawk. What we call ourselves." She slows down the word so me and Virgil can repeat after her. "You two may want to practice that." She laughs. "The printouts are in this box."

It's embarrassing that I never even thought about how to say Mohawk in the actual language. Though I know Wolfe Island is the traditional hunting lands of the Tyendinaga Mohawk, since Bailey told me it's important to know whose land we're on. Jacques's mom grew up here, and when she decided to downsize and get a condo on the mainland, Jacques and Izzy moved in and started the community.

"Sooooo," Mia says, sliding over to me. I stiffen, prepared for some awkward question about Virgil. Instead, she says, "Have you given more thought to our deal?"

"I have, actually." I sigh. "I'll do it."

She squeals, and Virgil looks over at us. I wave him away.

A MASTERY OF MONSTERS

I don't have any choice. Margot is already such a fucking hard-ass. I know if I don't get the knives sharpened soon, she's going to freak out. If I have to help plan a party, fine, it can't be that hard. "But!" I say, raising a finger. "I need them done now."

Mia scowls.

"I'm good for it!"

Now Virgil is paying attention.

"Mind your business," I tell him.

He tilts his head to the side. "I don't know that I want to."

Mia says, "August is going to help me organize a community dinner. We have to clean the barn and find a way to get some cheap tablecloths and stuff. Cheap but, like, nice, you know? And then decorate and get people signed up for the potluck."

The more she lists things, the more I'm starting to regret what I've signed up for.

"She's helping *voluntarily*?" Virgil asks.

I gesture to the booth. "I'm helping voluntarily right now."

"We have an arrangement," Mia says.

Virgil smirks at me, then says to Mia, "I actually know a guy who's good at thrifting stuff. He works at a secondhand place in the city. I could give you his number?"

"That would be great!"

"You're passionate about this, eh?"

"Yeah, I think it'll help everyone come together. Like, take today for example, half the people who live in the tiny house community aren't even participating."

I guess I hadn't realized. I keep forgetting that Bailey is a lot more involved and friendly with the Levesques.

Mia gives me a smug look. "See? This dinner matters. Community is something you make. You don't just sit back and wait for it to happen. Maybe some people can, but not everyone. Sometimes you have to go out and find where you belong. And if you can't find it, make it. That's why my parents started this in the first place. Not that they seem to remember." The last bit she mutters under her breath.

I still don't get Mia's obsession with this. I was always just fine with my family, and I don't even have that anymore. I spot Bailey with Izzy and Jacques, welcoming some people and pointing them over to where our booth is. Okay, I *almost* don't have family.

"You're right," Virgil says to Mia. "You have to actively participate if you want to see change."

"Yes!" She looks over at me. "He gets it."

"Good for him," I say.

People trickle in, and we get busy giving out shirts and accepting donations. More people than I expected show up and soon enough, we're surrounded by a sea of orange.

Izzy stands at the front of the group when it's time for the walk, poised with a megaphone. She clears her throat and consults a folded piece of paper, speaking in Mohawk. Or the Kanyen'kehá:ka language, I know now. The further she goes along, the less she needs to check the paper, and is soon talking without even looking at it.

Mia whispers to us that this is a shorter version of the Thanksgiving address that they learned—meant to express gratitude for all of Creation and help bring our minds together. From what I know, neither she nor Izzy grew up speaking their native language, but they've been taking classes for the past couple of years.

Izzy switches to English and says, "Thank you to everyone for coming out. Today we honor survivors. We honor the children who never returned home, their families, their communities, and their

A MASTERY OF MONSTERS

stories. We remember that every child matters, and when this day is over, we keep remembering and working toward reconciliation. Nyawenhkó:wa."

We clap, and the walk begins. The Levesques and Bailey go ahead, while me and Virgil agree to stay behind in case there are any stragglers who show up wanting shirts or to donate.

"We never participate in things like this," Virgil says, his voice so low that I almost miss it.

"Who's we?"

"The society . . . We're meant to set ourselves apart. All students should be equal. Participating in anything that specifies one people isn't allowed. You can do it in private but never publicly."

This is what Riley was talking about before. "But Corey's family teaches taekwondo, and that's fine. Doesn't that highlight that they're Korean?"

"It's a gray area since everyone can participate. It's not about her family being Korean. And I guess it doesn't remind people that we aren't actually living in equality in the outside world."

"You're just pretending that things like residential schools don't exist?"

Virgil hunches his shoulders. "No, we're aware of the world. And we could donate, even, but public displays are frowned upon."

"That's kind of fucked up."

"The society is a closed system. Our students don't participate in discrimination. If you acknowledge too much of the outside world or get too involved in it, you move further away from the society's teachings. That's why people come to us. To be loved and accepted as they are. It's always been that way, since Dr. Weiss founded the society."

"Then why are some of you being treated like volatile scum?"

"Because we've moved too far from his model. That's what Adam and Henry want to change. The Learners' Society is beautiful when it works the way it's supposed to work."

I don't know if anything shutting you off from other people and demanding that you stay in a closed system can be that great. It's one thing if it's your choice and another if doing that is the only way you get access to it. Especially when you teach people to be terrified of an apocalypse that only you can protect them from.

"Anyway, that's not what I came to talk to you about," Virgil says. "I still think it was a bad idea for you to join up with a QBSS member—"

"For fuck's sake—"

"*But* she had a good point about the fact that not everything in the society goes the way it's supposed to go. Exactly the way we were just talking about. I texted Henry about the Wilds. I dunno, I guess I thought he'd confirm what I knew from reading the society texts. He told me the truth. The Wilds *were* used for some . . . unsavory things. Though Riley wasn't exactly right. That happened before the agreement. It was part of the reason they rebelled. What Garrett signed with Cyrus actually stopped it."

"The assassinations?"

"Yes. I'm not surprised that Garrett is concerned about how things will go with new leadership and therefore wants more protections. I mean, they're owed that. Which is to say, I can admit when I'm wrong. And I get that it's not totally fair to you to do nothing to help with your brother until you win. Obviously, I care that he's okay. But I don't know that you think it's that obvious."

I scuff at the grass with the toe of my shoe. "He's not your brother."

"That doesn't mean I can't care about a human being. Or you."

"You barely know me."

"Are you serious right now?"

I shrug.

"I may not have known you for long, but I realize that your brother is important to you—that with your mom already gone, your brother being missing is even harder on you. I get what it's like to lose family. I wouldn't wish that on anyone. And I'd like to think that you, at least a little bit, don't want to see me in a prison cell."

I drop my chin to my chest so I don't have to keep looking him in the eye.

Virgil takes a deep breath. "Let me rephrase this so there's no confusion. I don't think we'll have access to anything helpful until you have a title, but if I can, of course I'm going to help find your brother. And even if I disagree, if you want to recruit someone like Riley to help, fine. But please be discreet. And you can ask me stuff too. If I can do something, I will. And if I can't, it's not because I don't want to, it's just because I can't. Okay?"

". . . Okay."

"And in exchange, can you try to think a little more about how what you do might affect me?"

"Okay," I say again, because it's the least I can do for this boy who's promised to help me find Jules. Promised to help me do the one thing that will guarantee that I don't help him in return.

Virgil opens his arms wide. "Now bring it in!"

I balk. "Excuse me?"

"Hug it out!"

"No!"

He sighs and raises a hand instead. "Handshake?"

I roll my eyes but reach out and shake his hand. Ignoring the insignificant and addled part of me that considered the hug.

Virgil grins, but I can't manage to return it.

He's helping me, and in exchange, I'm planning to betray him.

# CHAPTER TWENTY-TWO

I'm dying. And I don't think that's hyperbole. I'm confident that my heart is two seconds away from exploding as Margot blows her whistle for the millionth time. I run across the cricket field toward the monster truck–sized tire laid on the ground and shove at it with my shoulder, grunting and wheezing as I push it up, my arms shaking, my thighs screaming, and then flip it over. Again, and again, and again until I'm at Margot's feet.

What a way to spend a Friday afternoon.

I collapse onto the ground, my eyes closed and stars dancing in my vision.

Water splashes in my face as Margot pours the liquid onto me for not even the first time this session.

"Get up," she says.

I ignore her and stay where I am. I want to tell her to fuck off, but I can't even get the words out. And this is the woman who had the gall to tell me not to overdo it.

"You haven't been running every morning," Margot says, and I can picture her putting her hands on her hips even with my eyes closed. "I can tell."

How does she expect me to do all this? I'm supposed to run a 5k every morning, go to class, make time to study and perform well, and train for what's literally already a training session? This competition has eclipsed my life. I haven't even had a chance to get my braids redone. The sweat isn't helping. My edges are frizzy and mussed.

"You don't have anything to say?" Margot asks. "No defense? Are you just that fucking lazy?"

I bare my teeth and squeeze my eyes shut, balling my hands into fists.

They're the perfect words, really. Those are the words that make me force myself to stand and face her.

I walk away from Margot, nearly stumbling to the ground. I go to the other side of the field and drop down into a push-up and then jump to my feet and lift my hands in the air. I do ten burpees, my throat so dry that my wheezing has become near asthmatic coughing. I stumble my way back to the tire and go to push it.

I want to. Instead, I topple onto it and lie there.

Tears rush to my eyes, and I duck my head, letting the sweat stream down.

"I gave you a routine!" Margot's on a roll now. "You're the one who couldn't be bothered to follow it!"

"Stop." I don't look up, but know it's Virgil. I get to my feet, swaying. I can barely see him through my swimming vision, but maybe he's coming toward me? Very, very fast. When his arms grasp mine, I realize that I've fallen into him. "Are you trying to train her or kill her?"

A MASTERY OF MONSTERS

He picks me up with little effort, squeezing my arms and placing me back on my feet. He keeps his hands in place, as if afraid I'll fall again. I keep my head down because I physically can't lift it, and it hits his chest.

"If she'd done what I told her to, she would be fine. Take one look at her and you know she didn't!"

*Enough.*

My voice is dry and rough, but I still speak. "Just because I haven't suddenly lost fifty pounds doesn't mean I'm not doing anything. If that's what you wanted, you should have said so, and I would have told you I'm not doing that shit again."

There's a beat of silence where I keep panting, letting my breaths be noisy if that's what they need to be.

I'm thinking of everything I put into my mouth in the last month. Knowing that if I tracked it or skipped some of it, then I would probably look like everyone wants me to. I've done it before.

But I don't want to do it again. I want to stop. I want to be done.

I'm so tired of other people deciding what I do with my body.

"I never told you to lose weight," Margot says, her voice quiet for once.

"Bullshit," I spit, stumbling back from Virgil so I can look at her. "Has anyone ever called you lazy? Has anyone ever questioned if you're healthy, or if you did the workouts you were supposed to? You can tell I didn't do shit by looking at me? Are you serious?! If I had come to this training twenty pounds lighter, you wouldn't have had anything to say, and here's the kicker: if I *had* lost weight, I would be able to do even less than I can now."

"That wasn't what I meant," she says. "I meant the way you're performing. You're out of breath—this circuit shouldn't be taking that much out of you. That's all."

"It's *hard*! Of course I'm out of breath!" I sit on the ground, bringing my knees up and pressing my face into them. She doesn't get it.

"She's been running," Virgil says. I jerk my head toward him. He looks like he's two seconds away from tearing Margot's throat out. "I've literally seen her doing it because you gave her a route that goes past here. *You* don't even run that much. She's already done it this morning, and you expect her to not be tired for training? And that's not even getting into the bullshit she just called you out on."

Margot takes a long breath before sitting on the grass, splaying her legs out. "I'm sorry."

I say, "Wow, you can apologize?"

"I don't care what you look like, and even if I did, it doesn't matter, so I'm sorry. I didn't think about what I sounded like, or the shit I was saying, or how you felt about it." She scrubs a hand across her face. "I just—I want you to be prepared for this. They're going to run you harder, push you more, judge you harsher than anyone else because you're an outsider. You don't realize that they could destroy you and not even blink."

"Doesn't matter if you destroy her first." Virgil is the only one not sitting. He's still staring at Margot, eyes tight, muscles clenched.

"I know! I get it," Margot says. "I'm sorry."

I nod and stare at my lap. I don't want to be having this conversation. There's a magic invisibility in thinness. Nobody saw me. No one noticed when I skipped meals or tracked everything from oil in a pan to chewing gum. No one cared when I worked out for hours a day or avoided restaurants. And if they did realize what I was doing,

A MASTERY OF MONSTERS

they complimented me. Fatness is the opposite. No matter what I do, people have comments, and opinions, and assumptions. And somehow, I'm still the closest to real happiness that I've ever been.

But sometimes, times like this, I fantasize about going back to it. Buying a scale to replace the one I threw out, taking a new set of "before" pictures, and starting all over again. Not because it's what I want. But because it's easier that way.

People loved me more when I hated myself.

"I'm sorry," Margot says again. I don't know if she wants me to forgive her or if she isn't sure I heard. She can keep saying it if she wants. I want her to feel bad about it. I want her to keep feeling guilty for as long as I feel like shit. "I lost a lot of myself in this process. I forced myself to fit into the mold because I wanted to save my brother. I hated it. And . . . you don't need to copy me. That was my mistake." She pauses, but I don't say anything. "No more running. Use the weekend to rest up for Monday's training. We'll start on combat after the first cut." She stands and begins the process of collecting her equipment and loading it into her parked car.

"You okay?" Virgil asks.

I shrug.

He sits on the ground across from me, his legs crossed. Likely getting grass stains on his khakis. "Want to hear something messed up?"

"Sure," I say, glad for the distraction.

"After what my parents did, they wanted to kill me. I was four at the time."

"What the fuck?"

He laughs without mirth. "Yeah . . . Monsters get stronger with each generation, remember? I guess they worried I'd become too powerful and want revenge or whatever."

They were going to murder a child. I don't understand how Virgil can say stuff like this and still want to belong to the society. Then again, I guess he doesn't have much choice. Where else could he go?

He picks at the blades of grass without pulling them out. Just letting them slip through his fingers. "Henry stopped them. Adam backed him. And so, Cyrus backed him. And I was saved. Then every year, Masters would filter into McIntosh Castle to see how I was progressing. They didn't care if I could hear what they said. That I was lazy. Sloppy. Unkempt and unmotivated. That the wrong decision had been made." Virgil peeks at me through his lashes. "None of them knew me enough to assess my work ethic. And you know that I have impeccable style."

I snort.

Virgil smiles for a moment before it dims. "They just looked at me, a fat kid, and judged."

I swallow, and my mouth is so dry that I almost choke from it.

Back on move-in day, Corey talked about me and Virgil being similar, and I brushed it off. It's harder to do that now. I can't help but admit that we understand each other. Even more, I . . . feel something about it. I'm pissed that people would do that to him. When he was a fucking little kid.

Virgil says, "Even as a monster, nothing is more dehumanizing than having someone decide they know everything about you because of what you look like. I'm glad you said something to Margot."

I press my teeth against my trembling bottom lip, sawing back and forth. "How bad was it for her?"

"Doesn't excuse what she said."

"I know. But tell me."

"Not great. She was part of a particularly competitive year. Every test, she'd show up with new bruises. It was obvious that people were messing with her outside of them. Students complained about Henry training her, since nominators aren't supposed to. Your trainer is meant to be a more junior Master. Everyone Henry could get for her didn't want to rock the boat with their other society connections, so they said no. Henry tried to pay for private lessons, except everywhere in the city was full suddenly, likely because society members collaborated to take the spots. And so she had to do it by herself."

"They organized against her."

"Yeah. But she did it. She made it through. It's not like that changed everything for everyone, but some people took it as a positive. That, and the fact that others had interfered to make it more difficult for her came to light, and a lot of students didn't like that."

"Ah, because of the illusion of equality?"

"I know it's hard to understand, but—"

"No, it's simple. Not everyone actually wants the society to be equal, but they like to maintain the moral high ground."

Virgil's brow wrinkles. "Is Caden giving you a hard time?"

"Nothing I can't handle." He stares, and I stare back. "Don't look at me like that. There's nothing you can do. Trust me, even a tiny growl at one of those precious babies, and I'm sure they'd have you locked up." From the way Virgil's eyes drift away, I know I'm right. "Doesn't it bother y—"

"Of course it does. But you need to have a certain insulation to be able to fight back. Especially in my position and given who my parents were. We're on shaky ground here. When you become a Bachelor, it'll be different. Even that status can afford us so much more."

It makes me think of all the times I told myself that once I reached my goal weight, life would be better. When really, the only thing that changed was that other people were nicer to me. But I never felt better. If anything, it was worse. "Yeah." I get to my feet. "I'm gonna talk to Margot. I'll be back."

Virgil's eyes follow me as I make my way to the SUV, where she's struggling to lift the tire into the truck. I come up beside her and grip the other end, and together we get it inside.

"Thanks," Margot says.

"I get why you're worried. I can even appreciate you caring that much. But if you ever say that shit to me again, I'm done with you. I'd rather train alone."

She, of all people, knows how hard that is to do. "I won't." I nod and am turning to leave when she speaks again. "You're good, August. I know I don't say that enough or maybe even at all. But you're not a long shot. You have talent. You have the potential to win. Even Henry thinks so." There's something almost off about the way she says that last sentence. The tone and the twist of her mouth.

I'm still thinking about it once she's gone, while I walk back to my dorm, exhausted, sweaty, and a little bit triumphant.

# CHAPTER TWENTY-THREE

My backpack bumps against my body as I hurry toward the football field. My last lecture ran long since the professor got caught up in answering a bunch of student questions. I'm still early, but I want time to stretch and warm up. I dodge other students flooding out of their morning classes and heading to get lunch.

I'm walking so fast that I almost miss a guy saying, "Hey, Jules's sister." I skid to a stop and turn at the same time, almost toppling over.

The guy who spoke is some white boy I've never seen before. He half smiles like he's not sure if he should be. "Hey . . . We met, like, once, not sure if you remember me. Me and Jules were roommates in first year."

There is something semifamiliar about his floppy brown hair under a baseball hat. I *have* seen him before. I met him when we dropped off Jules in his first year. Mom had told him I'd be heading here next fall. We hadn't even gotten my acceptance yet.

The guy's name is something with a G. . . . Greg? "You're . . ."

"George." Not Greg. "I was surprised that he's not here this year. Or, I mean, I dunno, maybe not surprised."

"Not surprised?"

He shrugs. "I know he was struggling with school after the stuff with your mom. He was distracted all the time. I can't even imagine what that must be like. I'm sorry, by the way. Like, for your loss."

I don't tell him that Mom isn't dead because I'm so distracted by what he said. Jules doesn't struggle with school. He always does well.

My silence encourages George to keep talking. "I saw you and figured I'd ask if he's doing okay. I tried texting, but he doesn't answer. I feel bad 'cause, like, we asked him to join our house for this year, but he said he didn't think it would be a good idea 'cause of the academic probation, and he didn't even know if he'd be coming ba—"

"Academic probation?!"

*No.* There's no fucking way. To be on academic probation, Jules would have needed to be doing poorly in multiple courses. Absolutely not. I don't even think Jules has ever gotten so much as a B, and even in the days when I was obsessed with perfection, I'd gotten Bs.

My phone vibrates, and I check it, seeing an all-caps message from Virgil asking where I am.

"Fuck," I say. "I'm sorry, I gotta go."

"Wait, but, like, is everything cool with Jules?"

I don't have time to answer George, and even if I did, it wouldn't be the answer he wants. I race to the football field. Virgil, Margot, and Corey are in the stands along with a small crowd, I assume people who've come to watch the other competitors. Wonderful, now I have an audience.

I throw my bag into a pile with the rest of the candidates' stuff and yank off the sweatpants and sweatshirt combo I wore to class to expose the bike shorts and T-shirt ensemble underneath. I've barely put my arm over my chest to stretch when Perez is blowing his whistle.

I guess my run over is as close to a warm-up as I'm going to get.

And now I have George's words looping in my head. Jules was on academic probation? He never said anything about it. I'm a fucking walking, talking disappointment. If anyone would have understood, I would have. So why didn't he tell me?

"You'll be paired off several times today," Perez says to us, ignoring the onlookers in the stands. "Make no mistake—this is not just training, it's a competition, and that doesn't stop after you become a Bachelor. Head-to-head exercises are important. I'll pair you as necessary. First drills will be sprinting heats. Let's go. Black with Mosser. Sharma with Thomas." He continues to pair us off, and I fight not to groan as I line up beside Caden while Violet lines up next to another candidate.

"Can't wait to get paired with someone it'll look impressive to beat," Caden says, keeping his head down, I assume so it won't be obvious to the onlookers that he's talking to me.

I ignore him and kneel on the temporary marker for the starting line. It's just sprints. And there's not enough lanes for us to all go at once, meaning we'll probably run in heats and get breaks in between.

"On your mark!" Perez shouts. "Get set." He blows the whistle.

I take off, sprinting toward the finish line and doing my best to block out everything beside me. Caden. The other candidates. Everyone in the stands. Thoughts of Jules.

The whistle blows again, and I look around, but I can't be sure what I ranked. Caden probably can't either, because he's gritting his teeth. That means I stuck close to him. I smile a little. I walk with the others toward the benches by the stands, ready for my break before the next heat, but Perez calls me again.

I glance around to see if anyone else gets called again, but I'm the only repeat. I get back in line for another sprint. He blows the whistle and I run.

We move on to the next station, which is tire flipping. I guess I should be grateful to Margot. She said a lot of bullshit that day, but she also trained me accurately. Perez is new, but must be repeating exercises from last year.

I expect that I'll be benched for the first heat since I already ran twice in a row, but the professor calls my name again. Beside me, Violet's eyes dart from me to Perez and back again. I hesitate.

"Did I stutter, Black?" he asks.

I shake my head and get in position next to a candidate whose muscled thigh is roughly the size of my face. I peer down the line and notice that the others are paired more evenly.

The whistle blows, and I huff, jerking my arms under the tire and using my legs to help me shove it over. Meanwhile, the guy I'm up against is destroying me. Dude is a beast, flipping the tire like it's from a tricycle.

By the time we get to the end, it's obvious I've lost the heat.

I'm breathing heavily, and sweat is already dripping from my forehead. I head for the benches, but Perez calls my name again. I stop and stare at him, and he stares right back.

*This. Motherfucker.*

I get ready for the next heat.

And for every heat that comes, Perez pairs me up, and makes sure I'm matched with people who I realize are the top of the class in physical endurance. And unlike the first heat with Caden, every time it's obvious that I lose.

Over.

And over.

And over again.

Perez says, "Final exercise is a long-distance run, five laps. Get in line."

I line up with the rest of the candidates, and when the whistle blows, I'm the last to take off from the starting line. Almost everyone laps me. Some of them throw me pitying looks. And others are smugger. Violet and Bryce have the decency to ignore me.

I finish dead last.

As I walk over to get my bag, I'm confronted by Caden holding court near it.

I'm going to pick up my stuff and leave. That's it. I'm grabbing the handle when he says, "Better luck next year. Though I guess you'll need a new partner. I think yours will be underground by then, don't you? Maybe you can visit him. Since you get along so well with the monsters down there."

I crush my strap between my fingers. I stare at Caden, who's looming over me, a grin on his face, his buddies crowding around.

What's the point of holding back? He's right. I've lost. I'll be cut on Friday. This whole thing is by fucking design. Bernie was right. So why not take a couple slices of this piece of shit while I go? I have the knives for it. They're in my bag. Razor sharp thanks to

Mia. I know the exact one I'll choose to pop out those pretty baby blue eyes.

A hand lands on my shoulder, and I jerk back. "I got it," Virgil says. He pulls the strap from my hands and slings it over his shoulder. When he glances at Caden, the boy looks away. "Let's go."

I shrug his hand off and power walk off the field with tears pricking at my eyes.

I don't want to deal with Virgil right now.

"I know," I say when we're far enough away. "I sucked. I don't need to hear it from you."

Virgil stops, and his jaw drops. "Are you serious?" He points toward the field. "You didn't suck. That was bullshit."

My shoulders slump. I hadn't even realized that I'd hiked them up.

"You're the only candidate who didn't get a single moment to rest, and you were consistently paired with the people who are not just the most physically fit, they're literal university athletes. Most of the candidates he put you up against have already made varsity. Do you know how messed up that is? Of course you lost. Anyone else in that lineup would have lost too. But they never got a chance because he kept pairing them with you. Plus, they got breaks!" When Virgil finishes, his chest is heaving. "You did fucking amazing, and don't let anyone else ever tell you differently!"

It's like I've sunk into a hot tub. My entire body feels flushed, and my cheeks are, mortifyingly, blooming and getting bigger and fuller, and fuck me, I'm smiling. "That statement feels greatly inflated."

"Didn't I tell you not to let anyone say differently? That includes you, by the way."

I cross my arms. "Wow, bossy."

"Also, just so you know, Margot was like two seconds away from coming down there to strangle the professor. I didn't realize you could physically see veins throbbing on someone's forehead like that."

I laugh and wipe my eyes, the tears that were pricking there losing their fury and coming out in a rush of mirth.

Virgil continues, "You should have heard her. She was like a sports commentator or something. She was like, 'Look at her form! She's got perfect form! That asshole is lifting with his back. Look at the other lanes! She's destroying the people in the other lanes!'"

My face goes slack. "Wait, really?"

"Uh, yeah." Virgil adjusts his glasses like he can't believe he has to explain this. "Like I said, he only paired you with the best. And since you were competing with them, you were going way harder. You did a lot better than the others. Perez just pulled that shit so he could put on paper that you lost every heat. Fuck. The professors are supposed to be unbiased and unaffiliated. But I can't think that this is anything but a Traditionalist middle finger to Henry and Adam."

I shake my head. "It's too late, it's done. Do you think I'll fail because of this?"

"I don't know . . ."

Virgil doesn't need to be over here comforting me. It's clear Perez isn't going to give me that recommendation. If anything, Virgil should be dealing with his own grief about this. But here he is. Trying to make me feel better instead of mourning the loss of his humanity.

I may forever regret this, but with a sigh, I open my arms. "Hug it out?"

Virgil's jaw practically unhinges. I'm about to take it back when he rushes in, physically lifting me off the ground with the hug. I squeal, and he puts me down with a chuckle but doesn't break the contact.

His stubble is itchy against my cheek, and all I can smell is my own sweat. But it's otherwise exactly how I definitely didn't imagine. He's warm, and his body almost envelops mine like the perfect blanket. I can't remember the last time I hugged someone. I stopped letting myself. "If you tell anyone about this, I'll kill you," I whisper.

He chuckles, his breath blowing against my ear. "Noted."

# CHAPTER TWENTY-FOUR

Surprise!" Bailey exclaims when I open the door to my room.

She's beaming and holding a box with a few dusty photo albums and a plant, plus a bulky campus bookstore bag slung around her wrist. I shuffle aside to let her into the room, and she does a bunch of oohing and aahing like my room isn't in the exact same threadbare condition it was when I moved into it. Minus the random landscape print stretched on the wall behind my desk that Corey picked up at the poster sale because apparently my room felt sad. Mostly the space is "decorated" by the dirty clothes that have overtaken my desk chair to the point where I've started sitting on my bed to work.

Bailey sets the box and bag on my bed, taking out the plant and placing it on my windowsill. "It's a snake plant, so you don't have to water it often—once every two to three weeks. I should have brought it a lot earlier, but I wanted to give you time to settle in."

Really, she'd texted me multiple times about when she should come by, which I ignored.

"Glad you found the place okay. . . ." I hadn't told her my floor or room number.

"Yeah, the guy at the front desk let me know. I told him I was your aunt, and we have the same last name and everything, so he let me in."

Campus security is very permissive. I shift in place. I have to be at Summerhill in an hour to see if I made it through the first cut of candidates. I'm not exactly in a silly goofy mood and definitely don't want to chitchat with my aunt, but there isn't anything to do about it now.

"I thought this was such a cute set." Opening the bag, she reveals a pair of black sweatpants and a sweatshirt both with the Queen's University logo on them.

I pull the clothes to me and check the tags. They are my size and they do feel soft and comfortable. "Thanks."

She pushes the box aside so the area between us is clear and sets a photo album there. "And I found these and figured you might want to look through them. I try to print pictures as often as I can."

Bailey opens it, and I stare at the first photo. I recognize the spot. It's on campus, not far from Summerhill. And there, with his legs spread out and laughing, is Dad, and beside him, Mom. Her hair was relaxed back then and draped across her shoulders. She had bangs that she swept to the side. Bailey's there too, a little girl, tucked against Mom's side. If that's my parents' first year, Bailey would have been about eight, since she and Dad were born ten years apart.

"I idolized her," Bailey says. She flips the pages, revealing more shots of her with my parents and a lot more than expected of just her and Mom. "I begged Mike to propose to her within a week of them dating. She used to take me to all sorts of places. We went to the island, and historical sites around the city, and the haunted walks, and pumpkin patches and corn mazes in the fall. She was the big sister I always wanted."

Bailey and Mom were close? And there are photos to prove it. It doesn't make any sense. I barely talked to Bailey until this year.

She picks up a new album. It's a soft baby blue. Inside, there are pictures of us. Me and Jules. Tiny versions swaddled in blankets or held on laps. In one, Bailey's in a slinky black dress holding on to me, and there's a kiss mark on my forehead the exact shade of her lipstick.

"I have one of the three of you." Bailey pulls out another album and flips through it before exclaiming, "Here it is!" She takes out a picture and hands it to me. It's me, Mom, and Jules. I was probably four or so, making Jules five. This must have been right before we moved away from Kingston. "You can keep that."

"Thank you." I hold the picture in my hands. Bailey reaches for it, and I tug the photo away, my eyes going wide.

She holds up a frame. "Just . . . I thought this one would fit it."

"Right. Sorry." I let her take the picture and put it inside, then she hands it back to me.

She taps the box. "I can leave these here with you. Take whichever ones you want. Though if you stick them up, please use the sticky tack instead of tape. I packed those too." She rummages around in the box until she finds the white gummy stripes.

"How come you weren't around when we could actually remember you?" I ask.

Bailey bites her lip. "Busy, I guess. There's no good excuse. I was in school and trying to, like, be an adult or whatever, and you guys were always moving, and I never had the money to just go where you were. And Mike couldn't afford to pay for me to come. And then . . . I guess I was a little ashamed."

"Ashamed?" This woman drove a yellow Honda and put flowers in her hair unironically. What could possibly shame her?

"Annie was so brilliant. I wanted to be just like her, but I was a screwup."

Since when? Bailey is a little do-gooder. She lives in her tiny house community, and plants greens, and goes to protests, recycles and composts, and sells her serums and other crunchy granola stuff on Etsy, plus the whole YouTube influencer gig. And that actually makes her enough money to live. She's, like, successful and shit.

Maybe reading it on my face, she says, "Everything you see me doing now is pretty recent. In the last two to three years. It's why I could agree to have you stay with me. To be honest, it's probably the only reason Mike was cool with you living with me."

I scoff. "Like he cares."

Bailey sighs. "I'm not going to make excuses for him or speak for him, but I can say that *I* care. I meant what I said. If you need me, let me know. Not just if you're in trouble or struggling. But also, like, I dunno, if you want to go to the mall or, like, the knife store or wherever you get those knife throwing things. I know we don't know each other as well as we should, but I'm here for you." Bailey's eyes start to fill with tears. "You're my family, and I love you. And I want to know you. I loved your mom so much, and I let us drift apart. I don't want that. And I know you're doing better now, and you're committed to school and that's great, but that doesn't mean you won't need help."

"Don't talk about her in past tense."

A MASTERY OF MONSTERS

"I know, I know," Bailey says. "But she's not here right now."

I hunch my shoulders. Bailey's trying. She's been trying this whole time.

She brushes my braids from my shoulder. "I know it can be hard to let people in when you've lost someone. Especially someone you were so close to. But when you lock everyone out, all you end up with is yourself. And I never want you to be alone like that if you don't actually want to be."

I swallow. "I don't want more people to let down." Why am I saying this to Bailey of all people? Maybe because I waited too long to tell Jules.

"It's your life. Who cares if you let me down? I've let so many people down over the years. But the problem I needed to solve wasn't how not to let them down, it was how not to let *myself* down. Because that was who I cared the most about disappointing."

I stare at Bailey for a long moment. Yeah, she's cringey most of the time, but just now, she said something that made a lot of sense. "Okay."

"Okay." She tilts her head, staring at me. "You can also call me when you need your braids redone."

I scowl. "Wow."

"They're just looking a little . . . old." She picks at some braids where the split between my hair and the Kanekalon is becoming increasingly obvious.

"Could you do them this weekend? It's Thanksgiving. And reading week. I'm off until the twentieth."

"Of course!" She pauses. "Well, we're not celebrating the colonizers."

"Obviously."

"But we can still eat a lot and get this hair done. What do you want? Mashed potatoes?"

"And gravy. And chicken."

She beams. "And apple pie."

"A must."

She laughs, and we keep naming dishes, making our menu for the holiday weekend.

I even find myself looking forward to it.


The crowd in Summerhill is smaller today. Apparently the first cut isn't open to the entire society, who will find out at the next lecture on Monday. It's a small mercy that if I fail, at least it won't happen in front of everyone. But it means that me and Virgil are the only ones allowed into the room, and Margot and Corey are forced to wait outside.

We sit at a table near the front, which isn't my preference, but Virgil insists. I slouch in my spot while he keeps his body stiff and at attention. We're eventually joined by Violet and Bryce. And I'm actually all right with it. I like them, and they've helped me a couple of times now.

Or Violet has, at least. And Bryce is pleasant enough.

Only a couple of other candidates are attending with monsters.

"Have you guys not started looking for partners?" I ask Violet.

She shakes her head. "My dad said it's not worth it until you make it past the first cut. You'll see. A bunch of people will suddenly be paired after this." She waves at Virgil. "Hey, I'm Violet. This is Bryce."

Virgil clears his throat. "Oh, yeah, uh, hello. Virgil."

I side-eye him. "That was the worst introduction I've ever heard."

A MASTERY OF MONSTERS 249

He glares at me. "I wasn't expecting to be involved in the conversation." He sits back, crossing his arms.

"Are you two related, or . . . ?" Bryce asks, and my eyebrows go all the way up, while Violet groans. I take it back, Bryce has lost all the points. He holds up his hands. "No, no, I mean—not, like, 'cause you're both—" He takes a deep breath. "People who come to the candidacy already paired usually know the monster they're with really well. Often, they're family. I'm sorry, I worded that poorly."

Fine, Bryce points reinstated. But he's on thin ice. "Do people not just have monster friends?"

Violet shakes her head. "We don't go to the same schools. We often don't know each other unless we're involved in the candidacy or if our family members are Masters. For me, I'll be pairing with the daughter of my aunt's partner. But I've only had small interactions even with her."

It's so interesting how "safety" is used over and over again, but I've still not seen any violence from monsters in human form. And yet the one monster I was attacked by isn't even being investigated. "Me and Virgil have an arrangement. But no, we're not related."

"An arrangement?" Violet regards Virgil. "To be honest, I wasn't sure you would find a partner. I'm glad you two managed to pair up. I think it's unethical to hold you accountable for something you didn't do."

Swallowing, Virgil shifts in his seat.

He's saved from responding when the professors walk onto the stage, followed by Adam, James, and Carrigan. Just like Adam said, Carrigan is apparently sticking around. Adam smiles at us, while James keeps a more neutral expression. Carrigan is scrolling on his phone again. Wow. Why even stay if he's going to be so hands-off?

James steps forward to the mic. "Welcome, candidates. We are honored to learn with you."

"And us with you," the room says back. I find a spot on the table to look at so I don't have to say the words with everyone else.

James continues, "We will be announcing the candidates who have made the first cut, beginning with the highest scoring and ending with the lowest scoring. This will bring the number of candidates from twenty-five to fifteen. Your training scores will be scrubbed after this cut. Following the third test, the panel of Masters will award one point each to a candidate of their choosing. Multiple Masters may choose to award points to the same candidate. Therefore, the choice of the five who will go through the initiation will be decided by a combination of their test scores and their panel scores. Is this understood?"

A stiff "yes" resounds through the room. This time I naturally miss the cue on us answering in unison, so I'm looking up when it happens. James throws me an annoyed look.

"Let us begin," he says, and clears his throat, reading down the list from the top. We're forced to pause and applaud for each named candidate.

Caden is sixth, to the delight of his lackeys. If I thought I could get away with making a gagging motion, I would. Instead, I settle for sharing knowing looks with everyone at our table. It helps that Violet came in fifth. I clapped louder for her and do the same for Bryce when he comes in eighth.

The list continues, followed by applause. Virgil's fists are balled in his lap.

By his own admission, I did well in the physical endurance, but the reality is that I lost almost every heat. Besides, the professors never

A MASTERY OF MONSTERS

251

explained how they're creating these scores. If points for physical endurance come from winning, then I'll have the worst one, unless what I got from Bernie and Chen makes up for it.

Some girl I don't know comes in fourteenth, and we clap.

My head is both light and overfilled. I can barely keep it upright.

"In last place . . . ," James drones, his lip curling, "August Black." He gives me a pointed look that speaks to how absolutely delighted he is for me.

There's a smattering of applause, mostly from Violet and Bryce. Virgil is too busy gasping beside me to do any clapping.

Meanwhile, I stare at Perez, expecting him to have an expression of barely concealed rage. Instead this motherfucker has the nerve to grin at me. Like he did me some favor. Like he isn't the reason I almost didn't make it.

We're dismissed, but Virgil is having a small heart attack, so I stay where I am.

"You should have been ranked higher," Violet whispers to me before she leaves.

"It's fine." The training scores will be scrubbed anyway. All that matters is that I made it.

Finally, me and Virgil are the only two people left in the room. He turns to me, his face beaming and split wide. "Holy shit. You did it!"

"It's only the first round."

"I know, I know, but still." Virgil looks at the now empty stage and his smile dims to a frown.

"What?"

"You should have scored higher."

"Not you too. It's basically a miracle that I passed."

"This is supposed to be a fair process, but you were singled out. And you did everything right. You followed the rules." He jerks his hand around. "Even how James looked at you was ridiculous."

James is one thing. I know he hates me by association with Adam. "What's Perez's deal? I thought he was messing with me, but then he was happy I passed."

Virgil says, "Henry looked into things, and Perez may have Pro-Lib associations. Which is strange because why would that influence him to try to manipulate your results? What would the Pro-Libs want with you?"

"No idea."

For now, I've cemented my place in the competition, and that's what matters. I just have to last until I find Jules.

I picture Virgil's beaming smile falling when I drop out of the competition prematurely.

Hunching my shoulders, I stand and lead the way out of Summerhill.

# CHAPTER TWENTY-FIVE

Corey opens the door to McIntosh Castle and frowns at my outfit. She insisted on a theme of Victorian nightclothes for our sleepover. She has on a long white dressing gown that's somewhat sheer, exposing the shorter white dress underneath. She's also holding a gold candelabra that, while a prop, is probably also something that casually exists in her home. I'm wearing the matching pair of Queen's sweatpants and sweatshirt that Bailey got me. The spirit wear was a bit much, but they're super comfortable, so here I am.

"You couldn't have at least tried?" Corey asks.

"What if I told you I was filled with deep malaise?"

She examines me for a moment and then nods. "That does help. Come on, we're in my room."

I look at the other spaces on the main floor, several of which have their doors shut. Which maybe I could ignore if I weren't aware that they're talking about me in there. It's only hours after I made the first cut, and this was Corey's idea of a celebration, and at the same time, Henry organized a meeting to figure out next steps. I assume the fact that one of the professors may or may not have it out for me will come up. Only Bachelors and Masters are allowed, meaning I can't even attend the meeting that's about me.

"Margot will update us later," Corey says, following my gaze. "If it helps, it's not just about you. They're going to discuss the election, too. Let's go."

Feet trailing, I follow her upstairs. For some reason, the second-floor hallway has carpet instead of hardwood like everywhere else. And it's only the hall. As if they couldn't be bothered with consistency. Corey leads me into the first bedroom on the right.

It's maybe double the size of my dorm room with a strange triangular shape and high ceilings with a small skylight. The double-door closet is flung open to expose a wardrobe that mostly consists of neutral tones, and an old wooden vanity on the wall beside it with a bunch of books and skin care stuff on it. Corey's bed is a simple wood frame with plain white linens, though it does have what looks like a hand-knit blanket. The desk on the other side of the room is littered with papers both underneath and on top of a bronze MacBook. And of course, there are a bunch of bookshelves.

For the purposes of the sleepover, there's an array of pillows and blankets on the floor arranged around a massive wooden slab loaded with charcuterie beside a bottle of wine and some carefully placed glasses. There's also a projector screen on the wall playing a lo-fi video of a woman in a Victorian nightgown walking through hallways to piano music.

No one can say the girl doesn't stick to a theme.

I make myself comfortable on the floor while Corey shouts at

Virgil to come over. He leaves a bedroom across the hall.

Virgil has no qualms about the theme, because he's in his own white dress, though this one has buttons that go all the way down. This man even has a little Scrooge sleeping hat.

I look from Virgil to Corey. "Why do you have these outfits? You do know you gave me like an hour to fit this theme as if I just own this stuff."

Corey tilts her head. "You don't have costumes lying around? We've done a bunch of fancy dress gatherings. Victorian era—"

"Pirate themes," Virgil says. "Lets you reuse some of the frilly Victorian stuff."

Corey nods. "And I already have the peg leg."

I snort and then flush. "I'm sorr—"

"It's a joke, you're supposed to laugh." She smiles. "Also, both pirates and Victorian stuff can also be used for decade themes."

"Where are you doing all this dressing up?" I ask. "How many costumes parties could you be going to?"

Corey waves around the room. "We just do it here."

"You mean you have regular costume parties . . ." I look between them. "Just you two?"

Virgil opens his mouth and then scowls. "Okay, you're trying to make this into a sad, nerdy thing only the two of us do—"

"Am I making it into that or is it like that?"

Corey says, "Dr. Liu always says it doesn't matter what other people think as long as we're having fun." She furrows her brow. "Oh my God, was that to reassure us because he thought it was sad?!"

Virgil massages his temples. "Let's not dwell on it."

"Right." Corey nods to herself. She says to Virgil, "Why don't you give August a tour of your room? I have to get my prosthesis off.

I think I stood too long today, as my little leg is swelling. And I'd rather not flash everyone while I hike up my dressing gown."

Virgil makes a show of bowing at the waist and pointing toward his room. This boy is so cheesy. I ignore that I'm fighting a smile. Once we're in his room, I ask, "Is she okay? With the swelling?"

"Yeah, it happens sometimes if she does a lot of standing, that's all. She's fine."

Participating in the candidacy fundamentally changed how Corey lives. Corey, who is significantly more skilled than I am. My only saving grace is that I don't plan to go as far as she did. Ideally, she wouldn't have had to go that far either.

Virgil's bedroom is pretty much the same layout-wise as Corey's—that odd triangle shape and the abundance of bookshelves. Though his bedding is maroon. I spot a stuffed bird on his bed and give it a poke. It's royal blue and not much bigger than my hand. "I bet you named him."

"Reginald."

I pull a face. "You would."

"My mom named him, actually. My birthday was coming up, and she already had the present prepped. The name was in the card. Henry found it in their things." He stands next to me, looking at the bird.

"Why a bird? Isn't a teddy bear usually the childhood stuffed animal of choice?"

"Some of us like to break the mold." I throw him a look, and he laughs. He picks up the toy, staring into its beady eyes. "My mom used to tell me this story. She said that once upon a time there was a vicious little bird. It pecked at any animal or person who came near it, and the songs it sang were off-key. One day, it injured itself. No

A MASTERY OF MONSTERS

one would help it, for it had only ever made enemies. All except for a kind human girl. She fed it, even though it pecked her, and bandaged its wounds though it screeched at her, and showed it a kindness that the bird had never given to anyone. When it was well, she asked the bird to visit her daily and sing her a gentle tune. Every day it returned to her windowsill and sang her sweet melodies. Right up until the day it died. She stuffed the bird and immortalized it, keeping it on her sill until the day she died."

My lip curls. "That's fucking grim."

"It's a fable," Virgil says, rolling his eyes. "What matters is the message of the story."

"Which is?"

"That kindness deserves repayment."

I can't help the shocked laugh that comes out of my mouth. "And the bird deserved to spend its entire life repaying a debt to a stranger who helped it once?"

He shakes his head. "You don't get it. They became friends. No one liked the bird. It found someone who did despite what it was."

"Did it? Or was it afraid that if it didn't do as the girl said, the next time it needed help, she wouldn't come? Did you even ask why the bird was so unpleasant in the first place? Maybe the other animals were little shits. The girl trapped that bird and made it twist itself into something it wasn't for her."

Virgil stares at me.

Fuck. I don't know why I let myself get worked up about some silly story his mom told him. I push out a snort. "Your face! I'm not trying to ruin your childhood memory. I'm sure you're right. I don't think I'm a fable sort of girl."

He put the bird back down on the bed. "There was a note with the gift. The last words my parents left me." He met my eyes. "It said, 'Fly free.'"

"Meaning?"

"Meaning, I wonder if my mom felt the way you do. That the bird was trapped."

"But that's not what you think."

"No. We had very different ideologies, my parents and I."

"So what does that make me?"

"Dangerous, probably."

I lick my lips. "Do you know why they did it?" Maybe it's insensitive to ask, but we keep dancing around it. And I'd rather talk about them than me.

"Your guess is as good as mine."

"But the Doctorate can control them, can't he? Or their partners— didn't they try to stop them?"

"They drugged their partners, so they were asleep. Even the strongest Master can't exert control in that state. But with the Doctorate . . . well, they didn't have a chance." He shakes his head. "And they were smart people. Anyone could have seen that was a terrible plan, but they still did it."

"Maybe they thought they could manage somehow."

"Maybe." His phone vibrates, and he takes it out. As he stares at the screen, a little smile comes to life on his face. "Look." He shows me a picture of Isaac and Mia, of all people, in a furniture store.

Right, the stuff for the dinner. I guess Isaac is Virgil's contact. "Why would he send that to you?"

"He's been asking for tips." He wiggles his eyebrows. "For the ladies. He's basically in love with Mia."

"Again," I say, "why is he reaching out to *you* for that?"

A MASTERY OF MONSTERS

"Funny. I'd like to let you know that my rizz is strong."

"And that's my cue to go." I turn and head back to Corey's room.

"Don't deny my rizz!"

Corey's sitting on the blanket, pouring wine into the glasses. Her leg is in the closet with her other prostheses, so I guess she's keeping it off for the night. She raises an eyebrow at me, and I shake my head and plop down next to her. I refuse to get into a conversation about Virgil's skills with women. Yeah, okay, he's good-looking, but he's also a walking, talking sweater vest.

She holds out three bright packages with animal faces on them. "Pick the face mask you want."

"How is this Victorian-themed?" I ask.

She scowls at me. "It's sleepover-themed. Pick one."

I reach toward the rabbit, and her nose wrinkles a bit. I pause and move toward the tiger mask, and she relaxes. I reach for the rabbit one again and she tenses. "Do you want the rabbit mask?"

"I don't care which one I get."

"Bullshit."

"Okay, yes, I want it."

"Then take it!"

"But what if you wanted it? Or Virgil?"

"Corey!"

"Fine." She sets the rabbit mask aside, and I take the tiger. Virgil joins us and ends up with a bear. We carefully apply the masks to our faces.

There's a chorus of laughter downstairs. "They're all coming in now," Virgil says, plucking a piece of salami from the tray.

"Who are they?" I ask.

"Henry's Mastery group."

"That literally answered nothing."

"Basically, as candidates advance in the process by becoming Bachelors and Masters, older Masters start seeking people for their factions."

"The factions that aren't supposed to exist?"

"Correct. You want people on your side, and the new Bachelors and Masters want connections so that they have help achieving their various ambitions within the society. So certain Masters will have invite-only groups where they offer personal mentorship and help with networking, and it gives you a bunch of incoming Bachelors and Masters who have your back."

I purse my lips. "These are the same people who refused to train Margot?"

"Yeah . . . it didn't necessarily work out that way for her. That's how it's supposed to be, though. And Henry culled those people after that and replaced them with members more aligned with that goal."

There's a lot of talk of ambition for a society that's supposed to be equal. From the frown on her face, I wonder if Corey is thinking the same, even though she's used to this.

"Did Cyrus have a little group?" I grab a handful of grapes. They're perfectly crisp.

"No," Corey says. "That would be 'too far,' I guess, for a Doctorate to have one. But obviously there are Mastery groups affiliated with the factions of the candidates, so you could count that. Right now, I would say that James has more, but Adam has a younger and hungrier crowd. Hard to tell which is better for the vote."

Virgil shrugs. "What actually matters is that everyone can vote. Most monsters will vote Progressive."

A MASTERY OF MONSTERS

"Don't be naive," Corey says. Mine and Virgil's eyes widen, and she splutters, "Sorry, it's just—you can't pretend that there isn't a category of monsters who believe in the restrictions. Besides, some people were upset with Adam for nominating August. He's turned down several families' requests for nominations in the past, and now he's vouching for an outsider? No offense."

"None taken." I honestly can't bring myself to care about this whole voting thing.

Virgil glances at me sidelong. "You know this is relevant to you, right?"

"How?"

"If James becomes the Doctorate, he can implement whatever rules he wants. Including deciding that people who haven't been students for a certain period of time can't be Bachelor candidates. And the Doctorate vote happens before initiation night. It could very much affect you and me."

I dig my nail into the skin of a grape. "You can't just make up a new rule."

"You can when you're the Doctorate."

"I thought the Traditionalists wanted everything to be the same? Doesn't that mean not changing things? And wasn't this vote not supposed to interfere with the candidate process?"

Corey sips from her glass. "No one knows what James will do with the power. He's not above hypocrisy."

"Adam can do it," Virgil says, leaning forward. "The Pro-Libs will sway his way too."

Corey's grip on her wineglass tightens. "Because those are the sorts of people we want backing Adam?"

"Numbers are numbers."

I'm still trying to keep the factions clear in my head. "Progressives want fewer restrictions, Traditionalists want more restrictions, Pro-Libs want no restrictions, and the Scientists want a cure."

"Basically," Corey says. "But some people who work in the Scientist department still have other faction affiliations. They want a cure, but they believe the current system should be upheld a certain way."

"'Cause that's not confusing at all."

Knowing that a Master is behind everything with Sammie and Jules, I'm starting to wonder if this person's goals are less about them and more about what's going on in the society itself. All these factions and politics, and the fact that this is lining up with the election. Even if what happened to them started before Cyrus died, he was sick. They must have known he didn't have a lot of time left. And even if they didn't know about the election, he has three possible successors. No matter who's chosen, transitions of power are always unstable times. There would be growing pains. But then, why choose Sammie and Jules in particular?

"They'll work something out at this meeting," Virgil says. "Henry's going to pull on whatever strings he has to help Adam. And he's got a good amount."

Corey shrieks.

"What?!" I shout.

"I forgot the apricot jam!" She throws a stricken look at Virgil. "Can you go grab it?"

He sighs and heads to the kitchen.

I can't believe this girl screamed over jam.

"I'm going to the bathroom," I say, finishing up my glass.

I walk into the hall and across the way to the toilet. While I'm there, I take off the face mask and wash the product off. After I finish, I glance at Corey's room and then at the stairs.

Technically, I didn't lie. I did go to the bathroom.

Making sure that Corey isn't looking into the hall, I slip down the stairs. I step onto the main floor hallway on my tiptoes, pressing myself against the wall.

The Mastery group is meeting in the room on the right, and the kitchen is at the end of the hall. If Virgil catches me, I'll just say I wanted a different jam and was coming to get it.

Unfortunately, I can't hear much more than murmurs coming from the rooms. Until a door starts to open. I dart back around the corner, hopping up the first two steps, concealing myself in the stairway. I peek around the corner. Henry and Margot come out of the main meeting and walk across the hall to another room. I look down the hall to the kitchen, then upstairs.

No one.

*Fuck it.*

I move to the room Henry and Margot went into, pressing my ear against the door while I keep my eyes down the hall, alternating between looking at the room housing the Mastery group and the kitchen.

This close, I can actually hear the conversation.

Margot says, "This will come back and bite us. You must know that."

"You're being dramatic," Henry says. "I know that you in particular are risk averse, but this is worth the gamble. The winning pot is too much to pass up."

"And what about the people who get caught in the crosshairs?"

"All wars have casualties."

Margot scoffs.

"I know you can't see my vision—"

"Then tell me! Share the vision!"

Henry sighs. "You must trust that I am always working in our best interests. I'm not selfishly concealing truths to make myself feel better. This is strategic. We need to be careful. We're not the only ones playing a game here."

"Playing? I feel like I'm not even on the board! Do I just have to keep finding things out on my own?"

"There is an order to this! You want to speed things up? Make sure they win. Make sure Virgil comes out of this with full control of himself."

Margot starts to say something else, but Virgil leaves the kitchen, and I'm forced to straighten. He narrows his eyes at me, opens his mouth, and then decides better of it. He has a nicely arranged plate of snacks. He knocks on the Mastery group door, and I stand beside him. "What are you doing?" he asks.

"What are *you* doing?" I shoot back. "You're so transparent." I've never once seen this boy prepare charcuterie. He just wants an excuse to hear what they're talking about.

"So are you," he says.

I decide then not to remind him that he still has his bear face mask on.

The door opens, and Virgil makes a whole thing out of offering snacks.

Meanwhile, I'm distracted by a familiar person. "I know you," I say, pointing at a guy. He's a nondescript white boy, but I remember his smug little face. This is the ringleader of the group of guys who came after me in the park. This asshole is in the Mastery

A MASTERY OF MONSTERS                                              265

group?! He tries to avoid my gaze. "You, hey, I'm talking to you!"

Now the other members are paying attention. And Virgil's finally caught on. "You're the guy from the park!"

"Thank you!" I say.

Henry and Margot come out of the room behind us. He looks at the two of us. "What's going on here?"

"What's on your face?" Margot asks Virgil.

Virgil starts spluttering excuses for a bunch of things. I point into the room. "One of your guys in there was extremely rude to me. Not to mention creepy, dare I say *predatory*, and honestly, plain disgusting."

"You threw a knife at me!" The guy pipes up finally, looking around the room like someone is going to back him up before settling his gaze on Henry.

"Grow up."

Virgil says, "You did technically throw a knife at him."

"He deserved it. Besides, I only nicked him. Maybe next time he'll think twice before approaching drunk girls with his crew of dudes and suggesting that they're down to fuc—"

"Okay," Henry says, raising his hands. "I get it."

"That's what he said?" Virgil crosses his arms over his chest. "You cornered her by herself in a park with a group of your friends and made gross, sexually charged remarks, and *you're* upset she threw a knife that barely grazed you?"

The guy stabs at his ear, specifically at a scar so faint I have to squint to see it. "I had to go to the hospital! I got stitches! And we were just talking. We weren't going to do anything."

I shake my head. "You're so full of shit."

"You want me to deal with it?" Margot asks, turning to Henry.

"No, it's fine. Peters, come out here." Margot goes into the room and the guy, Peters, comes out. Henry motions for him to shut the door, which he does, and then he stands there shuffling his feet around. "Can we please move past whatever is going on so I can continue my meeting, and you two"—this with a look at me and Virgil—"can return upstairs where you're supposed to be?"

"Yes," I say. "We'll go back to being neither seen nor heard once he apologizes to me."

Peters gapes. "*You* threw a knife at *me*."

"And *you* were vile and predatory to *me*."

Henry massages his forehead. "I have no doubt that your encounter with Ms. Black was terrible, but I can assure you that any continued contact with her will be worse. And from what I have heard of the conversation, you were more in the wrong. Violence was not an ideal response, but you should have known better. Ill intentions or not, unless you were going over to help, you should have left the young lady alone. Quite frankly, I'm disappointed to hear of your behavior, and we will be discussing it at our next one-on-one. I'd advise you to make the apology and be done with it."

Peters turns wide eyes to Henry but then swallows and shifts his gaze to me. "I'm sorry."

"Sorry for what exactly?" I ask.

"For being, um, shitty and sexist?"

"Are you asking me or telling me?"

He grits his teeth. "I'm sorry for being shitty and sexist. That was poor behavior on my part. And I promise to do better in the future."

I beam at him. "Was that so hard?"

"Go away now," Henry says.

A MASTERY OF MONSTERS

"Gladly!" I walk back to Corey's room with Virgil trailing behind me.

"You're a terror," Virgil says, stifling a laugh. "You know that, right?"

"I'm a motherfucking delight."

When we enter the room, Corey and Virgil exchange a look, and she decides that it's best not to ask. Meanwhile, I'm thinking about what Henry and Margot were discussing. What exactly are they gambling on?

We watch a movie, and shortly after it finishes, we hear people leaving, and Margot appears in the doorway of the bedroom.

"So?" Virgil says.

"Perez doesn't have any faction links that we can find even after digging, and though his actions are confusing, you and August both said he was happy that she progressed. Whether that's an act or not, we don't know. We'll keep an eye on him. Either way, August will be judged by the panel of Masters going forward, not him. We've got at least four confirmed Progressives on there, so we'll see how it shakes out. Now for the bad news."

"That wasn't the bad news?" I ask.

"No," Margot says. "The bad news is that everyone is allowed a vote for the new Doctorate, but it's not equal. Votes from Masters with greater seniority will count more. It's a sliding scale. They're using the precedent that this is how voting is done in the Masterium."

I wrinkle my nose. "The what now?"

Virgil jerks to his feet. "Are you fucking kidding me?! The Masterium is voting only done by Masters. How is that relevant to a vote by the whole society?"

Margot leans on the doorjamb. "I know. But it's happening. This is how Cyrus set it up."

No one bothers to answer my question. Which is fair, given this new information. It won't matter if Adam has the majority monster vote. If he doesn't have most of the senior Masters in his pocket, he'll still lose. James could win. He could change the rules to suit him, meaning that even if I got through every test and came in the top five, he could disqualify me before I made it to the initiation.

Now I have more reason than ever to find Jules before it gets that far.

# CHAPTER TWENTY-SIX

I check the address in my phone against the house I'm standing in front of on Baiden Street. It's a classic two-story brick house. The grass is trimmed, and the wooden shutters on the windows look freshly touched up, matching the crisp white of the front door. Most of the Kingston brick homes have some wear and tear, but this one is in impeccable shape.

It's only when I get close to the door that I hear the hum of the music inside. I use the brass knocker and jump when the door is opened instantly. The Black girl on the other side is Janey, one of my old coworkers, who beams and ushers me in.

"Are you part of QBSS? I never see you!" There's a bit of a lilt to her voice that lets me know she's been drinking.

"No, uh, I'm meeting a friend. Riley?"

"She's upstairs." Janey leans against the wall. "What happened with Tim's? You just stopped showing up. Carrie was, like, feral over it."

"Some stuff came up." I point to the stairs and start moving toward them. "See you."

She frowns but doesn't stop me.

I don't have any issue with her, but the Tim's stuff feels like a lifetime ago now.

The vibe of this gathering is different than it was during the mixer at the beginning of the year. As advertised on their socials, this is the Homecoming party. The time of year just after the first reading week when alumni come back to visit, and everyone uses it as an excuse to get drunk. We were sent several emails about appropriate conduct during this week. Today's the last day, but despite it being a Sunday, there are still lots of parties happening.

But the ambience here is more than that. The mixer had a lot of awkward socializing, but now everyone knows each other. They have their own groups where they stand with their clear plastic cups talking or dancing.

Must be nice.

Not just being here but *choosing* to be here.

I'm glad at least that Bailey redid my braids over the holiday so I don't have to come into a room full of Black people with my hair a mess. Though my aunt mostly wears her hair out, she has a whole stash of Kanekalon in all different colors. So now I have burgundy strands mixed in with the black ones.

Someone walks past me, shouting at their friend, gold glinting in their mouth. Am I missing something? Are gold teeth the new thing?

I head up the stairs and text Riley on the landing instead of searching for her. I hadn't heard anything from this girl in a minute. Which was just as well, because I had training and midterms to deal with, and then taking a break. I tried to put more pieces together, but

A MASTERY OF MONSTERS

so far, I have nothing. Hopefully whatever Riley wants to talk about tonight will help.

The door to the left opens, and Riley sticks her head out. She's wearing her twists down, and her eyes are made up in a smoky look. She jerks her head into the room, and I follow.

The bedroom has a king bed covered in layered sheets of blue and yellow. There are floating shelves filled with trophies for track and field and gymnastics, and a converting standing-sitting desk in white that houses a giant blue iMac. The room is big enough that it has space for a chill spot with two couches and a glass coffee table. Riley sits on one couch, and I sink into the one facing her.

"You said you had a lead?" I ask.

"Hey, how are you, Riley? What have you been up to? Here's something that I have to contribute to the conversation."

"You're getting on me for not doing small talk?"

She sighs, crossing and then uncrossing her legs. "Look, I'm gonna be straight with you, and it's honestly because I've hit a wall. And you clearly need encouragement to find anything worthwhile, so it's better if I just say it."

"Okay . . ."

"I didn't pick you at random."

"I know that. You saw I was associated with the society."

"That was a bonus, actually." She leans forward and laces her fingers together. "I knew your brother."

"What?" The word falls limp from my mouth. "Wait, you knew him? This entire fucking time?!"

"Yes. He joined QBSS. He's in my year, but I didn't know him well. The president saw he had some potential, so he was recruited to a second level. We have . . . multiple sections, if you will. And we wanted him to join. He did, but then he stopped coming shortly thereafter. Then all of a sudden, he came back wanting a second chance. We said no. We don't do second chances."

My brain is trying to catch up with the information I'm learning. First, Riley knew I was looking for my brother and pretended she didn't know him. Second, if he'd joined QBSS, then that's an obvious link between him and Sammie. No wonder she was saying all that shit about the society targeting them. She already knew the connection was this club.

*That's* what this is about. Not someone targeting Jules or Sammie. They're targeting the Queen's Black Student Society. "You lied to me."

"I didn't know if you were trustworthy. And to be honest, I still don't. But I need your help. I'm giving a little so you can give a little."

"A little?" I laugh. "Sounds like a lot. So what? You denied Jules reentry into a club whose only requirement is that you're Black?"

"There are more qualifications needed for this particular section of it, and he knew that. The point is that you said he got an invitation, and the date on it is the day before he quit QBSS. So potentially whoever sent that to him sought him out because he was a part of it. Sammie also hadn't officially left and was in the special section. My theory is that the person behind this is trying to find people who might have information on us but are perhaps no longer loyal. Except that Jules tried to rejoin—why? Did they ask him to? And why did he disappear months later?"

I cross my arms over my chest. "Valid questions, but not an excuse for jerking me around. You think I have perfect trust in you? No. But I still told you everything."

Riley's shoulders drop. "I'm sorry, okay?"

I let the silence sit so she can sweat in it. When I decide she's had enough, I say, "So what's new now? You said you need my help."

"We've been doing our initiation for this separate section of QBSS. It wrapped just before the long weekend, and one of the guys didn't make the cut. And he basically did this rant on social media that made it clear that he was pissed. I snuck into his room this week and found an invitation."

"Is that how it went down with Jules and Sammie, too? Public disgruntlement?"

Riley frowns. "Kind of? Like, Sammie cussed out the president on her friends-only TikTok. I don't know who saw that. But Jules didn't do anything visible. And Sammie was being pushed out, same as this new guy. Jules leaving surprised us."

Meaning it's not 100 percent clear how this person is picking targets. Or maybe Jules is the exception. "This guy with the invite. I assume the meeting date is for tonight?"

She nods. "Different location, though." She clears her throat. "Are you coming or not?"

"Why don't you have your QBSS friends help you with this? Your boyfriend, even? Since you're the ones being targeted."

Riley clenches and unclenches her fingers. "I told them what I saw, Sammie's body, and . . . they don't want to get mixed up with the society. We maintained a peace with the previous Doctorate. The president doesn't want to rock the boat. He wants to wait and see how your election shakes out and then approach about Sammie. He would like us to focus on protecting each other instead of"—she pauses to grind her teeth—"digging up trouble and putting members in danger. And Jackson agrees. He doesn't want me to get involved."

"You're not supposed to be doing this with me, then?"

"No."

"What do they think we're doing meeting up like this?"

"I told them that you're my special project. That you're reluctant to commit, but I think you could be a great fit for the second level of QBSS, so I'm trying to encourage you to join. They know that Jules is your brother, which has helped add some legitimacy."

"Wow, you're real slick, aren't you?"

"It's a cover story. Chill." She spreads her arms open. "I wasn't honest with you, and that's fucked. I get it. But I have no one else. Sammie was my best friend. She didn't deserve what happened to her. Now we have a chance to try to catch this person. To stop them from doing this to more people, like your brother. And I need you for that. And I think you need me too."

Another person needing me. Another expectation.

But it's for Jules.

I say, "If I catch you in another lie, we're done."

"You won't." Riley stands. "We need to go. He's leaving." At my furrowed brow, she adds, "Security cameras on the outside of the house."

"Wait, he came to the party? I thought he was disgruntled."

"He is, but I begged him to come tonight with the promise of notes for a class I know he's struggling in. Most of his friends are in QBSS, so getting him to stay for a bit after I lured him here was easier. So let's not waste the opportunity I made."

The two of us head downstairs, where Jackson peels around a corner. He rubs his arm and looks between the two of us. "Hey, where are you guys off to?"

"Just going to grab more snacks!" Riley says. The way she puts on that grinning face in an instant makes me feel less bad for being tricked. She's no amateur. "We'll be right back. You want anything?"

"I could come—"

"We can't have both hosts running out, can we? We'll be right back."

His face falls. "Okay, yeah, cool."

We walk to the door at a calmer pace but once we get outside, Riley sprints for her car, and I hurry to keep up. It's a white Lexus SUV with leather seats. It puts both Bailey's Civic and Dad's CR-V to shame.

I look her up and down. "Are you rich?"

"Just get in!" I do as she says, and before I'm even buckled, she's peeling down the road. "I think he's gonna take the bus, so we can get there before him. But I need to park far enough away for him to not recognize my car."

"Okay, 007."

She rolls her eyes.

"Is that entire house yours?"

"My parents bought it."

Riley *is* rich. We drive down King Street past St. Lawrence and end up in a more residential area. She pulls up next to a set of houses where she parks, rushing me out of the vehicle. "We're on foot from here. We'll stay back a bit so we can watch him."

"Bossy," I mumble.

We walk on the sidewalk, clinging to the shadows, and I take the time to decide how much I want to trust Riley from this point forward. On one hand, she's brought most of the perks to this arrangement, and had she not specifically chosen me for my connection to my brother, probably could have shaken me off a long time ago.

On the other hand, fuck Riley for lying.

Virgil's been less helpful in making strides, but at least he's honest. He's always been up front about what's going on. And he even added some theories.

We made a promise to each other, and I know he'll do what he can to keep it. But Riley has her own motives.

I gnaw on my lip. I guess I do too.

"There he is," she whispers.

A boy in a hoodie hops off the bus. We keep back as he enters a parking lot in front of a wooded area. He disappears down a narrow path. There are signs marking this as the Rideau Trail and noting that it's closed after sundown.

Because the path is so narrow, we can't follow him right away. It would be obvious he was being tailed if he looked back, so we wait at the edge, glancing in every once in a while to see where he's gone. The next time we look, we can't see him at all.

"Shit," Riley says, and strides onto the path.

I follow her, looking from side to side to try to see him. On one side, there's a golf course, quiet and empty. But on the other, the trees are denser.

The sound of crunching leaves reaches us.

And then there's a louder sound. A massive smashing of branches and groan of trees.

The boy screams.

"Fuck!" Riley leaves the main path, running straight into the denser area, smacking tree branches out of her way and leaping over branches.

Damn, those track trophies weren't just for show. I rush after her, barely able to keep up, with a few slips and falls along the way.

We break out into a clearer section, where the trees are tall, their lower trunks naked and skeletal. The boy is on his knees, staring at a monster with wide eyes. I look at it, a fine tremble working under my skin.

This isn't the one from Big Sandy Bay.

Its body is covered in black fur that looks slick, and its eyes are bloodshot, the pupils blown wide around a ring of brown iris. It has the rough appearance of a bear, but there's a mane of bone around its neck, gleaming white. Those sharp ridges of bone are all over its body. They remind me of the way coral sticks to rocks. Sharp and unyielding.

The boy comes back to himself, scrambling off the ground and running. But he's going the wrong way. Farther into the trees instead of back the way we came. The monster tears after him.

Riley doesn't hesitate to take off after both of them.

"Oh, so we're chasing the giant monster?" I spit out between breaths.

"What else are we supposed to do?" she says. "We can't leave him to die."

We run through the trees, following the heavy sounds of the beast. This thing is massive. It should have easily caught that guy by now, but it hasn't.

"What the fuck?" I ask. "What's it doing?"

"I don't know," Riley says. "But it won't play with him like this forever."

A frantic cry echoes through the trees, and Riley runs faster. We come upon the monster with the boy pinned under one of its giant paws. The guy is bleeding from a scratch down one of his cheeks and someplace on his side too, judging by the wet spot on his hoodie. The creature turns to us and roars.

I stumble away from it. *Shit, shit, shit.* This is a terrible idea. I only have one knife on me. This girl told me to come to a party to talk. If Riley knew this was the plan, she should have said to bring more weapons. Then I would have my full set.

The monster increases the pressure on its paw. The boy's eyes bulge, tears streaming down his dirt-smeared cheeks.

"We need to do something. Distract it. Get it to focus on us," Riley says.

My mouth drops open. "And what are we supposed to do when that happens?"

"I got it. Just get it on us."

I swallow. I've already fought a monster. This can't possibly be as bad, right? I yank my blade out and throw it, aiming for the thing's eye. But it tilts its head at the perfect moment, and the blade smacks the hard bone around its neck and falls to the ground. It looks at me and snarls.

Well, it's paying attention to us now.

I step back as the beast abandons the boy and stalks toward me and Riley. "Okay, I did my part. This is where you do your bit." The monster picks up speed and rushes toward us. "Riley!" It's going too fast. "Fucking do something!"

"I got it," she says, her voice low and even.

A golden beam of light shoots from her chest, and the monster roars and reels back, using its paws to cover its eyes. Even I have to throw my hands up. Squinting, I realize that it isn't her chest glowing, it's that gaudy necklace she always wears. The one that doesn't fit her style.

She unclasps it, holding it in her hands, where it grows longer and thicker. The light fades, and she's holding a six-foot-long length of thick gold chain.

Before the monster can prepare, she whips it out, and it lengthens further and curls into a loop, wrapping around the thing's neck. The links glow. The beast howls and thrashes and bucks. And then it begins to shrink, smaller and smaller until it's a boy. No. Older than a boy but not a man, hunched over on his hands and knees, still bound by the chain.

He looks up, and I freeze.

"Jules?" My voice is small. Tiny. Insignificant.

Because I'm looking at my missing brother. Because the monster that rushed us, tried to *kill* us . . . is *Jules*.

His face crumples as he looks at me. All those sharp angles falling to ruin.

He snarls, fur bursts from his skin, and Riley's chain snaps. Monster once again, he turns and runs.

I drop to my knees.

My missing brother isn't missing after all.

And he might be a murderer.

# CHAPTER TWENTY-SEVEN

I keep playing the moment over and over in my head. The sight of that bearlike thing shifting and becoming my brother. Jules's sharp jaw and narrow eyes. It's the way he held his face so stiff and tight.

It was him.

He's a monster.

We got back to Riley's Lexus without seeing anyone else. The boy we'd dragged into the back seat was sweaty, bleeding, and near hyperventilating. I hadn't seen the wound on his side since Riley stripped off her jean jacket to put pressure on it. Understandably, she didn't have mental space for me. She ushered the boy into her house via the back door and told me it was best if I go. I made my way to Victoria Hall alone.

And now, the next day after classes as I'm walking toward McIntosh Castle, she finally texts me.

*There are two monsters, the one you saw at Big Sandy Bay and the one from last night, correct?*

Nothing about Jules.

*Yeah,* I reply.

And that's it.

I want to believe that Jules didn't kill Sammie. That he wouldn't have murdered that boy even without our intervention. But what proof do I have? He was failing out of school. He had time to leave a note. And the warnings he gave me . . . He was afraid. And he told me not to look for him. Is this why?

This isn't even getting into how he became a monster in the first place. He couldn't have been born that way like Virgil. I would have known. Wouldn't I? I mean, he was away for his first year, and he was struggling. It's possible he's one of those spontaneously born monsters without a bloodline, and that his turning was a surprise to him, too.

This changes everything.

I kept thinking that once I found Jules, I would disentangle myself from this whole thing. Drop out from the competition and school and go back to how things were. That's not possible anymore. Jules is in this. There's no way for him to stop being a monster. I don't know how to help him yet, but I do know I'll need a title. The power of it.

There's no quitting anymore. There's not even the option of skating by.

I have to *win.*

I barely notice when I reach the front door of McIntosh Castle. I stand there, thoughts whirling in my head.

Jules wouldn't choose to hurt people. I need to remember that a Master is almost definitely involved. No matter what he's done, it wasn't his fault. Someone must be forcing him. And they can't control him outside of his monster form, so they needed a different tactic.

That's why it attacked me. After all, I'm not in QBSS, so I wasn't a legitimate target. And even Virgil said the monster wasn't trying to kill me. It was a threat. And it worked. If I hadn't texted Jules, whoever is behind this probably would have told him. That's why Jules's note said I couldn't just leave Kingston. I have to stay here where I can be monitored. They're using me against him. Probably using Bailey and Dad, too.

The door opens, and I jerk away. Margot says, "Why are you just standing there?"

"Sorry . . . I . . ." She steps back, her brow furrowed, and I stumble in after her, swapping out my shoes for a pair of slides.

"Bring your shoes with you. You'll need them."

I follow her down the hall, carrying my sneakers as instructed.

She brings me through a door I've never paid much attention to that leads into a dark basement. The rafters are exposed and the lights hanging from them are dim. All the walls are the same stone on the exterior of the house and the concrete floor is shiny, like they smoothed lacquer over it.

Virgil is waiting there in the most casual outfit I've seen him in: a white golf shirt, *untucked,* and a pair of black basketball shorts.

There are a bunch of gym mats on the floor, which Margot walks over to. "Corey is finishing up a class, so she'll be by soon," she says. "In the meantime, you'll do some kickboxing drills with me, and then Virgil will be your moving target practice for your knives."

Once I've changed, put my shoes back on, and have my hands wrapped and in gloves, Margot runs me through the basics. I try

A MASTERY OF MONSTERS 283

to pay attention, but I'm picturing Jules's face. That pained way he looked at me.

What would Margot do if I told her? Tell Henry, most likely. And Henry might tell Adam. Maybe the society isn't paying much attention now, but once they have a name, will I just be making it easy for them? Say they lock up the Master partnered with Jules—what would happen to him? Would they pair him with someone else? Or put him in the Pen?

I just manage to dodge a punch from Margot. "Keep your guard up!" she says. "Move your feet more. Bouncing and staying light on them will help your speed."

I throw some wild punches that don't land. Then she comes back at me harder, and I'm stumbling on my feet trying to defend. I grunt as she catches me in the side and when I bend to block my body, a kick comes out of nowhere and sweeps my legs.

I fall with a hard *thump* on the mat.

"You didn't say we were doing kicks," I grumble, pushing to my feet.

Margot says, "It's *kick*boxing. Of course there are kicks."

She comes at me again, and again, and every time my defense is pathetic. When I do make my own offensive attempts, they fall short. I don't land a single hit, and the whole time I'm wondering where Jules is.

Margot grits her teeth and pulls off her gloves, shaking her head. "Knife throwing now. Get on your holsters."

I drag myself to my backpack and buckle the still too tight holsters onto my thighs.

Virgil pulls protective gear over his limbs and puts on a helmet. Margot straps a board with a target on it to his chest. "He's going to run around the room and move faster over time. Obviously, hit the target."

"Am I going to be throwing knives at people in the tests?"

"The first test will be some sort of navigation. We don't know what yet. Corey was dropped in a forest area. I got underground tunnels. And you may or may not need those skills for it. But yes, eventually, you will have to throw knives at people. Hand-to-hand combat is permissible by the second test. They add weapons in the third." She gestures to Virgil. "You run, and you"—a gesture to me—"stay in the center."

I expect him to jog around the small space; instead, Virgil moves at a near sprint, and I rush to throw a knife. I get one near the inner ring of the target. Then he speeds up. It's harder, but I manage another hit.

Then Virgil hits a speed that I can't fully comprehend. The instant I turn to him, he's already moving, and then I pivot, and he's gone again.

"Anticipate the movement!" Margot says.

I guess and throw, and the knife plinks off the wall. I try again without much success. Sweat drips down my forehead. I physically cannot move fast enough to both see him and throw accurately.

Finally, I run out of knives.

Margot claps her hands. "That's enough."

I hunch with my hands on my knees.

She says, "Do you know what I mean when I say anticipate his movement?"

"Somehow predict the future?"

"I mean stop and pay attention, and think with your brain. That entire time he was moving around in a predictable circle. All you had to do was wait for him to come around and throw. But you're not paying attention to anything. You're distracted. What's up with you?"

"Nothing."

Virgil's eyes dart from me to Margot and back. "Are you worried about the test?"

"No."

Margot mutters something under her breath and collects one of my knives from the floor, running her finger along the edge. "Sharp. That's good. But you'll need a new set. New holsters, too—you seem uncomfortable in those." She nods to Virgil. "You can ditch the protective gear."

"I don't need new knives." These are the ones Mom gave me. I don't want to go into these tests without them. Especially now that there's no exit plan. I'm in this, for real. *Fuck.*

"Yes, you do," Margot says. "Monster hides are tough. Only a few materials in the world can handle it."

"Mine are good!"

Virgil tosses off the last bit of gear. "I can get a test patch? We can see?" Before Margot agrees, he's pulling on a pair of slides and jogging up the stairs.

Once the door closes, she turns to me. "What's going on? You can tell me even if you don't want to tell Virgil. Or I can leave, and you can tell him if you don't want to share it with me."

"Nothing is going on!" Virgil is a rule follower. Loyal almost to a fault. He would tell Henry about Jules too. They all would. I wish I could trust the psychology professor as much as they do, but I don't know him. I can't put Jules at risk. "I just need to pay more attention, like you said."

When Virgil returns, he's holding a furry thing in his hand. He accepts the knife from Margot. She scowls. "It's not going to—"

He stabs the center and the fur splits.

It's a patch of a monster. Skin and fur in a neat square. "How did you get that?" I ask, my voice a whisper.

"It's collected. We need test patches to be sure of weapon strength. Your knives are good. I'm surprised . . ." He keeps talking about the quality of my blades, but I've already drifted away.

*Collected.*

Meaning, taken from a monster. I bet anything from the ones in the Pen. They went in there with a Doctorate, carved a neat square of flesh, and handed them out for testing.

That could be Virgil.

That could be *Jules.*

"Are you listening?" Margot asks. I nod. I know she doesn't believe me, but she continues, "You can't do anything significant until you have the serum, but doing the exercises to get into sync with each other will be useful. Better to start early in expectation of making it to the initiation."

Virgil reaches out his hands and I awkwardly set mine on his like we did during the monster affinity prelim. He must have already handed off the test patch to Margot. I don't know why we're doing this in the middle of a physical training session. He closes his eyes, so I close mine too. We're probably matching breaths again.

I should have gotten Greg or whatever's number so I could ask him more about how Jules had been. In February, he'd gotten that invitation, left QBSS, and then tried to rejoin. When I saw him this summer, he'd seemed fine, but his room was messier than usual, and apparently, he was on academic probation. Then, after

A MASTERY OF MONSTERS                    287

the Big Sandy Bay thing, he disappeared with that warning note.

I don't think it's far-fetched to link the monster at Big Sandy Bay, Jules, these invitations, and QBSS together. The trouble is figuring out what the links are. And why this stuff with Jules started in February but nothing popped off until months later.

"August, concentrate," Margot says.

Virgil keeps shifting around, which isn't helping with this breath-matching thing.

"*August*," Margot says again.

"I'm trying," I reply.

"Then why aren't you moving?"

I open my eyes. "Why would I be moving?"

Margot stares at me for a long moment. "I'm out. Deal with your shit and come back later. If I stay here a second longer, I'm going to lose it."

I stare slack-jawed as she gathers her stuff and stomps up the stairs, nearly running into Corey, who's coming down. Corey looks after Margot and then at us. She shakes it off and smiles. "I think I've had a breakthrough with Dr. Weiss's journal. I found this contact—"

"The exercise we were supposed to be doing was matching motions," Virgil says to me. "To help us sync movement. Which you would have heard if you were paying attention. You know, so you can develop techniques to keep me from ripping you apart during the initiation."

His tone is light, but the words are cutting. Virgil is the sort of person who holds on to his anger and releases it in sharp, passive-aggressive bursts. Possibly because overt aggression, as a monster, would make his life difficult.

I say, "Why are we even doing this now? I'm three tests away from initiation."

"Maybe because you weren't paying enough attention to physically train properly, so Margot was attempting to give you a break to be nice to you? Like she's putting in effort while you're apparently daydreaming?"

"I wasn't daydream—"

"Do you understand the seriousness of this? We need to have affinity in order to connect during initiation. Seriously, what is going on with you? If you tell us, then we can help instead of wasting time."

I could. I could tell him.

But then I think of Riley. She knew me from my brother this whole time. And then Virgil just happened to see me throw my knife at that guy? Was that really a coincidence? Or was it planned somehow? Is he keeping something from me?

I don't know these people.

What if me and my brother are pawns in a bigger game? In whatever Henry and Margot were talking about at that meeting.

Virgil's parents were monsters who killed people. They weren't sent to the Pen; they were murdered.

If Jules killed anyone, even if it wasn't by choice, it doesn't change the facts.

"Nothing is wrong," I say.

Virgil shakes his head. "Fine. I think we're done for the day."

I leave, walking past Corey, who stands with her head down. I know she said something about Dr. Weiss's journals, but I don't have the capacity to get into any of it.

I just want to leave.

A MASTERY OF MONSTERS

# CHAPTER TWENTY-EIGHT

The barn we're supposed to be using for this community dinner needs a lot more work than Mia advertised. It's big enough to hold maybe thirty people comfortably, and the ceiling is high, which is great, but it's also dusty and full of cobwebs, and it smells like it's recently had animals in it even though Mia insists that it hasn't for decades.

Mia says, "It had cows when Grandma was a girl, but not since she's owned it. And definitely not since we took over the property. Not yet, anyway. Mom's going to get chickens soon. We just have to build the coop. We have a lot of plans for the community." She wrinkles her nose. "Even though our plans don't always match up."

"In what way?"

She clears her throat. "Uh, you know, just, like, I'd prefer goats."

I laugh. "Okay . . . That's cool, though. Living here and making plans for the space. I mean, it's your people's land to begin with, isn't it?"

She nods. "We're back to being its stewards. Protecting the land and taking care of it so that seven generations from now, they have something better. Ideally, everyone would do that."

"Honestly, I don't even know if we'll still be here in seven generations with how things are going."

"That's kind of the problem."

Mia hands me a push broom, and I get to work on sweeping the floor. It's not my idea of a fun afternoon, but it's better than dealing with Virgil or Margot. Especially after what went down at McIntosh Castle earlier today.

"I'm gonna get more supplies." Mia leaves the barn, and I stare around the space.

There's no way we're going to be able to clean everything today by ourselves.

When the door opens again fifteen minutes later, I'm ready to tell her that we need to reassess what we can accomplish in an afternoon and evening when Virgil and Isaac walk in.

"What are you doing here?" I ask.

Mia pops out behind them. "Virgil said he would help, remember? And Isaac is helping too." She beams at the younger boy, whose expression becomes so sappy that I have to look away.

"Also, Margot has an evening class, so I said I would drive Isaac," Virgil adds.

Mia hands him a dustpan. "You and August can work as a team. She sweeps, and you dustpan. Me and Isaac will mop. I think we can clean the floor today, and I have a couple of poles that you can put a cloth on the ends of and extend them to reach the ceiling.

Me and Virgil work in silence while Mia and Isaac talk about some show they both watch.

A MASTERY OF MONSTERS

"Are you worried about the community dinner?" Virgil asks.

"No."

"Having trouble with schoolwork?"

"No."

"Family?"

"Stop trying to guess," I say. "I'm fine. Everything is fine."

I take out my phone again, but there's nothing from Riley. I texted her to get more information about how Jules acted when he was in QBSS, wondering if that would give me any clues about how he ended up the way he is. Also, to remind her that I hadn't forgotten about her shiny chain thing that made Jules revert to human form in the first place. Obviously, there's something deeper going on in her organization.

I have to figure out the Jules stuff without letting anyone in the society know, so she's the only source of information I have. I still think there could be a political component because of the timing of when Sammie was killed, but how is that linked to the QBSS stuff?

Jules must have been so confused and alone. When that invitation came, he would have gone. He couldn't have known things would go down like this.

"What's going on?" Virgil asks.

If the society knows about Jules, they'll put him underground. They haven't stopped that other monster yet, so why would they do it now? Meaning the deranged Easter Bunny and its partner will remain free. If Jules obeying whoever is controlling him is what's keeping me, Bailey, and Dad safe, what will happen if Jules is captured? Will it leave us alone or go after us as some sort of revenge for Jules failing them? I can take care of me, but I don't know that I can protect Dad and Bailey at the same time. It's not just bad for Jules. This is a shitty situation for us all.

"Please," Virgil says. "Tell me. I can help."

"How?! How can you help? You're part of a society that doesn't even see you as human. That would chop off little pieces of you to give out so others can test stabbing it."

He flinches. "They only do it to monsters with regeneration abilities."

"But it hurts, doesn't it? Or do they give them anesthesia?"

Virgil runs his hand over his head. "Look, I told you I would help, didn't I? I know I can't do anything society-wise right now. But that doesn't mean we have to do nothing. Tell me what you want me to do, and I'll help."

"I just want to find him." It sounds hollow even to my ears.

"We will."

Yes, we will. I already have. The problem now is how to save him. Especially since, while in human form, Jules is committed to avoiding help to protect me and our family, and in monster form, he's under the control of this Master. The only real solution is finding out who the Master is and dealing with them. Or *Masters*, since there are two monsters, and we've already decided Wilds are unlikely to be involved. Unless one Master can be bonded to multiple monsters. No one's ever talked about it, and I've only ever met pairs, not trios.

"Random question for you," I say, and Virgil perks up.

I swallow, hoping he won't read too much into this. "Can one Master ever be bonded to multiple monsters at once?"

His brow furrows. "It's not impossible, but it is—"

"If you say improbable, I'm going to scream."

". . . Unlikely. Some tests were done to explore that possibility. After all, it would be useful. But it created an imbalance of power. The Master's body would begin to break down, followed by their

A MASTERY OF MONSTERS

minds. They struggled to manage the abilities of both partners, and the partners in turn tended to have less control of themselves while in monster form. There have been a couple of rare cases of people who pulled it off, but it's so risky that it's not often attempted. You also need Doctorate approval, and in most situations, they have declined. It's why the Doctorate's ability is so impressive, beyond not having to bond with a monster to share control."

The question of why I'm asking this lingers in the air, and I ignore it, returning to sweeping. Thankfully, Virgil doesn't push me on it. And now I know that we're looking for two Masters. It's the more likely scenario.

We're able to finish cleaning the floors, and Mia sets Virgil and Isaac to using her extender poles to get at the ceiling. They set up a few ladders, with one spotting and holding the base, and the other doing the cobweb cleaning.

"What's up with you and Virgil?" Mia asks.

"I don't have the patience for this today."

"No, I mean, I know you're not dating or whatever. But you guys are weird today."

I shrug.

Mia shakes her head before surveying our work. "This is going to be good. It'll finally feel like this community means something, you know?"

"I guess so."

"You don't want to belong to anything, do you?"

I jerk my head toward Mia. "What?"

"I don't get it." She tilts her head to the side. "You have a family, and you avoid them. You have friends, and you're weird with them. Like, do you want to be on your own?"

"Why are you even bringing this up?"

"Because I don't understand it. And I guess I'm asking if you just don't think you belong anywhere." She waves around at the barn. "Because you can belong here, you know? That's the point of doing this."

Before, everything was different. I was a different person. I wanted different things. Now, I don't want to be that person anymore. I don't want to be anything. I just want to help my brother.

But also . . . I don't want to be part of the society. I don't want to be at Queen's. I don't want to be part of QBSS, either. And yeah, maybe I don't want to be part of my family. Because it's never just enough to exist. Everything comes with expectations, and rules, and pressure.

Then again, there's also what Bailey said. That I didn't have to care about what she expects. That I could just care about what I want. An echo of what Jules has been saying to me for years. And I know so many things that I don't want, but when it comes to what I *do* want . . . that's a lot harder.

"Isn't this a little too deep for a fifteen-year-old?" I say instead of answering her question.

Mia rolls her eyes. "Whatever, it's your life. I don't get it, but you do you."

The door to the barn opens, and Jacques enters, eyes darting around and lips pressing into a line. Mia's dad is huge. Like, he has to be at least 6'5", and he's built like a lumberjack and kind of looks like one too, with his brunette beard speckled with gray and ginger hairs.

He clears his throat. "I'm Jacques, Mia's dad. I thought I saw you kids coming in here." He looks directly at Mia then, and she

A MASTERY OF MONSTERS                                                      295

hunches her shoulders. Usually, Jacques is laid-back. He's anything but now, standing stiff in the doorway.

"Yup," Mia says, without any elaboration.

I look at Jacques and then at Mia, who avoids my gaze, and back again.

"And you are?" Jacques asks Isaac, who spends about a minute stumbling over his words to introduce himself, followed by a handshake in which Jacques's hand basically engulfs the boy's.

"Isaac works at that antiques place downtown," Mia supplies.

"The fancy one?"

"No, the cheap one."

Jacques nods in a sort of approval, then turns to Virgil. His gaze is somehow more intense for him than Isaac. There's a sort of sizing up.

Mia says, "That's Virgil. He's August's—" I give her a pointed look. She better not say some bullshit. "*Friend,*" she finishes with a grin.

Jacques offers Virgil a handshake that goes on a touch too long. Even Virgil notices, from the quick *what the fuck* glance he throws my way. Like I know. Jacques never struck me as the sort of alpha male type who would be aggro with his daughter's male friends, but I guess I don't know him that well.

"And what are you kids doing in the barn?" Jacques asks.

"Just cleaning up," Mia says.

"That's thoughtful." Jacques's smile is tight. "And altruistic. I didn't know you cared that much about the barn."

My mouth drops open. "Does he not know what we're cleaning the barn for?"

Mia makes a sound in the back of her throat.

I'm starting to think that when she discussed her parents' plans not matching up with hers, she didn't mean goats vs. chickens like she said.

Isaac's and Virgil's eyes dart from her to her dad, to me, and then start the cycle again.

Jacques blows a breath out of his nose. "Your mom and I spoke to you about this. We don't want to force people to—"

"Okay! But they might be into it, and we're not even using the barn for anything! And I've already started planning about furniture and stuff. I have allowance saved, and Grandad gave me birthday money. I can do it."

"That's not the point!" Jacques says, and I jump from the bass in his voice. "We said no."

The skin around Mia's eyes is tight. Shit, I hope she doesn't cry right now.

I should say nothing. Don't get involved. It's better for me anyway. This event will get canceled, and I already have my sharp knives.

Keep quiet, August.

Don't say a fucking word.

"We're just going to ask people if they want to participate," I tell Jacques. "Isn't it good if everyone who lives here gets to know each other better?" I feel Mia's gaze on me, which I ignore. "Mia's already done a bunch of work and even spent her own money. I don't see the harm in it. It could be nice. And if they say no, they say no. But I think a lot of people will like it."

Jacques regards me for a moment like he's only just meeting me. "Izzy and I—"

"Izzy's always trying to get me and Bailey to do stuff with her. It kind of seems like maybe she'd like this too. If the only hesitation is bugging people, we won't. We'll just see what they think. You two

A MASTERY OF MONSTERS                                      297

haven't even asked around. Maybe the community wants this too."

Jacques scratches his beard and then looks at his daughter's face. This girl pops out her lower lip without an ounce of shame. I have to respect it. Her dad groans. "Okay, okay. You can ask, but if people say no, I don't want to hear about you pestering them."

"We won't!" Mia is positively beaming.

Jacques nods, throwing one last searching look at all of us before he leaves.

Mia turns to me. "You were actually helpful!"

"Wow, thanks."

"August Black," Virgil says, a grin spreading across his lips. "Secret softie."

I hold up a hand. "Okay, no."

I resent the idea of being secretly soft, but I can be nice sometimes. Especially to the girl who sharpens my knives.

We finish cleaning and I get a ride from Virgil. I slouch in the back while Isaac asks for advice. Apparently, he saw them setting up a corn maze on the island, and he wants to ask Mia to go with him. I tune them out and only tune back in when Virgil's dropping me off at Victoria Hall.

"I mean it," he says as I go for the door. "I want to help."

It's reminiscent of Bailey dropping me off at the dock, and again in my dorm room with her box of pictures, and plant, and spirit wear.

"Yeah, I'll let you know when I figure out what I want to do."

It's a lie, but he doesn't know that.

Secret softie. Yeah, right.

# CHAPTER TWENTY-NINE

Riley doesn't look surprised to see me on her doorstep later that week. She just backtracks into her home and leaves the door open. It's different inside during the day without the partygoers. Similarly to Sammie's house, there's an assortment of shoes in the entryway, but they're neatly tucked into built-in compartments.

Riley leads me into the living area where I take a seat on the couch. There are two huge windows that overlook a small private garden in a side yard.

"Coffee?" she asks.

"Sure." I rub my eyes, which have been drifting closed all day, only to be forced back open. I spent most of the night pouring over Jules's invitation again, trying to find clues in the wording. I even held a flame under it, hoping to reveal hidden ink. There was nothing.

Riley goes over to an elaborate coffee station with a professional espresso machine, syrup pumps, matching white mugs, and shakers of labeled powders.

"Did you know my brother was a monster?" I ask.

"That's a complicated question. Do you like foam? How much espresso?"

"What does that mean?"

Riley turns to me. "Like, what do you want? A latte? Macchiato? Cappuccino?"

"A latte, whatever."

"Yeah, okay, get mouthy like I'm not making you a drink," she says. "Concerning your brother, anything was possible. I cared more about whether he was a victim or a perpetrator."

"Those aren't mutually exclusive."

"No, I guess not if Masters are involved." The machine hums. Apparently even expensive things are noisy. "Hot or iced?"

"Hot. If he had anything to do with Sammie, it wasn't by choice. My brother isn't like that."

He just needs help. This isn't like Mom. I won't be groping in the dark for months only to come up with nothing. I can get my brother back.

"But he had enough autonomy to write a goodbye note," Riley says. "Flavoring?"

"Surprise me." I stand from the couch. "I don't know what to say to you. He got the same invitation as Sammie and that boy. I'm sorry she died. I don't know why they got to liv—"

"He's dead," Riley says, her back still turned and working on the coffee.

I walk to the kitchen island, gripping the edge of the marble top. *"What?"*

"The guy we followed. Jacob. He was bitten. He died from it the same night." She sticks a mug under the machine, pouring milk into a separate metal canister and heating it. "Of course, that meant I needed help, so now everything's kind of fallen to shit. But your brother, he's alive and well."

"What are you trying to say?"

"It's suspicious, is all."

"You know what's suspicious? Your magic powers, which I assume you got from an artifact that you conveniently never mentioned."

The chain is back on her neck, looking out of place as usual. I expected the artifacts Joseph Lawrence had to be statues or something. Not jewelry. But what she did looked enough like magic that I can make the connection. I know I said I'd have to see it to believe it, but I never thought I would be seeing it.

She says, "The artifacts aren't any of your business. They were gifts from our founder."

"Stolen gifts."

Riley laughs and turns back to me, neglecting the steaming milk. "Wow, they got to you, eh? That organization was created by a white man, and yet you're looking at our Black society and think we stole shit from *them*? Because that's historically how that goes, isn't it?"

I swallow. I want to argue. To say that Joseph Lawrence is a traitor, but I don't actually know that.

"Here's something your little society won't tell you. Sure, Edward Weiss made space for people of color—celebrated them, even, which is a fuck ton more than a lot of white people did during his time—but only so long as they did what he wanted. And when Joseph Lawrence decided to think for himself, he was dead to dear old Eddie."

A MASTERY OF MONSTERS  301

She shakes her head and grabs my mug, pumping flavor into the coffee and stirring it around. She drops the milk and foam on top and sprinkles a delicate dusting of chocolate shavings on it. She slides the drink across the island to me.

"Thanks." I take a sip. It's good, because of course it is. "The monsters are looking for the artifacts, aren't they? It's the only reason they would be targeting QBSS."

"Ding ding."

"What exactly are these artifacts? No matter what you think, Jules doesn't know anything about this stuff. It has to be the Master who wants them. But why?"

"Incorrect. Jules does know about them, which is exactly why he was targeted. Sammie knew, and Jacob knew too. Specifically, they know some of the locations where we hide artifacts. Ones that aren't meant to be used day-to-day like my chain. And if they'd made it to the next stage, they would have earned their own artifact." I open my mouth, and she raises a finger. "Before you ask, I have no idea which one this person is looking for or why. If they wanted a weapon, they could take it from us. Kill people who are using the artifacts and steal them. Easy enough to spot because of that inane trend of putting gold in their mouths."

I gape. "That's what that is?!"

She sighs. "People who hold artifacts are required to donate bone to show their commitment. Historics like myself—" At my confused look, Riley adds, "People who have had at least three generations of QBSS members. We know to save our baby teeth. But people whose family weren't members typically don't have that information. They get a fresh tooth pulled, and someone started a trend of capping the fake replacement with gold in honor of the artifacts, which are all cast in the same metal." She adds in a wry tone, "Even some Historics have taken up the trend. It looks cool, but it's not exactly inconspicuous."

I shake my head. "What is up with these societies and cutting off pieces of your body?"

"As I was saying, if they wanted a weapon, they'd have their pick. But that clearly isn't the aim. They want something specific. But they're also not very smart. We would never tell newbies about the locations or existence of the powerful artifacts."

"You can't rattle a few and their abilities off? Maybe it'll spark an idea. Or something you might have missed that I could catch."

She peers at me. "Did you not hear me say we don't even tell newbies that? I would be happy to tell you at least what they get to know if you were a member."

I snort. "I thought you didn't want me because I'm part of the society?"

"I've reconsidered. It could be helpful to have an insider. A mole, if you will. Also, I've been told that I need to get you to join."

"Excuse me?"

"The president is now aware that you exist, that I brought you into this, and that the monster who bit and, perhaps inadvertently, but still very much killed a member, is your brother."

I rear back from the island. "You told him about Jules?!"

She slams her palms on the island. "No, Jacob told him before he fucking died!"

I take a big gulp of the coffee and end up with a scalded tongue. "You need me to join to cover your ass."

"I think you owe me that much. We found your brother, didn't we?" She narrows her eyes. "And he killed my best friend."

A MASTERY OF MONSTERS

"You don't know that. There are two monsters," I say. "He hadn't even run away when Sammie was murdered."

"Fine. He's only killed one person. Is that better?"

It's cramped suddenly. In the space. In my head. Everywhere. It was bad enough to get boxed into the candidacy process and school. I spent so much time and effort smashing my way out of these tight spaces of crushing expectation. Clawing to freedom, just to be folded back in like this.

"No," I say. "I'm not joining."

"Don't be a child. What do you think the Learners will do when they find out your brother is running wild like that? You think they'll protect him or you? We'll have your back."

"But only if I do what *you* say, right?"

"Do you think this is a game?!" Riley's voice is high and scattered. "Fuck! You're just like her. You would rather self-destruct than deal with a little hardship. What do you think is waiting for you on their side? I really want to know. Have those people actually done anything to help you? Because I know they haven't done more than I have. But the second I ask you for something, you couldn't care less."

"I'm leaving." I turn to the front door.

"Yeah, that's what I thought. Go! I'll be right here to say I told you so when you come back."

I stop and look at her over my shoulder. "How did that work out with Sammie? Did you get to say I told you so?"

Riley's eyes water. "Get the fuck out of my house!"

"It's your parents' house!" I slam the front door behind me when I leave. Then I open it and slam it again, just to feel it.

In a university town, Thirsty Thursdays can be as busy as going out on a weekend. There's some sort of theme running at Ale

House tonight, though I don't pay attention to it as I attach myself to a group of girls and flash my stolen ID. The bouncer asks us what we're dressed as, and the girls rattle off names of singers that I vaguely recognize. Eighties or nineties, I don't know. But they supply a bunch of people who I could maybe be, and I roll with it.

The floor is sticky, stale sweat is the scent du jour, and the strobe lights make all my movements look out of sync.

I'm four doubles deep in five minutes. It might be a record.

I don't have my job anymore, but I do have the credit card I was given for school and society-based purchases.

On the dance floor, I close my eyes and get lost in the music. My head empties and whenever a thought about Jules or Riley or Virgil comes up, I focus on the song instead. I sing though no one can hear me, the power of the speakers drowning us all out.

Here, I don't have a dad who doesn't care about me. I don't have a missing mom. I don't have a monstrous and murderous brother. It's just me. Me, myself, and I.

The great thing about ruining your life is that when it's ruined, there's nothing else to lose. No one else to disappoint. No way to fail.

So maybe Mia is right. I don't want to belong. Belonging is overrated. Belonging to the society got Virgil treated like less than human his entire life and got Corey thrown into a traumatic competition that destroyed her relationship with her family. Belonging to QBSS is how Riley lost her best friend. Belonging to my family is how I ended up here in the first place. How I lost Mom. Lost Dad another way. And now, thanks to trying to help Jules, here I am.

I'm eight doubles in when someone pulls at my shirt. I ignore it the first time. The crowd's gotten bigger, and I assume someone brushed against me.

A MASTERY OF MONSTERS

The second time the tug comes with an annoyingly persistent buzz that sounds a lot like my name.

I open my eyes.

Corey is there, looking distinctly out of place in her wide-leg trousers and trench coat. "August! Let's go."

I jerk my arm away. "I'm dancing."

She sighs and looks around the room, rubbing her arms like she isn't wearing a literal jacket. "Let me take you back to Vic Hall, okay?"

"I'm not going anywhere."

"Can you stop being so selfish for a minute?!" She falters and flushes. "I'm sorry, I—"

"I am selfish," I say because it's true. "I don't care, and I'm sorry you didn't realize that before. You should go."

Corey glances over her shoulder and groans as Virgil stomps into the club with a bouncer by his side.

That fucking narc.

The bouncer asks for my ID, and even when I tell him I'll just leave, insists upon seeing it, blocking my path out. Corey and Virgil hover as the man checks it and then looks at me. "You have another piece of ID to confirm this name?"

I press my lips into a line.

"I'm confiscating this."

I head to the exit without even bothering to argue. To my immense displeasure, Virgil and Corey follow me out.

It's colder now that it's late. I shiver and clutch my arms.

A coat drops onto my shoulders. Virgil stands next to me in just a sweater. I hold the jacket to my body and continue my walk back to the dorms without saying anything. I go through the side entrance,

306                                    LISELLE SAMBURY

like when Jules came and got me a couple of months ago, and use my student ID to swipe in.

A couple of months. That's how long it's been. It's too short.

When we reach my room, I flop down on my bed. The motion churns my stomach and I have just enough time to grab my trash bin before I puke into it.

Corey rushes to gather my braids and holds them out of the way, acquiring a scrunchie from somewhere that she uses to pull them into a ponytail. I expect that it's harder for her to do with the missing fingers, but she manages it like a skill well practiced.

I'm staring into the trash can at the mess and bracing myself for another bout as Virgil squats in front of my face. "After our conversation in the barn, I went to Henry and begged him to help us find some way to do more to find your brother. Not for the first time, either. No luck, but I figured maybe we could brainstorm something together. So today, I'm calling and texting you and getting nothing. Corey is worried, Margot is worried, and then Henry lets us know that your credit card is being used at a nightclub."

I assume I'm not supposed to say anything, so I don't.

"This is my fault," Virgil says. "I should have never believed in you. Then I wouldn't be disappointed. I know that now."

"Couldn't have said it better myself." Virgil stands, and I don't need to watch to know he's left the room. Corey brings over a water bottle, which I drink from. "Aren't you going too?"

"Why would I leave a friend alone like this?"

"We aren't friends."

Corey's eyes widen for a moment, and she stares at the ground. "If you want me to go, you can just say that. You don't have to try to hurt me."

"Then go."

I think she's gone until she speaks again, and I realize she was still hovering in the room. Silent. "You know . . . I put up with a lot of shit. And I know I shouldn't. That's how I got in that mess with the candidacy in the first place, because I just did what my parents wanted. Then I had Virgil, and I never wanted to lose him. And before I knew it, I was doing it again. Even though he always tells me not to. Virgil puts up with shit too. All the time. But when I met you, I thought, wow, this is a girl who does what she wants. I admired that about you. But you know what?"

"I assume you're going to tell me."

"You think what you're doing is not putting up with shit or being your most authentic self or whatever, but actually, you just don't care about anyone else. I'm here in the middle of the night trying to help you. But what have you ever done for me? We're not friends? Yeah, I guess we aren't. Because you didn't care that I had this breakthrough with the journal, and I'm sure you don't care that it turned out to be fake, and it doesn't even matter about Henry and his group and getting in by finding the journal because you're going to be the reason my actual best friend is locked underground for the rest of his life."

I wipe my mouth and transition to sitting on the bed. I wish Corey would leave.

She looks down at me. "No one would have blamed you for failing. We just wanted you to try."

"Are you glad you tried?" Maybe I shouldn't have said it. But Corey lost more than just half a leg and some fingers in that competition. She lost her family, too. She made so many sacrifices, and for what?

"Glad? No. But when I made the decision to save my brother, I stuck by it. I can see that we're two very different people." She picks up the water bottle and puts it on my bedside table before gathering the plastic bag of puke from the trash and putting a new bag in my bin. "Sleep on your side so you don't choke and die." She leaves with the bag of vomit.

I wait until I'm sure she's gone before I let myself cry.

# CHAPTER THIRTY

I wake to water being splashed in my face.

Margot stands over me. Clearly making use of the spare key that Henry insisted be given to her to help mind me. "Shower."

Whether it's because I'm confused, drowsy, used to listening to her, or all three, I drag myself out of bed and across the hall to the shower room. Margot orders a cold shower to help wake me up, but I take a hot one, because absolutely not. I brush my teeth and get dressed in a pair of sweatpants and an oversized T-shirt.

Margot presents me with a green smoothie, which looks like it would taste terrible but is delicious, along with a plate of chicken in some sort of sauce with rice. I devour both.

It's only when we're in her car that I realize it's nighttime again. I slept through a full day of classes and dinner.

"Those are for you," she says, motioning to the Gatorade bottles on the floor of the passenger seat. "Since you're so good at chugging drinks you shouldn't have any problems getting two down. Now."

I roll my eyes but obey.

I think of Jules, leaning against his desk with his arms crossed, asking me if I was happy living my life like this. Jules, his voice in that note, telling me not to look for him. Jules, in the forest wrapped in Riley's chain, staring at me like I'd caught him the in the worst moment and all he wanted was for me to turn away.

Dancing and drinking were great solutions when I needed to forget.

But I can't just forget anymore.

Every memory is sharp-edged, leaving tiny cuts on my skin that burn as if they were larger wounds. Corey's words echo in my head. She did everything she could to save a brother she didn't even have a good relationship with. I'm involved in this shit in the first place for Jules, and when I'm supposed to be working harder to make it through this competition, I got drunk, and now I'm hungover for the first test.

Turns out, it's easy to fuck up, and harder to stop doing it.

There's no escaping this. The plan had been that when I found Jules, I could back out. But now, finding him means the opposite. I'm in this, fully. I need some sort of foothold in this society, and this competition is my only way to get it.

At McIntosh Castle, we pick up Corey and Virgil, who say nothing as Margot drives to the ferry dock and we travel to Wolfe Island.

When we pull around the corner, I see the sign for a local farm and immediately know. Margot said the first test would involve navigation. "Corn maze," I say.

Margot presses her lips into a line. "I don't suppose you know anything about dealing with mazes?"

I don't dignify it with a response.

"Put your right hand on the right wall and follow it," Corey says

A MASTERY OF MONSTERS

without looking at me. "I read that once. But that's to get out. If you have to make it to the center, you'll need to visualize a mental map."

The Gatorade is helping with the dry, crusty feeling in my mouth, but my head feels like it weighs a hundred pounds. I couldn't possibly sleep more, but I desperately want to lie down.

Margot glances at me. "You need to get your shit together. The tests aren't like the trainings. You can get seriously injured. You're lucky the first one has the least risk."

"Didn't know you cared."

"You have a brother out there. An aunt. A dad. A mom. Don't you think they would care if you didn't make it out of this? It's a privilege to have that much."

Again, I say nothing.

We arrive at the parking lot and walk through to the maze. It's too large to see the full scope of it from anywhere on the ground. I know that sometimes they'll cut the corn into a specific shape or leave it as a giant square, and there's no way for me to tell from the tall green stalks.

The other candidates are limbering up for the competition, while a crowd of spectators sit in stands in front of mounted projector screens. I forgot about that. The trainings were mostly unattended, but any student is allowed to watch the tests. There's a more exclusive area at the top featuring armchairs with cupholders, including a small private box where the three Doctorate candidates sit along with Henry and a few others.

I should warm up with my fellow candidates, but instead I'm looking for a bathroom, partially because I needed to pee after drinking all the Gatorade, and partially because I think I might throw up a bunch of the sports drink.

I find the portable bathroom quickly. It's one of those fancy ones set up like a real public bathroom instead of a porta-potty, with sinks and separate stalls. When I get in, I do both pee and throw up. Through the second part is a lot less violent than last night and is more spit than anything.

*Fuck.* I shouldn't have gone out. It's the first time I've ever had that thought. Before, it didn't matter. Nothing mattered. Now . . . I force myself to take a deep breath and flush.

When I come out of the stall, there's a Black woman at the sink, reapplying lipstick. She turns to me with a smile. Natalie. The Pro-Lib leader. "Feeling better, I hope?" she asks.

"Yeah." I rinse my mouth out at the sink. A mint tin appears in my peripheral vision.

"Want one?"

"Thanks . . ." I take the mint and pop it in my mouth. I doubt the woman would try to poison me. What would be the point?

"That boy you're paired with," she says. "Hawthorne, right? Is he who you're fighting for?"

"I'm fighting for the title. Everyone is."

"Of course." Natalie tilts her head to the side. "But you're also battling for someone. There's a person on your mind. I can always spot that sort of candidate. You fight harder. And you lose harder too. It crushes you." She snaps her mint tin closed. "I had someone to fight for once. And he was taken away. I hope you won't suffer the same fate." She walks to the door of the portable without waiting for me to respond. "Break a leg!"

"You say that for performances."

She smiles. "I know."

I stay standing there for a few more moments. What is this

A MASTERY OF MONSTERS

woman's angle? I can't tell if she was saying cryptic shit to mess with me, threatening me, or just honestly wishing me luck.

When I come out of the bathroom, I barely have time to stretch before a sharp whistle blows and the candidates are being called to where the professors stand.

"Good luck." Virgil's voice is so low that I almost miss it. And when I turn around, he's already heading into the stands with Corey and Margot.

I gather with the others and look at the second portable not marked with a bathroom symbol. I assume that's where this panel of Masters is watching on video screens or something. They aren't in the stands. I assume if they were, there would be some special way to tell them apart, like the Doctorate's box.

According to Corey, a lot of them come to campus ahead of time. Could someone have been here early enough in the year to have sent Jules and Sammie those invitations?

Perez speaks into a microphone. "Welcome to the first test of this year's Bachelor candidacy. As you can see, it is a maze. Candidates will navigate to the center, where you'll take the bag with your name on it and a corresponding symbol. You must go through the maze and collect tokens. There are ten stations. You cannot gather tokens until you have your bag, and you can only take one token from each station. The player who exits the maze the fastest with the highest number of tokens matching the symbol on their bag will place first and be given a score of ten. Ranking to follow will be based on token amount and then on time, with second place getting five points, third place four points, and so on until it hits zero. Anyone ranking below will pass but receive no points.

"Candidates who break any of the stated rules will be disqualified.

314                                    LISELLE SAMBURY

Candidates who fail to collect at least five tokens or do not exit the maze in an hour will be disqualified. No physical contact with other candidates is allowed. This will also result in disqualification. As will false starts. Go on the long whistle only. You will hear horns marking the halfway point, five minutes left, and one minute left."

This doesn't sound that bad. There's ten stations, and you only have to get five tokens. I just need to find five as fast as possible and get out. Though there are the votes from the panel to consider. Maybe going for all ten would gain me enough favor for one to consider giving me a point at the end. But then again, they may already be planning to vote based on faction loyalty, even though they're not supposed to.

"Lastly," Perez says, "you may exit anywhere in the maze. However, if you can find your way back to your starting point and solve a puzzle, you'll get a bonus token. Therefore, eleven is actually the maximum number of tokens you can collect."

That would be a waste of time. The maze will be hard enough on its own, but with Corey's trick, I can exit wherever I want. The bonus could edge me into first place, since the tokens are worth more than finishing faster. But it might take too long to find my way back, and there's no guarantee that I can solve the puzzle. I should go for five tokens, assess where my exit is, and see what extra tokens I can manage nearby. Then at the five-minute mark, leave.

I'm led to an edge of the maze with half the candidates while the other half are taken to the opposite side. There are separate entrances for all of us. Unfortunately, mine is right next to Caden, who I ignore.

There are two short whistles; my toe twitches, but I don't move. And then the long whistle.

A MASTERY OF MONSTERS

I run into the maze, and my head rushes and swims. For a moment, I'm sure I'll throw up, but then I recover. The darkness obscures the corn, making it feel like I'm in a crowd of swaying people instead of crops. The leaves press me in on the already narrow path. The wind is crisp, making me wish I had gone for a sweatshirt instead of the T-shirt.

I remind myself of Corey's advice and slow down enough that I can think a bit more. There are supposed to be stations. I can't grab tokens until I have the bag, but if I note any that I pass, I can backtrack later. If there are at least five on the way to the center, I'm golden.

When I find the first station, which is little more than a patio stone on the ground with a swirl symbol on it, I grin.

Though my smile shrinks as I get deeper into the maze without finding any more.

I stop and shut my eyes, ignoring the rustling of the corn and the thumping sound of candidates running so I can try to cobble together this mental map. I entered on the left side of the maze, so I ran forward and was trying to stay straight to get to the center of the maze. I have to eventually reach it.

"Trust the process," I say to myself and keep moving forward and glancing down intermittently for any more patio stones.

This place has to be huge, because the sounds of running have died off now, like we've all gotten farther away from each other. Even though, if we're each heading to the center, we should be getting closer.

Overhead, drones whir as they broadcast our progress.

I make another turn to the left and stumble into a clearing.

*I did it! I actually did it.*

A horn blares, signaling that half the time has passed.

There's a wooden table in the middle, and when I run to get my pouch, six are missing. Shit. Meaning that out of fifteen, I'm currently in seventh place, and there's only thirty minutes left. I grab the blue bag with my name and a water drop symbol embroidered on it.

The problem is that I didn't pass by five stations on my way here, only one. I have to go a different way to get more.

With a sigh, I run down the next path over, hoping that maybe it'll end up close to my exit. Logically, I know I'll have to map my way down this path and come back to the center. But that wastes time. Ideally, I would find a way to connect back to mine if I want that bonus.

I can't think about any of that right now.

I race down one path, trying to keep the pattern in my mind and find one of the patio stones. I crouch and lift it, revealing a dug-out bit of earth with an open wooden box inside, filled with small circular tokens. I find one with my matching water drop and put it in my bag.

I get lucky, and down the same stretch, I spot another patio stone. This one is almost right in front of what I can see is an exit. But now, the exit has a small wooden box in front of it.

That must be our final task to do before we leave. But I know this isn't my exit, or . . . I think it isn't?

I abandon the patio stone momentarily and approach the box, which has a picture of a girl on it. I have no idea who she is, but then I pause—no . . . wait, I do. She was in the room when we heard about the first cut. But she's not a candidate, meaning she must be a monster. Then my box probably has Virgil's face on it.

That'll be handy for confirming which exit is mine. I go back to the patio stone, but when I search for my token, it's not there.

I stare at the pieces, looking through them again, and then checking the dirt in case it fell or something.

Do not all the boxes hold everyone's tokens? But no. There are fourteen tokens in there. Only one is missing—mine.

Perez said we could only take one token at each station. . . . He never said we had to take our own.

That's why we only need five to pass. And anyone who gets to the center early enough would be able to see the matching symbol with someone's name.

*Fuck.*

*Fuck, fuck, fuck.*

I try to think back and remember if I saw Caden's bag there. But I know I didn't. I would have noticed it whether I wanted to or not, since that shit stain asserts himself in my life so often.

He and his cronies are likely running around, fine with risking first place so they can sabotage me.

I shove the patio stone into its original position and sprint back toward the middle. I don't have any time to waste now. I need to go.

When the five minutes left horn goes, I'm on my knees, panting. I've gone to seven different stones and only have four tokens to show for it.

I need to go for the bonus. It's the only guarantee. Forget the score; if I don't manage five, I'll get disqualified.

I sprint back to the middle and wind my way down the original path I started on. The single benefit of having to search more often is that it's given me a more detailed mental map to work with. So I'm able to find my way back faster.

Dropping to my knees, I flip over that first patio stone I found.

But there isn't a water drop token inside. I grit my teeth.

All I have is the bonus. I sprint to my exit, where I find a box with Virgil's face on it.

Inside, there are more photos of Virgil, each with a different series of four numbers on the back, and an even smaller box with a lock code on it. Okay, I guess one of these opens the lock and the token is inside.

I peer at the photos. As I line them up, I notice that some are off. In one, his nose is oddly narrow. In another, there's a scar on his chin that I don't remember seeing. Even the one on the cover of the box itself doesn't look right.

I start eliminating the obvious ones and I'm left with three. I stare at them, trying to recall.

The horn sounds again.

One minute.

I looked at Virgil's face before I came ·in here. Just that brief glance as he turned away after wishing me luck.

I don't know why I tricked myself into thinking that me screwing up only ruined things for me and Jules. I promised Virgil I would think of him when I did shit. And Corey *is* my friend. A better one than any of those people from high school who called themselves my friends. Both of them were committed to helping me. And I spent most of that time planning to betray them.

I look at one of the photos, and just then, I know it.

That's him.

I know that Virgil. The same one who promised to help with Jules, who defended me when people were shitty even if it meant going up against Margot, and who came to help Mia clean just because he said he would. With his ridiculous outfits and that little grin that lights up his eyes behind gold-rimmed glasses.

I flip the photo over and enter the code.

When I open the box, it's empty.

The final long horn blares.

# CHAPTER THIRTY-ONE

I stare at the empty box.

Finally, I pick it up and exit the maze, stumbling out from the corn.

A South Asian–looking man comes over and holds out his hand. I give him the pouch and the empty box. He shakes the coins out and counts them. "Four. Disqualified."

"No," I say. "There's supposed to be five."

The man gives me an odd look. "Yes . . . but you only have four."

I stab my finger at the box. "I opened it, and nothing was inside."

There's a sharp laugh to my left. Caden is bumping fists with his friend. As if sensing me staring, he turns my way and smirks. "Better luck next time."

Just like I saw the box with that girl's face and knew who it belonged to, Caden also had access to my box. It's completely unhinged. He would have had to waste time sitting and figuring out which one was Virgil.

But this is the boy he hates. The one whose parents killed one of his. I'm sure he knows Virgil's face as well as I do. Maybe even better.

I stomp toward him, ears ringing. Maybe it's something in my eyes that makes Caden's smirk drop away, and before he can prepare himself, I lunge at him.

And am tugged back by my collar so hard that I fall on my ass with a grunt.

Behind me, Bernie winces and holds his hands up. "Apologies, no fighting. Fighting will get you disqualified." I have to close my mouth, which I didn't realize had dropped open. I wouldn't have guessed he had the strength to yank me back like that. But it's cost him. The professor has to take a moment to lean against the corn, gripping the stalk like a lifeline.

When the other professors come around the corner, Caden screeches at them, "She attacked me!" Accompanied by a helpful point.

Chen frowns and looks at Bernie, who says, "There was no physical contact, though Ms. Black is rather upset about something."

"Bullshit!" Caden screams, spit flying from his mouth. His friend beside him backs him up.

Perez says to me, "What happened?"

"He," I motion to Caden, "fucked with my box. It was the last token I needed, and when I opened it, there wasn't a token inside."

"That's a serious allegation."

"Roll back the footage." I wave at the drones. "You have it. Roll it back and you'll see what he did."

Perez regards me, crossing his muscled arms over his chest. "You're going to look ridiculous if you're wrong."

"I'm not."

The professors get into a small huddle and whisper for a bit. Finally, they declare that they're going to go check with the panel of Masters and head to the portable.

I throw a poisonous look at Caden, who glares back at me.

Margot, Virgil, and Corey come around the corner along with a few other trainers.

Caden spots them and says, "You need to keep your bitch on a fucking leash."

Virgil freezes and turns to the candidate. When he speaks, his voice has the texture of low grit sandpaper. "Excuse me?"

Caden shrinks like a kicked puppy, stumbling over his words. "She—she attacked me! She's out of control!"

That makes Virgil's face go slack, and he turns to me for confirmation.

I look away.

Corey sighs, and Margot swears.

"I didn't touch him," I say. "Bernie stopped me."

"Wow, so a real adult had to help you make a decent decision for once," Virgil says, shaking his head.

I don't know why I'm bothering to defend myself. "He fucked with my box. He took the bonus token, and it's the one I need to get five."

Virgil squints at me. "Hold on, you thought he did something that would get you disqualified, and so your solution was to do something that would get you disqualified?"

I hunch my shoulders. "I . . ."

"You weren't thinking about that, right? Because you never do. You never think about anyone but yourself. Even all this,

A MASTERY OF MONSTERS

323

which you're supposedly doing for someone else!"

"I know! I'm sorry, okay?"

"You're out of control, and I'm tired of watching it. Do whatever you want. I'll just wait to be taken to the Pen. That's somehow less stressful than watching you slow-motion fail." Virgil stomps away. Corey looks between us and then chases after her friend, leaving me and Margot standing there.

My chest is heaving, and I don't bother to hide it.

The professors come back around the corner. Chen says, "There should have been a token in that box, and we can confirm that before that point you had collected four tokens, making it your fifth. You'll be counted as a pass."

"What about the footage of Caden tampering with it?" I ask.

"It's a live video feed," comes a voice from behind them, and who should stroll around the corner but James Shaw. Margot stiffens beside me. He's dressed in a pair of slacks and a polo like he's off to a round of golf. "No one saw this alleged tampering. But there was an oversight in getting your token into the box. Easily solved."

The professors say nothing, but I notice the way Bernie's fists clench and unclench at his sides. I don't know if he's annoyed because James is lying and he can't dispute it, or if he's just frustrated. I know Bernie wants me to succeed because he wants Virgil to be saved. Caden being punished isn't exactly a part of that, but it's still annoying.

"Thank you," Margot says because I refuse to respond. "We appreciate the panel taking the time to look into this error and awarding August a passing grade."

"The girl is lucky she didn't get disqualified for attacking another candidate," James says.

"There was no physical contact."

"Yes, I suppose you would know all about that little technicality," he muses. "Isn't that how you avoided disqualification in *your* first test?"

I jerk my head toward Margot. *Excuse me?* Ms. Perfect almost got disqualified?

"I conducted myself within the rules of the candidacy," she says.

For a moment they simply stare at each other, and then James laughs. "Yes, yes, I can tell you're one of Henry's. He has that same sort of familiarity. You don't shrink in the presence of a Doctorate."

"Doctorate *candidate*," Margot amends.

The good humor on James's face sours.

"Would you care to meet more of the Bachelor candidates, sir?" Bernie asks, waving at the others.

James holds back a sneer, his lip curling ever so slightly. "Very well."

Bernie and the other professors leave with James.

Margot lets out a long slow breath before turning to me and saying, "Let's go."

I follow her because I need a ride back to the mainland, though I would have preferred to stomp off like Virgil. I look sidelong at my trainer. "That was kind of mouthy."

"Yes, I know. I am not immune to losing my temper."

"Kind of makes me feel better."

Margot sighs. "Virgil has spent his entire life holding everything in. He holds in anger and frustration, but also fear and disappointment. For him, these sorts of things should be second nature, and that's why what you do is so frustrating. He doesn't understand the idea of not being able to be restrained like that."

A MASTERY OF MONSTERS

I clocked that much. He's a strict little rule-follower. And I get it. He has to be. But he also can't expect me to be exactly like him.

And honestly, maybe I don't know how to hold myself in anymore.

At the same time, I know Virgil is right. Even Corey said it. I've said it myself too. I don't think about other people the way I should. Before, I thought about them too much. There's some sort of balance that I've yet to reach, I guess because I wasn't trying to. In fact, I was doing the opposite.

Margot says, "I had a Caden of my own. Several, actually. That first test meant navigating the tunnels that run under the city, searching for tokens again, and like you, I was targeted. But then there was this sewage pipe that led outside. Pretty steep drop down. One of them tripped. He was dangling over a ledge. I went to get help . . . taking my time. He was rescued. But he insisted that I tripped him. My disqualification was discussed heavily."

". . . Did you?"

"Obviously," she says, rolling her eyes. "But it was subtle. They weren't lying about the feed being live only. Dangerous to keep video proof of monsters. The panel can't notice everything. And yes, it felt good in the moment, but when my disqualification was being considered, and I realized that I could have failed Isaac for a tiny bit of revenge, I hated myself. That's the part that Virgil misses. 'Cause I know you feel like shit when you do this stuff. I know it affects you. And I know you don't do it on purpose. It just happens. I know, because I'm the same."

I kick at the grass. "How did you stop?"

"By trying. By trying as much as I could as often as I could."

"I don't want to be someone's perfect show pony," I say. "I want to be me."

326                     LISELLE SAMBURY

"Then be you! No one is asking you to become Virgil or Corey or whoever. Just find a way to do you that doesn't torpedo the things you actually want in your life."

It's hard to picture Margot as being anything like me, but I guess I see it. Like with the lazy comment shit. She got pissed and stressed and said crap without thinking. Instead of discussing it further, I say, "Caden wouldn't have been subtle. Someone saw him mess with my box."

"Almost definitely. He knows he's got some degree of insulation. His dad is high up, and his mom was beloved in life. His great, great, whatever grandfather even went to medical school with Dr. Weiss. That's why this is the hardest part of the process for us. Because you and I are no one. We only have four Progressives on the panel. They probably saw it. But they don't have the numbers for anything they say to matter, so they stay quiet. Especially if James is going to come and skulk around to see how they're proceeding."

"He wants me to fail."

"Yes. Because it makes Adam look bad. And James wants to win."

And here I thought these politics didn't have anything to do with me. Now I know the score. Caden and his friends can mess with me in the tasks with no consequences. Once again, I'll have to work twice as hard as anyone else to get ahead.

The same way Margot did.

I don't want to be here. I don't want this society competition to be the only way to help Jules, but I also don't want to do it Riley's way. I want nothing to do with anything.

But I can't do that anymore. I can't check out. I can't not care.

"What are we supposed to do if Virgil is giving up?" I ask.

Margot scoffs. "He'll come around. This is his life we're talking

A MASTERY OF MONSTERS 327

about. He's just not sure what to do with his emotions. He's never encountered someone like you, and he's learning how to navigate your relationship. He's throwing a fit over what he can't control." She glances at me. "Not unlike a certain someone who went clubbing I assume because she's frustrated with her lack of control over this process."

She's wrong, but she's also not.

"I'm gonna take a walk," I say, striding away from Margot before she can say anything.

In the parking lot, eyes land on me, and I ignore them, hunching my shoulders. A car horn beeps beside me. I jerk my head toward the sound, ready to snap at Margot to give me some space, but it isn't her.

It's Adam, in a green Jeep. He rolls down the passenger side window and leans over. "Need a ride?"

# CHAPTER THIRTY-TWO

Adam's music is set on low volume and doesn't have any words to it. But it's not classical either. It sounds more like lo-fi beats. The sort of thing you find on YouTube and play in the background while you study, and the screen is an anime girl sitting in front of a window with a cat, and it's raining or something.

I don't think I've ever been in a Jeep before, but it's nice. Black leather seats and enough space to be comfortable. It's too cold for the top and sides to be off, so I don't get the full effect of the vehicle, but it's nice.

"You passed," Adam says, peeling out of the corn maze parking lot.

People clearly know that this is his car, because everyone yields and makes space so he's not waiting in line.

"Yup."

"And almost started a fight."

I wince. "You saw that?"

He shrugs and smiles at me. "Henry learned about it, and I happened to be there when he was learning."

I sink into my seat. "Great."

"I know Henry is very much into the whole 'public persona' and 'reputation' thing, but I want to tell you that I think it matters significantly less than he assumes." That makes me look over at him. "I don't want you to feel weighed down by this pressure that your competition standing has the potential to set off all these things. If your performance is what makes someone vote or not vote for me, then I've not done my job."

Something releases from my shoulders. "Everyone acts like it's going to be this stain on your reputation."

Adam rolls his eyes. "It's not. People do care, of course they do. And sure, maybe some will question my judgment in choosing you depending on how you do in the candidacy, and perhaps that will make them think I'm not good at making choices. But that's such a small part of my campaign. Henry is a details person, so he thinks that every tiny piece counts. Like that single voter who swings away because of you will mean the difference in a win. But to me, it's not worth you struggling under that pressure. Trust me, I know a thing or two about the weight of expectations."

"Like being expected to fight for leadership basically from the time you were born?" I'm not trying to be mouthy, it's the truth. He's a Shaw. One of them was always going to be the Doctorate at some point.

"Yeah." The corner of his lip twitches. "I used to hope that my dad would live a long life, and by the time it could be any of us, we'd be too old, and it would skip to the next generation. James's daughter. Or that maybe one of my brothers would step up and become someone who I could fall behind."

"Too bad." James isn't exactly the sort of person to support in this. But what Adam said does make things confusing when it comes to his older brother. I thought James wanted me to lose because it would mess with Adam's reputation and make it easier for him to win. But if even Adam doesn't think that matters much, then what is James's issue with me?

Adam says, "I hear you didn't want to go to Queen's?"

"You hear a lot of things."

He laughs. "I do, that's true. But I relate in some ways. University isn't the only means of education. When I was your age, I wanted to be a sort of traveling scholar. Go around the world and learn from different people and experiences. It felt very much within the teachings of Dr. Weiss to be devoted to knowledge in that way. I was sure that was my calling."

"But you didn't."

"No. By then I'd already shown signs of having the gift. My purpose was set."

"How do you show signs?" I ask. "Like, you wake up one day and subconsciously control a monster or something?"

Adam laughs again. "No, no. Dad would take us down to the Pen every year on our birthdays and throw us into a cage."

"With a monster?!"

"Yes. He'd have control and he'd let it slip and slide, always saving us before anything happened. But the fear was fresh every time. And eventually, it was strong enough to push the gift out. Unfortunately, that's the way of monsters and Masters and Doctorates. Strength can only be gained through hardship, and suffering, and fear." He winks at me. "Or I suppose that's all we've tried."

"That's kind of fucked up." Maybe I should be more formal with a Doctorate candidate, but I get the feeling Adam doesn't want me to be.

"It is, isn't it? He always said there was a reason for his methods that he would explain at the right time to the chosen heir. Though the time never came. That's why I want to change things. Create a different sort of leadership with different priorities."

"That's why you're the candidate we like."

"I suppose so."

I look out the window at the wind turbines slowly going round and round in circles. "I didn't know your dad was like that."

"Cruel?" Adam asks.

I turn to him. I didn't expect him to say it outright.

He shrugs. "When he wanted a result, he did what was necessary to get it. In some ways, I understand. The rate of spontaneously born monsters suddenly shot up during his term too. He felt that the apocalypse was just around the corner. That's a lot of weight on one person to save the world. I think that's why he had multiple children in defiance of the rules. Dr. Weiss only ever mentioned one Doctorate when he spoke of the savior. But Dad knew how to spin things. Henry is like him in that way. I think that's why he was so willing to take Henry in and make him part of the family. I'm sure Dad often wished that Henry was his son instead of me."

I shift in place. What am I even supposed to say to that?

Adam pushes out another laugh. "It's okay, I'm fine with it. Especially since I know I'm not the only one who thought it. Henry was right there at Dad's bedside with the rest of us. Before the three of us were let in, Henry went in by himself at Dad's request. They had their own private conversation." The corner of Adam's lip twitches. "He requested no such thing with us. And as he died, Henry held his hand. And the other one, Dad held like this." He raises his right hand in a fist. "Whether on purpose or not, only Henry got that moment. Made for an awkward winter holiday, I can tell you that much."

"Winter holiday?" That makes no sense. Hadn't the Doctorate just died?

"Ah yes, I suppose Henry thinks that's more need-to-know information. It's more well-known among the senior members of the society. Dad died in November of last year. We didn't publicize the information until this year to give us more time to plan for the election. He didn't let us know that was his intention until shortly before his death, thinking he would hold on longer. There was also the issue of succession and setting things up to work in the interim so my brothers and I could split duties until one leader was decided upon."

November. He died in November. That means that if whoever is behind this stuff with Jules knew about it, they had more than enough time to prepare. Adam said senior members of the society knew. That's also in line with our theory that we're looking for a Master of some level of renown and status.

"And so," Adam continues, "James hates Henry, and Carrigan hates Henry too, but likes to pretend he doesn't care enough to hate him. And I . . . well, I love Henry. Like a brother. The one brother who I never have to be in competition with because he can't even participate."

I've been so involved with the "we love Henry" people, it hadn't occurred to me that other people might actively hate him. I think about the moment in his office when Adam essentially said the same thing in different words. That Henry is the best man for the job, but he doesn't have the birthright, so it doesn't matter. What must it have been like for Henry to grow up like that? And why is Adam telling this stuff to *me*, of all people? Though the answer comes quickly. I'm on Henry's side, but I'm not devoted like the others. And I'm indebted to Adam. I'm naturally on his side. And I'm an outsider. I don't know proper protocol of how I'm supposed to speak to him. I treat him like a regular person. If I were him, raised in his position, I would want that from someone.

"You don't want to hate Henry too?" I ask.

"No," Adam says. "Rather, I suppose I look up to him. Maybe a little silly since we're the same age. But I know he was the blueprint. He was what Dad wanted me to be. And I spent a lot of time trying to be like him, and then one day Henry said, 'You don't need to be like me when you can just use me.'"

"Sounds like him." The hard-edged bluntness of it.

Adam nods, drumming his fingers on the steering wheel. "I didn't like that word. *Use.* Like he was a tool. Then I got older, and I realized that everyone is using someone. That the best I could do was use someone kindly, with consent and respect. And so that's what I do. In return, he uses me too."

Like how Adam is using me now to vent and trauma dump. I wonder if he's self-aware enough to realize that. "Like getting you to nominate me."

"Henry is invested in you and Virgil. He cares, truly. Besides that, he doesn't like to lose, and he's chosen you now, so you're a valuable chess piece."

"What you're saying is that he's using me too?"

"He uses everyone. You have to understand, losing his family changed Henry. Life has to be a game. It can never be too real. For him, he would rather think of the Bachelor candidacy as a challenge to win instead of a high stakes situation in which he may lose the precious son of his friends. Virgil's parents, once upon a time, were very committed to Henry, and to me through him. We all wanted to change things. We just . . . We didn't think they would choose something as extreme as trying to kill my dad."

I shake my head, compelled to ask the same things I asked of Virgil. "Why would they even attempt it? They must have known he would just control them."

"The Doctorate is not as invulnerable as we make them out to be. Even Dad had his fears. I think they thought they had something over him, though I don't know what. They failed anyway. But what made them so loathsome, such villains to the society, is not just the people they killed." He looks over at me. "It's the fact that they nearly succeeded. They achieved more than any monster before. The chains of a Master are supposed to render monsters safe and harmless. They showed that even beasts in bondage can bite. The rebellion followed soon after. Some even say it was incited by what they did."

Of course, it's that simple. That's the way this entire society works. They use each other and they keep the monsters at the bottom. That sort of reminder, that monsters have the real power, would be hated by them. "And you're the candidate who wants to give monsters more freedom, so does that mean they hate you?"

"Some of them, but not all. There are others who can vote and who have influence."

A MASTERY OF MONSTERS

"Like the Wilds."

Adam grimaces. "Yes, well."

"Would it be so bad to let them do their own thing?" Especially now that I know how the society treated them. "Don't you think they're owed that?"

"They are. I'm under no illusion that what my dad and ancestors did was wrong. Everything they ask for is what we took from them." He smiles at me. "I appreciate you keeping me in check on that. Too many students are unwilling to see fault in the society. The struggle with the Wilds is that it's no longer enough for them to just be free. They want power."

"Power keeps you safe."

"It does, doesn't it? But I have to give it to them in the right way. You must understand that when you give one group power, the ones who've had power all along begin to feel threatened. They don't see it as bringing the scales to balance. They see it as an attack that hasn't happened yet."

We lapse into silence. Thankfully, we're in time to get onto the ferry, and Adam is able to drive on without any issues. They blow the horn, and the ferry takes off.

I glance at Adam. I know that Henry and probably everyone else would not want me taking things directly to Adam. But he's the one who offered me the ride, and I'm not going to miss a chance to help Jules. Adam's right. We all use each other. "You know about the stuff with my brother, right?"

"I do. Henry wasn't particularly forthcoming about it, to be honest, but he eventually shared the details with me. I wish I could devote resources to helping, but the election—"

"Yeah, I get that. What I wanted to ask about is that I think this person manipulating my brother is looking for an object. An artifact. Like what Joseph Lawrence took with him when he left. Do you have any idea what would be worth looking for?"

Adam shakes his head. "Our records from Dr. Weiss are a bit scattered because of the lending of his journals, and those would be where you might find answers. Or otherwise, from Lawrence's organization directly, though I know they don't much care for us. Reasonably so."

"Okay. Thanks anyway."

Useless. Another dead end. If the man whose ancestor knew about this stuff doesn't even know what it is, how am I supposed to figure it out? But I guess I don't need to. What matters is finding who's behind this.

The rest of the drive, Adam asks me about my classes and what sorts of things I like to do. It's kind of like having a conversation with a relative who you don't know well. They have to ask you a bunch of basic things, and you give basic answers.

When we stop in front of Victoria Hall, Adam says, "I'm aware that you're stocked up with mentors, but please know that if you need to, you can come to me for help or advice."

"Aren't you a little busy for that?"

"I can make time." The look he gives me is intense. I wait for the creeper feeling. Like, why is he interested in me at all? But I don't get those vibes. I do just think he's desperate for someone who treats him like a normal person. And I'm cool to be that for him if it gives me any sort of power in this society. For Jules's sake.

I thank him and leave.

He waits until I'm safely inside to drive away.

# CHAPTER THIRTY-THREE

I peel open my eyes to darkness. There's a rapid knocking on my door followed by hushed voices and a jiggling of the knob. I'm getting my bearings when the door is eased open, and the light flicked on. I put a hand over my face and groan. I'm still wearing my clothes from the first test, even though the outfit stinks of stale sweat.

I squint when Bailey crouches in front of me. She says, "We need to go, okay? Just get dressed. It's all right."

"If it's all right, why do you look freaked out?" My voice is sleep-addled, and I must have been less than coherent, because Bailey acts like she hasn't even heard me.

She returns to the door to speak to the campus security guy and a girl who I vaguely remember is my don. She's supposed to be managing the dorm floor, though I've talked to her maybe twice. The two of them leave, and Bailey shuts the door.

"What's happening?" I ask.

"I'll explain on the way. Let's go."

I press my lips into a line as Bailey gives me a pleading look.

"Fine," I say. "But I have to change."

She digs in my closet and grabs a pair of leggings and a sweater, which she tosses onto the bed.

"Sweatpants," I grumble. "New bra."

Bailey turns back to the closet and tosses over my Queen's sweats and then riffles around in my drawers, thankfully throwing me a sports bra instead of a real one. I shrug out of my sweaty clothes and change into the other ones.

She finds some socks stuffed in a pair of sneakers, which she starts to bring over, then she wrinkles her nose and tosses the socks for a new pair. I put them on and shove my feet into the shoes, wondering what I did to deserve getting woken up like this for the second time in the same day. "What's happening?" I ask again. "I'm dressed, we're going, just tell me."

Bailey bites her lip. "Your dad's had a heart attack."

Now I'm wide awake.

I stare at the shiny hospital floors as me and Bailey sit next to each other in comfortable but cheap chairs. The coffee in my hands cooled a long time ago, and my aunt slouches back with her head tipped toward the wall, her breathing long and slow. We've been here for hours. Night has already turned to day, and the hospital has resumed its daily routine of shift changes and appointments.

Dad collapsed in his bedroom, and his roommate called 911 and then Bailey. She tried contacting me multiple times, but I was passed out, exhausted from the test. So she went directly to the dorms and used those magical words: "family emergency."

A MASTERY OF MONSTERS

He's too young for a heart attack. Heart attacks are for people over sixty at least, and Dad is fifteen years too early. Though they stabilized him quickly, he isn't up for visitors yet. Bailey tried to send me back to the dorms a few hours ago, but I refused.

I look at my phone lock screen. It's black. I used to have a picture of me and Mom. I changed it because it got to be a lot to see every day.

I want to text someone. To tell them what happened. I want to text Jules. I want to text Corey. I want to text Virgil, who lost both his parents and probably would have something to say that wouldn't sound like bullshit.

Instead, I grip the phone in my shaking hand and squeeze my eyes shut.

Everything is so fucked. It started going downhill the moment Mom disappeared and hasn't stopped since.

I think of what Mia keeps bringing up. About if I want to be alone.

It takes a moment for me to clock the hand on my back. I snap my gaze sideways to where Bailey has woken up. She smiles, but the corners of her lips don't tug up. It comes out more like a grimace. The tears that have been gathering slip down my face. She pulls me into her, and I let her. She smells like spices, and flour, and weed. "It'll be okay," she says. "He'll be okay. It's okay."

I haven't done anything to deserve my aunt. But here she is.

I wind my arms around her back and cling to her. "I'm sorry," I choke out.

"You don't have anything to be sorry for."

But I do. She's tried time and time again to be there for me, and I wouldn't let her. Now here I am, needing her, and here she is, being here. And it isn't fair somehow. Like she should be gone too.

"Oh, hello again," Bailey says.

I look up from the cocoon of her arms to find Virgil standing with a bouquet of flowers. I didn't even notice his footsteps.

My aunt clears her throat. "I'm gonna go get some coffee." As if she doesn't already have a cooled cup of it at her feet.

Virgil takes her seat while I wipe my face. He hands me the flowers. "For your dad."

"Thanks. How did you know?"

He rubs the back of his head. "Henry. He's good at keeping tabs on people under his care."

Fuck, that man is well informed. I don't think I could spit without him knowing. It's unsettling, honestly. "Does this mean you're not mad anymore?"

"No, I am. But I'm come-see-if-you're-okay mad, not stay-away mad." He nudges my foot with the toe of his. Shiny leather shoes most people would wear with suits, but Virgil pairs with gray wool pants and a cashmere sweater. "Corey wanted to come too, but she has class."

I nod, picking pieces of fuzz off my sweats.

Virgil jerks his head at the door across from us. "He's in that room?"

"Yeah."

He closes his eyes, and I study him as he tilts his head. "Good steady heartbeat."

My mouth drops open. "You can hear it?"

"Yes. The closer I get to turning, the better my senses. Strength, too." He opens his eyes.

"How will you know when it's about to happen?"

"I'm not sure. Everyone says you just know. There's enough

A MASTERY OF MONSTERS

341

lead-up time to it either way." He nudges my foot again. I scowl, and he smiles. "I *am* still mad, but if things like this happen or you need help, text me anyway."

"Why?"

"Because I'll still come."

"Why?" I ask again.

Virgil stares at me. Our chairs are close together. I didn't notice when Bailey was sitting here, but I notice now. When he shifts toward me, our thighs and knees brush against each other. "If I needed you, and I texted, even if you were pissed, wouldn't you still come?"

My mouth becomes parched and dry. "Yes." And I'm surprised that it's the truth.

I don't know if I ever could have done it. If I could have found Jules and walked away from Virgil. I didn't know him, and I didn't owe him anything. But those facts have been changing. I know that Virgil loves sad boy lit fic and classics and will always go for the salami on a charcuterie board first. That he's not his parents, and that despite what the world has thrown at him, he's done everything he can to keep close the people in his life who bring him joy. He became a brother to a girl who lost her family, a cherished student to a man who lost his son, a ward to a man who lost his friends, and a partner to a girl who wanted to save the one person she had left.

How could I have ever abandoned the boy who saves everyone else, the one time he asked to be saved in return?

The door to Dad's room opens, and a nurse comes out. The man asks, "Here for Michael Black?" I nod. "He's awake now, so if you'd like to go in . . ."

"I'll wait here and let Bailey know when she comes back," Virgil says.

I thank him and follow the nurse into the room.

The bed is pushed upright so Dad can sit, though he's sunk into the pillows. His dark skin looks ashen and washed out, and his salt-and-pepper beard, which is always so neat, is straggly and unkempt. I know he has a bald spot he likes to hide with his hats, but apparently at some point he gave up entirely and shaved the whole thing.

I missed that transition.

He doesn't look like my dad. He looks like a copied version of himself. One done on a busted printer that can only manage grayscale. Smudged at the edges.

I stand next to his bed and set the flowers on a side table. I glance at his hand but don't hold it.

"Hey, Summer," he says with a strained smile. Dad always jokes that they named me August because there were too many Summers running around that year. Even though I was born in a completely different season. So, he made it a nickname. I haven't heard it in a long time.

"You overdid it." The words come out snapped and hard. "You always overdo it."

Dad's smile fades. "I do. I'm sorry."

I try to remember the last time I talked to him. Like, in person or on the phone. I suspect that I haven't since he dropped me off at Bailey's place in June. It's almost the end of October. Now Jules is . . . gone, but not missing. Though Dad doesn't know that.

No wife. No son. And no daughter.

"Bailey told me you're doing well in school," Dad says, his smile returning. "I'm proud of you. I did mean to stop by, but I got caught up in work. I was surprised that you decided to go after all, to be honest. But I appreciate you giving it a try. All I ever wanted you two to do is try." His eyes dart to the door for a moment, and I read it in his face.

Jules isn't here. He should be. But he isn't.

"No, you didn't. It was never enough to try. We had to *do*. And we had to do better than anyone else."

"Yeah," he says, looking down. "I guess I did make you both feel that way." He licks his lips and looks back at me. "You're going because you want to now, right?" he asks. "Not because of me or Mom?"

I say nothing, just stare at him.

"You said it yourself. I put a lot of pressure on you kids to do well. You tried so hard in school in those subjects we told you would be good, and I never thought about whether you actually liked them. You seemed to . . . but I didn't ask, did I? I was surprised about Jules's decision to leave so suddenly, but then again, I'd never asked him what he wanted either." Dad shakes his head. "I don't want you to leave too. So do what you like, okay? Whatever makes you happy, and I'll be happy too. I should have said that to you before. To Jules, too. Both of you. You guys and Bailey, you're . . ."

*You're all I have left.*

He's right. He never asked. He never asked whether I wanted to go to university, or if I wanted to study what they pushed me to in school. He didn't ask . . . and Mom didn't either. But she isn't here for me to punish.

"I'd like to be better," Dad says when I don't respond.

"Don't wait until you almost die to be better!" The tears that spring to my eyes are unfathomable. I don't know if they're because I'm upset or pissed or a combination of the two. "Now you want to tell me to do what I want? Now you actually care what I want? You're seventeen years too fucking late."

"You're right," he says. "I am too late, aren't I? I'd hoped not. But I am."

"Yeah, I know. And now I'm a disappointment."

His face crumples. "I was never disappointed in you."

I snort.

"I'm sorry I didn't make that clearer. I was disappointed in *me*. I . . . I thought things would be so different when I left school. I wanted to make a life with your mom. Instead, I got engaged and paid for the wedding with credit. Acted like I had more than I did. By the time you two were born, we were drowning in debt. Annie learned how bad it was when we tried to get a new car, not even a super nice one, and still failed the credit check. I couldn't manage any of the prestigious teaching jobs I hoped for. Annie had to support us with her consulting. I thought if I pushed you kids to be better than I was, that you'd avoid struggling like that. We worked so hard to hide how difficult it was from you. And then . . . and then she was gone, and I couldn't—" He stops for a moment, choking up. "I thought being with Bailey would be better than you watching me fall apart. And I could tell you were struggling, but I didn't know what to do, so I just stayed away, I guess. You had Jules and Bailey."

"I wanted my dad! I wanted you to try too!" I never said the words aloud before and hadn't realized that I wanted to say them either. That I meant it. "Do you know what it would have meant to hear you or Mom say you weren't perfect?! After you tried to make sure we were? It would have been a fucking relief to know it was impossible even for you. Instead, you pretended like you'd never misstepped in your entire life so that we could feel worse than shit when we did."

Dad winces.

I know that in some ways, he did try. He texted and called and even emailed. I don't know what I want him to do, but I want it to be better than that. Maybe I want him to be knocking down my door like Bailey. To insert himself. To read my mind and know what I want.

My hands tremble at my sides.

"I will," he says. "I'll try. And you, August, you're perfect just as you are. I'm sorry I made you feel like you had to do what I wanted. I just want you to be you. And I want you to be okay." He reaches out his hand to me.

I want to slap it away. To push him back. To avoid him ever wanting anything from me. But how can I, when what he wants is what I want too?

I don't want my family to keep shrinking.

I reach out and take his hand.

"I'm sorry for Jules," Dad says.

"He chose to leave."

"He was upset with me. About your mom. He kept asking me these questions about when I had met her, and the people she knew, and all this other stuff, and I didn't have answers for him, and he was so angry."

I frown. "Questions about Mom? Like, recently?"

Dad nods. "I think he was trying to look into her genealogy, but Annie's mother wasn't close wth her family, Annie didn't know her father, and she didn't have any siblings. She had some friends at Queen's, sure, we both did, but I didn't remember them, and she didn't keep in touch after school. They had some sort of falling out."

Why would Jules be interested in that stuff? And why would he be so pressed about it? "Jules never gets angry at you."

346                                    LISELLE SAMBURY

"Yeah. It was unlike him, but you know, he'd been having trouble in school." I hadn't known that, actually, but apparently everyone else did. "Then he had a tussle with that boy, and I had to bail him out."

"Wait, wait, wait." I hold my hands up. "Jules *fought* with someone? And got arrested?!"

Dad shifts on his bed. "From what I heard, it was pretty one-sided. It started as an argument but then got out of hand."

"When was this?"

"During the school year, a couple months after Annie . . ."

"Like February?"

"Maybe? I can't remember. I figured he was acting out. I was a little more permissive. But I don't know, now he's gone, and I can't help feeling like I didn't do enough."

"He'll come back," I say.

I'm working through the time line. The aggression that Jules was experiencing was out of character, but it wasn't abnormal for a monster getting close to turning. Which meant my brother was struggling with this for a long time. No wonder he was desperate enough to accept that invitation. And looking into Mom's history . . . Did he have some understanding of born and bitten monsters? It's not like you'd forget if you were bitten, and he would have transformed right away in that case, so he must have been chasing lineage. Maybe he doesn't know about spontaneously born monsters. But how did he learn about monsters at all? From QBSS?

The solution to all this is to find a way to communicate with Jules. But if it were that easy, I would have already done it.

I need help.

I think of Virgil out in the hallway.

# CHAPTER THIRTY-FOUR

I compare the house in front of me to the address Violet sent me. She texted yesterday to invite me to her Halloween party for candidates, partners, and a few other society people. She'd invited Corey and Virgil too, who confirmed that they would be coming. Thankfully, Caden isn't invited.

I feel like I missed the memo where every Learners' student casually has access to my contact details. I wouldn't be here at all if not for the mention of Corey and Virgil.

In the past week since Dad's heart attack, I've been visiting him at his apartment regularly between classes. Bailey stocked him up with a variety of soups and curries that Grandma taught her to make with what she termed "heart-healthy modifications." Technically, Grandma taught them both to make them, but Dad's never cooked a single Trinidadian dish for us. Mom does randomly have a fantastic jerk chicken recipe even though she's not Jamaican.

I've been so focused on Dad's recovery that if not for the

pumpkin-themed decorations staring me in the face, I might have forgotten about Halloween. I half expected that society students wouldn't celebrate it. But I guess they don't see it as culturally specific enough to avoid.

I walk up the stone steps to the gray brick townhouse that has flickering orange and black lights on the outside, seven different pumpkins on the stoop, and a wooden sign over the door that declares, ENTER, IF YOU DARE . . .

When I push open the door, I jump as a sudden loud cackling rings out. Sounds of talking drift from the living room accompanied by some sort of electronic version of the Monster Mash.

A bored teenage boy with floppy bangs in a black hoodie is slouched in the entryway on a chair. "Shoes off," he says. "There's candy if you want. Living room to the left."

Based on the family photo by the entryway, this is Violet's brother. I take a fun-sized pack of Swedish Fish and Fuzzy Peaches while I take off my shoes.

He looks me up and down. "Violet said you almost kicked Caden's ass at the first test."

I raise my brow.

Before I can answer, Violet comes around the corner in a long black gown. "Matt! You're supposed to tell me when people come in."

"I was going to," he says.

She gestures to me. "We're all over here."

I follow Violet down the hallway into a living room. It's cozy. The couch is a big sectional that looks pillow-soft, and there are matching armchairs. On the TV, the *Halloween Baking Championship* is playing while people chat and mill around.

I recognize some of the other candidates. I've only ever talked to

A MASTERY OF MONSTERS 349

Violet and Bryce, but most of the others have been friendly enough.

"Everyone," Violet says as I follow her in. "This is August. She's partnered with Virgil, who's over there." She points him out, though I spotted him the instant we walked in. Everyone pauses to wave at me, and I wave back. It's strange to party with people I'm competing with, but they don't see any problem with it.

Virgil is wearing suspenders with neon straps over a striped T-shirt and has changed out his usual glasses for ones with red frames. Corey, meanwhile, has dressed up as rollerblading Barbie with a pink unitard and neon green fanny pack.

I slide over to them, ignoring the muscles of Virgil's arms, which are usually hidden by button-ups and sweaters. "You guys didn't want to use the multipurpose Victorian/Pirate costumes?"

Corey shrugs. "Since we had the opportunity to go to a party of more than two people, we decided to branch out."

I nod and gesture to Virgil. "Who are you supposed to be?"

"Urkel."

I stare at him blankly, and he sighs.

Corey says, "I didn't get it either."

I swallow, building up to it. I can't not say anything about how shit went down that night at the club.

"It's okay—" Corey starts.

"No, it's not. I'm sorry. Like, actually. Obviously, we are friends. You're a great friend. Amazing, honestly. And I was an asshole." I glance at Virgil. "To you too. Sorry."

She beams. "Apology accepted. And I'm sorry for saying you don't care about people. I know that's not true."

Virgil, however, scowls. Corey nudges him. He sighs. "I guess I'm also sorry for not considering how hard it is dealing with everything that comes with the candidacy. And the extra crap, like Caden. I'm used to Learners' bullshit, but you aren't."

I straighten. "Thanks."

"Group hug!" Corey announces.

"No," I say. She pouts a bit but accepts it.

"You didn't mind the hug before." Virgil tilts his head to the side. *How. Dare. He.*

Corey looks between the two of us. "You hugged? *Without* me?!"

"What's going on with this journal you mentioned?" I ask her, smoothly changing the topic.

She lets out a long, dramatic sigh, effectively distracted. "I got this rare book dealer guy to talk to me, and the book he has looks like the other journals, so I buy it. But once I get it home to examine it, I realize the binding is too new. I thought that maybe he'd rebound it? But, like, the paper and the ink weren't right either. And I know it because I know books. TLDR, he doesn't want to give me a refund, and I'm right back where I started."

"Shit. I'm sorry. But, like, isn't this whole thing kind of unnecessary? You're good at researching, and you shouldn't have to impress Henry before he lets you into his little club."

She hunches her shoulders.

"That's what I said," Virgil adds, crossing his arms over his chest. Which, of course, makes the muscles bulge. He has to know he's doing it, right? He can't be that oblivious.

When both of them look expectantly at me, I realize I missed what he said when I was ogling his biceps.

A tiny smile starts to peel onto Corey's face, which I ignore. I say, "Sorry, couldn't hear over the music. What did you say?"

Virgil shakes his head. "I said, she should just ask Henry to be involved. It's not like he said she had to do this to get into the Mastery group. It's self-inflicted."

Violet claps her hands at the front of the room. "We're playing a game!" Half the room groans. "It's gonna be fun! I have cards with famous horror characters and people on them. Don't look at yours! Just stick it on your forehead—"

"With spit?" Bryce calls out. He's wearing a onesie with a skeleton design drawn on.

"Not with spit! It'll naturally adhere to the oils on your face—"

"Gross!"

And here I thought Bryce was just a nice, quiet guy. But it looks like he has a sense of humor. One that Violet is used to, because she plows on. "Go find someone and say facts about the person on their head so they can guess who it is. If they get it right, you take their card. Person with the most cards at the end gets a prize."

"What is it?" Bryce asks.

She rolls her eyes. "You'll know if you win."

"Booooooo!"

Ignoring him, Violet goes around the room handing out cards. Corey sticks hers on her head. "I have to win," she mutters, leaving us to find someone.

"Is she competitive?" I ask.

Virgil nods. "Yup. I stopped playing board games with her when we were sixteen. Too intense." He meets my eyes. "You're, like, super beautiful."

I choke on air. "What?!"

He points at the card on my forehead. "The person."

"That's a shit clue!"

"I don't know!"

352    LISELLE SAMBURY

Corey cheers from across the room. This girl already has multiple cards in her hands. I look at Virgil's card, which declares that he's Vincent Price. "I think you have a mustache. And you might also be dead?"

"I don't think we're good at this?"

I snort laugh, and Virgil smiles and leans against the wall. "How's your dad?"

"Great. He's getting a bunch of home-cooked meals from Bailey. And the college gave him some paid leave." I swallow. "We good?"

"Yeah. Also, I kind of don't have anyone else."

"Facts." I shove my hands in my jeans pockets. I settled on the solid costume of being the color black. "I don't have anyone else either." Riley has decided not to respond to my texts or calls, and I don't want to join this magic QBSS faction, so we're at a stalemate. Plus, I need this. I need to win. I push a breath out. "I saw Jules."

Virgil's jaw drops. "What?!"

I tug at the shirt tucked into my jeans. "Riley had a lead, so we followed it. And a monster appeared. I saw him transform back. It was Jules." Even if me and Riley aren't cool right now, I figure the magic stuff is supposed to be need-to-know. I trust Virgil with the truth about Jules, but Riley's secrets aren't mine to tell.

"When?" he asks.

"Like, a week and a half ago."

Virgil looks around the room and bites his lip. "Maybe we should go somewhere . . . ?" He glances at Corey, who's grilling Bryce. "Let's leave her to it."

The two of us ditch the cards on our foreheads and walk into the entryway, where Matt is still at the door, now giving out candy to some trick-or-treaters. "Hey, is there another room you don't mind us being in?" Virgil asks him.

Matt looks between the two of us. "Dude. That's bold."

"Not for that!" Virgil splutters. "We have to take a phone call."

"Oh." Matt's face drops. He jerks his thumb to a door across the hall. "You can go in Violet's nerd palace."

Violet's nerd palace is a small library that may have originally been a large closet. Half the shelves are filled with anime figurines.

Virgil says, "Jules was the monster at Big Sandy Bay?"

"No, that's another one. Jules was different. Kind of . . . uh, bearlike, I guess."

Virgil sinks into one of the plush armchairs, and I take the one across. "Two. *Two.* Obviously unregistered, and one is Jules. Bitten, I assume?"

"Actually, I was thinking maybe spontaneously born? It seems like it was a slow process, and bitten monsters turn or die right away."

"That's true, and a better theory. And this is why you asked me if one Master could bond to two monsters?" I nod. He attempts to look me in the eye, but I shift my gaze away. "And you didn't tell us any of this because . . . ?"

"I didn't want you to tell Henry. Because then the society would get involved. And what if they—" I swallow.

"Kill him?"

"Yes."

Virgil stares at me for a long moment before he says, "You think I would have done anything to put your brother in danger—"

"You follow the rules!" I say, voice rising. "You do what you're supposed to do. Are you telling me your first instinct when I told you wasn't to tell Henry?"

"He can help!"

"You think he would help? Or would he see the fact that I have a brother running around like that as an obvious stain on me and therefore on Adam and his campaign and want to get rid of Jules? Henry doesn't know me! He doesn't care about me, and he doesn't care about my brother."

"*I* care about you!" Virgil says, leaning forward. "So I'll *make* him care."

The room is too hot suddenly. I lick my lips, which only makes them drier.

Virgil clears his throat. "Like . . . we're partners and stuff. You're doing this to help your brother, so I wouldn't put him in a bad position, but I'm sorry I made you feel like you couldn't tell me."

The door opens, and Corey bursts in waving around a massive black bat stuffed toy. "Her name is Emily, and she wants to be an astronomer, and I love her!" She pauses, looking between us. "What?"

After we catch her up to speed, Corey sags against the door, hugging Emily the Bat. "Two unregistered monsters."

"Meaning two Masters," Virgil says. "It has to be people higher up, like we suspected. It's the only explanation for why the society isn't doing anything about it or is having trouble detecting them. Whichever it is."

I say, "A Doctorate candidate could still be involved indirectly. James wants to win the election, and he hates me. This stuff with Jules could be like a distraction or something. Otherwise, why wait until late summer to kill someone when Jules was bonded in February? Plus, Adam told me that Cyrus died in November. They've known about the election since then and waited until the Bachelor nomination to announce so they could prep for it. He would have had time to plan."

"Adam told you when?" Virgil asks.

I shrug. "He gave me a ride home from the first test."

"Adam did?!"

"It wasn't creepy."

"I didn't think it was creepy!"

"Let's refocus," Corey says. "What's being done with Jules isn't actually disrupting anything because someone in the society is making sure no one pays attention to it. What's the benefit for James?" She bites her lip. "The Pro-Libs used to create unregistered monsters. The serum is locked up tight now, but what if they kept some of what was originally stolen for the rebellion? Natalie still has power too."

I say, "I mean, it could work. She might have talked to the right people and found out Cyrus was dead early. It would explain why she's suddenly resurfaced. And she was arguing with Garrett at the nomination ceremony. Maybe she was trying to rope him into it. She also said something weird to me before the first test."

Virgil asks, "When did you talk to her during the first test? How are you having all these side conversations?"

"I don't know! People come to me. I was in the bathroom—" I clear my throat. "Using it."

"Not at all a suspicious pause, but okay."

"And she started talking about, like, how she had someone to fight for once and not anymore, et cetera. Then she told me to break a leg."

Corey squishes Emily the Bat closer to her chest. "There were rumors that Natalie and her previous partner were . . ."

"Intimate," Virgil finishes.

"I thought that was forbidden," I say.

Corey says, "It is. That's why it was a rumor and not a fact. A little while after the rebellion got broken up, Natalie was sent out on a mission to deal with a bitten monster. When she got there, there were six bitten and already transformed. They descended. It was a blood bath. When backup came, her partner was already dead."

"Shit," I breathe.

"There was some discussion about whether it was just bad circumstances or by design."

"As in, Cyrus punishing her or something?"

She nods. "But I don't know why she'd share that with you."

I shrug, choosing not to mention the additional things Natalie said about me fighting for someone. Technically she was right, I'm competing for Jules. But how could she know that? She must have meant Virgil. She'd obviously misinterpreted our relationship as more than it is, making some connection between me and Virgil and her and her rumored nonplatonic partner. Still, why was she even paying that much attention to me?

"What I don't get," Virgil says, "is how does that relate to targeting QBSS? What does Natalie have to gain?"

It's a question I don't have a complete answer for, but I do have some idea of motive. I just need to come at it carefully. "What about those artifacts that Joseph Lawrence took? Could someone want those? Maybe that's the whole point. To get their hands on those and do something with them."

Corey says, "There's been no evidence of them anywhere since he took them. QBSS might have them, but they might not. I think it's more likely that they're trying to stir up old resentments. Cause issues. Does Riley think it has something to do with the artifacts?"

"No, no, just spitballing." Fuck, it's complicated going at this while protecting Riley's shit. I've had to lie outright, which I didn't want to do.

"Either way," Virgil says, "we know that we're looking for two Masters."

Corey adds, "And once we find them, we can have the Doctorate break the bond between the Master and your brother."

"And once the tie is severed, what then?" I ask.

Virgil and Corey look at each other and then away. Corey says, "Maybe we should cross that bridge when we get to it—"

"No. Tell me. Tell me right now."

She swallows. "He'd be out of control again. He'll need to be bonded to someone new or they'll put him in the Pen. And that's assuming they don't kill him for his crimes."

I knew my fears weren't unfounded. Even if we save Jules, he'll immediately be in danger again.

"We don't know what will happen until we get these Masters," Virgil says. "We could make a good case for Jules, get him a new partner, and keep him alive. We'll prove he's innocent. We have Henry and Adam on our side. If you're okay with it, we can update Henry and Margot and see what's possible. I know you don't trust him, but trust that we—that *I*—wouldn't let him do anything to hurt Jules."

I look into his eyes.

Without even realizing, I created this expectation to save Jules with no help and was drowning under the weight of it. Under the pain of already feeling I'd failed. Already disappointing myself.

It's different now. I'm not the only one trying to save him.

I never had to be.

Jules was always the person I shared that burden with. The weight of what our parents wanted from us was less when we were together. With him gone, I assumed that was gone too.

Once upon a time, Jules was all I had.

But not anymore.

"Okay," I say.

# CHAPTER THIRTY-FIVE

Meadowbrook Park is sectioned off with road-blocks, and people in bright orange vests warn away civilians as we file into the competition area. What excuse are they giving for what this is? I guess if the society's been running this for over a century, they have a strong system in place. This test isn't that far from campus, but Margot still had to pick us up. It's only her, me, and Virgil, since Corey has a meeting with a new bookseller, and this was the only time they could do it.

The spectator area is in a clearing of trees, far enough into the park to keep it from prying eyes. It occurs to me that I've never considered how much it costs to run this every year. Not just operations but also the effort to conceal what's happening. But then again, most people ignore what they're not involved in. They probably brush this off as some sort of private event.

"Carrigan's here again," Virgil says, spotting the man in the stands. "I thought him coming to the first test was a fluke."

"Is there a chance he does want to win the election?" I ask. "Maybe he's trying to show face for the voters?"

Margot says, "Honestly, it's not a bad strategy to pretend he never wanted the title. After all, Adam and James targeted each other right away. They assumed he would pull out. And maybe he would have, but if the spontaneously born monster birth rates are increasing . . . Curing monstrosity is the only thing his faction cares about. Maybe he's feeling the pressure now. Leading the entire society would get him a lot more access to what he needs than working in labs and begging his brothers for funding."

It's not dissimilar to what Adam brought up that time in Henry's office. "Why don't more people support the scientists? I mean, a cure would be the best thing, wouldn't it?"

Virgil swallows and looks away.

"It would be," Margot says. "For us. But for the Masters who are making money on contracts to protect wealthy people in case of monster threats, or the ones whose power lies in the fact that people know they could command a beast to tear them apart, or even the ones who go on missions for the society to round up bitten monsters and are cared for by the coffers of the Learners? Not so much."

"Why have a cure when you could have control?" Virgil says, pulling forward to walk a couple of feet in front of us.

I know I'm supposed to be team Adam, and I do like him, but I'd rather see Carrigan win. And at the same time, I understand exactly why few will vote for him, for the exact reasons that Margot and Virgil said.

Monsters give Masters power. And there's no way they'll want to give that up. I'm sure there are even monsters who are partnered

A MASTERY OF MONSTERS

and benefitting who might not want the cure either. Like what Corey said during our sleepover. It's naive to assume all monsters want the same thing.

Farther in, the trees are tall, their naked trunks making them look skeletal, when really the leaves are just higher up, turned a burnt orange by the season, and also lying in piles on the ground, turning brown. There's a bite to the chilled air that teases the coming of colder weather. It'll start to drop significantly from here. I pulled out my insulated leggings for this test and am cuddled up in my sweatshirt. I'll probably have to ditch it before the test starts, since I assume there will be running. There's always running.

Margot and Corey's only inside information was that the second test allows combat between candidates. The format varies otherwise. In the last week, Margot focused our sessions on boxing. I'm not terrible at it. All the basic combat and acrobat flow things Mom taught me help with movement and evading attacks, but at some point, I'm forced to be offensive and strategic, and that's when things fall apart. My strongest offensive skill is knife throwing, and that requires distance. Close combat is not my thing. And most of what I have to show from training are bruises. Corey continued to try to help with kicks, too, and while I managed to get more power in, my form was, as she put it, "not great."

We reach a small clearing, where the remaining candidates are gathered. Now that the group is smaller, it's easier for me to identify the faces. The party helped with that too. There's Violet and Bryce, and Caden and his two lackies. I also recognize a Black girl whose hair is shaved on one side and braided on the other, a red-haired white guy, and two East Asian—looking girls who seem to be close friends, one who has a bob cut and the other a buzz cut. Most importantly, there are thirteen of us. Only two people were eliminated in the first test.

Today, everyone is accompanied by their monster partner. Just like Violet said, people paired up fast after the first cut. The dynamics between them are interesting. Some people, like Caden, have opted to ignore their partners, while others, like Violet, are more friendly.

The professors stand together. Bernie's eyes scan the group, and I smile when he reaches me, but instead of smiling back, he just passes me over. Okaaaaaay, kind of rude. Maybe he doesn't want to look like he's showing favoritism? Especially after he had to intervene during the first test.

Chen steps forward in a pair of boots that go all the way up and underneath her sweater dress. "Welcome to the second test. This one will be performed alongside your monster partner, who you should have brought with you, as instructed." She looks around at the group, nodding as she notices the pairs. "Shortly, you will be led to your separate starting points. From there, your objective is to find ten plastic eggs that have been hidden within the area. Anyone who doesn't have this minimum number at the end of one hour will be disqualified. And only candidates can touch the eggs and/or egg-holding sling bags. The winner of this challenge will be the one with the most eggs at the end. They will be awarded twenty points. Second place will get ten, and third, nine, and so on."

That's ten up from the first challenge for coming in first. Getting that many points could turn things around for me.

"Your monster partners will be blindfolded for the duration of the challenge. Removing the blindfold will result in disqualification. We do have surveillance set up, and we will see if you cheat." I scoff.

A MASTERY OF MONSTERS

Yeah, they can see cheating but won't do anything about it—at least not if it's done by the *right* people. "Candidates may engage in hand-to-hand combat with monsters or other candidates. However, monsters may only engage in hand-to-hand combat with other monsters. Monsters engaging with candidates will result in disqualification."

After the first challenge, I've learned to read between the lines. We need to collect a minimum of ten eggs, but to win, we'll need to steal eggs from the others. Or otherwise find a ton in the beginning and then spend the hour defending.

At the very least, Virgil has one of the larger builds out of the monsters, so I'm not worried about him engaging with them. I'm more concerned about the fact that he can't do anything against candidates.

Chen says, "The current rankings are as follows: in first place, Violet with ten points; in second, Charity with five points; third, Caden with four points; fourth, Bryce with three points; fifth, Peter with two points; sixth, Rae with one point; and the rest of you have zero points and are tied for seventh place."

*Fuck.* I knew things hadn't gone well, but I didn't think I did that badly in the first test.

Virgil says, "It's okay. Ranking better in later tests can help. We'll be fine."

Or Caden could win and get an even higher rank.

"Horns will sound at the halfway point, five minutes, and one minute," Chen says. "As a final note, there are one hundred and thirty eggs in play."

Exactly enough for each of us to pass. Meaning that if none of us engages with each other and none of us tries for more than ten, we can all pass equally. They'd be forced to give us each twenty points, and the rankings wouldn't change.

Something tells me that's not going to happen.

A volunteer in a red vest approaches me and Virgil to bring us to the starting point. I shrug off my sweatshirt and give it to Margot. I'm cold now, but that'll change soon. "Remember," she says, "protect your face and core. Try to put space between you. Keep your kicks strong. And you," she says to Virgil. "Don't let them bait you, because they'll try."

"I've been baited every day of my life," he says while giving her his glasses. "I can handle it."

Margot gives us both a quick once-over before nodding, and we follow the volunteer, who has us weaving through the trees on a path that's obvious to them and not us, before stopping in front of a tree with a red mark.

They give me a blue sling bag, which I attach to myself, and then bring out a pair of goggles with black lenses, which they put on Virgil with trembling hands before leaving. I assume it's more secure than a cloth blindfold, which might fall off during combat.

"We need a strategy for this," Virgil says. "We should team up with Violet and Bryce. They like you, right? If we run in a pack, we have a better chance."

"We're friendly, but I don't know if we're *team-up* friendly."

"They'll know that's the better strategy too."

"Fine. We'll have to find them."

Virgil nods. "But first, I think we should get our ten eggs as soon as possible. Then seek them out. This way, at least we'll have the minimum."

It's not a bad plan, but I need to score well to get my rank up. Assuming that all four Progressives give me their points at the end, that's only four. It could help in a close race, but I need to win to make any real progress.

A MASTERY OF MONSTERS

Just passing is no longer an option.

Virgil must pick up on my thoughts, because he says, "The alternative is getting eliminated right here, right now. Not everyone is going to make it through this. We need to manage the bare minimum first."

"Okay, okay," I say. "Do you have a strategy for finding these eggs?"

"Finding them is the easy part, trust me. This test isn't about that. It's not like the first one. It's about the combat."

"Uh, you and your blindfolded ass think finding them is going to be easy?"

"Yes," he says. "But we need to be fast. I'm not allowed to touch them, so you need to follow me and run. Trust me on this. We can't waste even a second, okay?"

"Okay . . ."

The sound of a short whistle goes off in the air, and I straighten. The second the long whistle goes off, Virgil runs.

It takes me a moment to get my bearings, and then I'm sprinting after him. He's fucking fast, which you'd think I would remember from when I failed so badly at target practice with him. It takes everything in me to keep up.

He finds a spot on the ground, pushes leaves away, and points at an egg. I blink at him. "Dude, what the fuck?"

"Don't waste time!"

I shove the egg in my sling bag, and we take off again, sprinting from location to location to location. I'm breathing hard, and I'm glad that at least I'm not the only one. Virgil is huffing too. I don't have the headspace to count how many eggs we're getting. I'm just running as fast as I can. He scales trees to shake down eggs, and digs holes, and directs me to fish around in the ponds. I'm a glorified gofer, stuffing the eggs in my pouch and rushing from spot to spot.

Then he stops suddenly, sweat dripping down his face onto the golf shirt this loser wore to the competition. "That's it," he says. "The others are already captured." He holds out the wrist his watch is on. "Time?"

I'm about to tell him when the halfway horn blares. Virgil swears.

I ask, "How do you know the rest are gone? Actually, how did you know where they were?"

"They smell like plastic," he says. "Fresh plastic, like, new."

"You can smell that?!"

"When I concentrate, yes. I can also smell the others, just like they can smell us if they've got a monster at all worth their salt. That's how I know all the eggs are claimed, because there are people scents mingling around them. How many do we have?"

I swallow, counting the eggs once, and then again. "Nine."

"Fuck. I tried to keep us away from other people. I hoped we could manage the ten."

"So we find Violet and Bryce now," I say. "And hope we can steal enough. You can sniff them out, right?"

Virgil scratches the stubble on his face. "That's not how it works. People, for the most part, generally smell the same. Maybe if they were wearing a specific perfume, or if I knew them well enough to recognize more subtleties in their scent."

"Does that mean you know my scent? What do I smell like to you?"

Virgil coughs into his fist and shuffles in place. "Is this really the time to get into that?"

"Didn't think it was that complicated a question."

"It's not what you're thinking. People don't smell like wood-smoke or thyme or whatever beautiful poetic descriptions that get put into books. And you smell to me the same way you would to any monster who knew you for long enough. Which is, honestly, like hair products."

"What sorts? Nice hair products?"

He waves his hands around. "You know, like shea butter, and almond oil, and mint sometimes that I guess is from your shampoo? And coconut and—" He stops and swallows.

"Sounds pretty poetic to me," I say, fighting the urge to rip off the blindfold on his face so I can see his expression properly. "Also, you listed a lot of things."

"Can we please move on?!"

"Fine, fine. So basically, we have to just accept encounters with random people until we find Violet and Bryce."

"Yes. I can tell some are smaller groups. I figure we can try those and see how things shake out."

"Awesome. Well, odds-wise, there's a redheaded guy and a Black girl who haven't formed any close attachments as far as I can tell. Caden has two guys, so he'll be in a bigger group, hopefully easier to avoid. And there are two girls I know are teaming up. That's, like, most people accounted for. Let's go for someone who's alone first so we can get our minimum. Then go to Violet and Bryce."

"I agree. Let's get going, then." Virgil rolls his neck. "You ready?"

"Sure."

"You've inspired so much confidence in me," he says and takes off running again.

We reach someone faster than I expect. It's the redheaded guy and his partner, a slim white boy whose fists tremble as he raises them when we come around the corner. I assume he's smelled us.

I pause. Virgil doesn't.

He drops the kid like a fucking hot potato. Just straight-up decks this dude in the face. Instant KO. My jaw is on the floor. "August!" he shouts. "Do something!"

I jerk to attention and move to fight the redhead. His partner was unprepared, but this guy isn't a pushover. I swing at him, aiming for his head and gut like Margot taught me, and kicking out intermittently.

"We don't have time." Virgil bounces from foot to foot in my periphery. "People are coming."

I weave out of the way of a punch. "Working on it!" Finally, I land a hard kick on the redhead's shin that makes him howl.

"Hurry," Virgil says. "We're going to be outnumbered soon. End it."

"'Cause it's so easy." I'm dripping sweat, and besides that one kick, not getting anywhere with this. I look at the guy, bobbing and weaving.

The problem with this is I'm fighting the way Margot taught me, which is all well and good, but I'm not Margot. And I don't have time to be this well-behaved.

I spit in the guy's face. He splutters and reels back, and I rush him, shoving him to the ground and slamming my foot down on his stomach. Once, twice, three times. While he curls into a ball on his side, I unclip his sling bag and take it, running into the trees.

There's muffled laughter behind me.

I glare at Virgil even though he can't see it. "What?!"

"Did you . . . spit at him?" he manages between chuckles.

"No!"

A MASTERY OF MONSTERS

"I heard spitting."

"*He* spat at *me*."

"Really? Because I swore I heard a spit and then he made a disgusted sound—"

"I thought we were running from people! Stop talking!"

Virgil pulls ahead again, and I let him lead me. And I guess we're far enough away, because he stops so we can catch our breath.

I open my bag and dump redhead's eggs into it. "Shit. He only had five."

"Not surprising. The egg finding puts a lot of pressure on the monster, and his partner wasn't very skilled. But we did it. You dealt with the candidate quickly too."

"Because you rushed me," I hiss. And it hadn't exactly been easy to do. We need to find Violet and Bryce.

A howl tears through the air. Not a monster. But a boy. A set of boys. Howling. "Come out to play, August!"

Me and Virgil look at each other.

We're so fucked.

# CHAPTER THIRTY-SIX

Caden obviously isn't worried about anyone else hearing him and his group with how loud he's being. Either he's just that confident in his abilities, or he knows he's in the largest group. They're crashing through the trees and shouting, whooping, and howling.

"How did they even manage to find each other that fast?" I ask Virgil.

"Wearing distinctive scents, maybe. If they assumed a team-up in at least one of the challenges, they could prepare that way."

"Let's run." It's the only solution. If they find us, we'll be easily outnumbered, and it isn't like I'm the best even in a fair fight. I only managed with the redhead because I fought dirty, and he hadn't been expecting it. "At least then we have an actual chance at finding Violet and Bryce."

Virgil nods and takes off at a jog, and I hurry after him. It's bright daylight but that isn't making navigation any more helpful.

And there's no way for us to shout for Violet and Bryce without alerting Caden of our position.

Not that it matters, because they aren't getting any farther away.

Caden shouts, "We can smell your fear!"

"We can't smell emotions," Virgil says. "Maybe they can hear our heartbeats, but there's no way to differentiate them."

"I don't know that he cares about the specifics of it," I say. "But how is he tailing us this well?"

"Because we're one of the few pairs who didn't team up. It took him a bit to get to us. He probably already confronted the others who are alone."

We can't keep up with this. I doubt that fourteen eggs will be enough to rank well. I can basically only guarantee that I'll do better than the redhead.

I stop running. "Virgil."

It takes him a moment to realize I'm not following, and he has to double back. "What?"

"Let's fight them."

His jaw drops. "It's three on one! We'll get slaughtered."

"There's no other option."

"Yes, there is! We run, we find Violet and Bryce, and we do the fastest all-out brawl we can manage."

"We can't play it safe this time. We can't just follow the rules and skate by. And honestly, when has that ever worked for you? You did everything they wanted and you're still here with me, fighting for the chance to live."

"I *know*. I didn't always, but I do now. And I still think this will give us the best chance. But if we don't find them by the five-minute horn, then okay, we'll fight Caden."

"Fine."

We increase the pace of our running, though Caden is still gaining on us. The only benefit is that they must be as tired as we are, otherwise they would have caught up. I can't picture them drawing this out and wasting time. Also, they've stopped shouting things, so they must be conserving energy now.

"You'd think it'd be easier to spot Violet 'cause of the dark colors," I say, panting.

Virgil jerks his head toward me. "Wait, was she wearing her lipstick today?"

"I don't know. Probably. She always does."

He veers in a new direction. "She's smart. No wonder she's in first place."

"Care to share with the class?" I gasp, struggling to keep up.

"The lipstick. It has a scent. She, like Caden, must have anticipated a team up. She wears it all the time, so it's easy to forget that it could be distinctive unless you know to search for it."

We round a corner and nearly smash into the exact people we're looking for.

"Do you want to team up?!" I shout the question so fast that I barely understand it as it comes out and have to repeat myself.

"Yes!" Violet and Bryce reply at the same time.

Violet waves to her partner, a South Asian—looking girl whose hair is cropped shorter in the front with curtain bangs and longer in the back, brushing the nape of her neck. "My partner, Frankie. And Bryce's partner, Mitch." She gestures to the short, stocky white guy beside Bryce. "Obviously you can't see them, but this is Virgil and August."

"We're familiar," Frankie says.

Instead of his usual glasses, Bryce has a pair that look like

A MASTERY OF MONSTERS

swimming goggles with an elastic strap. He says, "Caden is looking for you. We saw him and his group go for Jerri, who was alone. We thought he'd pivot to us, but they left, and he was shouting your name."

That confirms Virgil's theory that they were focusing on candidates who were alone, hoping to make it to me. "I know," I say.

And then the boy himself comes crashing through the trees with his two buddies, a wolfish grin on his face. He was all childish jibes and comments before, but now he's been given permission to hit me, and that changes everything. Their partners trail behind them. I recognize the white girl as Caden's partner, her dark hair up in a ponytail. The others I hadn't paid attention to, but I notice now. An East Asian—looking boy and a white boy. Neither of them is particularly bulky, but they're tall, and they immediately drop into fighting stances.

I roll my shoulders back and shake my legs out. This was inevitable. I can see that in Caden's face too. He already made one attempt to get me out of the competition, and this is his chance to do it legitimately.

Caden jerks his head at the guys beside him. "You take the other two."

They don't need any more instructions, and I don't have time to prepare as Caden comes flying at me. I pull my block up, getting my forearms in front of my face, but his punches are hard and direct. It's not like training with Margot, where she's at least wearing gloves. This is bone-to-bone contact. I swear that my forearms crack as he swings at them. I try to dance back to get some distance, but he's relentless in his pursuit. I even try spitting again, and he not only lets it hit his cheek, the little shit spits back at me and doesn't falter in his attack.

I spent this whole time thinking of Caden as a schoolyard bully, but he hasn't been ranking the way he has for nothing. He's better at this. He's stronger than me. And maybe with my knives, I could even the score, but that's not what this is.

The last punch does crack something, and I scream, dropping the block and hunching, and Caden uses the opportunity to drop his elbow onto my head. Stars explode in my vision, and I fall to my hands and knees, gasping.

Caden whips out his leg for a kick. I flinch, but it doesn't connect.

I'm crawling around on the ground, shaking.

When I finally get my wits about me, I realize that Virgil is in front of me with Caden wailing on him unrestrained. I thought Caden would be too scared of Virgil to ever hit him. But Virgil isn't allowed to fight back. And no matter how he tries to pretend, Virgil isn't indestructible or incapable of being hurt, because he's wincing and his face is bruising, but he's still taking every hit.

For me.

Because I wasn't strong enough.

I look at the other fights happening around us. Bryce is a fucking beast. He's more than the guy who hangs around Violet. He's fast and his kicks are strong—when they land, they make loud thwacking sounds. And Violet, as expected, is brilliant and brutal. She's dealing with the other lackey, punching and kicking until he's backed against a tree.

Their partners are similarly skilled. Frankie moves at a speed I can barely follow, and her opponent can't seem to keep up either because he keeps taking hits. And she does it all with a little grin on her face. A few feet away, Mitch is throwing punches so powerful that I'm sure the only reason the guy he's fighting doesn't have broken ribs is because he's a monster.

While I've been getting my ass handed to me, the rest of our impromptu team have been kicking ass.

And then there's Caden's partner, leaning against a tree, doing nothing. Which explains why Virgil can be here with me.

I get back to my feet and refocus. "Move," I say to Virgil. "I can take over."

"You're just getting knocked around," he grunts, continuing to block me from Caden.

"Then let me get knocked around. You can't take every hit. We're supposed to be partners, so we should share the beatdown, okay?"

"That doesn't make any sense! I can handle it."

I kick Virgil in the shin to put him off balance, and he falls backward. I swing at Caden. The boy sneers and jumps back. He was having a great time with Virgil, apparently.

"Are you even thinking?!" Virgil scrambles off the ground.

I can't look away from Caden. I bring up my block again. He smashes a fist into it, and I grit my teeth. I can barely get a breath in, much less have time to argue with Virgil.

Violet shouts, "Stop, Caden! Look around!" I gasp at the reprieve as Caden eases back. Violet has her foot planted on one lackey's stomach, and the other is on the ground near Bryce, knocked out. Frankie's opponent is also unconscious, while Mitch has his in a headlock. "You're outnumbered. You can keep fighting with us until we take your eggs too, or you can leave now with what you have."

Caden turns a spiteful gaze to me, his jaw tight.

I know the last thing he wants is to leave me here. But he is, unfortunately, smart. He knows he's in a losing position.

"Why are we letting him go?!" I ask Violet. "Like you said, we outnumber him."

"You're not in a position to dictate how this goes." Her voice is even and cold. This is not the Violet who handed out Pillsbury cookies with pumpkin designs on them. This Violet's eyes are sharper, and her tone doesn't leave room for argument. "Make your choice," she says to Caden.

"How can you help them?" Caden asks her. "His parents murdered people in cold blood. Tried to kill the Doctorate! I'm not the only person who grew up missing a parent." At that, he looks at Bryce.

I gape at the boy. Mitch bristles but Bryce's expression remains neutral. "You can't punish someone for something they didn't do."

"Can't you?!" Caden says. "When the apocalypse comes, are they who you want at your side? Are those sorts of people the ones you want to bring into the new world? That's why the society exists. We are choosing the best students to protect." He points at Virgil and me. "*They* are not worth protecting. Right here, right now, you're making a choice."

The horn blares.

Bryce shakes his head. "No. We already made our choice."

"Now run," Violet says.

Caden sneers at them before turning and sprinting into the trees. His partner follows at a more leisurely pace.

"You should have let me handle it," Virgil says, whirling on me.

I narrow my eyes at him. "What do you think being partners means? We fight together. It's one thing to take hits to give me time to recover, and it's another to take them because you think you deserve them." He looks away, snapping his mouth closed. "Because you don't," I add. "But . . . thank you, anyway. I . . . I wasn't prepared."

"It's fine," he says. "And, yeah, okay. I get it."

A MASTERY OF MONSTERS

"What was up with Caden's partner? Did you fight her at the start and she gave up, or what?"

"She didn't fight at all," Frankie says. "She tried, but Caden told her to stay out of it. I don't think they get along well."

Mitch releases the guy from the headlock, and he slumps to the ground. Mitch sits next to the defeated monster with a sigh. "Not our problem."

"Let's count what we have." Violet rips open the bag of the lackey she was perching on and empties the eggs into the middle of the area, throwing the empty bag back to him. He clutches it to his chest and curls onto his side.

Bryce grabs the eggs from the unconscious guy.

I walk over to them, my mouth set. "Why did you let Caden go?"

"Because I don't want to have him as an enemy," Violet says. "As I'm sure you've experienced, he's like a dog with a bone. You make enemies in this competition, and you make things harder for yourself. I grew up with him. He's an asshole, but I did him a favor. He'll remember that."

"You think he cares about that stuff?"

"Yes. He does. Like I said, I've known him much longer than you. We don't have time to discuss this. We need to sort the eggs."

Violet and Bryce both empty their bags, and they have the same amount that I do. Me and Virgil did better than I thought.

Violet says, "Dump yours in too."

I add my fourteen. Both of them nod approvingly, and I hold myself a little straighter.

Violet says, "We have sixty-two between the three of us. That leaves sixty-eight in play. Vince has zero. Hudson has zero—"

"Oh yeah," Frankie says. "I think one of the pairs left when you were talking. Can't hear that one guy wheezing anymore. Does that matter?"

Violet's mouth drops open. "Why didn't you say anything when they were actually escaping?"

"Was I supposed to? Mitch didn't either."

Mitch shrugs. "I heard someone, probably his partner, dragging him away, but it's cruel to kick a guy when he's down."

"It's fine," Bryce says with a sigh. "Actually, this is better. Caden will have to share eggs with him."

"You guys think the sun shines out of his ass," I say, awe obvious in my voice. I can't picture a single scenario in which Caden risks his rank to help his hanger-on.

"It makes sense," Virgil says. "He might need someone in the third test. Just weighing odds, it could be worth it."

"Not even that complicated," Violet says. "Hudson and Caden are besties. If Hudson asks, he'll give him the ten. Vince, he might have just let lose, but not Hudson. He may hate you, but he does like other people." She points at the eggs. "Hudson will have ten, leaving Caden with at least ten himself. We cleared Sasha. We saw Caden and crew clear Jerri. Did you clear anyone out, August?"

"Redhead. He had five."

"Chase. Peter and Charity placed, so they'll likely have a good amount. I'm sure Felicity and Rae would have just gotten their ten and hid, but they could have been found and cleared too." She bites her lip and looks at Bryce. "I don't know, what do you think?"

"Thirty to August, sixteen for each for us," Bryce says. "That'll keep us in the middle of the pack at least."

"Yeah, I think that'll work best."

A MASTERY OF MONSTERS

Before I can even say anything, Violet and Bryce start counting out the eggs and distributing them into our bags.

"You don't have to give me your eggs!" I say. "I'll probably be okay with fourteen."

Violet smiles at me as she packs the remaining eggs into her and Bryce's bags. "I like you, August, I really do, but I don't like you that much."

Frankie snorts.

"... Thank ... you?"

I look at Virgil, and the frown he wears suggests that he doesn't understand any more than I do.

"We were trying to find you since we needed the numbers to deal with Caden, but to be honest, we have an ulterior motive. There's someone who wants you to come out of this on top who has the sort of pull we need. And coming first means they can't dispute you. Numbers are numbers, and there are no rules against sharing eggs with teammates."

"Henry," Virgil says.

Violet grins. "He's got the best Progressive Mastery group on campus."

"And he's got an in with Adam, who might be the future Doctorate," Bryce adds.

*Fucking Henry.* "How long ago did he make that offer?"

"From the start," Violet says. "But we couldn't actually help you until now." She meets my eyes. "We're not lying. We do like you. I don't care for this cloak and dagger stuff, but we weren't one hundred percent sure if we were on board. We wanted to take a bit more time to feel you out."

That puppet master motherfucker. I want to be annoyed with

Henry for playing this game, but he did pick the right people to approach. I like them, their partners seem cool too, and they cared enough to make sure I was an okay person before helping. They weren't ready to do anything for anyone to get into his group. Though I don't like that, just like with Riley, I got put into this position of having to prove myself to someone to be let in on the secret.

The final horn sounds.

Unlike the end of the first test, I have some hope when I hear it.

# CHAPTER THIRTY-SEVEN

Corey insists upon another celebratory sleepover for what she calls "our triumphant return to friendship and to kicking Caden's ass!" This time there are no meetings downstairs, so we're set up in one of the sitting rooms, where she's covered the entire coffee table with snacks and a "make your own Caesar" drink station that includes bacon strips, mini pickles, and more. Though Caesar is a generous term, since there's no vodka, so it's basically Clamato. Apparently, a glass of wine is acceptable underage drinking and hard liquor is not. I can't wait to turn nineteen next year and be legal.

But even more unfortunate than the lack of alcohol is the giant banner strung up that says, HAPPY BIRTHDAY!

Which I am currently scowling at.

Corey has also mysteriously left the room, which I worry means a surprise is coming.

Virgil nudges me in the shoulder. "Are you seriously mad that we're celebrating your birthday?"

"I knew it was sus that she picked this date for the party." I hadn't told any of them my birth date to avoid this, but I shouldn't be shocked that they found out.

I was glad to have spent the last few days since the second test licking my wounds and training for the final one. I hoped I could let this particular day pass by. It's why, when Bailey called to set up a family get-together, I pushed it off to meeting for breakfast on the weekend.

Last year, Mom made a big deal, as she did every year. We went for dinner at a fancy restaurant, and I ordered this expensive steak and got a free slice of chocolate ice cream cake. I took two bites of the cake and pretended to be full.

I thought about the cake that entire day and night. Before the meal, about whether I would let myself eat any of the cake. During the meal, about if the cake would come or not, because I wasn't going to order it, but if someone else did, I was obligated to eat some. That would make it okay to have. Then when the cake came, carefully controlling how much I had. Savoring the two bites. Forcing myself not to eat more. Offering it to Jules, and Dad, and Mom to have some to be sure they'd finish it, and I wouldn't have the option to go back for more. Then that night at home, thinking about the cake while I stared at the ceiling. Wishing I'd eaten the whole slice.

A week and a half later, Mom was gone.

That was the last day I really spent quality time with her, and all I was thinking about was cake.

"Speaking of birthdays . . ." Virgil holds out a card to me. "This came in the mail for you."

"To McIntosh Castle?"

A MASTERY OF MONSTERS

He shrugs. "Probably a society person. Bernie maybe?"

There's no return address on the envelope. Inside there's a card that says, *Happy Birthday!* on the front with a bunch of cartoon balloons. I open it and stare at the words, reading them once and then again.

Virgil, of course, is too polite to peek. "Is it from Bernie?" he asks.

I shake my head. "It says, 'There once was a man who thought himself a God. He wrote his lessons as a God. He led his people as a God. He was revered as a God. And then one day, that God died. That was the day we learned that any God can be killed.'"

"What does that even mean?"

"How should I know?" It's creepy as hell. I wouldn't put it past Caden to figure out my birthday and send some weird card in the mail to mess with me. He must still be pissed about the second test. I toss it onto the coffee table and rub my bruised forearms. Caden hadn't actually broken any bones, but even five days later, they still hurt.

Virgil watches me. "Still bad, eh?"

"I couldn't keep up with him. It was pathetic."

"Caden's had years of practice. If it had involved knife throwing, you would have done way better. It's a skill set thing. Margot can't make you into an expert overnight."

"Maybe I could with the right pupil," Margot says from the door with a plastic bag in her hands.

I gape at her. "Wow, you accepted a party invite?"

"I heard it was someone's birthday, so I made an exception." She tosses me the bag, and I manage to catch it.

Inside there's a pair of fingerless leather gloves with long fabric attached that also has some sort of cushioning. "You got me something?!"

"Wear the gloves for combat. The padding goes down your fore-arms, so you don't get hurt blocking again. It's also fishnet, since that's in line with your style."

It is. They're, like, actually cute. "Thank you."

Margot makes a noise in the back of her throat and looks away from me.

"Happy birthday to you . . ." Corey comes around the corner with a cake covered in black icing with red lettering on it.

Margot shakes her head. "No one wants that."

"Thank you!" I say, even more enthusiastically than I did for the gift.

Corey rolls her eyes and stops singing, setting the cake down. Then she spots me with the gloves. "You started gifts without me?!"

"Relax," Virgil says. "Let's do the cake first."

I'm tasked with cutting the cake, and I make sure to give myself a nice big slice with plans to eat absolutely all of it. Halfway through my portion, I get a video call from Riley. This girl hasn't so much as texted me since we fought at her bougie ass house and now she's video calling me out of the blue? "I gotta get this," I say, and go out to another room. I answer the phone, and Riley pops up. "Did you call to say happy birthday?" I ask.

"What?" She scrunches her face. "It's your birthday?"

Okay, I guess that isn't why she's calling.

She says, "Another invitation was sent out. The meet-up spot is the same. I don't know if they're trying to tempt us into going back or what. Now that things have escalated, QBSS will be going, and the plan is elimination. If the society won't put down a murderous

A MASTERY OF MONSTERS                                                                385

monster, we will. If you want to have some say in what happens to your brother, I would get down there. And be discreet! The note says to meet at midnight this time." She hangs up.

I stare at the screen, open-mouthed.

They're going to kill Jules.

"August?" I jump and whirl around. Corey is standing in the doorway. She looks from the phone to my face. "Everything okay?"

"Yeah, for sure. It was just my dad." In reality, Dad called earlier in the day to wish me happy birthday.

Back in the room, I eat my cake. I put forkful after forkful into my mouth, tasting it less with every bite.

Corey tells me I have to wait until the end of the semester for her gift. Virgil hands over a box he pulls from behind the couch.

I unwrap it and stare at the black leather and the rows of dark metal beneath it.

Virgil shifts in place. "I figured that since Henry took away the credit card, you didn't get a chance to buy holsters that fit. Also, an extra set of knives, because retrieval is hard with knife throwing. And I know you care about your set. I figure these are ones you can throw without worrying about losing them."

There aren't just holsters for my thighs, but also ones to go around my chest and back, and some that work for boots too. I can carry an exorbitant amount of knives with these. I run my fingers over a stamp in the leather. A. B. "What if I have a middle name?" I ask.

"I checked with Bailey. She said you don't."

Of course he did. "Thank you," I say, my voice quiet and my eyes on the leather. I'm supposed to use these to fight so I can help Jules. But none of that will matter if he doesn't make it through the night.

I choke back a sob. Virgil's eyes widen, and he starts waving his hands around. "It's not that big of a deal! I didn't even use my own money! And you needed it—"

"They're going to kill my brother tonight."

"This is so cool," Isaac says. "I've never been to a stakeout."

We walk together through the trees, already off the main path. I have my new knives strapped to me with the new holsters. It's more weight than I'm used to, but I'm managing. We move slowly, trying not to make too much noise, since Riley gave me a heads up about being discreet. Though I don't know how possible that'll be once they go after Jules.

Margot made us walk in a formation with her and Isaac at the front, me and Corey in the middle, and Virgil bringing up the rear.

"Is any of this looking familiar?" Margot asks, pointing ahead.

She may as well point at the sky for all it helps. Everything is cloaked in darkness, the same way it was the first time I came with Riley, and I was running then. "Not really."

Margot sighs. "Okay, let's split up."

"As a Black person—"

"It's strategically the best idea, since you don't know where we're going." She jerks her thumb at Virgil and then Isaac. "You two try to sniff out the Masters." Isaac opens his mouth, and she cuts him off. "I know it's not that easy, but the QBSS members will be together in clumps, so it should be feasible to avoid them. The Masters will be nearby and on their own. Try to see who you can find that fits. Or any scents that are out of place and might be them trying to cover theirs. Besides, this might be a setup, so both monsters could be in play. Splitting up could help us force *them* to split up too. If you find the Masters, do not engage. We just need identities. The rest can be dealt with later. August, Corey, and I will focus on stopping QBSS members from killing Jules and also stopping Jules from killing QBSS members. Good?"

Virgil shoves his hands into the pockets of his slacks. "I could handle looking for the Master alone. That way you guys can keep Isaac with you."

"No, because of the reasons I just said," Margot replies. "And you can't turn. You need some protection too—that's Isaac."

He bites his lip, looking at me and Corey. "We'll be fine," I say. "Go."

"Corey?" he asks.

"I'll be okay," she says. "I have August and Margot."

Virgil hesitates for a moment again before he takes off with Isaac. Leaving the three of us alone.

Corey shakes out her left leg. Instead of her usual prosthesis, she's wearing one with a curved blade on the end, like the kind I've seen athletes use in the Olympics.

"Why not use the leg you do taekwondo in?" I ask.

She bounces a bit, the leg flexing and bending beneath her. It's taller than her usual prosthetic leg too, making her gait uneven as we follow Margot into the trees "This one is best for running. As I'm sure you've noticed, it's awkward to walk in, but I'll be glad to have it if we're being chased."

I glance at where Virgil and Isaac disappeared before following. "Hopefully we won't be."

"Hopefully."

After a few minutes of walking, I start to recognize the foliage. "I think this is it," I say, and Margot stops. She motions for me and

Corey to crouch behind a cluster of trees, her eyes on the clearing. We stay in position, waiting to see if anyone shows up.

I'm almost dozing off when finally, someone appears. But it's not some random QBSS member; it's Riley. Her hair is tied up, and she's shivering and rubbing her arms, hunching in on herself. As if she hadn't confidently attacked Jules a few weeks ago.

Corey says, "It's August's hot friend." She pauses. "Hot and single, or . . . ?"

"She has a boyfriend."

She groans. "They always do."

"Focus," Margot says.

A massive form pushes through the trees. My breath catches in my throat, where I hold it. It's that same bearlike form from before with the bone accents. My brother is somewhere inside there. The brother who was always willing to put himself out if it meant helping me, who pushed me to chase after what I wanted instead of what our parents did, who was the only one to still believe in me when no one else did.

I lean toward him. "I need to do something. Try to talk to him or—"

"Absolutely not," Margot says. "He's under the active control of a Master. It's too risky. Wait and see what QBSS do. If he's in danger, we'll act. Until then, we stay hidden."

Beside me, Corey's shaking. She was joking a few moments ago, but now there's a monster. She couldn't even watch Isaac transform. I don't know that she's ready for this. Even if we need her. She catches me staring. "I'm fine," she says.

"What do you want from us?" Riley asks Jules. "Are you looking for our artifacts?"

A MASTERY OF MONSTERS

Monsters, to my knowledge, can't talk in that form, and Riley should know that. Jules kind of stomps around in place and throws his head. Is it annoyance or frustration? But he's keeping his distance. He must remember what she did with the chain.

"I know where they are," Riley says. "Maybe even the artifact you want."

That's when he stops moving.

"I could take you to one if you transform back and explain some of what's happening."

He tilts his head almost as if he's considering it.

"Here, I'll even do this." Riley removes the chain from her neck and tosses it into the grass. Jules's head jerks to follow the motion.

He starts moving closer and closer. *Too close.* He's charging her!

I jump out from my spot and throw two knives in quick succession toward his head. He reels back to avoid them.

"August?!" Riley shouts as she ducks and rolls out of the way.

We don't have time to talk because Jules charges again, snarling with a mouth full of sharp teeth.

Margot leaps over us and slams her fist down on his snout. Red sparks flash, and Jules roars as he falls on his back.

I scream, "Don't hurt him!"

She glares over her shoulder. "He's an eight-foot-tall monster. He's fine." She slams her brass knuckles together, and more red sparks dance across the metal at the contact. Even the metal itself is tinged crimson like heated steel. I think of the sizzling of Isaac's drool. Heat-based. Right, bonded Masters and monsters can share abilities. I've never seen it in action before.

"What the fuck are you doing?!" Riley says, then points at Margot. "Why did you bring her? How much have you told them?"

She spins around and spots Corey. She's still in the trees, crouched on her knees, shaking and staring at the ground. "Her, too?! How many of you are here?!"

I say, "Wow, okay, how about a thank you for saving your life?"

"It's a setup! Which you ruined. Fuck! I knew I shouldn't have told you about this. I just wanted you to have a chance to watch out for your brother if things got out of hand, and this is what you do?" Riley's eyes are darting around the bushes as if she expects someone to jump out . . . and maybe she does.

"Where are the others? Aren't they supposed to be here?" I ask, but she just scowls at me. "Why wouldn't you tell me everything that was going to happen?!" This girl really wanted me to read her mind.

"Because you're not a member! You are, in fact, basically the opposite, and *they*"—she points at Margot and then Corey—"are *definitely* the opposite." She scrambles around in the grass. "Help me find my chain."

I use my phone light to help search.

In the background, Jules is getting back up. He sets his sights on Margot and runs toward her. She dodges out of the way and lands another punch on his face, but this time, he's more prepared and doesn't go down.

"Fuck," I mutter, searching for the necklace. If we make him transform back, we can end the fight. "Here!" I pick up the chain and immediately drop it. It *pulsed* in my hands.

"Where is it?!" Riley asks.

I point at the spot on the ground where I dropped it, and she snatches it up.

I stare at my hand. Did that really happen? Or am I just freaking out?

A MASTERY OF MONSTERS

Margot flies past us and lands with a thud on the ground.

"Margot!" She's not getting up. Fuck, she's not getting up.

Golden light beams as Riley's chain expands, but Jules isn't giving her a chance to use it. He's already running toward us, head down, sharp bone mane pointed out.

I'm frozen. Even if I reach for a knife now, it'll be too late, and it won't do anything.

A flash of clothing appears, and all I see is a blur of metal.

Jules screams and rolls to the side.

It's only when I see Corey skidding on the grass that I realize it was her. She kicked him in the face. Really hard.

Gold pieces fly and gather around Jules. Riley's chain. The links bind together and tighten, wrapping Jules up, forcing him into human form. Except, it isn't quite working. His head is human, but the rest of his body is stuck between forms.

Riley winces. "Stop . . . fighting . . ."

I rush to my feet and go to Jules. He's twisting in the grasp of the chains. Snapping and growling. "Who's doing this to you? What's going on?"

"August," he gasps.

I grab his arm. It's a mix of skin and fur and bone, pinned to his sides by the chain. "Yes, it's me. Who's controlling you?"

"Can't . . ." Veins bulge from his neck as he struggles. "You know . . . you know . . . you know . . ."

A screech so shrill that I flinch sounds in the trees.

Riley's head snaps toward it, and her shoulders tighten.

"What was that?" I ask.

She swallows. "Team two. They were looking for the second monster."

The sound's done something to Jules. His eyes are rolling, and he keeps muttering, "Have to go, have to help, have to go." He bucks and roils against the chains.

"Get them off," Margot says, coming up behind us with blood on her temple.

Riley snaps, "You don't get to order me around!"

"You're forcing him to disobey the person controlling him. You're going to either kill him or make him lose his mind."

I say, "But he's partially in human form, right? He can't be controlled like this."

Margot shakes her head. "It's not enough. He's still partially monster. The control is holding."

I look at Riley. This is exactly what QBSS wants, for Jules to die. My bottom lip trembles. "Please, Riley."

She grits her teeth and glances into the trees again. "Ugh! Fine!" The links fly apart, and Jules explodes into a mass of teeth and fur, returning fully to his monster form and running away into the night.

Margot slumps to the ground, and I go to her. She waves me away. "I'm fine, just a little dizzy."

"I'm sorry," Corey says, coming over, tears streaming down her face. "I—I—I couldn't move, I—"

"You saved us." My voice is firm. "You saved us, okay?"

She nods, wiping her face with her hand.

"You good?"

"Yeah, yeah . . . landed weird because of my balance issues, but otherwise, fine." She looks at Riley with a furrowed brow. "Shouldn't someone else have been here to make sure *you* were okay?"

Riley crosses her arms over her chest. "They trusted me to handle myself." She narrows her eyes at me. "And I'm glad they weren't here to see that you brought the Learners into this."

"One of them is," says a boy as he emerges from the trees. He looks like he's around our age. Riley stiffens beside me. He's tall and dressed in black sportswear. His dark skin shines in the moon-light, and he wears a thin chain around his neck with a pendant in the shape of a scythe. I get flashes of gold as he speaks. A capped right canine. "I'd love to hear your explanation for this, Riley. Poor Jackson was so distraught to leave his girl and tend to team two, so I said I would come back and check on you."

Riley casts her eyes down. "I— This is . . . I didn't bring them, I—"

"That's enough, I think," he says, and she falls silent.

He stops in front of me, Margot, and Corey, looking us up and down. He dismisses me and Corey immediately. "The famous Margot Bouchard."

"The infamous Malachi Jones," she says.

He chuckles and then casts his eyes to me. "Riley has kept some questionable company over the years, but I must say that you, Ms. Black, are the worst."

"Thanks," I reply with a grin. "It's nice to have fans."

"The next time we encounter your brother, we will kill him."

"The fuck you will."

He smiles, slow and languid. "You keep thinking you have a say in that." He nods to Riley. "We're leaving."

There's nothing further to the conversation. Riley turns on her heel and follows him into the trees.

I wait until they're gone to ask Margot, "Who was that?"

"Malachi Jones. He's the president of QBSS, and his threat was very real." Margot sighs. "Let's meet back up with Virgil and Isaac. Maybe they'll have some good news."

When we get back to the car and see the expressions on the boys' faces, it's clear that they don't have anything helpful to report. They heard the scream of the second monster but avoided QBSS as instructed. They couldn't find any Masters hiding nearby. Though they admitted that there are a lot of scents layered over each other in this area, which makes it especially hard to pick out people. No wonder Jules and the rabid Easter Bunny keep having their meetings here.

Basically, it's a bust.

All that, and the only clue I got from Jules was, "You know . . ."

# CHAPTER THIRTY-EIGHT

The morning after our failed stakeout, I adjust my backpack on my shoulders as I walk toward Humphrey Hall. All the pretty autumn leaves have come and gone. The weather has descended into a dry chill, and the puffy jackets have come out. I've begun to almost exclusively wear sweatpants in a desire to both keep my legs warm and expend as little effort as possible.

When I get to the side door of the building, Virgil, Corey, and Margot are already there. Henry sent us a message that we were required to attend his office hours today. Something I haven't been ordered to do since the beginning of the year. And from their grim faces, I expect that he's not going to be asking how our classes have been going.

"Wow," I say. "Everyone looks so cheery." Though I'm sure my expression isn't any better. I've been turning over what Jules said in my mind incessantly, and I'm no closer to figuring out what it means than I was when he said it.

Margot squares her shoulders and says, "When I updated Henry on the situation last night, he said that we were not to go. I obviously didn't listen—"

"Oh my God," I gasp. "You didn't listen to Daddy?!"

"August!" Virgil gawks at me, aghast. "Really?"

"I'm sorry, was I not supposed to acknowledge the strange pseudo-parent thing you all have going with him? Okay."

"May I remind you that this was for your benefit?" Margot says.

"And I appreciated it!" It's kind of wild. I thought she had this unflinching and complete loyalty to Henry. Then again, she's also had times where she didn't seem to trust him. So maybe not.

Margot continues, "I figured it was best for plausible deniability to simply not tell the rest of you what he said. This will be a dressing down. Just let me take the lead, because it's for me."

"But what is he actually going to do? Turn us over his knee and give us a good spank—"

"Please stop," Virgil groans. "Henry is helping us, remember? We're operating under his good will. We kind of want to keep that."

"Yeah, but he's not going to stop helping. Because of his reputation or whatever, and he's literally your guardian. We're just going up there so that he can yell at us and feel a bit better."

Corey hunches like being yelled at is, in fact, the worst possible thing she could experience. Virgil's not far off either.

I guess it makes sense. None of them are used to letting people down. But I'm a pro. "Let's just get it over with," I say, taking the lead and walking into the building.

When we reach Henry's office and knock on the door, Laira greets us with a grim expression. Which is basically a confirmation that we are about to be yelled at.

A MASTERY OF MONSTERS

The four of us file in like naughty schoolchildren. At least Margot keeps her head high like me. Corey stares at the floor and Virgil does that thing where it's like he's looking at you, but really, he's looking at something to the left of your head to avoid direct eye contact.

Henry sits in his chair with his hands resting loosely on top of the desk. "Explain."

Margot sets her shoulders. "There isn't any explanation that I think you'd find satisfactory. I assessed that August's brother might be in real danger, you told me not to get involved, and I chose to do so anyway. I didn't tell the others what you said. They operated under the assumption that everything was fine."

I open my mouth, and Henry throws me a sharp look. "You don't talk. Do not say a word until I ask you to." I scowl, and the pleading look from Virgil is the only thing that stops me from speaking. I stand by what I said. Henry's not going to do anything. This is about the illusion of punishment. It only works if you feel guilty.

I press my lips together and mime zipping them.

From his expression, Henry doesn't appreciate the gesture. He turns back to Margot. "Have I ever, in the history of us knowing each other, forbidden you to do something when it was not in your best interests?"

"No," Margot says.

"Have I ever advised you in a way that you felt was not in your best interests?"

"No."

"Then what would possess you to go against my instructions?!" He rises from his chair so abruptly that it rolls back and hits the wall. Margot doesn't flinch. "We are on the brink of taking the first real steps to achieving the sort of freedom and liberation that you told me you dreamed of for Isaac. And you are running around creating conflict with QBSS and getting involved in this unregistered monster conspiracy theory for what?" He points at me. "For *her*?!"

"Henry—" Virgil starts.

"Did I ask you to speak?!"

Virgil stands straighter and keeps going. "It's her brother. They were going to kill him. If Margot hadn't been there to intervene, they might have. You don't think she has a sort of sympathy considering that she joined the society to save her own brother? You think it would be acceptable for us to step back while August might lose a member of her family? Shouldn't you of all people know how precious family is?"

I stare at Virgil, my heart rate faster than it was a moment ago, but he's focused on Henry.

Corey doesn't say anything, but she steps up next to her friend, nodding to show her assent.

Henry stares back at Virgil, unblinking, then he throws a venomous look my way.

I see everything in it.

The fury at himself for letting Virgil choose me. The anger at watching his pseudo-children disobey him for my sake. The rage at not being able to get rid of me without losing Virgil.

Adam said that Henry uses everyone. Sees them as pieces to move in his game.

A wild card. That's what Laira called me the first time we met. The unaccounted-for piece that's thrown his careful arrangement out of order.

If he comes down hard on me, if he pushes that stance of not helping my brother, then he risks losing them all. Maybe at the start this was just about a bargain. But it's different now. There's loyalty in play.

I try to pull it back, but I can't. The corner of my lip twitches into a slight smile.

Henry closes his eyes and takes a deep breath.

"Can I talk now?" I ask. Not because I care. More because the speaking is technically breaking his rule. But, like, in a polite way.

He doesn't open his eyes. "Fine."

"I appreciate how you've helped me and Virgil in the candidacy. Even I know that we'd already be out of the competition if Violet and Bryce hadn't been *encouraged* to help us. And I know that both Margot and Corey are committed to helping you. But I think we'll all be better served to work together on the two things we want: for Adam to win, and for my brother to be safely removed from this shitty situation he's gotten into. Besides, Adam himself said he doesn't think what I do is feeding into his reputation anywhere near as much as you think it is."

That makes his eyes open. "When exactly did Adam say that?"

I shrug. "He gave me a ride home after the first test. We had a chat."

Henry's face goes still. It takes him another few moments before he speaks again. "Here is what we will do. I will continue to focus my efforts on Adam's campaign and success. And you four can do whatever you want. But do not expect my support or assistance in this business. I have told you, multiple times, to wait until the election is over to sort this out. I promised my help. I promised Adam's help if you would only wait. Clearly whoever is using the boy needs him. He will not be killed. I can see this for the distraction that it is, and I will not fall into this trap. But if you want to, fine. And if, in the process, this pursuit affects your performance in the candidacy, then that will be your burden to bear as well. Dismissed."

I look at the others. "Does that mean we can go or—"

"Dismissed!"

The four of us leave the room, and Laira follows. "I'll escort you out," she says.

We know the way but don't fight it.

"I think that went well," I say.

Virgil shakes his head at me. "Better than it could have, I guess."

I ignore the fluttering in my stomach. Virgil talked back to Henry. *For me.* He wasn't just saying shit on Halloween. He followed through.

"How do you think it went?" Margot asks Laira.

The older woman shrugs. "I think he just wanted to yell at you and feel a bit better about you disobeying him."

"That's what I said!" I throw my hands up.

Laira grins at me. "He does usually like a bit of pushback, though. Appreciates the critical thinking and all that. But I think the election has him too stressed out. He just wants everything to work neatly now. But of course, people aren't like that." She pats Margot on the shoulder. "He'll be fine. You're still his favorite protégé."

Margot scowls. "If he would delegate more, then he would have less on his plate."

"But then he'd have to share his secrets," Laira says. "And here we are!"

We file out the door, and when I look back, Laira is still standing there with that smile plastered on her face.

A MASTERY OF MONSTERS

# CHAPTER THIRTY-NINE

I leap back as Margot darts toward me, swinging at my body and head in quick succession. I've gotten faster, because it's not as hard to duck out of the way as it used to be. I see an opening and take it, driving forward with an uppercut. I get her, but all she does is grunt and kick my shin. I'm expecting it and jump. She raises an eyebrow, and I grin. I'm rewarded for my confidence by a kick to my opposite shin, which lands. "Don't get overconfident," she says.

We're training on Wolfe Island today, because we're supposed to be doing the bulk of the setup for the community dinner next Saturday. So this Saturday, the secondhand place where Isaac works will be dropping off everything, and we're going to head over there after.

Corey and Virgil are on standby for the second and third portions of my training. And since Isaac was already coming to help Mia, Margot insisted that he participate too.

Margot comes at me again, and I lift my guard up, bouncing on the balls of my feet. The moves don't feel as foreign anymore.

She says, "The last test is always a monster run. You have the basic building blocks of everything you need, but you have to go harder. They're going to throw in a bunch of experienced Master-monster pairs, who will become obstacles. But your real challenge will be the other contestants. This is full combat. Meaning anyone can come at you with weapons. The society never wants to lose potential Masters, so the aim is for you to focus on the run, but if Caden decides he wants to waste time trying to kill you, they won't stop it."

I falter. "You think he'd go that far?"

Margot throws a hard right hook, and I duck out of the way. "It would not be the first or last time a candidate tried to permanently retire another one."

Great. And Virgil won't be in this test with me, so if I go down again, I'll be on my own.

"Corey," Margot calls, backing off me.

"Yup!" Corey stands, and we bow to each other before we begin. She's got on the prosthesis she uses for taekwondo. "Let's see the high kick. I'll demonstrate, and you go after." When she shoots her leg up, she's able to keep her form and balance better than the first time she showed me. "Now you."

I stifle a groan and tilt my body, lifting my leg up as high as it'll go while she walks around me and checks my form. "Not as straight and I'd like, but you could make up for it with power."

She runs me through drills and then calls out forms while I do my best to keep up. It's all things we've done before, but her standards for me are higher. Boxing is difficult because I have to use every ounce of my concentration to counter and anticipate the next move.

A MASTERY OF MONSTERS

But the kicking drills are exhausting and repetitive. Even so, like with Margot, I know that I'm getting stronger.

"Don't forget your kihap," Corey says.

Sometimes I get distracted and forget. I was kind of skeptical of it when she first explained kihap to me—the shout as a focus of energy and power, and an intimidation tool—but I do feel like I kick harder when I do it.

Corey has us do a couple of spars to break up the drills. She's at a disadvantage, since she can only kick me with her right leg. A kick from the prosthetic leg might do some unwanted damage. Still, it's difficult to keep up and counter. She's fast and when her balance throws her off, she recovers quickly. I feel like I've gotten faster as a result of training with her.

After we finish our last spar, she crosses her arms.

"What?" I ask.

"You need to go to classes when we have more time. My dad would freak out if he knew I was teaching you piecemeal like this. You only know basic forms—"

"Not the time," Margot interjects.

"It hurts my soul," Corey groans.

"I'll go to proper classes after!" I say.

She beams at me. "Good. Next drill!"

While I run through it, Margot continues to discuss the test. "At the beginning of the run, a bunch of monsters will appear and try to stop you from getting past them. Avoid them if you can, and if not, only fight enough to slip past. You're not at a level to beat anyone. The challenge is that we don't know who will be there, and their monster partners will have different specialties."

"Like your sparky fists?" I grunt, jumping with a kick.

"No. My 'sparky fists,' as you so elegantly called them, are a monster evolution three ability. Not relevant to you until next semester, and Masters in the run don't have clearance to use any evolution two or three abilities. Meaning they won't use speed or strength either. It's unfair otherwise, since you won't have even achieved the first evolution, so don't worry about it. This will also be the best time to team up if you're going to."

"I'll text Violet and Bryce," I say. She presses her lips into a thin line. "Is that a problem?"

"No. It's fine. Henry's seen to their loyalty." I don't miss the bitter edge to her words.

After we finished the second test, me and Virgil learned that Margot also wasn't aware of what Henry set up with them. I don't know why he wouldn't tell her, and maybe she doesn't either.

"Good enough," Margot says. "Thanks, Corey." Me and Corey bow to each other to finish. "Virgil, get on your gear and get into position. Isaac, you'll need to transform. August is going to run down the middle of the field, and you two try to stop her."

While Virgil gets suited up so he doesn't get stabbed when I throw knives, and Isaac sets about shifting forms, I catch my breath and stretch. It's strange to try to act normal while a person is becoming a giant dog, but I do my best. I've been wearing the holsters and knives for all of training, and though they're lightweight, they're still a weight, and it gets draining after a while.

Margot continues, "After you get past that first hurdle of monsters, the Master-monster pairs are going to break out into different sections. Do not forget that, first and foremost, this is a race. Do whatever's necessary to rush to the finish. Avoid conflict as much as possible. Do you remember Corris from the nomination ceremony?"

A MASTERY OF MONSTERS

"The one you said to avoid?"

"Yes. Do that. No one ever gets past him. If you see him, backtrack and try another route. He's the only Master who I can guarantee is in it."

"He's that strong? What makes him so special?"

"Despite being on the smaller side, his partner is very good at defense. Their size is a strength, actually. They're faster than larger monsters would be, and that also means you can't dart between their legs. And the tusks on them are the worst bit. Any way you get close, you're more likely to get skewered. Plus, they're not offensive. When you go on the offense, you also leave yourself open. They never do. It's like combating an impenetrable wall. You're more likely to both waste time and end up exhausted. It's better to just run. Depending on your second test scores, you might not even need panel votes if you come first."

I wish they would release the scores at the end of the test so I would know where I stand. Instead, I'm in this weird limbo. Not unlike everything with Jules, which I've been avoiding thinking about so I don't get distracted. But it's hard not to. Virgil and Isaac didn't find anyone. The other monster and Jules got away. And the only thing I got is "You know." What does that even mean? I know what happened to Jules? Or I know who the Masters are? Or I know who the other monster is? Or I know . . . something else?

"Let's run it!" Margot directs me to the beginning of the long expanse of field. Virgil and Isaac are positioned at different spots. I swallow, looking at Isaac in his monster form staring down at me. Even knowing he wouldn't hurt me doesn't change how unsettling it is to be face-to-face with a monster. "It'll be wide open like this to start. You'll have foliage cover after to help, but this will be the roughest bit." Margot blows the whistle around her neck, short first, and then the long one.

I dart forward and am immediately met by Isaac, who I throw several knives at as fast as possible. As he moves left to avoid them, I sprint right. But he's unfazed and spins around and gives me an almost insultingly gentle shove with his front paw. I stumble back onto my ass, caught off guard.

"You can't fall," Margot says. "It is extremely difficult to get back up. Any candidate who wants to take you out will have an easy job if you fall. Restart."

Isaac gives me the most ridiculous sad puppy dog look. I'm being pitied by someone who currently has almost as many teeth as a shark.

"Stop looking guilty! She's training!"

We set it up again, and this time when I start the run, I stick with the strategy of unleashing my knives. None of them actually hit, but they're good distractions. I also keep one in my hand to make Isaac evade while I attempt to sprint between his legs. He stumbles, and I falter to avoid cutting him.

Margot says, "He's a monster! He's tough! There's no time to hesitate!"

For my concern about him, Isaac rewards me by sweeping my legs out from underneath me with a casual swish of his tail. I go down.

"You can't f—"

"I know! Fuck." I get to my feet and start again.

And we do this over and over. I finally manage to dart between Isaac's massive legs and reach Virgil when someone barrels into me from the side. I tumble onto the grass. I look up, my mouth wide open at Corey.

"Sorry," she says, holding her hands out in front of her. "Margot told me to."

I glare at my trainer.

"Pay attention to your surroundings!" Margot says. "You think Caden won't use this chaos to take you down? Restart!"

By the time we finish, my legs feel like Jell-O, I am bruised, and any ego I developed in the beginning of the session when I realized my progress has died a long, painful death.

"I think you did pretty good," Corey says as we pack into the car.

I shoot her a look. "How did that meeting with the book guy go, by the way?"

She rolls her eyes. "He didn't show."

"Seriously?" Virgil asks.

I say, "So is the one you have a fake or a copy?"

Corey asks, "What do you mean?"

"Well, does Henry want the authentic book to collect, or does he just want to know what's in it?"

She bites her lip. "He never said. I assumed he wanted the actual journal, but if it's about subject matter . . . then I just need to confirm the contents. August! You're a genius."

I grin. "I know."

When we arrive at the barn, Margot zeroes in on Mia, crossing her arms while she watches Isaac almost fall over himself rushing toward the girl.

"Are you going into battle?" Mia asks, and I look down. Shit, I forgot to change out of my holsters. I guess I'm getting more used to the weight than I thought.

"Just practicing," I say.

She slips one of the knives out of a holster and runs her finger along the edge. "I can sharpen these for you too." I ignore the aghast look that Margot throws me.

Mia tests the weight of the blade in her hand, and then tosses it hard at the opposite wall.

It sticks. And though she did it fast, I swear she had perfect form.

I stare at her, open-mouthed. "You can throw?"

"Beginner's luck," she says with a smile, then whispers so only I can hear, "Also, don't tell anyone, but I kind of wanted to impress his sister."

As Mia retrieves my blade, I glance out of the corner of my eye at Margot, who's appraising the girl differently now. Mia hands it back to me with a smile, and I slip it into my holster.

I'm shocked that she's actually into Isaac. I hate to say it, but maybe Virgil did successfully teach him something.

Or Mia just likes nice boys who work at antique stores.

Still . . . that throw was a lot more than beginner's luck.

"How are you doing?" Virgil comes up next to me. Mia is doling out orders, and we've been tasked with helping move in the tables. Virgil lifts one with me, though either of us could have done it alone.

"Fine, I guess." Though he's checking on me, Virgil himself isn't looking too hot. For one, his pants are wrinkled instead of perfectly pressed with a crease down the front, and there's a strain around the corners of his eyes. "You?"

He shrugs. "You know, exams coming up. Though I guess that's more for you. Lots of essays for me. Also, a test that'll determine the fate of my life."

"Right. How's stuff with Henry? Is he still pissed?"

"I haven't spoken to him since, but I'm sure he's fine. I know it's taken me a bit to come around to it, but some rules are meant to

A MASTERY OF MONSTERS                    409

be broken." His eyes meet mine, holding my gaze. "Sometimes it's worth it."

There are multiple feet between us, but it's like we're only an inch apart.

My hands get sweaty, and I struggle to keep a hold of the table, licking lips that aren't even dry.

I need to win on Friday. There's no other option.

I can't lose my chance to help Jules.

And I can't lose Virgil either.

# CHAPTER FORTY

The final test is on Wolfe Island. The sky overhead churns with gray clouds. The chill in the air is crisp and biting, and the ground is covered in a thin layer of frost. We're in a stretch of forest not far from where we've done a lot of my training, except the area now has the addition of a spectator's section—rows of tall metal stands already filled with people and several projectors set up to broadcast the test.

I stand with Virgil and Corey as Margot goes over to the stands to chat with Henry. He's sitting in the special box with Adam. Though when he spots Margot, he excuses himself and goes down.

Adam gives me an enthusiastic thumbs-up. I manage a grim smile in response.

I don't know what to make of the man. He's kind but in a sort of unreliable way. Like his offer to help. The same as Henry, he can't deliver on it until after the election. He's not that different from his friend. He just presents better.

It's been over a week since the last time I saw Jules, and he hasn't resurfaced. Margot promised that she and Isaac would keep an eye on the area so I could concentrate on training, but nothing.

I've decided that Jules must have been telling us that we know the person who's controlling him. That *I* know. And I only know a limited number of Masters to begin with. But then again, I could have encountered someone at the nomination or first cut and still not really *know* them. Or maybe Jules is *assuming* that I know someone.

I stare at the crowd. James, obviously, could enlist any Master willing to help in whatever way he likes. Just as people want Adam's favor, James has his loyal followers too. Maybe I know someone pretending to be a Progressive who's actually working for the Traditionalists.

Then there are the Wilds and Pro-Libs. I spot Natalie and Garrett separately in the stands. Their groups worked together before to push their own agenda. Why not do it again? After all, the Pro-Libs have experience with unregistered monsters, meaning they could be responsible for Jules, and the other one could be a Wild. It would be a huge risk for the Wilds, like Corey said, but maybe it's worth it for them now. It would also mean the Pro-Libs forcing a monster to work with them, which goes against their stance on monster liberation, but a lot of people sacrifice morals when it comes to getting what they want. Maybe something about this artifact could tip the scales of power in their favor?

If only we knew what the artifact was. That could help us narrow things down.

Virgil nudges my shoulder. Without even looking, I know it's him. Because it's the same way he always breaks me out of my thoughts, that gentle push of his shoulder against mine. "You can't think about it right now," he says.

"I know."

Corey says, "Everything will work out."

I don't think I believe her, but I appreciate her. "Yeah."

I watch Margot and Henry have their conversation. Part of me is expecting an argument, but they seem cordial. They finish, and Margot comes back down.

"What was that about?" I ask.

"A statement of intention, I suppose," she says, as if I have any idea what that means. "Believe me when I say I don't trust a lot of people, and I put my faith in even fewer, but I believe that you can do this." I'm too shocked by her words to say anything, and she plows on quickly. "Let's warm up and do a couple drills."

Margot helps me stretch and pushes me to run a couple of laps around the small trainee waiting area. Then Corey has me do some kicks and checks my form. Margot even has us do a short spar to practice. I can tell that Corey is taking it easy on me, either because she only has on her everyday prosthesis or because she doesn't want to send me into a test with a bruised ego, maybe both.

When we finish, Corey's eyes go to the stands where her parents sit. They throw strained smiles their daughter's way and wave. I expect to look back at Corey and see her eyes averted, but instead, she's staring back at them.

Just a few years ago, she was down here, waiting to go into the third test. Fifteen years old. Desperate to prove herself. Even though she's eighteen now, I don't know if that feeling has ever gone away.

"You good?" I ask her.

She nods. "Yes."

A MASTERY OF MONSTERS

There's a crackle, and Chen's voice comes through the loud-speakers. "We will now announce the current candidate standings. These are the cumulative scores of both the first and second tests."

Looking around, I count six other candidates gathered in the area. Meaning that six didn't get their minimums in the last test and were disqualified. Unfortunately, Caden is still here along with his buddy, Hudson. The Black guy. And the only lackey left. Violet was right. Caden's an asshole, but he's a loyal asshole.

Virgil swallows, bouncing on his toes.

"In first place with twenty-five points, Charity; in second place with nineteen points, Violet; in third place with twelve points, Bryce."

Shit. I didn't rank first for the second test. I got zero points in the first test, but if I came in first for the second, I would have twenty now and be in the lead.

"In fourth place with eleven points, Caden; tied for fifth place with ten points, August and Peter; and in sixth place with seven points, Hudson."

Ten points. I came in second that last round. I glance across the training area at Charity, who I've previously never paid much attention to. She's a white girl, bulky in the shoulders like a swimmer, with dark brown hair cropped short. I don't think she came to the Halloween party.

I need to get first. Meaning that she just became my competition. This is a race, but if I can slow her down from the onset, I'll give myself a better chance. And from the way the other competitors are looking at her, they're thinking the same thing.

"Maybe it's good you didn't come in first," Corey says. "In my year, a bunch of candidates went for the guy in first as soon as the whistle blew. Held him down and broke his legs and arms."

I shake my head. "That's fucking horrific."

"People get desperate in the last test."

My eyes stray to Caden. Even if Charity is the better target, I know he's still going to come for me.

Instead of dwelling on him, I nod to Violet and Bryce. We agreed to help get each other through the first rush of monsters, but from there, we'll go our separate ways. They need to hold on to their ranks, after all. No point in having a spot in Henry's Mastery group if you can't get to the initiation and become Bachelors.

"This is good." Virgil wrings his hands. "You're within the top five. You just need to keep that spot. They make the panel break ties, so that's not ideal, but we're in a strong position."

Chen continues, "The winner of this test will receive thirty points, the second-place winner fifteen points, third place, fourteen points, and so on. At the end of the test, the cumulative scores will be shown on the board, and then we will have a final announcement for the scores with the addition of panel votes. This final score will determine the five candidates who will proceed to initiation.

"This is the monster run. Competitors will race from the start to the finish line, encountering various obstacles on the way. These will be in the form of Master-monster pairs who have volunteered for this test. The fastest time wins. Anyone who, due to forfeit, injury, or death, cannot complete the race will be disqualified. Anyone who does not finish the run within the hour will be disqualified. Combat of any kind, be it hand-to-hand or weapon-based, between candidates is allowed for this test. As usual, you'll have horns for halfway, five minutes, and one minute.

A MASTERY OF MONSTERS 415

Candidates, please proceed to the competition area now."

"It's time." Margot adjusts my holsters herself. It reminds me of the first time Mom helped me into a set. Showing me how to loop the belts and testing the sizing even though I could have done it myself. I knew it wasn't for me. It was for her. "Keep your guard up. Stay alert to your surroundings. This isn't just a physical test. Keep your mind sharp too."

"I will."

She swallows and steps back.

Corey comes forward to give me a hug. Her fingers shake where they press against my back. "Don't forget your kihap."

"I won't."

She and Margot head for the stands, leaving me and Virgil alone.

"Fuck 'em up," he says.

A laugh bursts out of me. "Wow. That is the most un-Virgil thing you've ever said."

He gives me a sad smile. "I'm glad you're the one I came this far with. Even with everything. Both your and my bullshit. I don't think I would have gotten to this point with anyone but you." He glances over at the other competitors, who are still saying their own good-byes. "Let me teach you something quick."

I raise an eyebrow but nod.

He holds out his hand, his fingers facing up. "You do the same thing." I copy him and he grasps my fingers, tugging me in close until our forearms are pressed together. I manage to suppress a gasp, but I still feel breathless. "They used to do this back in the day. Master and monster. For good luck. It showed that they were the same. I never hoped for that. I planned for the bare minimum. But you and I, we're different."

I can't even make myself swallow, my throat is so dry. I stare into Virgil's eyes. "We're better."

The corner of his lip jerks up.

I pull away, our fingers falling from each other at last, and join the rest of the candidates, leaving Virgil to go to the stands. When I turn to check on him, he's looking back at me.

At the starting line, our professors stand together and drones hover above us. Perez looks like his usual pretty boy self, and Chen is styled perfectly, but Bernie looks . . . to be honest, like shit—haggard and worn out. I know sometimes people with long-term health issues can have good and bad days, but Bernie seems to have only had bad ones lately.

From inside the trees, howls, croaks, and cries explode.

I don't shake or jump. I keep my body tense and still. Then I allow myself a nice long deep breath to let my muscles loosen.

We're arranged in a line facing the open field. It's not as bad as where we practiced. There are some trees; they're just more spread out than the dense forest area farther on. The candidates are spaced only a few feet apart. Anyone could close that gap. I look down the line to Violet and Bryce. Violet has a bow and quiver of arrows strapped to her back while Bryce has gone for a large sword. We were allowed to bring only weapons, weapon holders, and water.

I run my fingers along the metal of one of the knives at my right thigh. It's the one I threw in the park that day and Virgil stole. That first one Mom gave me.

Blades are meant to sever, but this one formed bonds.

I grip the metal hard, feeling the coolness of it.

The short whistle goes. And then, the long one.

I jerk to my left and sprint to Violet and Bryce. At the same

A MASTERY OF MONSTERS 417

time, several monsters burst out from the forest area into the field. Scaled tails, frothing mouths, bulging eyes and veins, and a fuck ton of sharp teeth and claws.

"Go for the ferret!" Violet says. "You two distract it, and I'm going to put up ropes in some of the trees. We can get in the air and go over. There's no way it can jump, and we can't go through the legs. Good?"

"Good!" Bryce and I say.

I aim for the monster Violet was talking about. It's got a long body covered in fur and a rodentlike face, but it has far too many legs, scuttling like a centipede. And some of the legs have mini ferret faces with jaws full of teeth at the bottom instead of paws.

"I'll go high, and you go low?" I ask Bryce, and he nods, tugging the sword from his back. It's all silver, from the hilt to the blade. He rushes at the legs, hacking at them while I zigzag run, throwing blades at its main face.

As the monster grapples with us, Violet ties the rope to an arrow and shoots it at a tree, and then again with another, wrapping the rope around.

There's a scream from across the field. When I whip my head toward the sound, Charity is on the ground, both her legs twisted and bloodied with Caden and Hudson looking down at her. They wield giant sledgehammers.

The girl is trembling and crying on the ground, reaching shaking fingers out to her legs.

"Focus!" Bryce says, and I throw more knives, trying to check my count and retrieving what I can while I watch for Caden.

He tries to come our way but is distracted by dealing with his own set of monsters. And it looks like he and Hudson are having some sort of disagreement. Snapping things at each other that I can't hear. The lackey is rebelling, it seems.

"Let's get up!" Violet says. "I'll go first. Cover whoever is on the rope."

She's been able to use her arrows to rig up a system of ropes through the trees so we can navigate at a height instead of on the ground. Me and Bryce focus on the monster while she shimmies up into the trees. The ferret is an expert at evading us. And when my blades do hit, the thing is barely affected.

Violet gets up, and Bryce motions for me to go. I work to climb the rope as fast as possible. It's not exactly light exercise. But I've had a lot of training since prelims, and I manage to make it in a decent amount of time. I join Violet in covering Bryce, and eventually, we're all up.

Then it's just a matter of using Violet's ropes to get from tree to tree—hanging by our arms and legs and moving across.

Technically, it's working. Violet was right. The monster can't jump. But this method of travel is also draining and slow as shit.

Peter slips through the legs of a monster that Caden and Hudson are dealing with and takes off.

*Shit.* I was tied with him. Now he's already ranking higher.

My eyes dart around the space. Then I look down at the monster below me. "This isn't working," I say aloud. All those legs . . . and it's fast, too. "We have to ride the monster," I say, trying out the words.

Bryce whips toward me with wide eyes. "You're not serious."

"I think I am."

Looking back at the area, Caden and Hudson break away for a moment, but a monster pursues them, cutting the duo off again. Meanwhile, Peter is still running, and the ferret has turned in his direction.

I hand out two blades each to Violet and Bryce. It's the most I can do in the time I have before I jump into the air, a blade in each hand. I land on the beast's back, my knives digging in to keep me secure. The fucking thing doesn't even notice. It's focused on Peter.

I, however, do notice the twin thumps behind me just before the ferret takes off after the boy. It's really, *really* fast. It tears across the field after Peter, and it's all I can do to stay on.

"Get off now!" Violet says, and I don't think, I let go of the blades and tuck. I hit the ground hard but manage to roll and spring to my feet.

Meanwhile, the monster is still concentrating on Peter, giving us time to run before it notices. We take off into the trees, stopping once we're safe under their cover.

"You're really something, you know that?" Violet pants, shaking her head at me. "But thank you."

She doesn't waste any more words, and she and Bryce disappear, splitting to the left and right of me. I go to the left too but down a different path from Bryce. I could go straight through the middle to get to the end, but it's too simple. Too predictable.

I can't make it easy for either Caden or a monster to find me.

I take the potentially more difficult path with the hope that it's worth it in the end.

# CHAPTER FORTY-ONE

I sprint between the trees, following the path forward. Trying to remember everything that Margot and Corey drilled into me and avoiding thinking about the time and who's ahead of or behind me. The cold is welcome to me now, the frigid air cooling my skin and sharpening my focus.

I stop for a moment, ducking behind a tree and slinging my water pouch to my front, chugging down a bunch and splashing some on my face. Margot said this test has two phases: the initial rush of monsters and then more buried on the way to the finish.

This is a race, and I need to go.

I run forward again. My heart pounds in my ears, and I force myself to regulate my breathing. I'm in the middle of an inhale when I'm struck in the stomach. I double over and fall to the ground, rolling to the side to get out of the way and jerking myself back up, Margot's voice in my head screaming that I can't fall.

When I look around, there's nothing and no one.

"Awesome. Just fucking awesome."

I slip two knives into my hands from the holsters on my back. I'm out on my left thigh and side. I move, this time paying more attention to my surroundings. But the hit comes again, so fast that I can barely track it. I cry out and slice wildly but don't manage to catch anything.

This time I glimpse the slick appendage slinking away.

*Calm. Down.*

I run again, jumping at random intervals and weaving back and forth. The thing shoots out again, but it misses my stomach and hits the edge of my foot instead. I keep up with the strategy, and eventually I reach a forked path.

When I whip my head back, the thing is retreating. I shudder. I never got a good look at it. But apparently it's not following me beyond here.

I get it now. They all have their own boundaries. That ferret monster followed Peter but likely only would to a certain point. Just like that second thing I encountered. I don't know how many monsters you have to pass to make it to the end, but I have to keep moving. I don't have time to slow down.

The horn blares.

*How the fuck is that possible?!* There's no way it's already been thirty minutes. Shit, shit, shit.

I take the right fork, hoping that'll direct me back toward the center so I don't get too off course. Eventually I find myself in a clearing where a single man waits in a formal pair of black slacks with a tucked-in blue-patterned dress shirt and a navy suit jacket, all of them topped with a peacoat. It's more like he's expecting to perform than fight.

Corris.

Margot told me to run if I saw him, but I can't. I don't have time to go around. We're already at the halfway point, and if I want a firm chance of being in the final five, I need to rank high. I can't count on panel votes.

I plant my feet.

"I hoped it wouldn't be you," he says with an air of genuine regret. "I wanted you to make it."

"I *am* going to make it," I say with a grin, gripping my knives.

He shakes his head. "Not against us." He sits cross-legged on the ground. "Your challenge is to cut me. If you can do that, we'll let you pass—"

Before he's even finished his sentence, I've thrown a knife. A massive leg comes out in front of him, and the blade sinks in deep. From behind the trees a monster emerges, covered in fur with a trunk. It's only maybe six feet tall. It's the smallest monster I've seen, with patches of what look like green moss on its fur. On either side of its trunk are sharp protruding tusks that I have no doubt could run me through despite its size. If not them, then the two horns on its crown would do the job.

Corris laughs. "I knew I liked you. You're eager."

I immediately see all the issues that Margot presented. Unlike Isaac or the other monsters, I can't get through its legs. I would have to get on the ground and crawl, and at that point I'm more likely to be crushed. And those tusks. They come out at least three feet from its body. Close combat is impossible. Plus, it should have evaded the knife, but instead it took the hit. The other monsters I've encountered are physically stronger, but this one is a logistical nightmare. I can't use the same strategy that I have been.

It's fast, too. I try to run around the perimeter, but it races ahead and blocks me. I thought Isaac was fast, but I did successfully get past him. And Virgil in his human form is even faster than Isaac is because he's not moving a giant body. That's where this monster has the advantage.

I throw a couple of blades, hoping maybe I can throw quicker, but they're both knocked aside by its tusks. The knife I threw earlier is still sunk in. That means my weapons can still be effective. But does that even matter if I can't get to Corris? That's what complicates this even more.

An impenetrable wall. I get it now.

Margot said I can't hope to beat any of the monsters in this race, but I don't know what other choice I have. It has to be taken down so I can reach Corris. It's too fast for me to hope to sneak past. I'll have to be direct.

I charge, raising the knife with the intent to stab it in the eyes. But when I look at them, I pause.

The hesitation is enough, and the monster turns and kicks me with both its back legs, sending me flying into a tree.

I lie against the trunk, gasping. My head and back throbbing.

It takes me a minute to regain my bearings enough to stumble to my feet and get grounded. I'm fighting a monster woolly mammoth thing, and it has human eyes.

Of course it does. Like Isaac. Like Jules.

I forgot so quickly. The instant I was thrown into that melee, I went at the monsters like beasts. But they're also human. I ran around slicing and stabbing like it wasn't a big deal. I know monsters are tough, Margot said as much, but still.

"You okay over there?" Corris asks.

"Fine," I manage to spit out.

I need to figure out what to do. The mammoth looks over at me, stomping its feet like it's impatient to get back to fighting. "Can you cut me some slack?!"

It makes a soft sound and ducks its head.

I freeze.

What the . . . ?

It looks . . . sheepish? Like it feels bad about it. Not unlike how Isaac looked guilty when he pushed me over.

I raise my knife and its eyes sharpen. It lifts its trunk menacingly.

I'm considering another ridiculous idea. It may be a complete waste of time, but now that the thought has entered my mind, I can't unthink it.

I lower the knife and stick it back into my belt. "Hey," I say, making sure the monster knows I'm talking to it. "Could you let me get close to your partner if I promised just to give him a very tiny cut?"

The mammoth tilts its head.

I swallow and take a couple of steps forward. My head throbs, and I wince. It's worse when I bend. Something on my left side is not okay. "Just a little cut on his finger. I *need* to win." I look at Corris, who is studying me but isn't doing anything to stop me. "My friend is a monster too. And if I don't win, they'll lock him up."

The mammoth makes a deep crooning sound, and its eyes dip down.

"He doesn't have anyone else who can help him. It has to be me. I *have* to get past you two. Could you let me, please, and I'll give him the world's smallest cut, okay?" I keep creeping closer. "I promise."

This time, the mammoth doesn't move, just observes me as I

A MASTERY OF MONSTERS

425

come forward. I slip around it, and it lets me but follows me carefully with its eyes. I have to edge past its tusks and do so with my breath held, letting it out only once I'm past. "I'm taking out the knife now, okay?"

The glint of the blade makes the mammoth stiffen, but it doesn't stop me. I slowly bring it to Corris's finger and poke him with the point of the blade, enough to draw a pinprick of blood.

I wait, looking from him to the monster.

He winks at me. "I've done this same test for the past four years, and not once has anyone ever gotten past me. Certainly no one has ever tried to talk to my partner."

"It listened to me," I say.

"She did," he says. "She's only eleven. She's used to listening to adults, but only if they're nice and reasonable." An amused smile crosses his face. "Unless they're her guardians trying to get her to eat more vegetables."

The mammoth lets out a huffing breath.

Back when I first met Corris at the nomination ceremony, he said he'd left the kids at home. She must have been one of them.

Eleven years old. Fuck. And she's been doing this for four years?! "That's too young." I stabbed an eleven-year-old. "Why would you volunteer her for this?" My lips twist as I look at him.

"It's not so much volunteer as it is volun*told*. Some Masters and monsters go on missions or have private security gigs, and some of us have to do this to keep our place in society. But it sounds nicer to pretend it's a choice. Besides, she transformed early and didn't have anyone to look after her. I was one of the few Masters without a partner available to take her in. She's not exempt. Monsters must compete, and they have to perform their duties."

I stare at my knife, still stuck in this little girl's flesh. "If I'd known, I wouldn't have—"

"I know," he says. "You're probably the only candidate who doesn't know. I assume Margot didn't tell you so you wouldn't hesitate."

No. Margot told me to avoid him. She made it out like it was because I couldn't beat him, and maybe she did think I couldn't, but part of me wonders if she also wanted to save me the moral dilemma of realizing I'd fought a child.

I reach out to the girl, and she blinks at me with those huge eyes. "I'm sorry," I say to her, and pry out the knife as gently as I can. She doesn't even squeak. I use the knife to tear the bottom of my shirt into a strip that I tie around her leg. It barely fits.

"Usually, the medical team helps with that," Corris says, and I jump because I didn't realize he was so close to me. "But we appreciate it nonetheless." He tucks his hands into his pockets. "But you're supposed to be racing. And I would hate to see you do anything other than finish in the top five. Lucky for you, I was your last obstacle."

My brain catches up to what he's saying. The race. I need to finish.

I sprint past him but make time to shout over my shoulder, "Thank you! Both of you!"

I'm rewarded with joyous trunk honking.

Never again. I can't let myself forget there are people inside those monster bodies.

I'm going to do it. I'm going to finish. Hopefully I'm fast enough to place well.

It's only Margot's warning to be vigilant that makes me check the trees as I run, just in time to duck as a sledgehammer speeds toward my face. I roll on the ground and spring to my feet, my thighs screaming as I do so, my side aching, and my head spinning.

I spot Caden coming out from the trees. His lip is split, and he licks away the blood as he grins at me. "Found you."

# CHAPTER FORTY-TWO

Caden swings the sledgehammer again, and I jump back. I get a knife out and flying through the air, where it slices across his cheek. He doesn't even wince. He darts at me, managing the heavy tool with a lot more dexterity and ease than it should warrant. It's not even like he's a big guy, but you don't need bulging muscles to be strong.

I look behind him, but Hudson's nowhere to be seen. "Where's your buddy?" I ask.

"He thought chasing you was a waste of time. He's got a lower rank, after all. He has to focus. But I can always make time for you." He swings and the edge of the sledgehammer catches me in the side. And of course, it's the same fucking side that already aches. I cry out, twisting away from him.

The hammer thumps on the ground as he pauses to take a breath. "Where's your mom?"

"What?!"

"Your mom. Did you grow up with her? Is she in your life? Alive?"

He is the last person who I want to speak with about Mom.

Caden doesn't care either way. "Mine was doing research at Summerhill. She took me along because my dad had to work late. When she heard them coming, the screaming and the snarls, she tugged a bookshelf out from the wall and pushed me behind it, piling up books in front to hide me. I wasn't allowed to come out."

I take a chance and try to run away while he's busy talking. But he's not having any of it. He rushes me, abandoning his weapon, and slams his body into mine, sending me to the ground with him on top of me. I attempt to shove him off, and we end up grappling. He manages to get a hand on the side on my face, shoving it into the dirt as he straddles me.

"Rude," he says. "I was talking. Anyway, I'm hiding behind these books, and I'm four years old. No idea what's happening. And then these monsters storm through. And one of them crushes her under his foot. Her body just fucking bursts. Like smashing a watermelon." He lets out a hysterical laugh. "And it wasn't even on purpose. I guess they didn't see her. And there was pancake Mommy on the ground. Blood syrup, and guts for butter, and crushed bones like little chocolate chips."

I manage to slide a knife free, and I stab the closest bit of him that I can get to. Caden swears, and I become frenzied, striking wherever I can.

He scrambles off me, and I jump to my feet and whip out my leg. But he's faster and gets a block up. I let loose more knives, but he's too close. I can't get a good throw in.

"Do you know that born monsters look like their parents?"

Caden retrieves his sledgehammer. "Their monstrous forms. When Hawthorne turns, he'll probably look like them. Or some mash-up of them. Stronger than both." He glares at me. "You think I want to see a stronger variant of my mom's murderers? You think any of the victims want to see that?!"

He charges at me, and I'm on the defensive using my knives and wrist braces to block, hoping for an opening, but none comes. He's stronger than me. It's the second test all over again.

Caden screams, "He belongs six feet under, just like them! But if I can't have that, I'll kill you and guarantee that he's underground." He laughs harder, spit flying onto my face. "Actually, that would put him more than six feet under. Perfect."

The next time he swings, I duck out of the way. He almost got me. A proper direct hit from that thing will break bones. I can't get hit. But I also can't just keep defending. I need to do something.

When he raises his weapon again, I jump back and throw a knife directly at his hand. He shouts and pulls back. I scream and kick out in a roundhouse, catching his other hand and making him drop his weapon.

I use every kick that Corey has ever taught me to drive him back. Shouting louder with each and every one.

I am so fucking tired of this kid. He lost his mom, I get it, it's horrible. Worse to watch her die in front of him. At least I can still believe that my mom is out there. But Virgil lost both his parents. His family is gone, and he's been villainized and ostracized from his own community his entire life for something he had no role in. He's lost enough.

And still, people like Caden insist on punishing him more so they can feel better.

A MASTERY OF MONSTERS

He recovers, rolling away from me and getting his sledgehammer back into his hands. But I'm right on top of him, rushing in fast. In a panic, he raises the thing high over his head—the first mistake he's made this whole fight. He shouts, "I'm going to finish th—"

I lean back, pull my leg close to my body, and shoot it straight up with a cry. My foot connects with the bottom of Caden's chin and shoves it up. He drops the sledgehammer. Blood spurts over my face as he falls.

He's clutching his mouth, which is bleeding profusely, and he's choking and searching around.

That's when I see the bit of pink muscle covered in dirt.

"Nothing more to say?" I grin at him. "Cat got your tongue?"

He moans, but he's too occupied with his pain to do anything else.

There's nothing I can tell this boy to make him see Virgil as anything other than the son of the monsters who killed his mom. And it's not my job to make him understand or learn or do better.

I just need to beat him.

I take off into the trees, running as fast as I can, leaving Caden howling behind me.

I break out into a clearing, passing the white spray-painted line in the grass. I skid to a stop.

I'm alone.

I'm . . . I'm last. Or, second to last.

Tears spring to my eyes, and I hide my face in my hands. I don't want the drone whirring above me to capture this moment.

Caden delayed me just enough.

"You did it! You did it! You did it!" That voice is . . . Virgil.

I pull my face away from my hands, and he's running around the corner with a huge grin on his face. He slams into me like a ton of bricks, lifting me off my feet and spinning me around. "You fucking did it!"

"What?" I croak.

"You did it!" His breath is warm against my ear.

"But . . . I'm practically last."

"What?!" Virgil pulls back from me and shouts in my face. "August. You're *first*! And you got past Corris, which no one has ever managed in the candidacy. *Ever.*"

My mouth is wide open. A dude with a camera appears and is shoving it in my face. Asking me how I feel to have come in first and how I knew the trick to beating Corris.

Fuck, my head hurts. My side hurts. My everything hurts.

"Give her some space!" Margot says, coming over with Corey, who squeals and hugs me.

I wince.

"Sorry!" Corey steps back. "Do we have a medic?"

I'm still in a daze when we get into a thing that Virgil says is a side-by-side vehicle, and it takes us around the grounds. A medic is in there, asking me questions and checking on me. I answer without even paying attention. He says something about my ribs being bruised but not broken.

*First.*

I came in first.

Thirty points. If Charity hadn't been taken out in the beginning and had come in second, we'd be tied. But now that means I'm first. Violet could beat me if she got all ten panel votes, but I don't give a shit about that. I'm in the top five for sure.

"Virgil." I turn to him. "I'm in the top five."

A MASTERY OF MONSTERS

He rolls his eyes. "That's what I've been trying to tell you."

Tears spill down my face. "You should be crying too!"

"He already did," Margot and Corey say together.

"Okay." Virgil puts up his hands. "You guys were too happy about getting to say that."

"He cried like four separate times watching you," Corey says, grinning. "I guess he's out of tears now. But more importantly, you did the kick!"

"I did!" I'm laughing, the mirth spilling out of me.

I know this isn't the end. There's still initiation. But in the words of Virgil, I fucking did it.

"The powers that be are pleased," Margot says, as the vehicle turns the corner and we can see the crowd. They explode into cheers when I come into view. Henry and Adam are both beaming and clapping.

But it's not just them. So many people in the stands look excited for me.

Margot meets my eyes. "I know it can feel like a lot. That sudden shift. When they see you as one of them instead of an outsider. But you showed them who you are. That you belong." She mutters, "And Caden showed his ass."

"Could you hear what he was saying?" I look over at Virgil.

He shakes his head. "No. There are no mics. Just the footage. Why? What did he say?"

"Nothing. Just bullshit." If he didn't hear, then I don't want him to know. Virgil already carries enough guilt over what his parents did.

When we get off the side-by-side, a bunch of people come over to congratulate me. Virgil and Corey stand beside me while Margot rattles off everyone's names. Chen gives me a self-satisfied nod, and I nod back. Perez comes over to congratulate me too and seems genuinely thrilled for me. I think during the training he was just trying to put me in a position that would make it impossible for people to deny that I deserved to get through. But that begs the questions of why? Why try that hard to legitimize me? I don't even know him.

I look around for Bernie, but he's hunched over on a bench. "Is he okay?" I ask Virgil.

Virgil bites his lip. "I told him that he should go home, but as a professor he's supposed to be observing. I think this is going to be his last time doing this. He's been struggling all year."

I turn away from Bernie and watch the screens. There are several showing the live footage and another updating the scores as we place. Someone is commentating over the loudspeakers about their progress. I'm currently in first with forty points.

And I guess Violet and Bryce must have just come through, because she's in second with thirty-four points, and he's third with twenty-six. Suddenly, the scoreboard changes. Caden appears in fourth with twenty-four points. I guess he dragged himself to the finish line.

At the bottom of the scoreboard, Charity and Peter are under disqualification. Hudson is still doing the run.

"What happens if Hudson doesn't finish on time?" I ask Virgil. "We wouldn't have five finalists."

"It happens sometimes. There are five spots, but they don't always get filled if there aren't enough candidates who qualify."

Right. There's no way the society would give them a free pass.

We sit in the stands, where I'm given water and an impressive cheese plate. When the hour is up and I've been suitably stuffed,

A MASTERY OF MONSTERS

we're made to wait another half hour while the panel of Masters casts their votes. I get medication for my head, which still hurts, but the medic said I don't have a concussion, at least.

Finally, James, Adam, Carrigan, the professors, and a woman I've never seen before gather. The camera guy perches in front of them.

The mystery woman accepts a microphone. "I am the representative from the panel of Masters, and I am here to announce the candidates who will participate in the initiation. Due to disqualifications, there will be no fifth candidate. In fourth, Hudson with twenty points. Tied for second place, Caden and Bryce with twenty-eight points."

The crowd starts buzzing.

"What the fuck . . . ?" Virgil looks at Margot. "What's happening right now?"

Margot is staring at the woman, her brow furrowing. "Just stay calm."

"How?!" he shouts, and I jerk toward him. It's the loudest I've ever heard him speak, even when he's been pissed at me. "Can't you see what they're doing?!"

Some people in the crowd have started looking his way, and for the first time, Virgil doesn't care.

He's reading the writing on the wall in real time, the same way I am.

"And in first place with fifty-three points," the woman says, making her voice louder to be heard over the murmuring crowd. "Violet!"

The crowd erupts. There are screams and cries and boos.

It's not what Violet deserves, but I can't even turn my mind to her.

The woman on the mic is half screaming into it. "August Black has been disqualified. It was noted that in the second test, she took the bag used to hold the eggs from another candidate, therefore making it impossible for that candidate to continue participating in the test. It was being discussed whether or not this should be grounds for disqualification, and the decision was finalized today. The panel voted six to four that she should be disqualified. The two panel members who gave her their votes for the final score refused to reassign them, which is why the numbers are as they are."

Virgil rushes toward the woman.

Margot sprints forward and tries to pull him back by his arm, but he's incandescent, tugging her along the ground. Corey has to grab his other arm to stop him, both of them working in tandem to keep him from getting to the lady with the mic, who's stumbled back.

"It's bullshit!" Virgil screams. "She won! You know she won! She won!"

Henry comes down from the stands and gets in front of Virgil, speaking to him in a low, urgent tone, but even he's not helping calm him.

It's like I'm watching the scene through a TV screen.

Remote and separated.

His entire life he held back so he could be saved. And in the end, they showed him the truth. They were never going to allow him to ascend in this society. Not me, either.

And isn't this how I knew this was going to end? I tried my best. I did everything I could, and still, this was the result.

Now I'm going to lose them both.

Virgil to the monster.

And Jules to the Master manipulating him. Or if not them, then to the society whenever they get around to dealing with what's happening. Or to QBSS, who plans to kill him.

A MASTERY OF MONSTERS

It's worse now, worse than it's ever been, because I wanted this for myself too. I wanted to win. I wanted to save them. And I wanted to show these people that I could do it.

I leave without looking back.

# CHAPTER FORTY-THREE

If I had it my way, I would skip the community dinner. But I promised Mia, and without her help with my knives, I wouldn't have even made it through the test yesterday. Not that it mattered in the end.

When I step into the barn, the afternoon sun is high in the sky. It's a bright, sunny day, making the cold more bearable. Proof that the world moves on no matter what's happening in your life.

My eyes widen at the setup. I was expecting to have a lot to do, but most is already finished. The linens have been put onto the tables and chairs. The centerpieces of mismatched candles arranged. Even the heaters have been put up, though they're not on yet. And swathes of cloth have been hung from the barn loft.

Mia and Isaac are arranging heating lamps on a table for the food. When she spots me, she says, "You're here! And . . . I think most of the stuff is done."

When I reach the two of them, I avoid looking Isaac in the eye.

I know he won't talk about the candidacy with Mia here, but I don't want to see whatever emotion he has swimming there.

"Virgil came early and did all this on his own," Isaac says. "I guess he let himself in."

"You saw him?" I ask, staring at the table.

"No. He texted after to say he helped set up. It was like this when we came by. Except for the rafter stuff, we hung those."

I guess he wanted to keep his promise too. But without having to see any of us. Without having to see *me*. I scratch at the tablecloth, imagining ripping a hole into it just to hurt something.

"Isaac was saying he might not come by at all since he's sick," Mia says. And there's something about her voice that makes me look up. She's staring at me, her expression flat. "I texted to see if, since he was feeling well enough to help, he might come tonight."

Isaac looks at Mia and then at me. Again, I turn away. "What can I do?" I ask.

"Come learn how to sharpen knives with me." Mia turns to Isaac. "You don't mind finishing with the heat lamps?"

"Uh, no, that's cool."

"Thank you!" She hooks her arm through mine and drags me over to the shed behind her house.

My eyes bug out when I see inside.

The walls are packed with weapons. No firearms. Just row after row of knives, swords, axes, and more. "Told you he had a nerd collection," Mia singsongs. She leads me to a table at the back, where she pulls out some small tools. "These are whetstones. You can come in here whenever—just text me, and I can let you know when's a good time so you don't get caught by Dad and end up suffering his admiration."

"You'll lose leverage by teaching me."

"I don't need leverage anymore."

I stare at the arrangement of tools. I really thought she was out here with one of those medieval wheels, since I'd never actually watched Mom sharpen.

She instructs me, handing me a dull blade to practice. I'm curious about how it got dull in the first place but don't pry. I know how she threw that knife wasn't a fluke. The same way that Virgil knew when he watched me throw.

"Your dad taught you how to use some of this stuff, didn't he?" I ask.

"Mom taught me traditional medicine and Dad taught me blades. Between you and me, her lessons were a lot more practical. But I do use some of his moves in hockey."

"My mom taught me." I move the knife the way Mia showed me across the whetstone. "Which I guess most people think is weird. But I don't know. She wanted to share a hobby with us. It's not that strange."

"Is that what you think?" Mia leans her hand against her palm.

"Don't you?"

"I don't think my parents would teach me anything they didn't expect me to use."

We stare at each other for a moment. I turn away to the wall of weapons and notice that one of the swords has initials stamped on it. I peer closer. G. T. M. "Was this someone else's before?" If it belonged to Jacques, it would be J. L.

"Yeah. Grandad. My dad's dad. He made some of these—that's how Dad got all obsessed. G. T. M. Garrett Thomas Murphy."

My fingers clench around the handle of the knife.

*Garrett Murphy.*

"You okay?"

I relax my grip. "But . . . your dad's last name is Levesque."

"Yeah, it's his mom's maiden name. He had this whole falling out with Grandad and changed his name, and they didn't talk, like, my whole life, and then this year he started coming back around. They were arguing for a bit there, but I think they worked it out." She shrugs. "Family, right?"

I force out a laugh. "Yeah, right."

Mia doesn't know about the Wilds. Otherwise, she wouldn't be speaking this casually about Garrett to me. She would know I'm part of the society. Or that I was, anyway. Just like born monsters, not every Wild family has children who become Wilds. Maybe it didn't happen to her, and so Jacques decided to use his mom's name and live like a normal family. That was why he was so weird in the barn. It wasn't the event itself, it was the fact that Virgil and Isaac showed up. Maybe even just that Mia was spending so much time with me. Monsters can't sense each other or anything, but Garrett's been at the nominations and tests. He would know I'm a candidate. And he would know Virgil because of his parents.

*You know.*

I know Jacques, but I didn't know Jacques was a Murphy. Maybe he's like Mia, not a Wild. Or maybe he is. He and his dad have been repairing their relationship this year. The same year Cyrus dies, and the Wilds' agreement becomes null.

"You should ask Virgil to come tonight," Mia says, and I jump, shocked out of my thoughts. "I don't know what's gone down between the two of you, but I know him being sick is bullshit. If you ask him to come, I bet he will. You guys can work things out."

I hunch my shoulders. "He already has an invitation." Part of me wants to see him, and another part of me never wants to set eyes on him again.

Because the next time I see Virgil, it'll be to say goodbye.

The barn is unrecognizable by the time people start filtering in for the dinner. The lights strung from the rafters have been turned on and add just enough to the space. Not too dim and not too bright. Everyone's dishes are laid out on the tables under heating lamps, and people help themselves to drinks from the refreshments area. Music floats through the space from a sound system that one of the residents donated to us for the event. Margot's been invited alongside Isaac, and though I personally avoid her, she's getting along well with everyone else.

There's a hum in the air of people talking and laughing. That buzz that makes a room feel full.

I didn't appreciate how many people live here until I saw everyone who turned up for the event. I sit next to an older Black woman named Opal. She's one of the people whose door I knocked on to invite to this, and it's nice that she came. I'm pretty sure everyone we invited is here tonight.

We moved so often, and when we did interact with neighbors, it was brief and perfunctory. Mom liked for us to keep some distance. We never had anything like this. I bite my lip, considering what Mia said earlier about how her parents wouldn't teach her something they didn't expect her to use. Why would her dad think she would need to use weapons like that, and why would Mom think I would need knife and combat skills? But then, I did need them.

I eye Jacques from across the space. Could he be a part of

everything going down with Jules, or am I being paranoid?

Mia stands at the head of the room. Like her mom did before, she has a paper that she reads from in Mohawk. She uses it the whole time but speaks just as well as Izzy, only stumbling over her words a couple of times. In English she adds, "Thank you so much to everyone for coming. It means a lot to gather here with you on the traditional lands of my people. My parents wanted to transform this place from something owned to something shared." She nods to Izzy and Jacques, the former of whom is misty-eyed watching her. "I didn't get to know my maternal grandma. My mom didn't either. We've had a lot of things stolen from us that can never be given back. But we've also been trying to recover what we can. And community is a part of that. People who know each other, and support each other, and live together. That's what tonight is about. I'm thankful to the Creator, and my parents, and my friends who helped, August, and Isaac, and Virgil, and all of you who've come here today. Nyawenhkó:wa."

There's a round of applause, and she beams.

I never wanted to be a part of this community that Bailey found her way to, and I definitely didn't want anything to do with the Learners, but I like being here with these people. With Mia. And I like being with Corey, and Margot, and Isaac. Violet and Bryce. Riley, too.

And Virgil.

When Mom disappeared, I turned around, and the people who used to surround me were gone too. Everyone except for Jules.

I feel it happening again now.

And I don't want it to.

"August?" Bailey asks.

Tears slide down my face. I wipe them away. "Sorry, I'm fine."

"You sure?"

"Uh, no, but yeah." I manage a smile.

"I know what that feeling is like." She reaches across the table and grasps my hand. "You don't always have to be fine."

The rest of the night goes well. Mostly everyone's food is great. There's a mac and cheese with what looks like a frozen vegetable medley mixed into it that I avoid, but it's otherwise perfect. I meet everyone who lives here, and Mia does several rounds of icebreaker games to make triple sure we become familiar with each other.

People begin to fill the dance floor, and I watch Isaac stammer his way through inviting Mia to dance with him. To their credit, her parents get busy rearranging the drink section during the exchange. And the two manage to get onto the dance floor, swaying to the music, Mia's head laid on his chest.

Margot sits in the seat across from me. I stiffen. I expected her to come over at some point. I don't want to talk about the candidacy right now. I don't want to see the disappointment in her face.

She tilts her head away from me to watch her brother spinning with Mia in a slow circle. "I forgot this is what I was fighting for. Still am. This is why I'm on Henry's side. Why I'm working so hard for him. Not just because I didn't want to see my brother in the Pen, but because I wanted to see him like this. *Living*. Being a normal teenage boy." She turns to me. "You did everything you could for Virgil. Don't ever let anyone suggest otherwise."

With that, she stands, ready to head back to her own table.

"Thank you," I blurt out, and she pauses, meeting my eyes. "Thank you. I know you did everything you could too."

She gives me a small smile and then stops, turning toward the back of the barn. "Well, look at that." I follow her eyes, and there he is: Virgil, walking over to us. Margot raps her knuckles on the table. "I'll leave you to it," she says before heading back to her spot.

I don't know why I stand. I just do, and he comes up to stand beside me. He nudges his shoulder against mine. "Sorry I'm late."

I swallow to wet my throat. "You don't have to be here."

"No," he says. "I do. I just didn't know if I would."

"Then why?"

"Because it was harder to stay away than to come." He forces a smile. The corners of his eyes look strained, his skin dry and ashy.

"You look like shit," I say.

He laughs. "Wow, and I was planning to say how nice you looked." He clears his throat and holds out his hand. "Dance with me?"

"I don't know how to dance to this music." It's slow and gentle. I'm used to thumping beats so loud they vibrate through my body.

"Lucky for you, this is the only music I know how to dance to."

I take his hand.

Instead of bringing me to the dance floor, we make our way to a separate corner of the barn. It's darker here, lit only by twinkling fairy lights. We interlace our fingers, and he slides his other hand to my lower back. We sway, moving slowly in a circle. It hurts still to be this mobile. My side throbs, but it's worth it.

I allow myself to lay my head on his chest, resting it there. His heartbeat is too fast for the music.

Virgil says, "I did everything by the book. Followed all the rules. Dealt with everything they threw at me. And it didn't matter. I had so many people trying to help me. Amazing and talented people. And that didn't matter either. The second my parents stormed Summerhill, they changed my life forever." He sucks in a breath. "I . . . I believed in you. And you fucking did it, and they still—" A sob cuts him off.

I look up from his chest, and his eyes sparkle with unshed tears.

"I'm sorry," I say because there's nothing else to say.

"*You're* sorry? *I'm* sorry. I'm sorry I dragged you into the candidacy and acted like this was a fair place. Like we could do something or change things. But we can't. This is how the system is built. The society wasn't made to save monsters, it was made to elevate Masters. It's right there in the name. There is no equality. There is no fairness. And Adam is trying, but it's not enough, and it never will be."

I know I should say something contrary to make him feel better. But I can't lie to him. Not now.

Virgil pulls his hand away from my back to scrub at his face. "Margot and Corey are still going to help with your brother. Me too, however I can."

"The deal—"

"The deal was that you would win, and we would help you. And you won. But I have a request."

"A new deal?"

"Sure."

"What?"

"Don't act like I'm gone while I'm still here." He peers down at me. "I know you don't owe me anything, but we're . . . we're friends, at least, aren't we?"

Tears build behind my eyes.

"So be my friend until it's over."

I break from Virgil's arms and step back. I don't have to do this. It's a request. That means I can say no. I can back away from all this. Try to manage helping Jules on my own. Stop speaking to Virgil.

A MASTERY OF MONSTERS

Avoid everything that will come with watching this boy walk down a steep set of stairs to the rest of his life as a mindless monster.

Because what if I can't be there for him? What if I mess that up somehow? And then that's the last thing I ever do before losing him. Because this time, losing Virgil is guaranteed. No matter what.

After Mom disappeared, I thought that it was better to expedite that process. Skip the part where they expect anything of you, disappoint them first, lose them before I could love them. Before it could hurt.

That's what I should do now. Say no to Virgil. Deal with the hurt now. Move on.

But I can't do that anymore.

Because even after everything, even after having gone through the whole competition, it's still worth it. It was worth it to know him. Even if I ended up disappointing him somehow. Even knowing that I'll lose him. It's still worth it.

*He's* worth it.

"Until it's over," I say, holding out my hand, arm bent.

Virgil clasps my fingers, and we pull close to each other, our forearms and elbows touching. I lay my forehead on his. The closest I'll allow myself to be.

"Until it's over," he repeats.

# CHAPTER FORTY-FOUR

The next three weeks are lost to a haze of both preparing for and taking exams. It's that time of the year when everything goes faster because the days are shorter. Everyone is rushing toward the end of cramming information into their brains and wishing for the winter break. I listen to my peers make plans to go home and become the subject of their family's attention as they reflect on their first semester.

Me, I don't want the semester to end.

I kept my promise to Virgil. I'm still keeping it. And he's spent the time pretending that his isn't running out. Studying just as hard as me and Corey, pulling all-nighters to get his essays done, and sometimes, avoiding everyone altogether. Those days, Corey will text me about scratching and growling coming from his room.

And this Saturday, after the final exam, the initiation will happen without us. Bachelor titles will be handed out, and other monsters will be saved.

But not Virgil.

He only has until the end of the year. That's the deadline for monsters who participated in this year's candidacy but didn't reach the final stage of monstrosity. It's meant to give them the opportunity to be approached by a senior Master, which won't be the case for Virgil. After all, that was why he needed me. And that's assuming he can hold out until then. Anyone who shows too many symptoms or turns is taken underground immediately.

I flop onto my bed face down. I'm one of the lucky people who had my last exam this afternoon on the Monday.

This is the part where I'm supposed to feel relieved. Where I pack up my stuff and go to Bailey's place, ready for rest and relaxation. Maybe she'll cook some of that macaroni pie she gave Dad when he was sick. And Jules will come home, and Mom will be there too, and she'll make her famous jerk chicken. Mia's already organizing a holiday meal for anyone not leaving the tiny house community during the break. We'll have some sort of New Year's gathering too. I could invite Virgil, and Corey, and Margot, and Isaac. I'd even try to invite Riley, though I haven't heard from her. We'd go into the next semester together.

In reality, Virgil will be sent to the Pen to live out the rest of his life in the dark. Only given a respite during training sessions for the next batch of candidates. And Jules . . . I don't know. He hasn't resurfaced. And no matter how long I turn it over in my head, there's no way to know for sure who he meant.

But I'm still here because I want to be. I want to keep trying to help Jules. And I want to stay with Virgil. Not just for them, for me too.

I make a sad attempt to clean up my room and uncover the box of pictures that Bailey brought me. I drag it over to my bed, pulling out the albums and flipping through them.

I frown at one of Mom and a guy. He looks South Asian and has dark curly hair that reaches his shoulders, which he's tucked behind his ears. Mom's beaming and holding on to him. I squint. He looks like someone. . . . Who does he look like? I pull the photo out and flip it over. It just has the year, 2000, and a bunch of hearts. Maybe an old boyfriend? I find more photos of the two of them, but also some of the two of them with Dad. I take a picture and send it to him. *Who's this?*

Dad answers back with an eye rolling Memoji. He's updated his to be bald now because he really is that cheesy.

*Not an answer,* I text back.

*He was your mom's best friend but clearly in love with her. I admit that I was jealous for a bit. But then they had a falling out when we finished school. I think he was upset about us getting married. Though she still sent him the odd invite. To baby showers and birthdays, but he never showed. Carl something? Carlton?*

I can't believe Dad is acting like he's not still jealous with that Memoji choice. Or with his "can't even be bothered to remember this man's name" performance.

Though that doesn't answer the question of why the guy looks familiar.

There's frenzied knocking at my door. I jump off the bed and go to it, and when I pull it open, Corey walks in and starts saying a bunch of things very quickly.

I raise my hands. "Stop. Restart. Slower."

She takes a deep breath and holds up a book—leather-bound in an older style but shiny. "It's a copy! It's a fake, yes, but it's an accurate copy."

A MASTERY OF MONSTERS

"Um . . ."

"It took *forever*, but Henry was able to let me take a look at some of the journals Adam has access to, and it was the same style of writing and cadence. I figured there was something more there, so Henry gave me the funds to pay off the guy who ghosted me and he cracked. Apparently, he was supposed to repair the original. The person who requested the repair paid a *lot*, and that made him think it was valuable. He photocopied all the pages, and then copied them by hand to make a fake! But the information is correct, so Henry can use it! Well, except for a few pages that were too mangled to copy. That's what the repair was for, fire damage. Someone did a poor job storing it."

"Who dropped it off?"

"He doesn't know. They left it in his mailbox, and for pickup he put it back in the mailbox, and they grabbed it later. And they used a fake name, too."

"If it's so valuable, why did they give it to this random guy to repair?"

"He's not random! He's pretty reputable for Kingston. That's why I was so shook that he stopped texting me like that. It's surprising that he copied it at all, but I think he's somewhat aware of society people. He said this wasn't the first Dr. Weiss journal he'd seen. But because of how much the person offered to rush the job, I think he saw an opportunity. He did also say business had been slow lately." She rolls her eyes and says in a mocking tone, "No one reads anymore!"

I laugh. "And what did Henry think?"

Corey collapses onto my desk chair. "Yeah, um, well . . . I kind of spat out the same story I told you, and then I yelled at him and left. So . . . he didn't get to say anything."

"You did *what?!*" I drag her chair close to the bed. "Details!"

"I told him what you and Virgil said. That I was happy to help him with this, but that I shouldn't have to prove myself to get involved in making change. I know he didn't say I needed to do this, that I put it on myself, but he encouraged it. He made it seem like a condition without explicitly saying so. Which I know now was unfair. And then when I got to the end, I realized that I was shouting." She drags her hands down her face. "Oh my God, I yelled at him."

"I honestly think not enough people yell at him." She glares at me and then catches herself and balks. But I just laugh again. "It's called standing up for yourself. And it's amazing that you're doing it."

"And now I have to finish my essays." She sighs and leans back in the chair. "I got caught up in this journal stuff, so I'm behind." She looks at me with wide eyes, slapping her palms together. "Can you please proofread my essays? Just to see if they make sense to you? Pleeeeeeeeeeeease?"

The absolute last thing I want to do is more schoolwork.

She pulls out the pout. I groan. I haven't built up Virgil's immunity to it. "Fine."

"Yay! You're the best!"

"You have to feed me, though."

"Deal!"

We walk together to McIntosh Castle while Corey talks about some of the things in the journals. It all pretty much goes over my head. It's Dr. Weiss waxing poetic about the place of the Learners' Society in the world and preparing for the apocalypse. More about the warning signs of the spontaneous births. Things we already know, but I guess it's interesting to find that this particular journal was the source of that information.

We open the door to distant booms and smashing sounds.

Me and Corey look at each other. She's about to call out when I put a hand to my lips, and she falls quiet. I reach back, patting the knife on my belt before creeping forward. We pad up the stairs. I keep my body tense.

Once we get to the upper floor landing, it's obvious that the sounds are coming from Virgil's room. I reach for the knob and twist it the slightest bit, but it's locked.

Corey waves me away. I step back and she jumps, shoving at the door with the heel of her right foot. It swings open. She grins. "And that wasn't even the metal le—" The words die in her throat as we get a good look inside the room.

It's carnage.

Bookcases are overturned, and their contents strewn around the room. Ripped pages fly through the air. There are chairs on their sides, one with a broken leg. The mirror that was leaning against the wall is shattered, splinters radiating out from the middle, with pieces lying on the floor and reflecting the boy in the center of the room.

Virgil pants, his chest heaving, his mouth overcrowded by teeth, his lips bloodied, and tear tracks on his face. He stares at me and Corey, his eyes darting.

He brings shaking hands to his face. "They won't go back in." His words are muffled by the teeth, and his fingers are cut up too.

I move forward and pull his hands away from his mouth, getting blood on my hands. "Just breathe, remember? Like Henry said." The only advice the professor gave was to try to keep Virgil calm. Knowing that eventually, it would get to be too much. Our goal is to get him to the end of the year.

454 LISELLE SAMBURY

"I don't want to go," he chokes out.

I shake my head. "It's fine. They'll go back in. Just brea—"

He stumbles away from me. "I'm so fucking tired of holding everything in!" he screams. "I don't want to go! This isn't my fault!" He grips his hands into fists. "I don't want to go like this. They treated me like shit my entire life, and I never fucking once got to make them pay for it. Not those assholes who came here to 'assess' me when I was a kid, not those people who glared at me in meetings and lectures, and not even Caden, who actively tried to kill you! None of them! And now I have to go underground, and they get to keep going?" He shakes his head. "No. Fuck that. Fuck them."

He opens his fists and there, sprouting from his nails, are black claws. "Go get someone," I say, glancing at Corey.

"But . . . ," she says, staring at Virgil. "But . . ."

"Go. Please."

Corey starts to tear up. "I can't just leave him."

"I'm here. He's not alone. Find someone who can help."

She bites her lip before nodding finally. "It's going to be okay," she says to Virgil, who laughs in response. It comes from somewhere deeper in his throat. Rough and raw. She turns and rushes down the stairs.

"I can't calm down," Virgil says. "I won't. Not this time."

"Fine," I say. "They don't deserve your restraint. They never did."

Virgil's eyes widen a fraction.

"You're too good for all of them. That's your problem. You're just . . . too good. So be mad. Be angry. Smash things. Go tear them apart. It's what they deserve."

Virgil hunches over and screams again, clenching his fists until

A MASTERY OF MONSTERS 455

they rip into his skin. It hurts to hear it. Not just in my ears. It tears through my entire body, drawing shakes, and making my eyes water. He drops to his knees and huddles into a ball.

A hand lands on my shoulder, and I jump, whipping around. Bernie smiles at me, his breathing heavy and face pale, like he ran. "I'll talk to him. Just give me a bit, okay?"

He puts his hand on Virgil's back, whispering too low for me to hear.

"We should eat," Corey says, tugging at my arm. I didn't even realize she'd come back too.

The last thing I want to do is leave Virgil.

I guess I know how she felt now.

And for the same reason she did, I go with Corey down into the kitchen and eat in silence while we leave Bernie alone with him.

It feels like hours later when Bernie comes back down the stairs. Me and Corey both jump up from the kitchen stools. "He's sleeping. He's okay. He's back to normal."

I grip the edge of the counter to keep myself steady. Henry said even juvenile monsters can handle some pretty severe symptoms. But I'd never seen Virgil with actual physical things like fangs and claws before. "What did you say to him?" I ask.

"Just spoke. Told him stories about his parents. Not that I knew them well. They were Henry's friends, but I knew enough. Told him things about Davy. Just anything." He wrings his hands. "I know how it goes, so I have some practice. But . . . I don't know if he'll make it to winter break, much less the end of the year."

I swallow. It's not what any of us want to hear.

Bernie says, "I would give him some space right now. Wait until the morning to talk to him. I'm going to head home."

Corey walks Bernie out while I stare at my empty plate, grains of rice stuck to the white porcelain.

Me and Corey try to get through the rest of the evening. I read over her essays which are, as far as I can tell, perfect. Though she still makes some additions. I stay up until the eleven o'clock deadline when she submits them.

I'll be sleeping in the guest room, as usual. I lie there, attempting to rest. At midnight, I give up and leave the room. I tell myself to get water, but instead I end up back at Virgil's door. I press my ear against it, hoping to hear soft breathing or snores.

When there's nothing, I turn the knob. It gives immediately. Corey broke the lock when she kicked it open.

I stare at Virgil's bed.

Virgil's bed where Virgil is supposed to be.

Instead, the sheets are tossed aside, and the bed is empty.

# CHAPTER FORTY-FIVE

Bernie lives on King Street, only a few blocks over from McIntosh Castle. It makes sense, since it's close to both the museum that he and his wife run, and campus. The street is quiet and abandoned. It's a Monday night after midnight, and though students live in this section too, there are enough non-student residents for it to be calm at this time.

"It's this one," Corey says, looking up from her phone. She's been texting and calling Bernie to see if Virgil might have said anything suggesting that he'd run away. We haven't heard back.

Meanwhile, Margot is getting ready and rousing Isaac, and she's supposed to drive over and meet us so we can search for him. "Any updates from Margot?"

"Yeah, she said Henry is getting his people to check the security footage on the house to see which way Virgil went, but they're having issues."

Right, the cameras. "Wait, they're Henry's cameras?"

"Yeah. Who else?"

"I thought they were the society's or something. Since it's one of their properties."

Corey shakes her head. "No, Henry had them installed because he was worried about someone coming after Virgil as revenge for his parents. People in his Mastery group watch them." She walks up the steps of the house and knocks on the front door.

Bernie's house is one of six or so identical brick townhouses that line the block. They all have three stories and a basement entrance.

When no one answers, I come up next to Corey and try to peer through the glass doors, but there's nothing but darkness. I knock harder on the glass, and Corey winces beside me.

I glance up and down the street, but no one's come out or is paying attention to us. I search their front porch, but there isn't anything that looks like it could be holding a spare key, including no front mat or even a ledge for a spare to rest on.

"You think he's asleep?" I ask.

"Probably. It's past midnight, and he's been having health issues all year. And then I came over here and made him run with me to help Virgil. That probably took a lot out of him."

She has a fair point. And he's been looking worse lately.

I walk down the stairs and into the narrow alley between the houses, looking through the windows there. But it's too dark in every single one.

Corey swears behind me, and I turn to her. "What?"

She's looking down at the lit-up phone in her hand. "Someone took out the cameras at McIntosh Castle."

"Took them out?!"

"Smashed them. There's no footage."

A MASTERY OF MONSTERS

I stuff my hands into my jacket pockets. "Virgil."

"He would have known where they were."

Even a day ago, I wouldn't have believed that he would run. But how he was earlier today . . . desperate and angry, it was different. I've never seen him like that before. "Fuck. What is even his plan? I would understand if he went to Henry or us or something, but this . . ."

I narrow my eyes at the window, and Corey must read something in my face, because she starts to shake her head. "August . . ."

"He's the last person who talked to Virgil. Don't you think these circumstances are dire enough? Henry can pay for the damages."

Corey swallows before sighing. "Okay."

"Keep a look out." The last thing I need is some neighbor calling the police to say a Black girl is breaking into someone's home. I don't see that ending well for me.

It's an awkward angle because the window is high. I take out my knife, aim handle first, and slam it into the window. Having never purposely broken a window before, I'm surprised when the whole thing shatters. Loudly.

I take my jacket off and use it to scatter the debris, then lay it on the ledge. "I need a boost! Quick! Before someone comes."

Corey helps boost me in, and then I drag her through the window after. We're in their ground-level bathroom. "Sorry, Bernie," she mumbles. We go into the hall and head up the stairs to the main floor.

"Bernie?!" Corey calls out, but no one answers.

The first door we open is a small bedroom. Davy's, I assume. It's been preserved. Everything left as is, made obvious by the thin layer of dust on the surfaces. We get to the main bedroom, and it's empty too.

"They're not home," Corey says.

"After midnight on a Monday? When he told us he was going home? What could he and his wife possibly be out doing?" I think back and say, "He also told us not to bother Virgil until the morning. The only reason I realized he was gone was because I didn't listen to him."

She shakes her head. "No . . . no . . . Why would he . . ."

"Virgil wouldn't run on his own. He's too pragmatic for that. But if someone promised to help him . . ."

"Shit."

"Yeah, shit." I look around the room, seeing if there's anything in there that might hint at where Virgil and Bernie went. "It's weird that his wife is gone too." I riffle through their closet, but it's just filled with clothes. No false back to it either. Not even shoeboxes that might hold something hidden.

"There's a basement." Corey starts toward it without waiting for me. I turn and rush after her. Both of us have to duck on the staircase because of the overhang, and neither of us is even that tall. There's a door at the bottom of the stairs without a lock on it. But when I push, it won't open.

I look at Corey with a raised brow.

"You do know that *you* can kick doors open too, right?" she says.

"But you do it so well."

She rolls her eyes and kicks at the door, but instead of it busting open, her whole foot goes through the thing. "Shit!" She loses her balance, and I grab a hold of her, helping her stay upright while she pulls her foot out.

"That did not happen last time," I say.

"No, it did not." I let her go, and Corey kicks again and again.

It's a normal hollow interior door, made of thin wood that splinters under the pressure of her attacks. She opens up a hole big enough for us to crawl inside. Once we're in there, it becomes clear why the door didn't just give. There are three deadbolts on the other side.

"Deadbolts on a cheap hollow door." I shake my head. "I guess they didn't expect anyone to physically attack it."

"But they also didn't want anyone to come in."

It's a mundane room. They seem to be using it as a sort of flex/rec space, though it's not much bigger than the main bedroom upstairs. There's a stacked washer and dryer on the far end, a squishy couch, a double bed shoved in the corner, and even a tiny, unfinished bathroom. The drywall hasn't been painted or anything. Just naked sheets, screwed onto two-by-fours.

Corey goes over to the bed and grabs the duvet, shaking it out and then lifting it to her nose.

"Is there a reason we're smelling the bedsheets?" I ask. "Or are you about to reveal a fetish to me?"

She scowls. "They're sweaty. Someone's been sleeping here recently."

"Why would they sleep down here when there's a perfectly good bedroom upstairs? Unless Bernie and his wife are fighting, and this is his man cave or whatever."

Corey moves faster around the room, going over to a chest of drawers and opening it, staring at the contents, and then grabbing another shirt from the floor. She snatches up more things in the room. Some random acoustic guitar and then drawings. And the more she does it, the paler she gets.

"What is it?" I ask.

"The clothes . . . they're like . . . graphic T-shirts and hoodies. And they smell. Someone's been wearing them. Have you ever seen Bernie wear clothes like that? He doesn't draw or play guitar . . . but . . . but Davy did. He loved art and music."

I chew on my bottom lip. A secret room in the basement. If it were locked from the outside, that would be suspicious, but from the inside . . . and the feel of this place, like it was built in a hurry. I look at the windows. They're not just covered with curtains, the curtains have been nailed into place, like someone wanted to be sure they wouldn't fall.

"How is he getting out?" I look around the room. "The door locks from the inside, and it was still locked. But no one is here."

"How is he alive is a better question," Corey says, wrapping her arms around herself. "We were sure he was dead. They went after him. They reported him dead."

"Was there a body?"

Corey sighs. "I mean, no."

"There was no body, and no one questioned that?!"

"Sometimes you never get a body, and you still know someone is gone!"

I grit my teeth. I know that, of course I know that.

She continues, "They found evidence that Davy had been camping, way over on the island. Probably trying to get on the ferry to New York, cross the border. But it was below freezing. He wouldn't have survived the night, and even if he had, he would have turned. He was already on the edge. We would have noticed a sudden uncontrolled monster popping up. They didn't need a body."

"Let's just keep looking for how he got out."

Corey joins me as we search the room more aggressively, pulling posters off the wall and shoving furniture, and then finally, I find it.

A trap door on the floor behind the couch. When I open it, there's a ladder leading into the darkness.

"I'm going in," I say.

"No, you're not. We need to call Henry and Margot."

"Fine, you stay and call, and I'll go in."

"You can't go in alone!"

"And if we both go and are viciously horror-movie killed, no one will know what happened. You wait, and I'll go."

Corey groans, squishing her cheeks with her hands. "Okay, okay, fine. You go. Fast! I'll call. Any sign of danger, come back right away."

I don't waste any more time and start climbing. Once I'm down the ladder, I use my phone to light the way. It's damp, and the space is huge. So much bigger than I thought it would be. I look back up at the hole I came out of, and it's rough. The edges aren't smooth the way they are in the rest of the space. Like someone forced this hole. Even the ladder is just something from a hardware store. Bernie must have made this setup himself. And I guess he isn't much of a handyman. He couldn't even finish the bathroom and didn't think of using a steel door for the basement.

I walk several feet down the tunnel, shining my light on the walls until it illuminates something that makes me stop in my tracks.

A cage.

A cage that looks exactly like the ones in the Pen. I run my hands over the lock on it. It's been smashed and melted, and replaced with chains and a padlock that are open. Inside, there are scratches and claw marks. And just outside the cell . . . dried blood.

Laira said that when senior Masters get a new partner, they put them in a cage so it's easier to do the flesh exchange part of the bonding. They skip the initiation. All they would need otherwise is the serum. The heavily protected serum. Except perhaps if you were a professor monitoring the candidacy. They would need the serum for initiation. Bernie must have found a way to use his position to get some.

His son was never missing. Bernie saved him. No one ever saw Davy turn, so they wouldn't know what his monster form looks like. Bernie got hold of the serum and has kept his son hidden and alive this whole time.

Bernie, who helped raise Virgil. Who's been so invested in Virgil's success. Who loves Virgil like a son.

I sprint back down the tunnel and up the ladder, already shouting to Corey. "Bernie is going to bond with Virgil! Just like he did with Davy! But I don't know how he'll handle two mon—" The words crumble to nothing as I pop my head into the basement and spot Corey standing with her hands up.

I turn and see an East Asian–looking woman holding a shotgun. She says, "Get the rest of the way up here, slowly. Then put your hands up, just like Corey."

"Ms. Mathers," Corey tries, but the woman cuts her off.

"Quiet." Ms. Mathers. Bernie's wife. Davy's mom. "I can't let you leave. I can't let you tell people about Davy."

"We wouldn't—"

"Don't lie!" Her lip trembles, and her grip on the shotgun tightens. "It was bad enough the first time when he had to do it. And now he's getting mixed up in trying to save Virgil, too! I left for twenty minutes. *Twenty minutes* to try to stop him, and in that time, you broke into our home, and you know everything, and I can't let you leave."

*Had to do it?* I assume she means that he had to save their son. But the tone is off . . . like it's not something she wanted. But she's aiming a gun at us to protect Davy, so obviously she wanted Bernie to bond with him. "You're going to kill us?" I ask.

She flinches.

I say, "We're Virgil's friends. We don't want to see anything bad happen to him. We wouldn't tell. We won't tell about Davy, either."

"You're lying! I know about protecting your own. You don't abandon family. Isn't that why you're here?! You stay put, and I'll tell you where he's taking Virgil, and you call Henry and make him stop Bernie from bonding with him. It'll kill him. Another monster will kill him for sure this time." Tears slip down her face, and she steers the gun toward Corey. "Call him!"

As Corey slowly slips her phone out of her pocket, I go back through everything Ms. Mathers said. She's desperate to stop Bernie from bonding, obviously because handling multiple monsters hurts people, and he's already sick. But she also said "this time."

It will kill him for sure *this time.*

*I know about protecting your own.*

*You don't abandon family.*

I was wrong. So, so wrong.

Bernie's already bonded with another monster. That's why he's been so sick. And he's been like that all year.

Jules was sent an invite in February.

*You know.*

"Bernie," I choke out. "Bernie bonded with Jules. He's been controlling Jules. Two monsters . . . We thought it was two Masters, but . . ."

Ms. Mathers's eyes widen. She thought we were here rooting

through their stuff because we'd figured everything out. She didn't know we were only here to find Virgil.

I take that moment to throw my knife. It hits her shoulder, and her grip on the gun slackens. It's more than enough time for Corey to run forward and knock the gun out of her hand before slamming a knee into the woman's gut. She goes down with a cry.

I expect the gun to go off as it falls and brace for it, but nothing happens.

In fact, it sounds almost hollow. I pick the thing up and peer at it. "It's fake," I say, a little giggle coming out.

Ms. Mathers whimpers from her spot on the floor.

Corey looks over at me, her own eyes filled with tears. "It's Bernie?!"

"It's Bernie," I repeat.

The same man who helped and supported me during the candidacy. The reason I didn't get disqualified right from the first task. The one who had such a big hand in raising Virgil and was the only person who could calm him down enough to hold on to his human form. This is the man who enslaved my brother with the promise of helping him, who ordered the murder of multiple QBSS members using not just Jules but his own son, and who now is trying to acquire a third member of his deadly group in Virgil—a boy as desperate and trusting of Bernie as the two who'd come before him.

# CHAPTER FORTY-SIX

Well, this is a mess," Henry says as he gazes around the basement.

Ms. Mathers sits on the lumpy couch, staring at her hands. Corey's call to Henry went through, but she hadn't started talking, and then I threw the knife. Henry recognized the voice of Bernie's wife on the phone and came straight here with Margot and Isaac. By the time we went to contact him, he was already on his way.

Now we're all in the basement, along with Laira, trying to figure out our next move.

"We need to go help Virgil," I say, and Corey nods vigorously.

Corey says, "If Bernie bonds with Virgil, he'll use him for whatever he has going on. And once Bernie's injected him, we can't get Virgil back."

Henry sighs and massages his temples. "From what you said, Virgil is already on the brink. The bigger issue is anyone finding out that he voluntarily ran away and tried to illegally bond with Bernie. The society will kill him for that. He wouldn't even get the privilege of being held in the Pen."

I always knew Henry cared about Virgil, but watching him like this, actually seeing the concern, is different. More human. Like a worried parent. We all want to get Virgil back.

I turn to Ms. Mathers. "Tell us where they went. You must know, since you said you left the house to try to stop him. You don't want Bernie to bond with Virgil either."

"If you find him, he'll be dead anyway," she says, playing with her hands. Her hair falling out of her bun. "Him and my boy."

Margot says, "Yes, but you'll still be alive. If you cooperate with us, we can let the society know. They'll be more lenient."

The woman lets out a dry laugh. "That won't protect me."

"Won't protect you from what, exactly?" Henry comes to stand in front of her. "Is Bernie working with someone . . . or rather, for someone?"

The way she talked, it's more likely the latter. But who? I think immediately of Natalie. The Pro-Libs have created unregistered pairs before. Besides, Bernie has always been sympathetic to monsters. Maybe he was secretly a Pro-Lib even though he said he didn't like politics. We're not in a position to believe much of what he said anymore.

Ms. Mathers hunches in on herself further. Henry sighs. "I'm afraid we don't have time for this. I'm sorry, Eleanor. I do hate to do things this way. But Virgil means too much to me." He turns to Laira, who's been quiet this whole time, and she pushes off the wall.

"Do you have a plan?" Margot asks Henry.

"Possibly. Do we know who the real target is? Who Bernie's after?"

"QBSS," I say, and hope I won't regret it. I want to keep Riley's secrets, but I need to help Virgil. "He wants an artifact from them."

"And you know a girl from QBSS, don't you?" Henry tilts his head. "Use her to lure Bernie out."

"*Or*," I reply, "I can ask her if she'll help us like a normal fucking person."

Laira snort laughs.

"Fine," Henry says. "I'll continue to question Eleanor and text the location to Margot once I get it out of her. Hopefully you'll be in time to grab Virgil before Bernie can put the serum in him. And as long as you have the QBSS girl and Bernie has a chance to get what he wants, he won't run away. Do your best to incapacitate him." He meets my eyes. "This is enough evidence to save your brother. I promise to speak on his behalf."

"I thought you didn't want to get involved with my brother."

"And like everything else, know that I am offering this not for you, but for Virgil, who begged me to help when he's gone." He jerks his head to the door. "Now go."

"Come on," Margot says, heading up the stairs.

Isaac and Corey immediately follow. I'm the last one to start out of the room. Ms. Mathers's eyes widen as she realizes we're leaving to go after her husband. The broken door swings shut as we walk up the stairs. "What if he can't get the location out of her?" I ask.

Margot looks back at me, her expression flat. "He won't. But Laira will."

From below us, screams explode to life. Hysterical and pleading.

Corey curls in on herself, and Isaac pulls his hood up, tightening the drawstrings.

I've never thought of myself as a fundamentally good person.

And now I know that I'm not. Because I'm unwilling to go back down there and stop what's happening. Not when Virgil's in danger.

Margot grits her teeth. "Let's go."

We leave Ms. Mathers screaming in the basement.

I knock on the door and wait. Part of me is thinking that this is the worst idea I've ever had, and another part of me knows that I need to at least try.

Riley opens the door and stares at me. "Wow. I shouldn't be surprised, because if anyone had the audacity, it'd be you. But somehow, I'm still—"

"We know who's controlling the monsters. They have Virgil, and they're going to use him too. We have a plan to stop them, but we need you." I hunch my shoulders. "You helped me, and I didn't realize what it was costing you to do it. I get it. QBSS is your community. You wanted to do something without losing it, and that's why you couldn't tell me everything. And it isn't just that we need your help. This is your chance to help bring the person responsible for Sammie's death to justice."

Riley's swallows. "I can't go. . . . I—"

There are footsteps behind her, and a man calls out, "Who's at the door?"

"Your boyfriend?"

"Him . . . and Malachi. My parents offered this house up to QBSS. The current sitting president always lives here."

*Shit.*

The footsteps come closer, and the two men appear behind Riley.

The president's gaze hardens when he sees me, and he gives Riley a disapproving look. "I can't wait to hear the explanation for this one."

"She just showed up," Riley says. "And I know her. It's not against the rules to know people outside of QBSS."

"Riley . . . ," Jackson starts.

A horn honks behind me. I can't stay here. We have to get to Virgil. But we need Riley for this plan to work. "I need to know right now if you're in or not."

Her eyes fall to the ground.

I can't blame her. I'm not Henry. I won't try to force her hand so I can use her. We'll have to figure something else out.

As I step back, Riley steps forward. Her eyes widen like even she's shocked.

Jackson lets out an involuntary giggle, on the edge of hysteric. "You're going with her? Riley. You're a Historic. It's okay if you want friends outside the club, but she's not it. She's not the—"

"Not the right sort of friend," Riley finishes, turning to face him. "I know. You said as much about Sammie."

He cringes. "I'm sorry about what happened to her. But she was on a collision course all on her own."

"Oh, so it's her fault she was murdered? Is that what you're saying?"

"No!"

"Enough," Malachi says. "Whatever this girl is mixed up in is her business, not yours. Unless it concerns her brother, who absolutely needs putting down. Not that you helped with that. Jackson is right. You're prone to bad influences."

Riley's lip curls. "Sammie was trying her hardest to fit in, and none of you ever gave her any slack. She was a sweet girl. She cared about people. You could have helped her. Instead, you treated her like she was *nothing*. Don't you wonder why we get so many recruits who leave? Do you ever question yourself?"

"You're not going to continue to associate with a society member. I am doing what I should have done a long time ago. I'm putting my foot down. Leave with her now, and you won't be invited back."

Jackson splutters, "Wait, what do you mean?"

But Riley knows exactly what he means. He wants her to choose. Go with me and be expelled from QBSS, or leave me alone and stay with QBSS.

Riley straightens her back, and the chain around her neck glows. This time, the color carries to her eyes, making the brown irises shine molten gold. Jackson stumbles back, but Malachi stands his ground. "I am a motherfucking *Historic*. My family has protected these artifacts and followed Joseph Lawrence's teachings for generations. We have given bones since before your grandparents were born." The clasp holding her passion twists snaps and her hair falls, coiling around her body. "You do not have, nor have you ever had, the power to tell me what to do. I deferred to you out of respect. But you are *not* my better. And you certainly cannot kick me out of the organization that was founded to protect *our* people." Now the chain links glow, separating into individual links floating around her.

Malachi reaches for his scythe chain, and Jackson shouts, "No!" and tackles him to the floor.

Riley flicks her wrist, and the links rapidly increase in size and fly across the threshold to bind Malachi and Jackson together. Slamming them against the wall and locking them in place. She walks forward and tugs the chain off the President's neck. "I'll be keeping this for a bit. And when I get back, when I have brought Sammie's and Jacob's killers to justice, we'll have a vote, and we'll see who gets to wear the sickle."

"You're a traitor to the bones," Malachi spits.

Riley's lip curls. "And you don't even understand what it means to give them."

Jackson struggles against the restraints. "Riley, please! Don't do this!"

"We can talk about it when I get back." She walks out the front door and pulls it closed. The remaining links floating around her rejoin and shrink, settling against her neck as a chain once more.

When we enter the car together, it's silent for a few moments.

Until Corey says, "Holy shit, that was so cool."

Riley flips her hair over her shoulder. "Not that big of a deal."

Isaac snorts from up front, and Margot pulls away from the curb. "We have the location from Henry. They're in the underground tunnels. They have a few entry and exit points they use: the one in their house, another in Murney Tower, and a final one in the Marshlands."

The eyes. Way back in the second group training at Murney Tower, I swore that I saw eyes down there, and then I talked myself out of believing what I saw. But it turns out a monster was down there all along. . . . Davy? No, Davy had a comfy chill pad in his parents' basement. I press my hand to my mouth. *Jules.* It was Jules. It must have been. Bernie wouldn't have been able to control Jules all the time. He would need to sleep. And that's where the threat to me and the family came in. That could keep Jules in line even without active control. But still, Bernie likely wanted to maintain authority over Jules as much as possible. Making the tunnels connected to the tower a convenient place to keep him.

I found my brother months ago and just didn't know it.

Not to mention City Park is near both the tower and Bernie's house. That must have been why they were initially meeting there. I think back to that guy who winked at me. . . . Could that have been Davy? Maybe he meant to attack me back then, but those guys showed up and interrupted him. They must have been desperate to proceed with their plans for Davy to risk following me to Wolfe Island to get Jules in line. Then later they switched to the Marshlands, where there would be fewer people and less chance of having their operation interrupted.

I clench my hands into fists. I'm going to have some words with Bernie when we get to him. "That's why Jules and Davy kept showing up in the Marshlands. They were using the tunnels."

Margot nods. "Apparently we'll have the best chance if we go in from that entrance and try to grab them. Bernie had to go and get more serum, which is what his wife went to stop him doing. She came back home because he wouldn't be persuaded against it, and she was risking getting him caught."

"How could he get the serum in the first place?" Corey asks. "The security is ridiculous. There's no way he's casually managing that, even if he's a professor."

"I thought professors had special access or something," I say.

Margot shakes her head. "No. They have a separate security team who delivers the serum for the initiation. Professors don't have any clearance. Someone is helping him. Henry is pushing Eleanor for a name now."

"Aren't there, like, laws and stuff against confessions given under duress or whatever?" Isaac asks.

"Technically, yes. Even in the society. But we can worry about that later. What matters is that Bernie going to get the serum has bought us some time. He has to do that and then travel back through the tunnels to where Eleanor said he's keeping Virgil, and he's not well, so he's not moving fast."

A MASTERY OF MONSTERS

"I need my running leg," Corey says.

"It's in the trunk. August's holsters and knives, too. Henry made us stop at Victoria Hall and McIntosh Castle to grab them. He's nothing if not prepared."

And we're better off for it. We're also lucky that it's so late, because Margot speeds through the streets and runs more than a couple of red lights getting us to where we need to be. We're forced to stop the car eventually and get out on foot. At which point Corey switches legs and I get my gear on.

We haven't been to this part of the park before, but it looks like the others—lots of tall trees and bushes. Ten minutes later, Margot says, "Here!" and points at the stone tunnel entrance. It's huge, big enough to tower over our heads, and has caution tape and construction signs out front prohibiting entrance. There's a shallow pool of water and muck on the ground that only gets worse as we enter.

"Gross," Corey whines. But that doesn't stop her from sprinting through the wetness.

The tunnel encloses us in darkness, the light from the entrance getting dimmer with every step. The dampness is like a wet towel on the back of my neck, but I ignore it and push forward.

Margot says to Isaac, "You're fastest. Run ahead!"

Her brother nods and races into the dark. The rest of us pant as we keep going, the light of Margot's phone leading us forward.

We have to get to him in time. We *have* to. I know that losing Virgil is inevitable. From the moment they disqualified me, it was the only possible ending. But that doesn't mean I'm prepared for it *now*.

"He's here!" Isaac shouts from ahead of us.

Suddenly we're all moving faster. Me and Corey are at the front of the pack, running with everything we have until we reach Isaac. He's in front of a cell like the one I found in the tunnel in Bernie's house.

Inside, Virgil gapes at us. He's sitting on the floor, still in his human form.

"You asshole!" I scream through the bars, and he flinches. "You should have told us. We would have helped you!"

He averts his eyes from mine. "I didn't want you to be implicated. I wanted you to be able to say you didn't have anything to do with this. Bernie said for that to happen, you couldn't know anything. Any of you."

"Bernie is not trying to help you. He's trying to use you."

Virgil's brow furrows, and he finally looks at me.

"How do you know I'm not trying to help him?"

We all whip toward the other side of the tunnel, where Bernie appears in the darkness, cradled in the arms of the same rabbitlike monster that attacked me at Big Sandy Bay. The one I now know is Davy. And from behind him, Jules emerges in his monster form.

We're officially out of time.

A MASTERY OF MONSTERS

# CHAPTER FORTY-SEVEN

Virgil clocks the monsters, and his warm brown skin goes chalky. He rises from the ground on shaky legs. "Bernie . . . what is this?"

He must recognize the deranged Easter Bunny that attacked us way back at Big Sandy Bay. I wonder now if the reason he retreated was because Virgil was there. He was coming after me with clear intent. Who knows? Maybe the plan was to kidnap me or something to make Jules cooperate. Bernie couldn't have guessed that I would know Virgil. And then he met me the next day when I was at McIntosh Castle. Said that shit about family, even.

Bernie was playing the long game. Now he walks toward us, holding a syringe of a thick pink fluid. The serum, I assume. He stops short when we don't move. "I thought you wanted to save Virgil," he says to me.

"Not your way," I say. "You'll just use him to keep killing QBSS members."

"It's a small price to pay for freedom."

"I'm not killing anyone!" Virgil says from the cage.

"You said you understood there would be a cost to doing this."

Virgil lets out a shocked laugh. "Yes! Running away and living my life hunted. That was the price. Helping you deal with the burden of two monsters. Not . . . not this, and you . . . That's Jules. *You're* the murderer. You're the one . . ." He shakes his head. "*Why? Why would you do it?*"

Something twists in Bernie's face. "I am helping you help yourself! Look around! This entire society is corrupt. The fact that I've been able to do this much proves it. The fact that August should have placed first overall but lost proves it. There is no fairness, no equality. You're so afraid of being a monster that you don't realize you're already in a cage!"

Virgil grips the bars. "*You* put me in here!"

Bernie laughs. "Ah, so you want to be literal. Here's another fact for you: without my help, you will rot in the Pen. Your only savior will be the apocalypse when the Doctorate throws you at the masses to die for his victory. Even if you leave now, they may still kill you for running in the first place. At least your parents died for something. This system cannot be fixed, and they knew it. You have to burn the whole fucking thing to the ground!" Spit flies from his mouth, and he doubles over, coughing. When he's recovered, Bernie looks up, not at Virgil, but at Riley. "Well, this is a positive result, at least. I figured I would have to dangle Jules in front of August as incentive to get you here, but we're skipping a step."

"What is wrong with you?" Virgil chokes out. He rattles the bars, sharp teeth bared. "How could you do this? You were like family to me! I trusted you!"

A MASTERY OF MONSTERS

Bernie throws a sideways look at him. "We *are* family. That's why I have to do this for your own good. You stay there while I take care of this." He pulls a box from his pocket and places the needle inside. He looks pointedly at Riley. "Now that I finally have your attention, we can get to the artifact."

"Have my attention?" Riley says.

He smiles. "Did you think I believed that any of those QBSS members would actually know where anything of value was? If they did, wonderful. But I suspected any real information would need to come from someone with a lot more power. Like the girl whose legacy stretches right back to Joseph Lawrence. But I couldn't risk attacking you directly. Would get very messy very fast. A bunch of Historic alumni would get involved, possibly an all-out war between you and the society. Not ideal. I knew with some encouragement, however, I could catch your interest."

"Sammie," Riley breathes.

"She definitely got your attention." Bernie tilts his head. "I considered your boyfriend, but he's a Historic too, so I thought it best to avoid him just in case. Besides, you don't even seem to like him that much. Not as much as you did Samantha. I'm sure that didn't bother him at all."

I watch Riley fall apart in front of me, her eyes cast down, tears building. All this time, Sammie was never a random victim. If Bernie had Jules on his side, he could have easily asked who Riley cared about or spent time with.

Bernie moves on, like he hasn't just crushed her. "Bring me to the artifact or I'll kill them all, right here, right now."

"No!" Virgil says.

Riley shakes her head. "Which artifact?!"

"You know the one," Bernie says.

"I actually don't!"

But Bernie isn't listening. Davy is already taking several menacing steps toward us, and Jules isn't far behind. They box us in from the two sides.

Isaac is attempting to shift, but it's taking him time. He can't do it instantaneously, and the monsters don't want to give him the chance. They lunge, and he gets distracted dodging them.

His back is half split open, and he's leaking blood on the ground. Anytime he attempts to make progress, the monsters leap forward and stop him.

Virgil keeps shouting and smashing against the bars, trying to get out, but even if he could, what could he do?

We're free and somehow just as trapped. We need to separate the two monsters to increase our chances of dealing with them. We also need time so that Isaac can transform, and we don't have either of those things at our disposal.

"Take him to the artifact," I say to Riley. "There's no point in lying anymore."

If there's one thing I can say about Riley, it's that the girl is a good liar. And that's what I need from her now.

Her face twists into one of shock and betrayal, and Bernie's eyes light up. "I knew it! I knew you knew. I knew you would be the one. I just couldn't get you, but now you're here, and you don't want your friends to die, do you? You can't be responsible for the death of more people."

I give Riley a hard stare and hope she understands. I need her to go along with this.

She holds my gaze for a moment and then looks at Bernie,

A MASTERY OF MONSTERS

grinding her teeth. "Fine." She points at the open end of the tunnel. "It's out there."

"Lead the way," Bernie says. Davy retrieves his dad, picking him up and cradling him between his front paws. "Drop the necklace." She obeys, and Davy maneuvers Bernie so he can grab it.

Riley walks toward the tunnel exit, and the rest of us follow. We have no choice because Jules is bringing up the rear.

I take one last look at Virgil, still gripping the bars.

I hope he knows that we'll be back for him. That we won't leave him.

Once we're outside, Riley says, "It's easier if I just tell you from here." Bernie beckons her forward.

She steps up to him, coming in close. "I wouldn't miss a chance to look into the eyes of the man who killed my best friend." She whips out a blade hidden in her sleeve, aiming for Bernie's eye. But Davy's too fast. He hops out of the way and snarls at her.

Bernie shakes his head and tuts. Like he's admonishing one of his students. "That's not very nice. Trying to trick a man in pain. We'll have to punish someone for that."

Jules jumps into action and headbutts Isaac, sending the boy flying into the trees. Margot screams, but when she tries to go after her brother, Jules blocks her.

"Finally!" Bernie says. "Someone has learned to be proactive. You know, Jules, when we threatened to kill everyone you loved, you came around pretty nicely, but I always had to *push* you. Now you're starting to understand the stakes a little more, aren't you?"

My eyes dart to where Isaac is. When I look to Jules, I can see him inside there. His eyes, staring at me. Why would he choose this moment of all times to cooperate with Bernie?

"Now," Bernie says. "The artifact. For real this time."

Davy and Jules loom over us as we follow Riley. Margot looks back at where her brother landed. There's no movement.

After walking for a bit, Riley stops and starts digging around on the ground, ripping up grass and earth.

She's not going to find anything. And now we don't even have Isaac. But we need to do something.

Bernie watches her intently. Davy, too, keeps his eyes on the progress. Even Jules. In this form, he's under Bernie's control. But if we could get Riley's necklace, we could force a shift and neutralize him.

I'm thinking about how we can make a distraction when the monsters swivel to the left as a creature bounds toward us.

A massive dog with a lolling tongue.

I shoot a look at Margot, who meets my eyes with a wicked grin.

She knew Isaac was okay the whole time.

He just needed time to transform. Jules . . . That was why he did that! To give Isaac time!

I could hug my brother, but not now, because he's still under the control of a murderer. And he immediately goes after Isaac.

Leaving Davy with us. Davy, who apparently was also thinking ahead, because he drops his dad and takes a hold of Riley, pressing a sharp claw to her throat. Bernie laughs from the ground. "Can you believe they would have just wasted him in the Pen? My boy is talented!" He jerks his head to Margot. "Stop Isaac, or we'll slit her throat."

"You won't," Margot says. "You need her."

"Fine. We'll maim her until she wishes she were dead."

"This isn't you," Corey cries. "Please, Bernie."

"Tick tock," he says, ignoring her.

We're fucked. We're completely fucked. Davy is too alert for me to get a knife off.

Something barrels into Bernie from behind at an alarming speed. The man is tossed off his feet, and Davy screeches, dropping Riley to get his dad.

The thing stops, and it's not a thing at all.

It's Virgil.

His mouth is too crowded with teeth again, and his fingernails are too long and sharp. But he's here. And he's struggling, breathing heavily and falling to his knees.

When Davy goes for him, I jump into action, whipping out a knife, which embeds itself in Davy's snout. He screams, and Margot jumps forward, smashing him in the face with her fists. Corey isn't far behind her, helping land kicks and focusing even though I know she's probably terrified. Not just of the monster, but for Virgil.

Riley is on her knees digging around in the grass.

The necklace! Bernie must have dropped it when Virgil hit him. The man in question is still struggling on the ground, coughing and spitting up blood. If we find the chain, we can restrain the monsters. I get down too, trying to help her look while Corey, Margot, and Virgil deal with Davy.

"Found it!" I grab the necklace. Again, a pulse shoots through my hand.

"August!" Virgil shouts.

I look up as Jules dives at me. He must have gotten away from Isaac. Out of instinct, I jerk my hands up to protect myself, and the chain in my hand glows bright gold, thickening and lengthening. The flash of light doesn't throw Jules off this time. He keeps coming. I'm still recovering from the shock of the chain transformation when my brother opens his jaw around my face.

I squeeze my eyes shut, but the bite doesn't come.

I open them and Jules is hovering there, his teeth surrounding my head, frozen in place.

Bernie's screaming at him to do it, crimson spit flying from his mouth, but Jules won't. My brother refuses to kill me.

Carefully, I take the chain in my hands and loop it around his head, and slowly, he shrinks into himself. Fully human and back in control.

In the background, Isaac takes Davy to the ground, savagely ripping into his fur. Where his teeth don't pierce, his drool lands, sizzling and burning. Davy's screaming and screaming and screaming. White fur stripped away to expose pink bubbling muscle.

Riley calls the chain to her. It flies off Jules and binds Davy. Already bleeding profusely, he's unable to fight the transformation. He's human once more, the burns on his skin so severe that I find myself looking away. It's like staring at charred meat, pink and black and raw.

Bernie crawls to his son, crying for us to leave him alone, clutching the boy's naked body, whispering Davy's name. Begging Davy to stay with him.

Jules mutters something in my ear.

"What?" I ask, turning to him.

"It wasn't me."

"What do you mean? What wasn't you?"

"I didn't stop myself. I . . . I was going to kill you. Just like he wanted."

*What?* I look over at a sobbing Bernie. He wanted Jules to kill

A MASTERY OF MONSTERS      485

me, so if it wasn't him and it wasn't Jules, what stopped him?

What saved me?

"It's okay, calm down," Corey says. I turn toward her, and she's attempting to approach Virgil. He looks up and snaps at her, and she jumps away, her eyes wide. She physically shakes herself, grinding her teeth, and keeps moving toward him.

His entire body is trembling. The claws are longer and a shiny metallic black. There's something far away in his eyes.

"August, no," Jules says. "He's turning. Stay away from him."

I don't listen. I move beside Corey, and together, we crowd around him.

"Virgil," I say. "It's fine. You're okay. We're here." Bernie is a piece of shit, but he was able to do this for Virgil. I have to try. After all, Virgil must have overexerted himself to get out of that cage, and that's why he's like this. He sacrificed his last moments of humanity to help us. "It's not time yet. You need to calm down. I mean, you haven't even handed in your last essay yet." The laugh that comes from my body is choking and tear-filled. "And you want to see Adam win, don't you?"

He snaps again, and Corey flinches but stays steady.

I take hold of his right hand, and she takes his left. Even when the tips of his claws scratch me, I don't let go.

"I still have the serum," Bernie says. I whip my head toward him. He holds up the case with the syringe in trembling hands. "Get him back to the cage, and you can bond with him before the society dogs get here. You can run away, the two of you. If you do nothing, they'll take him to the Pen. You've already lost the candidacy. Even if by some miracle you got nominated again next year, Virgil will have already transformed, and you'll have lost your chance. Do it now!"

"No!" Virgil says, and it comes out like a growl.

Corey sobs into his clawed fingers.

"They don't deserve you," I say to Virgil. "You don't have to keep following their rules."

"You . . . trouble," he manages between his oversized teeth.

We could do it, Virgil and me. Even if he doesn't want this. We could force him back into the cell. I was never a real part of the Learners' Society. We could run, like Bernie said. I could disappoint him right now by doing what he doesn't want and hold on to him.

Corey turns to me with tear-filled eyes. "What do we do?"

I grip Virgil's hands harder. "If you don't want me to give you the serum, if you don't want me to get myself in trouble and give us both a future where we're on the run, turn back! Turn back right fucking now! This is a threat, by the way. Don't think I won't do it. I'm a fantastic rule breaker. But I know you're too good to let that happen. Too good to let me suffer because the one time you decided to break the rules was the absolute worst moment." There's a strange sound coming from the back of Virgil's throat, and it takes me a second to realize it's a laugh. "I'll do other terrible things too. Maybe I'll go on a spree and murder some of those people we talked about. The shitty dudes who came to McIntosh Castle and were mean to you. Caden, definitely. He's first on the list. I'll fucking dance naked on his grave, you know I will—"

"Stop," Virgil says, and his voice is normal again.

During my tirade, his nails shrank, and his teeth receded.

He's Virgil again.

I pull him against me, and he sags in my hold, tired and spent.

Corey sobs and clings to him, the three of us locked into the group hug that I denied once upon a time.

A MASTERY OF MONSTERS

"I'm okay," he murmurs. "I'm okay."

Bernie shakes his head. "It won't last forever."

I know.

But I don't give a shit about disappointing Bernie.

I have my brother back.

And I'm still holding on to Virgil.

Right now, those are the only things I care about.

# CHAPTER FORTY-EIGHT

This time at Summerhill we aren't in the formal meeting area. Instead, we're ushered into a smaller side room that has a long conference table. There are pitchers of water set out alongside coffee pots and mugs. There are no windows to speak of, and there's a cool staleness to the air as if this room isn't used often.

Me, Virgil, Corey, and Margot settle in the chairs, and I look hopefully at the door. They're supposed to bring Jules out. The others busy themselves with getting water or tea while I tap my fingers on the table.

Virgil's shoulder nudges mine. "He's coming. It'll be fine."

"Yeah."

Virgil looks away, but I keep staring at him out of the corner of my eye.

It's surreal that just yesterday we fought Bernie and his giant monsters, one of which was my own brother. Margot called Henry once we'd incapacitated Bernie and Davy, which got Adam involved, which got James and Carrigan involved, and suddenly Jules was being taken away. The only reason I didn't start fighting them was because Henry assured me he wouldn't let anything happen to my brother.

I'm not Henry's biggest fan, but he's a man who knows how to come through.

Henry and Margot also had a hushed conversation that culminated in us agreeing to a lie about how Virgil got involved in the fight. Officially, the account is that Bernie tricked Virgil by pretending to need help with a possible lead on Davy, and then the two monsters forced Virgil into the cage. The intent being to add him to Bernie's roster of monsters. We noticed Virgil was gone, went to ask Bernie about him, found the secret basement tunnel, etc., etc. It was important to avoid any impression that Virgil had run away. It's our word against Bernie's and his family's, which are good odds, especially since we have Adam on our side. Jules agreed to the lie as well. And still, however despicable the man turned out to be, I don't think Bernie would contradict us. Even at the end, he wanted me to save Virgil.

We also had to say that the lock of the cage Virgil was in was melted and had been relocked with a new padlock by Bernie, exactly like the cage under his house. Isaac went and broke that open, freeing Virgil, and they both came to the fight. Isaac is faster in monster form, which is why he was first on the scene.

Unofficially, Virgil bent the bars of a cage that is specially formulated to keep monsters in and has been doing so for over a century. And he did it while in human form. Or, I suppose, a semimonstrous form. Henry had to get a welder in under the cover of night to bend the bars back into shape before the society could investigate our claims. The man was bribed to never mention the job, nor the underground cage.

No one had an explanation for why Virgil did something that is supposed to be impossible.

The door on the other side of the room opens, and James, Adam, Carrigan, and Professors Perez and Chen file in.

"My brother—" I start.

"He'll be brought in when it's time." James tugs at his clothes and sits down, adjusting himself frequently as if this is his first time sitting.

Meanwhile, Carrigan runs a hand through his curls and slouches over the table. Looking for all intents and purposes like he does not want to be there.

Adam says, "Thank you all for coming today. We also have the candidacy professors with us, as they worked closely with Bernie, and anything you say may help in adding to and/or supporting their accounts. Now, August, when did you become aware that your brother was an unregistered monster?"

"He'd gone missing. I was trying to find him, and I followed a lead with a friend who brought us to the Marshlands, where I saw him transform."

James says, "This friend being the QBSS treasurer, Riley Townsend—a Historic and a direct descendant of Joseph Lawrence."

Well, shit, I didn't know she was a direct descendant. That explains a lot of what she shouted at Malachi. I can't believe that fool thought he could kick her out knowing that. "A friend," I repeat.

"And you didn't report this unregistered monster sighting," James continues, eyeing us. "None of you did."

"With all due respect, sir," Margot says. "It is not our job to keep track of monster registration. It was our understanding that monsters running around in Kingston would have obviously been known to the society. Especially considering that this has been going on for a long period of time. Besides that, we *did* make reports early in the summer and got no response to them. We assumed that meant it was being handled. Furthermore, there was no reason to think Jules was unregistered. We suspected that his partner was not exactly acting with proper decorum, but we had no proof of this to report it. August investigated on her own time while participating in the candidacy, on top of her studies, when it should have been detected and handled by the society."

*Damn.* Margot is scary when she's mad at you but badass when she's angry on your behalf.

James glowers at her. "I don't know that I like your tone."

"But she's correct," Adam says, looking sidelong at his brother. "I'm interested in how this went undetected for so long, especially given that reports were made. It's clear to me that there was no nefarious intent on Ms. Black's part."

"We'll see what the boy has to say." James presses the intercom button on the table. "Bring in Mr. Black."

The door opens, and Jules walks in. He looks much better. He's standing tall with his shoulders back and his chest out. And they haven't put handcuffs on him or anything. He's dressed in a shirt and joggers that are a bit too big for him. He pauses for a moment in the doorway, staring at the Doctorate candidates, his eyes darting from one brother to another before he shakes himself out of it and sits down next to me.

I glance at him, but it's not like I can ask what's up right now.

I remember in that moment that tomorrow is his birthday. I

almost laugh. He'll be the same age as Davy, who I learned is only nineteen.

Adam nods to Jules. "Mr. Black, please tell us how you came to be partnered with Bernie Mathers."

"I was struggling. . . . I'd had an encounter and been bitten. I thought it was some sort of giant animal."

*Bitten?* I swore that Jules must have been a spontaneously born monster because of all the problems he'd had in the lead-up to February. But maybe that was just him dealing with Mom's disappearance. Still, a bite would have turned him right away.

"Did the monster who bit you have any distinguishing markings?" Chen asks, leaning forward. "Or an animal it looked like?"

Jules shakes his head. "It was dark. I didn't get a good look at it. I just know it had fur. But it wasn't Davy."

I swear that Carrigan's more alert. He's in the same slouching position, but before he was looking at the table or playing with his mug. Now, he's rapt with attention. This, he wants to hear about.

James looks like he's about to say something but holds himself back for once. Maybe he doesn't want to be too antagonistic?

"You were bitten," Adam says. "And then?"

"I started to notice changes. I was more aggressive. I had strange dreams. I craved raw meat. To be honest, I kind of thought maybe I was becoming a werewolf." He laughs, and the sound is hollow.

"Ridiculous," James huffs. "If he was bitten, he would have turned right away. And from his story, he hadn't even met Mathers yet, so how could he maintain control?"

I hate to side with James, but that was my understanding of bites too.

"Not necessarily," Carrigan says. "We've been having more

spontaneously born monsters in the last couple of decades. He might have already been slated to turn without knowing it and then was bitten. The effects of the bite on someone who already has the mutation are not predictable. Sometimes, yes, the bite can immediately activate an existing mutation. But other times, the bite simply exacerbates the onset of symptoms. I wouldn't expect anyone outside of my faction to be privy to that information, however, so your ignorance on these facts is understandable."

It's the first time Carrigan's spoken. I guess it shouldn't be surprising that, as an expert on monsters, he's decided to pipe up to correct things. And unlike James's interjections, it's actually helpful information.

James glares at Carrigan but doesn't try to clap back.

"Please continue," Adam says.

Jules nods. "I joined the Queen's Black Student Society just to make friends. But then Malachi said he could see something more in me, and I was recruited into their advancement program. While I was there, I was sent an invitation to meet and discuss my 'current circumstances.' I was desperate for answers, and so while it was vague, I went anyway. I met Bernie, and he knew everything I was going through. He explained that it would get worse and that he could help me control it. Like I said, I was desperate, so I agreed, and we bonded. This was in early February."

"Can you explain the details of the bonding, please?" Chen asks.

"He put me in that cage under his basement, I guess so I couldn't hurt him. He injected me with the serum and then himself. I don't remember anything after, just that when I came back to myself, I was in a monster body, and he coached me into transforming back into human form. I had control again. By that time, I'd quit QBSS because I knew how they felt about the society and monsters. I hadn't said anything to Bernie because honestly, I didn't think he would care. It was irrelevant. But he was upset when he learned I was no longer a member and tried to get me to rejoin. But they wouldn't take me. He said that was fine, and I believed him. Then he said he'd have to 'figure some things out,' and I was supposed to be on standby to help him."

"Did he say where he got the serum?" Chen asks.

Jules shakes his head.

Perez says, "On standby to help him . . . Help him how?"

"I don't know. Before the bonding, he acted like it was a no strings attached thing. Then, in August, he told me and Davy that we'd be hunting the members to find some object."

"Do you know what he was looking for?" James asks, leaning forward.

"Sometimes I felt like not even he knew what he was looking for."

"And the young girl who died first?" Chen says. "Samantha."

Jules casts his eyes down, and his hands roll into fists on the table. "That was Davy's doing. Bernie had originally suggested intimidation, not murdering people. That was when I said I wanted out. He couldn't control me in human form, so I thought I would be fine. Obviously, he had a plan for that. Bernie said if I didn't transform when he told me to, he would kill my whole family. I think that's why he sent Davy after August. To prove that he could easily get to them. I wanted to tell them to run away, but I was worried that would also provoke him to violence. I figured it would be easier on them if I disappeared. Keep them as far away from my shit as possible. I didn't know any other way to protect them."

I guessed as much, but it's still a lot to hear. I wish Jules had told me. We could have worked together to protect Dad and Bailey. He didn't need to do this alone.

"How did you get around the city?" Perez asks.

"The tunnels. They connect to all sorts of places. I think the Pen, too."

"Isn't that your domain, James?" Adam asks, sliding his eyes to his brother. Everyone in the room concentrates on the man. "I remember you pitching a revitalization project to Dad."

James rolls his neck. "Yes, when he was alive, I wanted them to be better maintained. But he passed, and I became preoccupied with my campaign."

"Well, we'll have to see who was supposed to be keeping an eye on them," Adam says, adjusting his collar. "Thank you for all this information. We're going to take a moment to deliberate."

"Are we not going to discuss the matter of how Mr. Hawthorne got mixed up in this?" James asks, looking at Virgil.

Adam says, "We already have their accounts. Mr. Hawthorne trusted Bernie and was manipulated."

"Has that been confirmed by Bernie? And his boy and the wife? By someone who is not personally invested in protecting Hawthorne?"

Virgil is stiff beside me but doesn't say a word.

"You will need more evidence besides witness accounts to bring a case against Mr. Hawthorne to vote. If you can provide a sufficient amount, we can include it." Adam looks his brother in the eye as James's lip twitches, like he wants to frown or spit. He knows he has nothing. Adam does too.

"No, I don't think that will be necessary," James says finally.

I fight not to exhale and slouch back in my seat.

The five of them leave the room and note that they'll be having some sort of wider meeting, and we're supposed to be "on deck" in case they need us.

Virgil sighs and leans back in his chair.

I say, "What—"

Margot shakes her head at me. We sit awkwardly in silence for over ten minutes before I realize that they might be watching and listening to us in this room. Hence why we can't discuss what happened.

Finally, after another half hour, we're brought into a larger room filled with people talking and shouting.

"They called a Masterium?" Corey says, looking around the room.

"What is that?" I ask. They'd mentioned it once before without explaining.

"It's a significant gathering of Masters. At minimum, all the ones in the province, but sometimes it's everyone in the country. A bunch would have come to watch the candidacy, so that's probably why it's so crowded. Usually, it's mostly virtual attendees. These happen when the Doctorate doesn't want to decide alone. James, Adam, and Carrigan must not be able to come to an agreement. The Masters will vote on what happens next."

"What are they voting on?"

Corey bites her lip.

Virgil swallows before he says, "They'll vote on if Jules gets to live."

"No!" I shake my head so hard that my braids whip me in the face. "He didn't do anything. It wasn't his fault."

"I should have known better," Jules says from beside me.

"How could you have known?!"

He shrugs and stares at the ground. He's always too hard

on himself. Like he's responsible for everything, even when it's impossible.

How fucking dare they play judge and jury with my brother when they didn't even notice what was happening until we brought it to their attention? This isn't just Bernie. It can't be. Someone was helping him get that serum, and someone was messing with the society internally to suppress reports. They may not have been doing the dirty work, but they were involved.

"I have to go to the bathroom." I speed walk out of the room and to the toilets. I splash water on my face and try to calm down. I can't lose Jules. I *can't*. But I don't know what I can do to stop it.

I come out of the bathroom and head back down the hallway. Just as I'm about to go into the room, I catch Carrigan coming out a side door. He pulls out a vape, taking a hit off it.

Something about the way he's leaning solidifies the thing that has been poking at my mind.

Before I can think better of it, I walk over to him. "I think you knew my mom." I hold up my phone with the picture I sent to Dad.

Carrigan glances at it with the same disinterest he goes about his whole life with. Except when he was listening to Jules. He cared about what my brother had to say. Was invested. Almost . . . like he knew who Jules was. "Annie, correct?"

"That's her."

He shrugs. "We were friends when I attended Queen's. She started to date your father, who was jealous and insecure." If he notices my scowl, he ignores it. "And didn't like her having male friends, so I distanced myself. She graduated and I guess went on to have children. And I took my place in the Learners' Society. We don't tend to keep nonstudent friends for long, so it was bound to happen."

"You're saying she wasn't part of the society?"

"No, she wasn't."

"Strange . . . Doctorate's son, wouldn't it make more sense to have society friends?"

"Clearly you have no concept of what it means to be the Doctorate's son." He jerks his head toward the door. "Look at Adam. Henry is his only real friend. Can you imagine that? A man with that much ambition leeched onto you. Invading your family. Becoming your father's favorite. Everyone in the society is ready to use you. I was fortunate to only have to deal with an emotion as petty as jealousy."

"And yet you still kept tabs on her. You knew who me and Jules were before we walked into that room, didn't you? You always did."

Carrigan laughs. "Yes, I did. Because dear Henry prepared a neat little dossier on you. Couldn't have his precious Virgil pairing up with just anyone, could he? And this was passed to Adam, and then passed to me and James before today's meeting." He leans toward me. "So perhaps consider who exactly you should be interrogating."

With that, he turns and enters the room via the door he came out of, and I'm left to stand alone in the hall.

Classic. Of course Henry did research on me. On Jules, without either of our consent. But still, I don't fully believe Carrigan. I remember how he stared at me at the nomination. I think he knew me even before Henry's helpful dossier. But why pretend otherwise? Because he's embarrassed about being hung up on Mom? Or some other reason?

I slip back into the room and join the others at the table as Adam and James are getting onstage. Carrigan takes his time, walking on several minutes after.

A MASTERY OF MONSTERS

"Order!" James booms at the front of the room. Everyone falls silent and sits down. Henry comes over and settles beside Margot at our table.

Adam says, "We're here to vote on four items based on the evidence you have seen thus far. Item number one, in regard to Bernard Mathers, raise your hand to vote him guilty of illegally bonding with two monsters and the misconduct of using said monsters for two counts of homicide, in person if you are here or online for virtual attendees."

I want to turn around to see the hands raising, but Margot gives me a look that keeps my head straight.

"Guilty. Sentencing to follow at a later date. Item number two, monsters bonded to Bernard Mathers, David Mathers and July Black, shall be unbonded via Doctorate. Raise your hand to vote yes on David Mathers."

Virgil stiffens in his seat.

"Wouldn't he obviously be unbonded via the Doctorate?" I whisper.

"No," he says. "You can also be unbonded via death, remember?"

Jules swallows beside me.

Adam says, "The vote passes for David Mathers to be unbonded via death."

*What the actual fuck?* They literally just voted to kill a nineteen-year-old boy?!

I start to rise, but Virgil grips my hand. "Anything you do could sway their vote."

"Raise your hands to vote yes on July Black being unbonded via Doctorate." Adam squints into the crowd. "I need a second confirmation of the in-person count."

Someone starts pointing at the hands, physically counting them. All I can see from my vantage point is that Henry's hand is up. It was up for Davy, too, though, and that didn't exactly go well. What will I do if not enough people vote yes? There's no way that I'm going to let that happen. I'll fight whoever it takes to save him.

"August," Jules says. "If they vote death, let it go."

"No."

"You have your whole life ahead of you. Don't ruin it for me. My choices led me here. It's not your job to fight for me. I never wanted you to be involved in this. That's why I left. That's why I told you not to look for me. I wanted you to live your life the way you want. Not to live it for someone else. You've done enough of that. I should have protected you then, and I didn't. So I'll do it now." He reaches for my hand, holding it in his grasp. It's trembling.

I gnash my teeth in my mouth. *"No."*

I appreciate that he wants to protect me, but I get to protect him too. That's my right.

Adam says, "July Black shall be unbonded via Doctorate. If he cannot secure a partner before the unbonding two weeks from today, he will be held in the Kingston Penitentiary until it is time to perform his duty in the apocalypse, a Bachelor or Master obtains special permission to partner with him, or his natural death, whichever comes first."

I exhale so hard I'm almost gasping.

Jules looks at me with tears in his eyes, a shaky smile on his lips. I squeeze his hand.

"Item number three, we have heard the concerns about corruption within factions and allegations of coconspirators in regard to Bernard Mathers. We are voting as to whether a further investigation will be made. Note that this investigation may delay both the Doctorate election and the Bachelor candidacy. Raise hands to vote yes on the investigation." Adam pauses for the count. Neither of Adam's brothers have been participating in the voting. I suppose that Doctorates can't, but I wonder what they would choose. "Yes passes—an investigation shall be conducted, and any delays will be handled as necessary. Finally, the last item is in regard to the Bachelor candidacy. Due to allegations of possible coconspirators of Bernard Mathers being on the panel of Masters, we are voting to decide if the panel should be scrubbed and a new one assigned. This new panel will recast their votes, which may affect the outcome of the Bachelor candidacy. Raise your hands to vote yes on scrubbing the panel." Another pause, and then, "Yes passes. The panel will be scrubbed. We will assign replacement Masters within the next twenty-four hours. They will likely be chosen from those who have joined us as spectators in the candidacy, as there are no filmed recordings to review."

Corey lets out a small squeal and beams at me.

"I . . . I was disqualified," I say. "They won't count me."

"They can do whatever they choose," Henry says, adjusting his tie. "Including reinstating any candidates who they feel were wrongly disqualified."

Me and Virgil look at each other.

I could be reinstated as a candidate.

I could still become a Bachelor.

# CHAPTER FORTY-NINE

I don't get to see Jules on his birthday, and the day after, I'm summoned to the Kingston Penitentiary. Both Margot and Corey have exams to sit, so only Virgil is with me. We get off the bus and cross the street to the building. He's been quiet since everything that went down with the vote, I assume thinking about the fact that his whole life could be turned around again if I'm reinstated as a candidate. I can't manage to consider the possibility like the others. I guess I'm already used to the Learners letting me down. I don't want to hope for anything.

We go around to the same side entrance I went to during the monster affinity training, where a white woman greets us and walks us down the staircase I mistakenly went down before. She uses a flashlight to guide us in the dark. Now I can properly see the monsters in their cages. They look drunk—slumped over and droopy-eyed. Do they drug them? Virgil's eyes linger as we pass, and I swallow.

"You didn't have to come," I say.

"I wanted to. You shouldn't have to go alone."

At the end of the hallway is a door where the three Doctorate candidates stand. Or two of them stand, as Carrigan is more slouched against the wall than anything.

Adam smiles at us. "Thank you for coming. We're still proceeding with the investigation, which is nearly complete, but Bernie has requested to speak with you, August."

"Me?" I ask, then look at Virgil. He's the one who was friends with the guy. And yes, I'd liked Bernie before I found out about his involvement in all this, but I hadn't know him that well. Clearly.

"We're hoping that since he made the request, you might be able to glean more information from him." He waves to the woman who brought us down and now holds an electronic device. "Lydia will get you miked, if you don't mind."

"Uh . . . sure." I let Lydia tape a mic under my clothes while everyone else politely looks away. There's equipment set up on the side featuring multiple headphones, which I guess they'll use to listen to Bernie's and my conversation. Lydia finishes up and hands me her flashlight.

I can't help but look back at Virgil, who gives me an encouraging smile. "It's just Bernie."

Right. It's just Bernie.

James opens the door for me. "Third cell on the right." His eyes follow me as I walk past him.

The door shuts with a soft *whoosh*, and I hold the flashlight out in front of me. I count the cells as I go. They're all empty except for Bernie's.

Ironically, he looks better than ever. There's a fresh pinkness to his skin, and he's not coughing or needing to lean against something for support. The only sign that anything is off is the redness of his eyes.

Davy died yesterday.

Was killed, technically.

Now Bernie is only partnered to one monster. Though Jules is, thankfully, outside of his control. Either way, the physical strain of being bonded to two partners is over.

"You came." Bernie's perched on the single bed. As far as cells go, it's a lot nicer than the Penitentiary was historically. The toilet has a privacy screen, and there's a mini fridge and a TV. I guess when it comes to people, the Learners suddenly know how to be humane.

I nod to the TV. "You get Netflix on that?"

"To be clear," Bernie says, his gaze on the floor, "I only called for you because I can't bring myself to face Virgil or Jules."

"Maybe try being less manipulative and homicidal next time."

A tiny smile blooms on his face, and he looks at me. "Perhaps. It wasn't personal. Though it's clear to me now that even that girl, Riley, didn't know what I meant or where the artifact was. I'm not sure any of them do."

"What artifact?"

"Now, isn't that the million-dollar question?"

So he doesn't know. I'd already gathered as much, but Bernie has just confirmed it.

He says, "Please convey my apologies to them. Jules and Virgil. I feel bad for what I did to your brother, but I feel worse about betraying Virgil. I've known him most of his life. Came to love him like a son. I admired his parents, too."

I don't know that I care for Bernie's brand of fatherly love. He wielded Davy like a tool and would have done the same with Virgil.

A MASTERY OF MONSTERS

"You admired the parents whose actions led to Virgil having a lifetime of being ostracized?" Honestly, it's on brand for Bernie.

"They dared to challenge the status quo. It's not fair that my boy was—" He sucks back a breath. "This entire society is predicated off of the belief that we are creating a fair system. But it never was. Virgil's parents knew that. They sought change so their son could have a better future. My Davy played by the rules for a long time, and look where it got him."

"Are you saying you decided to do this to . . . what? Disrupt the society? Is that what the artifact was supposed to help with?"

But then, Bernie doesn't even know what this artifact is, so why was he chasing it? He could have just lived quietly with his family. Instead he risked exposure to go after QBSS. "Your wife, she said you had to do this. Why?"

"Why did you have to join the society?"

"To help my brother."

"For family," Bernie says, staring at his lap.

We know that someone else helped Bernie . . . but even that doesn't make sense. They must have been getting something out of the exchange. Otherwise, why use their power and influence like that? What if they didn't just help? What if they were the reason Bernie was involved in the first place?

I stumbled onto the truth that Bernie had saved his son accidentally. It's not so far-fetched that someone else could have discovered what Bernie had done. "Someone found out about Davy, didn't they?"

Bernie gives me a small nod. "I knew you were a smart girl."

"Who?"

He laughs. "If only it were that simple."

He doesn't know. Or he does, but he won't say. Davy may be gone, but Eleanor is still alive. The only family he has left. "Why didn't you say something about this earlier?"

"It wouldn't have saved Davy. They were already going to kill him for the illegal bonding. If anything, it might have made things worse."

"Then why say it now?"

"Because maybe telling you will make the society take the protection of my wife more seriously."

"A name would be ideal."

"And I've already said it's not that simple. Let me ask you a question: When do you think this started?"

"February."

"Wrong. How do you expect that I got the serum to bond with Davy in the first place?"

I cross my arms over my chest. "You stole it?" It sounds weak even to my ears. Someone helped him recently for sure, but for Davy . . . I don't know.

"How? The serum is held under lock and key. Us professors don't even get access to it. When it's time for the initiation, it's taken from its secure location—which is not even known to us—with multiple witnesses to sign off, and transferred via armored truck straight to the Pen. There it continues to be monitored until used. And if any dose is missing, a red alert goes up. Let me tell you, Dr. Weiss was stolen from once in the past, and he refused to be stolen from again. The amount of people, power, and coordination you would need could never be satisfied by just me."

"Someone got it for you, even back then."

"Presented it as a prize. It was right there. Special delivery to my home. So I used it. Then all that evidence of Davy camping and this plan to run that neither he nor I had ever conceived suddenly appeared. A cover story." Bernie licks his lips. "I was naive. I thought there wouldn't be a cost to that decision. But of course there was. In February, I was given the name of a boy to seek out, along with the goal of acquiring an artifact."

"By who?" He has to know *something*.

"Listen!" he snaps. "Listen to me and use your brain!"

"I'm listening! You went to get serum that night for Virgil. Who did you go to?"

"I went to beg a ghost! And wouldn't you know, I guess I'm a believer, because once again they delivered."

A ghost . . . Holy shit. "You really don't know," I say.

"There she is. You can do it when you apply yourself."

I scowl at him.

*We're not the only ones playing a game here.* That's what Henry said to Margot at the Mastery group meeting weeks ago. And that's exactly what this feels like. Players and pieces being moved around and around.

But what do they want? I thought this was about the election, but Bernie's son was missing before Cyrus even died. That can't be discounted. The election is part of this, but with this much advance planning, that can't be the only goal.

"Someone manipulated you."

Bernie shrugs. "Why stop at one? Like I said, this requires coordination. This is not something that one person could do alone. And yet there must be someone at the helm. That's the question you should be asking." He spreads his arms open. "Go forth and cut those strings, Ms. Black. I'm already dangling because of your efforts.

It's almost curtains for me. But you need to keep going. Cutting and cutting and cutting until you get to the puppet master."

"How do I know you're not just saying bullshit to bait me?" I ask.

"You think I don't know that they're going to kill me? Even if the Masters vote in my favor, I'll still die. That's the only way you can be sure a secret stays safe."

I'm not naive enough to dispute what he's saying. Not now that I've seen how the society handles things. There's no saving Bernie, and I don't even know if that's what I want for him. But this is my last chance to learn what I can from the man. "You don't know what the artifact is, but do you know what it does?"

His lips spread into a wide grin. "It's a God killer."

# CHAPTER FIFTY

The next day we're summoned to Summerhill to vote in the Doctorate candidacy. Meaning the investigation has ended. Today is also the day we'll learn whether the new panel of Masters has made any changes to the ranking for the Bachelor candidacy.

"This seems fast." I play with the ends of my braids. "I thought an investigation would be a week or more. Especially given what went down yesterday."

"Clearly, the Masterium felt they'd seen everything they needed to see," Virgil says.

"Are they looking for this puppet master person?"

"We don't know," Corey says. "We can ask Margot when we get inside. She must have heard some things from Henry."

Virgil says, "If we knew what the artifact they were looking for was, it might help with motive and figuring out who would want it."

"It would, but Riley's not sharing more." Which I understand.

She's got her plate full right now with QBSS having their own vote to decide if Malachi will remain president or be replaced. And that's not even to mention the reckoning going on with her relationship.

Virgil glances at me sidelong, and I wonder if he's remembering that I was able to use Riley's chain the same way she had. I've been wondering about that myself. I'll definitely be having a conversation with Riley when she's free again.

"This might still shake out in Adam's favor. People are having conversations about factions creating unfair advantages now," Virgil says. "The factions aren't even supposed to exist, but now everyone's seen the bias firsthand. Most of the people in charge of the departments who failed to detect Bernie were Traditionalists. And the fact that August was disqualified on some after-the-fact technicality in a council that's Traditionalist stacked hasn't gone unnoticed either."

"Yeah, but people aren't going to vote for Adam because they're mad I didn't make the top five."

"*They might.* The candidacy is supposed to be fair. That's why they have a panel of Masters in the first place, to avoid professors playing favorites. Even if the system is rigged, there's an illusion of fairness, and they pulled the shroud away. It also means your chances of being reinstated are looking good." He stares at his hands and takes a deep breath. Over the past few days, he's done stuff like this a lot. Turn away from me and act like he has something to say but never says it. I guess now is the time. "And then . . . you'll have a decision to make."

I glance at Corey, who avoids my eyes.

"What does that mean?"

"Your brother needs a partner, or he'll be put in the Pen. Jules is now seen as a murderer, even though it's not his fault. And he's not a part of the society. No one is going to step up as a partner for him . . . but you can."

"But then you—" I hadn't thought through to this possibility because I hadn't expected to have any real chance of being put back into the candidacy. Virgil is right. I did all this to help Jules, and now I'm in a position to save him. But that leaves Virgil with nothing and no one.

"I've known what was coming since the investigation started. I would never expect you to choose me over your brother, and I wouldn't let you anyway. I refuse to compete with him."

I don't want to think of Virgil down in the Pen, but what else can I do? I know already that I would choose Jules over Virgil as my partner. And so Virgil's taking away the choice.

I can't believe that there's nothing else for him. There has to be something.

He shakes his head as if he can hear my thoughts. "I'll try to hold out until the end of the year. That's all I can do—" His voice cuts off. "I . . . I just need a minute, okay?" He walks out of Summerhill.

I look over at Corey, and she has tears in her eyes. "I wish I could try again," she says. "I would try again for him. I would. But I don't think he has that sort of time."

"He said that sometimes the society will sanction having two monsters. That means it's a possibility, right?"

"You saw what it did to Bernie. They've approved it before, but it was for a seasoned Master, and it was overseen carefully by the Doctorate, who was prepared to sever the bond if necessary."

"Then it's possible?"

"Yes, but—"

I rush out of the building. Corey calls after me, but I don't listen.

I find him on the grass, sitting with his legs sprawled out. I kneel in front of him, reaching out and grasping his hands. "Wait for me. I don't care how long it takes. I'll become a Bachelor. I'll become a Master. I'll get strong enough to have two monsters. Henry and Adam will back me because it'll be for you. You already know I don't like rules. If anyone can handle two monsters, it's me, right?"

This is something I don't know if I can ever achieve. I'm probably just setting myself up to disappoint Virgil. To let him down with this ridiculous goal that I've set for myself. But I want to do it. I want to help him in any way I can.

Virgil's shoulders shake, and he stares at the ground.

"It's me, right?" I say again, louder. "If anyone can do it, I can."

He looks up, smiling through tears. "That's right."

"I won't leave you down there. I promise."

Virgil squeezes our tangled fingers. "Okay . . . I'll wait."

"Promise," I say.

"Promise," he repeats.

Corey runs out. "Voting is starting!"

We're about to enter Summerhill again when someone shouts Corey's name. We stop and turn to where her parents are hurrying up the hill.

Ms. Yang says, "We heard you fought with Bernie and that you—you—"

"I'm a good fighter," Corey says, looking toward the escape of Summerhill.

"Of course you're a good fighter!" her mom shouts, and Corey lurches back. "But you could have been hurt! Something could have happened, and the last thing I would have said to you was that we had leftover gamjatang in the fridge." She ducks her head and wipes her eyes.

Mr. Yang rests a heavy hand on his wife's shoulder. "We thought . . . we . . ." He sighs. "We know we did wrong by you. We just wanted to protect both of you."

Corey stiffens. "But you didn't." Her voice rises as she speaks. "You protected *him*. It was always *him*. Everything was about him. I was just collateral. And then I come back, and you look at me like . . . like this. The *pity*."

Ms. Yang shakes her head. "No, we never pitied you. We were . . . we were ashamed."

Corey gapes at them.

"We almost lost you," Mr. Yang says, eyes shining. "Both of you. And you got hurt. Really hurt." He looks at Corey's left leg and then away. "It's our fault."

It feels like we shouldn't be here for this. "Maybe we should meet you inside?" I suggest, but Corey shakes her head. I glance at Virgil, who nods. If she wants us here, then we'll stay.

"That's why, when you said you wanted to go live with Dr. Liu, we agreed," Ms. Yang says. "And when you stopped talking to us, we didn't push back. We never wanted to lose you. But we almost did. We don't deserve a daughter as good as you." Her mom loses it then, dissolving into sobs and pressing her hands to her face.

"I . . . I . . ." Corey swallows. "I need some space." She walks away from her parents into Summerhill.

"Corey?" I ask, keeping my voice low.

"I just need a moment," she says.

"Okay."

We join the line of voters. It reminds me of when I've tagged along with my parents to vote. It's the same sort of mundanity. Checking of IDs and registration with the society. Confirming of status and designations. People chatting in line and speculating on the results.

"Have you forgiven them?" Corey asks me. "Your parents?"

"We're different people."

She shakes her head. "I shouldn't have said that—"

"Yes, you should have. And you were right. Even if our lives have similarities, they aren't the same. You don't have to do what I did. And honestly, I dunno, maybe I haven't forgiven my parents. But I want them around. Even if I only have one right now. But if you don't want the same, that would be fine too."

She bites her lip and looks at Virgil. "Would you think I was an asshole for it? I have two parents right here. Not everyone has that choice."

"It doesn't matter what I think," Virgil says. "And you can always change your mind. Or take it slow. Or cut them off. They didn't do what they did to me or August—they did it to you."

Corey nods to herself and enters the voting booth.

Virgil has his turn, and then me.

It's my first time voting, and it's for an organization that I only joined this year. My pencil hovers over Carrigan's name. I know I'm supposed to vote for Adam, but I can't help thinking about the things Bernie said. He was a snake, obviously, but some of what he said rang true. Our priority should be a cure. Not attempting to reconstruct a broken system. But I know Carrigan won't win. He doesn't even want to. Adam is at least willing to do something. There won't be another chance at this. There are no terms. There will be no new candidates.

I color in the box next to Adam's name. If Virgil and Corey and Henry and Margot and all these people can put their faith in him, I can too.

Summerhill is the most crowded I've ever seen it. There's barely any sitting room when we leave the voting area and most of us are crammed in with each other, the round tables loaded with extra chairs. I search around the space for Jules, but I can't see him. I assumed they would let him out for this vote, but maybe not. At least he's not in a cell like Bernie. They've set him up in a guest room in Summerhill for the time being.

Me, Virgil, and Corey find the table where Margot is already sitting with Isaac. The tables around us fill up quickly, and I spot Corey's parents looking for a place to sit. They pass by us, giving tentative smiles to their daughter.

"You can sit with us if you want," Corey says to them.

They sit down, almost rushing to the seats.

Corey adds, "This isn't me forgiving you."

The two of them nod, and Corey's shoulders relax. She introduces all of us to her parents properly.

"Good form with your kick in that last test," her dad says to me.

My face heats. "Uh, yeah, I had a good teacher."

Corey beams.

The doors at the side of the stage open and James, Adam, Carrigan, and the professors walk onto it. Our professors approach the podium.

Perez taps the mic and asks for attention, and eventually the chatter dies down. "We are honored to learn with you." The crowd gives the usual response. "We would like to make an announcement regarding the Bachelor candidacy. As you know, our former colleague Bernie Mathers was found to be traitorous. Due to suspicions of him being aided by Masters on the panel, which was confirmed in the investigation, it was dissolved, and a new one was created from those who attended the tests and were found to have not been involved in Mr. Mathers's crimes."

"So they found other Masters helping Bernie?" I whisper to Margot. "Do they know who they were working for?"

"It was just like Bernie. They got their instructions anonymously. All of them were being blackmailed. None of them knew who else was involved."

My first instinct is to say that the person behind this is James. He's a Doctorate candidate and therefore has the power to coordinate this. Plus, most of the people involved were Traditionalists. But at the same time . . . why would he blackmail his own faction into doing his dirty work? Aren't they loyal to him? If I were him, I would have picked Progressives so that if they got caught, it would make Adam look bad.

Perez continues, "The new panel has reevaluated the results of the tests and made their own point allotments. As such, the final scores have been affected and recalculated. The new rankings of the top five who will enter the initiation are as follows. . . ."

I want to hold my breath and not let go until he says all the names, but instead, I'm breathing too fast. Five candidates. That means a disqualification must have been reversed. It could be me, but it could also be anyone who was eliminated on a technicality early on. With a missing spot, they wouldn't even need a lot of points to make it.

"In fifth place with nineteen points, Hudson Barlowe. In fourth place with twenty-six points, Bryce Clark. In third place with twenty-seven points, Caden Mosser. In second place with thirty-seven points, Violet Sharma. And in first place with forty-four points . . ." He pauses for dramatic effect, and I imagine throttling him. "August Black."

The building erupts into cheers. People actually stand and clap. Properly this time. Not the weak half-assed ones I got at my nomination.

I'm looking at Virgil, and he's looking at me. "You did it," he says, a soft smile on his face.

"Yeah, I guess so," I say, still struggling to believe this is really happening.

Perez and Chen move to the side, and James, Adam, and Carrigan approach the podium.

James comes forward first. "We're pleased to welcome you to the first ever vote for Doctorate and are excited to share the results. You have seen each of us over the course of this year, and we've had a chance to share with you our vision of the future of the Learners' Society."

He steps back and lets Adam have the mic. "It was our father's will that our people be given this chance to select their leader for themselves. We are confident that whoever is chosen will lead us with the wisdom, care, and dedication given by the Doctorates who came before."

Adam gestures to Carrigan. The man sighs and approaches the podium. "I have nothing to say."

Everyone but me at the table cringes.

James doesn't even attempt to hide his fury, and Adam sighs. Their brother steps back from the mic with his arms crossed over his chest.

Adam returns to the podium. "The results are on their way. It should only be a few more minutes. We thank you for your patience."

Carrigan, apparently done with the whole thing, leaves the stage and ends up in a conversation with Henry, of all people. I haven't forgotten what he said about the psychology professor. Henry is definitely not his favorite person. I'm surprised that he's even giving him the time of day. And more curious is why Henry wants to talk to him at all.

While people chat among themselves, I notice Jules slip into the room. And he's not alone. Natalie is beside him, wearing a long shawl over a loose black dress.

I wave Jules over, which means both he and Natalie settle at our table. Corey's parents squirm in their seats. Isaac keeps looking at Margot as if to check that this is okay. And Margot herself stares down Natalie. I get that we're kind of the outcast table, but I imagine having Natalie sit with us is a whole other thing. Corey and Virgil both don't know what to make of this development and sit stiffly. I feel a little weird about it too, but I want to know why she and Jules are walking around together.

Jules says, "August, this is Natalie Soer."

She smiles. "We've met."

Jules's brow rises. "Oh. Okay."

"You can call me Nat if you like. Jules does."

I will not be doing that. Why are they so familiar with each other? What does Jules even know about her? I can't help but think of what Bernie said about the puppet master. Natalie is well-known as the leader of a faction that shouldn't exist, doesn't have the benefit of being the Doctorate's son, and still avoids any consequences for it. She's not an amateur. She led a rebellion and came out alive on the other side. A rebellion that had the means to steal highly protected serum.

"Nat has agreed to partner with me," Jules says.

My jaw drops. Someone at the table stifles a gasp.

Natalie laughs. "What a fun reaction."

"What does that even mean?" I look between the two of them.

"We'll be bonded." Natalie adjusts her shawl. "They've scheduled it for the same night as your initiation, actually." She flashes a smile. "Assuming you still go through with it." Several heads swivel to Natalie when she utters that last sentence.

"That's what I want to talk about." Jules leans in. "You don't have to do it for me now. You can drop out."

"Excuse me?!"

"Why don't we talk in private?" He gets up from the table and ushers me into a corner. I follow, scraping the chair back and not bothering to push it in. Once we're alone, he narrows his eyes. He's making his "stern" face. "Forfeit the candidacy and get as far away from these people and this monster bullshit as possible."

"And you get to decide that for me? Weren't you telling me not to live for other people just a few days ago?"

"Exactly! Now you don't have to throw away your life trying to save me."

I shake my head. "I can't leave Virgil. Not now, when I'm finally able to help him."

"A boy you met this year?! He's not worth it. These people are dangerous."

I reel back from him. "You don't know anything about him."

"You could die! Is he worth dying for? Is he worth your life?"

"He's worth trying to save. And I have no plans to die. Thanks for your vote of confidence." My brother stares at me like this is the first time he's ever met me, and I've started off the introduction by slapping him across the face. "You wanted me to live for myself. This is what I want to do. Are you going to be like Mom and Dad? Disappointed in me because I didn't do what *you* wanted?"

Jules deflates, his shoulders hunching. "Did you ever think that I just don't want to lose you too?"

"You won't."

"You can't guarantee that."

"Then believe in me."

Jules's eyes shine. "I always believe in you. You know that."

Adam taps on the mic and gestures to a Black woman holding a white envelope. "Mina is going to read the results."

Me and Jules look at the stage as she steps up to the podium and opens the envelope.

She smiles into the crowd. "The seventh Doctorate is Adam Shaw."

Everyone is cheering and screaming and hugging each other.

I'm watching the stage, where Adam is beaming, and find myself distracted by Carrigan, whose lips twist into a scowl before he turns away to hide it. James wears his disappointment plainly, but the brother who supposedly never wanted this has to hide his.

Maybe Natalie isn't the only person I should be suspicious of.

A MASTERY OF MONSTERS

# CHAPTER FIFTY-ONE

I went from being consumed with the realization that I could help Virgil right now to the realization that I will be doing the most life-threatening part of the candidacy without any of the preparation time that the others had. Shortly after Adam's win was announced, it was confirmed that the initiation would happen tomorrow as it was originally scheduled.

In less than twenty-four hours, I have to either bond with Virgil or potentially die trying.

Jules doesn't come with us to McIntosh Castle despite getting an invite. Apparently, Natalie owns a house and has offered him a room there. She has a dog. A detail that I could tell delighted my brother, because he's already sent me several pictures of the husky. They'll be living together for the foreseeable future, and he'll be reenrolled at Queen's for the winter semester.

When we get to McIntosh Castle, Corey and Margot make an excuse to leave the front sitting room. It's bullshit, but I don't call them on it.

Virgil crouches and plays with the fireplace, opening the gold-etched glass door and then closing it. Rearranging the charred logs inside. Fiddling with the poker. All while never touching the box of matches meant to light it.

I ask, "Are you going to tell me not to do it?"

"I'm not that selfless," he says over his shoulder. "It was easy to be when the choice was between me and your brother. He was the obvious pick. It didn't take much for me to tell you to choose him. You were going to anyway. But now . . . I mean, this was always the plan, wasn't it?"

It was, but still, Virgil's brow is furrowed. "What?"

"I won't tell you no, but you know that you don't have to do this, right?"

"I'm going to—"

"I get it," he says. "My life is on the line and all that. But I don't want to just be another person heaping something else on you. Because your life is at risk too."

I understand what he's saying, but it's not going to change anything. No part of me is prepared to let him rot in an underground prison, stripped of his humanity.

Virgil's shoulders slump. "It doesn't stop here, you know? After initiation, you'll still only be a Bachelor. You'll have to fight for the Master title. And then fight the next year to defend it."

"I know."

"I can at least promise to fight with you. Not just for the things in my life but in yours, too. Whatever it is. If you want me to spend a lifetime sniffing out your mom, I will. If you want me to keep an eye on Jules and Natalie, I will. Not because I owe it to you but because we're a team."

I suck back tears. I'm tired of crying. I remember thinking that at some point after Mom left. I was so exhausted from it that I stopped doing it. And when that happened, I stopped looking for her. But I never accepted her being dead. Virgil knows that. "We should also promise not to die."

"That would be ideal," Virgil says with a small smile, standing and leaving the fireplace be. "Let's get Corey and Margot so we can talk through the initiation."

I slump onto a couch while he goes and gets them. When they return, he sits next to me, and Margot and Corey sit across from us.

Margot looks between us and must assess that we're all right, because she launches into it. "The initiation happens in the tunnels of the Pen. You'll need to buy dry-fit clothes in the morning. It's cold down there, but you'll sweat. You'll be led inside, blindfolded so you can't see the route out, and then you'll both be given the serum."

Virgil shifts in place beside me. I wonder if he's thinking about how close that serum came to being in him when Bernie had it.

"Let's get to the flesh exchange stuff," I say. Besides being chased by an out-of-control monster, it's the part of initiation that disturbs me the most.

Margot gives me a grim look. "You'll have to eat a part of his body, and he eats a part of yours."

"Just some light cannibalism. No big deal."

My leg starts to bounce without my permission, and sweat builds on the back of my neck, even though I suddenly feel cold. It was one thing to hear these details way back when we started, when I never expected to be here, and another to hear them when this is what I'll be doing tomorrow. Cutting off a piece of myself. At no point in my life was that ever something I even had to consider, much less follow through on.

"And it has to be the monstrous flesh that you eat," Corey says. "It won't be considered that until he's fully transformed. It will actually scar him, so ideally you want to go for a tail if he's got one."

Margot says, "Unless you notice that he's got a regeneration ability. Some monsters do. That means anything is fair game, which would make things easier for you. But if it's life or death, regeneration ability or not, take what you can take."

"I'm not picky." Virgil plays with the edge of his shirt. "I'd rather lose something than have you die."

"You'll also need your own sacrifice." Corey lifts her left hand with its missing fingers. "I don't recommend fingers unless you're desperate. Hurts like hell, and you lose a lot of blood."

Sometimes, I don't know how Corey can be who she is given everything. She went into that competition, watched her brother consume her leg, had her relationship with her family destroyed, and then she left home to live in a library with near strangers. And she's still here, potentially retraumatizing herself to help me and Virgil.

"She's right," Margot says. "It's best to do your sacrifice closer to the end of things because of the potential dangers of blood loss. And this isn't a closed course. Other monsters will be able to get to you. Blood is a very distinct scent. It'll stick out like a beacon. Wear a scrap of fabric, headband, or something you don't care about so you can dress the wound. One, it'll help stanch the blood, and two, it'll block the smell somewhat."

"Exactly how much flesh are we talking about?" I ask.

Corey tilts her head. "It's unclear, honestly. I know people have used toes successfully. But don't do the baby toe because it might mess with your balance later."

"No stomach or thighs, you might bleed out," Margot adds.

Did not think I would be debating which part of my body to feed to Virgil tonight but here we are. Bile coats the back of my throat. "Why don't you just tell me what's best?"

"Ring toe, probably," Corey says. "There will be cold water somewhere down there. It can help numb it. But ideally, you can give yourself time to peel off a bit of skin from your arm. The toe is just faster."

I look over at Virgil. "And he has to eat it? How do I get him to—"

"It won't be an issue," he says, folding his hands together and gripping them tight. "Just throw it my way. I will, technically, already be trying to eat you."

Right. Well, at least that's an easy part.

Margot says, "After you've exchanged flesh, the mental connection will be made. From there, it's up to you two to sync together. Stay calm and match your breaths. You'll know the connection has happened right away. There's no mistaking it. But you don't have a lot of time. Once the exchange occurs, the serum will start to metabolize the flesh in both your bodies—that's what allows the connection in the first place. And it'll happen much faster on Virgil's end than yours. Once it's fully metabolized, your chance is gone. You have maybe five minutes. The serum becomes inactive at that point, and you won't be getting a second dose."

"And in that case," Corey says. "Run back to the starting point as fast as possible. Or, if necessary, crawl. If you can't do either, hide until the time runs down." She meets my eyes. *"Survive."*

The grandfather clock in the room chimes midnight.

Margot stands. "You should get some sleep. I'll see you tomorrow." We say our goodbyes to her as she leaves.

"Eat something before bed," Corey says to me and Virgil. "I'll heat stuff up for you."

"I'm not hungry," Virgil says, walking out of the room.

Corey sighs as she stares after him, then turns to me.

"I could eat," I say.

She smiles, and we go to the kitchen together. She pulls out a container of leftovers and opens it to reveal what looks like sushi—seaweed-wrapped rice with fillings. She sets a pan on the stove to heat, and grabs some eggs from the fridge, whisking them in a bowl with a pair of metal chopsticks while she adds salt and pepper. "I saw someone do this online with leftover kimbap. It's pretty good." She dunks the kimbap—not sushi, I know now—into the egg mixture and puts them in the hot pan.

When it's done, she brings the plate to the counter and gets us both new clean chopsticks. I start eating, and after a few seconds, Corey does too.

She's always said that Virgil and Dr. Liu eat what her mom brings. Never her.

"Both of you have to come back," Corey says. "Promise that you'll come back."

I swallow. "I promise."

I hope that it's a promise I can keep.

The Kingston Penitentiary is worse at night. They lead us around the back, but this time we go to a different entrance. This one has several locks and chains on it, and the stonework is especially dark and dingy. The professors go down there to prepare, leaving us waiting.

No one is interested in talking to each other. All of us are in our huddles of three: candidate, monster, and trainer. Even Caden doesn't have time to be his usual asshole self. Instead, he stands next to an older man who must be his trainer. His partner, however, is far away from them, crouched in a corner by herself.

I wish Corey could be with us, but she isn't allowed to come. There are no spectators for initiation. Instead, she's waiting in Margot's SUV in the parking lot.

I shiver in the cold. I brought my jacket specifically for this waiting period, but I can't manage to get warm. I'm sure it doesn't help to have a bunch of cold mental knives strapped to my body. And there's the phantom feeling of my phone vibrating in my pocket. I put it on silent because Jules was sending so many texts asking how I felt and if I was okay, and saying it wasn't too late to back out. He should be concerned with his own bonding.

Virgil is staring at the door the professors disappeared into. Has been since they left.

"What are you most afraid of?" Margot asks me.

I shift in place, tugging on my jacket.

"Go on."

I think about those tunnels and what I expect to meet down there. I'm scared of a lot of things. That I'll die. That I won't be fast enough cutting my flesh. Of the pain of that. But mostly . . . "That I'll fail."

Virgil looks away from the door to me.

"And you?" Margot asks him.

He swallows. "Of losing myself. Of not just becoming the

monster, but what I'll do then. Hurting August. And just . . . not knowing or caring."

"Henry asked me that question on my initiation night. Asked it of me *and* Isaac. And he never gave us an answer to our fears. I remember in the moment that it pissed me off. I didn't understand what the point of it was. And I could do the same and say nothing to you now, but I'm not Henry." There's something about the way she says that, like disappointment but also like resignation. "You two will need to join together during a time of heightened fear, so use that fear to your advantage. All you need is one point of connection to forge the bond. Don't forget what you said here."

The professors reemerge from the tunnels. Chen says, "We'll take the candidates and their partners down now. Trainers will be led to an observation room shortly thereafter."

I shrug off my coat and hand it to Margot. My fingers tremble, betraying me.

"Everyone is afraid when they go into this," she says. "There's no shame in it."

I look at Margot standing there, holding my coat in her arms. I think about if this is the last time I'll see her. We've had so many ups and downs, but she's a fixture in my life now. She fought for me, just like Virgil, and Corey, and Riley. I don't want to say goodbye, but I also don't want to lose my chance to say goodbye if I need to.

"I'll see you after," Margot says, deciding for us both.

"Okay."

Virgil's hand finds mine, and he squeezes. "Thanks, Margot. For everything." He takes off his glasses with his free hand and gives them to her.

She tucks the pair into my jacket pocket. "You're welcome."

A MASTERY OF MONSTERS

It's the last thing we hear from her before we descend, the only ones who do so with our fingers laced together.

We walk down a long hallway and stop in front of five doors.

Perez says, "We will be bringing each of you through your own door to a different starting point. Once there, a volunteer will deliver the serum. We've been able to advance to a formula that will have a delayed effect to give our volunteers time to exit the area."

"The trial will begin five minutes after injection," Chen says. "However, if your partner begins to turn before this time, consider it having begun then. You must exchange flesh in order to create the bond. Successful candidates will use this connection to bring monsters to the fourth and final stage of monstrosity, and the first evolution. Please note that this is a joint effort. The Master gives the monster their humanity, but the monster must use that clarity to return to their human form. Even if you've bonded and your partner is docile, if they cannot return to human form, you will both be disqualified. Do you understand?"

We all intone some version of an affirmative.

Perez picks up where she left off. "There is an hour time limit. This has been upsetting to some candidates in the past, but it is necessary. The apocalypse will not wait. We want our strongest soldiers to fight. If you cannot succeed within the hour, then you cannot wear the title. However, this time limit is simply for transformation. Monsters must be in human form once the hour is up, but you do not need to have reached the starting line. At the end of that hour, our Doctorate will keep all those who remain in monstrous form under control. Unsuccessful monsters will be transported directly to their cells. At this point, medics will also enter to provide emergency care, but only after the hour. If you require care or wish to forfeit during the initiation, no one will be coming. You will have to make your own way back to the starting line and come through these doors to get help."

If I fail but can stick it out for the hour, at least I'll be rescued. But glancing sidelong at Virgil, I know that's not a viable option. We need to succeed.

"I speak for both of us when I say that this has been a difficult candidacy, but we're proud of all of you who have made it here. And we wish you luck." Chen smiles at all of us then. "There is a learning in this."

"There is a learning in all," the candidates and monsters mumble. I move my lips without saying the words. None of us smiles back at our professor.

We're blindfolded and led through the doors by volunteers. I try to keep track of the twists and turns, making a mental map in my head. But we loop around a couple of times, and I wonder if that's purposely to confuse us.

Something pierces my arm, and I wince. The next thing I know, my blindfold is yanked off, and I'm watching the back of the volunteer as he runs away. Virgil presses a hand to his bicep.

"That asshole just stuck us both with a needle and ran away," I say.

"I guess he doesn't want to waste time."

I know I should stretch or something, but I can't bring myself to move.

Virgil grasps his elbows, holding his arms close to his body.

"We can do this," I say. "We just have to work together."

"How am I supposed to work with you when I'm like that?"

I nudge him in the shoulder. "Just like the second test. We'll each take some hits, and we'll walk out together, okay?"

A MASTERY OF MONSTERS

He can't manage a smile, but he tries.

We lapse into silence, and I'm about to fill it just to do something when I notice Virgil's breathing. I thought it was getting heavier from anxiety, but now it's built into panting. Teeth start to crowd his mouth and sharpen. He tries to say something but fails, instead crying out and clutching his stomach, bending onto his hands and knees.

I stumble back, cold sweat breaking out on the back of my neck.

Virgil screams, and as he bends over, his spine tears from his back, the white bone shredding through the fabric of his shirt and sticking in the air, growing flesh, lengthening and becoming thick. He spits as he tries again to say something.

His face cracks in two, the eyes bulging and seeping with something thick and pale yellow.

And finally, he manages to speak, in something that's part word and part growl: *"RUN!"*

# CHAPTER FIFTY-TWO

My feet thud on the concrete as I sprint through the maze of tunnels. They're large enough to accommodate the beasts roaming within them but still have a good number of sharp twists and turns. But there isn't much else. At least the second and third tests had hiding spots and foliage to blend into. This is all stark concrete and metal bars. The way this is made forces you to interact. I also have to deal with the potential of running into the wrong monster.

A roar sounds behind me, ripping up goose pimples on my skin. It could be any of the monsters, but it *feels* like Virgil.

I try to remember everything that Margot and Corey told me.

Flesh exchange.

I had to run because I needed Virgil to be fully transformed, but now that he is, I have to figure out how I'm going to do this. I also need time to slice my skin.

Which is impossible to do when I'm running. At the very least, there shouldn't be anything distinct in my scent. I'll smell sweaty, like any other candidate. In the morning, I even slathered on a leave-in conditioner that I don't usually use to confuse him. The pungent sewer smells are a natural cover too. I need to find somewhere to hide and prepare. Because once I cut myself and he smells the blood, it's over. It'll pierce through all that.

I scan the walls. There has to be something to help. They wouldn't just throw us in here with nowhere to go.

Finally, I spot a grate in the ground. I stop and lie down on my stomach, peering into its depths. The hole is small. Enough for me to fit, but definitely not enough for Virgil to fit.

I slot my fingers into the grate and tug, squatting around it and using my thighs to push myself up. But it isn't moving. I run my fingers over the sides, scrambling to find some sort of trick. Though at the same time I'm wondering if I'm wrong and this is just a drainage grate, and it isn't meant to be any sort of hiding spot.

Until my finger slides over a screw. It's a flat head. I yank out one of my knives and slide the tip in, turning the screw as fast as I can. When it falls out, I could cry. Instead, I move to the next one.

The ground trembles under my knees, and I work faster, sweat slipping down my face as I twist my wrist and another screw falls.

The same guttural roar sounds again, but this time it's like the claws are working at my throat. The sharp tips grazing the skin. Too close.

I'm turning the last screw when Virgil comes around the corner.

Even without having ever seen him in this form, I know him. Those are his eyes. Dark amber.

He walks on all fours, and he's at least eight feet tall and covered in thick wiry black fur. His tail is long and has metal spikes running along the full length. The metal is so shiny that it looks almost like a gemstone. The long nails on his paws are made of the same thing. His face has transformed into a long snout, packed with those rows and rows of teeth like a shark, his maw stretched and distorted to accommodate them all. As he spots me, the tips of his triangular ears twitch.

He makes Isaac's form look like a docile puppy instead of a hell hound. Virgil is the sort of beast that brings you nightmares.

And though the eyes are his, there's nothing of Virgil in the depths of those irises.

He's gone.

The monster is here.

*Who's afraid of the big bad wolf?*

He races toward me, bounding on all fours as I struggle with the last screw, turning it as fast as I possibly can. In the end, I don't even get the thing fully off before I rip up the grate and jump inside, landing hard on my knee with a cry and dropping the knife. I scramble forward in muddy water and scream as something slices across my back.

I keep moving forward, eventually getting my feet under me, and crawl to the far corner of the underground space. It isn't a tunnel, it's a fucking hole. There's nowhere else to go.

I've trapped myself.

Virgil roars from above me and his tail whips down into the space, attempting to lash at me, but it's about a foot too short.

I press myself against the damp wall, huddling my shoulders and reaching tentatively toward my back. There's a long slice, its edges ragged. I whimper as warm blood flows onto my hands. I try to slow my breathing, taking a long deep breath in through my nose and holding it, then pushing it out through my mouth.

I reach under the fabric, feeling along the wound and find the spot that hurts the most, where a piece of my skin is flapping free.

"Motherfucker." I clench my teeth against the pain.

Virgil must have caught me with the tip of his tail, which, as I watch it probe down into the space, has a sort of bulbous growth covered in fur and dozens of those metal spikes. Like a goddamned medieval mace. It's shining with my blood.

"Just breathe, just breathe," I chant to myself as I hold the dangling flesh with one hand and reach back with a knife with the other hand. I take a breath in and slice the skin free. Mercifully, it comes off with a single cut, but I still scream as I do it. It falls with a wet plop into the shallow, murky water that fills the hole.

I retrieve it and lay it on my palm to check the size. It fills the area. More than enough.

I strip off my sweatshirt and rip it up, tying the fabric tight around my body. I still have the dry fit shirt on that I was wearing underneath.

Unless I want to either bleed out or have Virgil eat my corpse, I need a plan. A way out.

Squinting, I look around the hole, hoping for some sort of opening to reveal itself. There has to be something, right?

But the more I look, the less likely that possibility becomes.

I have my bit of flesh, but I need some from him.

Virgil's tail is a terrible option. Fur and barbs and spikes. Anything I get is more likely to kill me as I try to swallow it. I need a better piece, but I also have no way to get around that fucking tail.

I slide along the wall, feeling for a notch or something that might hint at a secret exit. There has to be something down here. I don't believe they'd put a hole in for the sake of it. This is supposed to be a test, after all.

I fail to find anything, but Virgil does.

He's still whipping his tail around in the space, trying to get me, when he hits something on the far wall that flies off, revealing a small tunnel.

A tunnel to freedom.

A tunnel to freedom that will require me to get past that tail.

I gnaw on my lip. If I try to run past that thing, he could spear me in my gut without a second thought, ripping out entrails as it comes out.

Somehow, I need to distract him. I look at the piece of skin in my hand. I cut it in half. I throw a piece into the water, where it lands with a wet plop. Virgil's tail pauses its probing and then slices straight down, sticking its spikes into the skin and whipping it up and out of the hole. I don't hear any chewing, though there also wasn't much to chew on. But when the tail returns to the hole, the skin is gone. Assuming typical monster behavior, he should have eaten it.

Unfortunately, that also means it's currently metabolizing. I need to move fast.

I hold the other half in my hand. If I cut it up smaller, he might not be able to find the pieces, and I don't know if the half I threw is enough for bonding. I need to toss this and then go for it.

I'm trembling. One wrong move and I'm dead.

I toss the piece of skin, and the instant Virgil's tail moves for it, I hold my breath and shimmy past the barb toward the tunnel. Moving quickly enough to get to it in time, but not so fast that Virgil's more distracted by my movement than eating the skin.

A MASTERY OF MONSTERS

His tail disappears, bringing the skin up.

I leap into the tunnel just as the tail comes shooting back down. I swear I feel his fur brush the back of my neck. I drag myself through the tunnel and hope it goes to something useful. At the end of the space is a piece of metal that I manage to kick out. In that room, there's another grate overhead, with footholds on the wall leading up to it. I almost start crying but stop myself. I'm doing something right. Handholds mean these spots are supposed to be used. I squat in the water and splash it onto myself, ignoring that it's literal dirty sewer water, and hoping it'll cover the blood scent. I know blood is the stronger smell, but the wound is wrapped, which helps.

When I pop my head through the grate, Virgil's still bent over the original grate.

He doesn't turn.

I plant my feet with intention, inching up close to him and unsheathing two knives, one for each hand. My eyes rove over his body. I don't know that I have room to be picky. But a chunk of his back should work. I need to jump on him like with that ferret centipede monster in the third test. Give myself time to get a piece of flesh and hope he won't risk stabbing at his back and potentially hurting himself.

I'm so close. So very close.

My fingers inch toward his back.

The toe of my shoe scuffs against the floor. He whips around, opening his jaw and lunging for my face.

I jump and stab out with both knives on instinct, and they both lodge into his right eye, each downward at a diagonal. The perfect angle to take out a chunk. He growls and bats me away with one of his paws. I fly across the hallway, landing hard on my back, the wind knocked out of me. I twist onto my side, gasping. Virgil is crying and whining, scratching at his face with his paw.

My knives are on the floor, and maybe a foot away from me is a chunk of white flesh with red veins. Still struggling to breathe, I scramble on my knees to it, grab the piece of eye, and shove it between my lips. It bursts against my tongue, filling my mouth with a thickness that I want more than anything to spit out. I fight a strong wave of nausea.

Virgil's tail whips out and spears me in the shoulder. I manage to keep one hand clamped around my lips when all I want to do is scream. It's the worst pain I've ever felt. The metal spikes dig into muscle and break bone. I bite my tongue multiple times chewing. My vision goes in and out.

I swallow.

He rips his tail out of my shoulder, and the pain is so exquisite, so complete, that I don't even scream. I just drop forward onto my front, forehead smacking onto concrete, blood pooling around me, my body getting cold.

I don't want to die.

Not now.

Not like this.

I close my eyes and try to even out my breathing, the way Chen taught us, but I can't do it. I can't calm down.

I'm sobbing. Everything fucking hurts. I don't want to be here. I want Mom. I want her now more than I've ever wanted her.

*"You're too afraid to fail," Mom says, frowning as I drop from the slack line. We've been at this for hours. I can't get the hang of it. "If you're too scared of failing to try, you'll never be able to do anything."*

She was wrong, though. I wasn't afraid of failing. I was afraid of her *reaction* to my failing. I wanted to prove to her that I could do it. To avoid that frown and her shaking head. I wanted her to smile at me. To tell me I was good enough. To stay with me.

Virgil howls. It's not like before. Not aggression and wildness. It's long and drawn out. Like the choking, sobbing breaths I took on the second day when Mom didn't come home.

I open my eyes, and he's there. One of his eyes is bleeding, missing a chunk of itself.

It doesn't matter. In there is the snarling beast that Virgil was so afraid of becoming. Somehow, staring into his eyes, I know it isn't the monster form that he was really scared of. What Virgil is afraid of is the child inside him. The one who was shunned because of his parents. The one who hated that they were taken from him. The one who wanted to lash out. To hurt. To maim and kill. To make them all pay. The part of him that he shoved down no matter how much he wanted to set it free.

This is what the serum let loose.

I have it too. That monster lives in me. I hurt people I loved to keep them away. And if I had the power, I would have done more. Would have made Bernie pay for what he did to Jules. Would have made Caden suffer for the way he treated me. Made the Masters on that panel who disqualified me writhe in pain. And if I got a hold of whoever is to blame for Mom being gone, I would tear them to shreds.

Dr. Weiss said we all have this shadow inside us. The invisible monster. He wanted it controlled. Tamed. Well-behaved.

Virgil wants that too.

But I don't.

I *can't.*

I won't be the good girl again. Desperate for praise. I won't be boxed in. I won't be what is expected.

I don't want to tame the monster.

I want to use it.

In the distance, at the end of the hallway, a monster whips around the corner. Blood on its jaw, hackles up. It sees me lying prone on the ground, an easy target.

My eyes slip closed, but I'm not gone.

Virgil steps forward on fur-covered legs. The world is darker with him over top of me.

Shadows were never meant to stay in the darkness.

They can only truly be seen in the light.

When I scream, it isn't just me. It isn't just Virgil. It's more. It's the officer at the door saying they need to close Mom's missing person file. It's Henry cupping his hands around my face while he explains that Mommy and Daddy won't be coming home. It's my "friends" turning away from me in my grief. It's the people who sneer at me in Summerhill and mutter that I shouldn't be alive.

And it's not a scream.

It's a *roar*.

A roar that makes the wall shake. That makes the lightbulbs flicker. That sparks in our blood like a flame and burns in that perfect middle of pleasure and pain.

This is how me and Virgil become Master and Monster.

# CHAPTER FIFTY-THREE

I'm startled awake by a horn sounding. I have no idea for what time. I stumble to my feet, gasping. My body is too warm. I turn to the left and meet a pair of huge dark amber eyes. Perfectly intact and self-aware. He's curled up beside me. Tame as a puppy.

I don't need Virgil to tell me that he stayed in this form because I was vulnerable.

I look down the hall. The other Monster is gone. It ran away when it heard the roar.

We should have ripped it apart.

Virgil could. I'm aware of every bit of taut muscle in his body. Of the strength and deadliness of his tail.

The only reason we didn't is because I know Virgil wouldn't have liked that.

And so, we didn't.

This isn't what I thought the bond would be like. Knowing things like this.

Seconds later I understand that it's because our bonding is so fresh.

"Change back," I say. Or I think I say it. I might also just think it.

I walk toward the exit. Not with a mental map. I can smell them, where they're gathered, so I follow my nose. I don't need to look back to be aware of Virgil behind me, but I check on him anyway.

Each time I look over at him, something has changed. Less fur. Smaller teeth. A face slowly knitting back together.

We pass a smear of flesh and limbs on the floor. I stare at it. Beside it lies a sledgehammer, the wooden handle broken.

Caden.

I want to squat and scoop bits of him into my mouth. To smear the blood and entrails on my lips. Just the thought holds something euphoric. Like a bite into a perfectly ripe piece of fruit.

"August," Virgil says, and I turn to him.

He's in human form again and naked. Though in this moment, I don't care. It's like getting excited about seeing your own body in the mirror. It's not novel or interesting.

I look back at the mash of flesh.

"Don't."

I lick my lips.

"Don't," he says again, and I snarl at him. He snarls back.

We stand there, staring each other down.

Another horn sounds and breaks me out of my thoughts.

Too close together. That must be the last one.

When I turn back to the mess that was once Caden, vomit crowns at my throat, and I can't imagine how I wanted to eat that seconds before. Medics rush toward us, and I let them treat me. Not that there's much treating to be done. My shoulder is numb, and the bleeding has stopped. Same with my back. I don't notice the pain either. They tell me that's just adrenaline.

Satisfied, the medic lets us go. He gives me and Virgil shiny blankets to cover our skin. We exit the tunnels with them, returning to the hallway with its five doors where we started.

On the other side, Hudson, sweaty and bruised, rushes to the door we came out of. Caden's door. I wonder if that was Caden's partner with bloody teeth who we scared away. She's gone now. They'll be taking her underground.

Caden never even gave her a chance. So she didn't give him one either.

"Your buddy's a smear on the ground if you want to go get him." I love the way Hudson's chin trembles when I tell him. Almost as delicious as it would have been to taste Caden's corpse. "You can definitely get some into a jar and follow that around if you'd like."

"August," Margot says, coming forward with my jacket.

"What? You don't think if our places were switched, Caden wouldn't be laughing about my death with his buddies? But I have to be the bigger person?"

Margot and Virgil share a quick look.

There's a crust of blood around the insides of her ears. "What happened?" I ask.

"You did." She massages her forehead. "Don't worry about it. Just . . . chill, okay?"

Virgil says, "She's still coming down."

"I hope you're right," she replies, handing him his glasses.

I don't like the way they're talking about me. Virgil's worried about what other people will think. I don't care about other people.

Margot takes a deep breath. "How you act right now is as much of a test as that initiation was. And they would love to put you down. To put you *both* down. So shut your mouth and breathe."

She can't tell me what to do. We could fucking crush her in an instant.

I squeeze my eyes shut.

*No.* I don't want to crush Margot. We wouldn't do that.

I breathe. In and out. In and out. In and out.

And something monstrous bleeds away from me.

But also, some of it stays.

The medical team does one final check before letting us leave.

We're in the parking lot, a few feet away from the car, when Corey runs out of it. I don't think she's supposed to run on that leg, but she does it anyway, crashing into both me and Virgil and pulling us in close. The three of us stay like that for a moment before Corey pulls back, wiping tears from her eyes.

The car door opens again, and my eyes widen when Riley comes out. "Glad to see you alive," she says.

"Sorry I forgot to send you an invite," I say. "Thought you'd be busy."

"I'm never too busy to see if you do or don't get eaten. Thankfully, someone thought to call me."

I glance at Corey, who flushes. "I thought she would be invested in knowing how you were doing. Then she insisted on coming."

I tilt my head. "And how did you get her number?"

Corey grins. "I asked."

No one can say that girl is shy.

Riley says, "Corey offered to send me regular updates about what's happening with the Bernie stuff since you" —this with a point at me—"needed space to deal with what was going on with your brother and this death tournament."

"Well, I'm alive," I say.

Virgil shakes his head. "You should have stayed with the medic longer."

"He bandaged me up and said I wouldn't die. It's fine."

Virgil's regeneration ability extends to me, though not as strongly. I'll definitely have scars. Virgil's eye, however, is in perfect condition. Better than perfect. I stare at the glasses on his nose and then snatch them off, a realization dawning on me. "Wait, these aren't real?!"

He rolls his eyes. "Of course not. You thought I had heightened strength, hearing, and smell, but somehow poor vision?" He takes his glasses back, settling them on his nose. "They're *aesthetic*."

"You fucking would."

"You're taking the survival of your imminent death in stride," Riley says.

I shrug. "I'm a go-with-the-flow sort of person."

"Of course. Well, since you're fine, I'll head out." She fingers the chain at her neck. "But the two of us are going to have a conversation about this."

"I'm not joining QBSS."

"Did I ask you to?"

"Well, actually—"

Riley waves her hand. "I'll reach out. We'll do coffee."

"What about Malachi?"

She grins at me. "Oh, he's been demoted." She pulls another necklace out from under her shirt. This one has a tiny sickle pendant. I originally mistook it for a scythe. But when Riley holds it, it's just as deadly. "Looks like they'd rather be led by the girl who was trying to solve the murders instead of the guy who wanted to pretend they weren't happening."

She was dangerous enough without a blade.

Riley gives a final wave goodbye before walking over to her car, pulling out of the parking lot unnecessarily fast, and driving away.

"And she's siiiiiiingle," Corey sings.

"I'm glad you took the time to get that information."

She presses a hand to her chest. "She supplied that all by herself." She spots the blood on Margot's ears. "What happened to you?"

"A roar," Margot says.

Corey laughs. Margot doesn't. "Wait, are you serious?"

"Our roar." Virgil's eyes flick back to me.

"But roars are like . . ." Corey throws me an apologetic glance. "No offense. But it's historically a shitty ability as far as defensive stuff goes. It's just intimidation. It doesn't actually hurt people."

"Theirs was different." Margot's forehead wrinkles. "And of course, they had to show it off. So now we'll have to deal with the fallout of that."

"It's not that serious," I say. But it's Virgil's skeptical thought laced with anxiety.

"Don't worry about it now. Rest. You did it. Both of you."

I think of what Virgil said yesterday before we got into this. That this isn't the end of the fighting.

It's just the start.

# CHAPTER FIFTY-FOUR

If I never see Summerhill again, it'll be too soon.

We're brought to a room with the other successful candidates. Corey came through with her late birthday present, a beautiful black gown for the Bachelor ceremony. I have no idea how she found out my size and perhaps don't want to know, but it fits perfectly. It's strapless but tight enough that I don't feel like I'm going to fall out of it, with a double slit up the sides that exposes the fishnet tights I chose to pair with it, finishing with my shiny Docs. Virgil is in a matching all-black suit that has been tailored impeccably. I can begrudgingly admit to myself that he was right about good tailoring. He's like a dashing dark knight. It fits for someone like him, so willing to fight for everyone else. I don't know what that makes me. The sword, maybe. Essential for his survival and liable to cut.

I touch the chain at my neck. It came in a package delivered to me at Vic Hall with a note from Riley that said, *I figured you'd prefer it in black.*

The necklace doesn't warm every time I touch it, but it can. Maybe I shouldn't have taken this. It's a promise of sorts, I know. But I would make that promise without it. Because it's for Riley. I trust that she has my back.

Everyone's heads turn as me and Virgil enter the holding room.

Hudson immediately looks away from me. Between the two of them, I would have expected Caden to be the one standing here. Alive. About to be given the Bachelor title. Instead, it's his underling. Thankfully, he doesn't want anything to do with me. To be honest, I think he's afraid of me now.

As Virgil greets the other Monsters, Violet comes over and folds me into a hug.

"Glad you didn't die," she says.

"Same to you."

She has a bandage over her temple and is now less the ring finger on her left hand. When Bryce joins her in congratulating me, he's limping. He might have lost a toe. I congratulate them in kind. It'll be nice to go into the next semester knowing there will be decent people besides Margot in Henry's Mastery group.

"And not a scratch on you." Violet looks me up and down. Then she pauses as she spots my shoulder. "Or almost."

"Better than it could be."

I have scars on my back and shoulder, but they look like they've been there for years. Not something that only happened yesterday.

Violet leans forward. "I heard the roar was you guys."

"It was so loud, I thought you two must have been, like, right next to us," Bryce says.

I nod. "Yeah, that was us."

Violet says, "Holy shit. My trainer said because they were

wearing headphones in the observation room, they got it way louder. I felt the shaking and knew I heard something, but I was also kind of preoccupied trying not to get eaten."

"Understandable."

I'm starting to feel a bit of Margot's and Virgil's anxiety. I didn't think people would make such a big deal out of the roar thing. Then again, I don't see how it could hurt us.

The door opens, and Chen sweeps in. She's in an emerald gown that brushes the floor. "We're going to put you all in separate sections, so you enter from different points. Symbolic of the tests, you know? Professor Perez will call your names, and you will present yourselves. Follow me. I'll get you in place."

Me and Virgil are shoved into a tiny room with thick velvet curtains in front. It's dim. The only reason we can even see each other is because we're standing close.

The knowing of everything has gone away. Virgil is back to having his thoughts private. And it's the same for me to him.

"We did it," I say, as if just realizing.

Virgil holds out his hand. I clasp onto it as if we've been doing this for years. Pull our forearms close.

It's not enough.

I let go of his hand and tug him to me fully, winding my arms around his neck, and he brings his hands to the small of my back.

I meet his eyes.

There's a danger in this. He knows it too. I don't need our minds to be connected to sense that.

"Aren't you a rule breaker now?" I ask. "Break a rule with me."

"This isn't the one to break," he breathes.

I begin to pull away, but he keeps me close. He presses his

forehead against mine. His glasses brush against my cheeks. "So we can only do it this one time. Once, and never again."

"Once," I repeat. "And never again."

No sooner are the words out of my mouth than Virgil is pressing his lips to mine. It's not just a kiss. It's him and me, and me and him. It's everything that we are to each other now. Not just Monster and Master. But Virgil and August. This is the boy who fought with me and for me. I'm the girl who fought with and for him. We would have died for each other. Not even out of anything sentimental. Not because we're in love but because we didn't want to imagine a world without the other.

When we separate, it's only because we need air.

Our foreheads stay connected, panting loud, our breath mingling with one another.

Once is never going to be enough.

"August Black and Virgil Hawthorne!" Perez calls from the other side of the curtain.

I swallow and turn toward them as the fabric is swept aside. I step forward. Virgil steps behind me. I turn to him. "What are you doing?"

"Monsters walk in the back."

"Fuck that." Virgil gives me an exasperated look, but there's a smile on his lips too. Now I know how they taste. The fullness of them. "You worked just as hard for this."

I can never again think of the marker "Monster" in lowercase. I didn't do that test alone. If I get a title, he should have one too.

I hold out my arm and he takes it, and we walk into the ballroom side by side.

The curl of James's lip when he sees us is worth it.

A MASTERY OF MONSTERS

He's not the only one irked at our departure from tradition. More than a few Masters toss us sneers or turn up their noses. This isn't like when I was reinstated as a candidate to cheers and applause. Most of those people were students. At the lowest rungs of the society. These are the elite. And it seems that they are not so easily impressed.

Adam, however, beams at us from the table at the head of the room between his two brothers. I can't help but seek out Carrigan's face, looking for some sort of reaction, but his expression is placid and bored.

The room is filled with faces both new and familiar. These are senior Masters and Monsters, people with power and sway in this world, and now we're only a few steps removed from being just like them.

An usher leads us to our table, which includes Margot, Isaac, Corey, Henry, Laira, and Jules. I stiffen, watching my brother, but all he does is hold his fist out for me to bump.

"I wish you hadn't done it," he says as we tap knuckles. "But you did it wonderfully."

"Thanks." I sit between him and Virgil. "You and Natalie are bonded?" I eye him like I'll be able to physically see a difference now that he has a new partner.

"Yup. A much easier process than what you went through." He straightens his tie. "The Doctorate broke the bond to Bernie right before. They were only keeping him alive until I was bonded to someone new. I guess he won't be for long."

I exhale. I can't make myself feel bad for Bernie, even knowing he was manipulated. But I do feel for Davy. For his son who's already dead because he dared to try to live free.

Virgil nudges me and points to Adam, who is standing from

his seat. He opens with the usual call and response before launching into his speech. "Congratulations to the candidates who are to be seen and acknowledged henceforth as Bachelors. These brave pupils put their lives on the line to become strong enough to protect our society, both Bachelors and Monsters." There are some titters from the crowd. I assume they don't like the Monster acknowledgment. But now Adam is the Doctorate. He promised real equality. Things are going to change. At least, I have to believe that. "Tonight, I hope you'll enjoy this meal with your friends and families, and the honored Master and Monster pairs who were invited to join us. These people are now your peers and potentially your future mentors. I wish you all luck next semester in the Monster's Ball."

Adam sits down to a chorus of applause, and food is brought out. Once he's seated, his smile drops and settles into a flat line, only reappearing when someone turns to speak to him. I frown. He won. You'd think he would be happier.

"What exactly does the Monster's Ball entail?" I ask Virgil. I know of it, but we never got into the details.

"People say that if the candidacy is the test for Masters, then the Monster's Ball is the test for Monsters. You're put into direct competition with every new Bachelor in the province. We'll be in a bracket and forced into one-on-one showdowns. The expectation being that Monsters evolve significantly between competing in their first Monster's Ball and defending the next year. And lucky for us, Ontario always has the highest-level candidates." He doesn't bother to hide his grimace.

"Fantastic." That is something I will be avoiding thinking about until after winter holidays.

As servers move around the room, Henry clears his throat and looks at me. "I know that you and I didn't get off to a great start, but you've done something very impressive. You too, Virgil. It's not simple to participate in these tests, and even more challenging to pass them." He nods to Margot. "Margot has done a wonderful job training you, but next semester she'll be preoccupied with her own preparations to defend her title at the Monster's Ball."

I look over at Margot, alarmed. I mean, I knew she would be busy. But I didn't realize that meant she wouldn't be my trainer anymore.

She straightens in her chair. "I could maybe—"

"Don't overextend yourself." Henry slides his eyes to her. I still don't like him, but more on principle than for something he's actually done. If anything, he's only helped. Not every time he should have, but enough. "It's best to let Margot concentrate so she can achieve what's needed for Isaac."

Isaac hunches his shoulders, and Margot stares at her plate. Neither of them speak against Henry.

He continues, "Pairs need to place inside the cutoff twice— once as Bachelors, and once as Masters. When you do it in two consecutive years, you have more opportunities, which is what we want for Margot and Isaac. The worst-case scenario, of course, is failing three times. Those people are stripped of both their title and partner like our disgraced colleague, Bernie."

Bernie, who's sitting in a cell somewhere waiting to be killed. I say, "I'm not giving him excuses, but he didn't do it by himself. He was being directed by someone else."

"Yes." Henry adjusts his tie. "And trust me, the society is looking into it. Adam is readying a task force."

"The same society who didn't even notice what was happening until we dropped it in their laps?"

There's shifting at the table. Virgil fiddles with his shirt cuffs. We're silent until the server has left.

"Use that," Henry says. "That rage. That feeling of injustice. That is what will serve us as we reshape the Learners under Adam. Even if he does not want to move as quickly as we'd like . . . Sometimes justice is slow, but—"

"Slow and steady wins the race," Margot says.

He grins. "Exactly."

"You have a lot to say," Jules muses, meeting Henry's eye. "But you don't like to just say it."

"Welcome to the Learners' Society. Though I'm curious to hear your point of view."

"Bernie was a sad man who loved his kid. Davy is dead. His dad will be soon. And even though someone else was pulling the strings, they're either too crafty or too high up to be punished. You act like that's going to change, but you can't promise it."

"Who says I can't make that promise?"

Jules raises his brow. "You're going to guarantee them being brought to justice?"

"Yes. Because I believe in what we're doing here, Mr. Black. And change is made by believers. An opinion I thought your partner held as well."

"If she does, she hasn't shared that with me."

"Interesting. Well, in any case"—Henry turns back to me—"I would like to invite you to join my Mastery group in the new year alongside Violet and Bryce. We'll get a chance to work closely together on making sure you all succeed in the coming trials. Corey will also be coming on board as a research assistant."

"Part-time," she adds, straightening. "I'm going to restart classes at the dojang. I want to brush up." She eyes me. "And I've already signed you up."

"I know, I promised."

She's acting casual but, in a couple of sentences, she stood up for herself against Henry and noted that she'll be going back to her family's dojang. I haven't wanted to pry, but I know she's been tentatively talking with them again.

"Right, part-time." Henry gestures to Jules. "I would offer to take you on board as well, but your partner already has an assured title, and the group is for prospective Masters and Masters-in-training. What do you think, August?"

Virgil is practically vibrating beside me. This is exactly what he wants. I level my gaze at Henry. "Thank you. We'll be happy to join."

Under the table, Jules grips my hand.

After dinner, Henry excuses himself to mingle with the other guests, and Virgil makes me walk around the room doing the same thing. We repetitively introduce ourselves and accept congratulations. For every pat on the shoulder, there's a ghost of a knife at my back. For every connection made in the society, you make an equal enemy.

"Oh!" Virgil says. "There's Corris. I'll be right back. I want to pick his brain."

I'm glad for the moment to myself. I hang around the dessert table, trying to figure out what I want to try.

"I hear the Basque cheesecake bites are delicious." I whip around at the smooth voice and come face-to-face with Natalie. I didn't see her earlier and assumed she wasn't here. But of course she is.

"Congrats on bonding," I say. "I appreciate you pairing with my brother."

"It's my pleasure. I get a lot of joy in helping young people. Speaking of . . ." She tilts her head to the side. "Did you get my card?"

"What?"

"The birthday card I sent."

I set my plate down on the dessert table a little too hard. The weird card with that story I assumed was some prank of Caden's— I'd forgotten about it until this moment. *That was the day we learned that any God can be killed.* I think of what Bernie said only days ago with new interest. "You know about the artifact? The one that kills Gods?"

Natalie leans forward. "The what now?"

Is she really going to play this game? "What Bernie was looking for. The artifact."

"Oh, is that what he wanted?" She laughs. "Silly. You kill a God with your teeth and claws, not a tool." She gazes across the room at Virgil. "Let me give you some advice that I wish I'd been given. When you're told a story, think about who benefits from that narrative."

"Like your story from the card?"

"Yes. Here, I'll tell you one more. Once upon a time, there was a woman who wanted to see the man she loved live free. She joined a group that believed in it. Eventually, she became the leader of that group. They grew stronger, and they started to make progress. Real progress. Not a cure, but a way to break the chains her lover wore. Another man didn't like that very much. He sent them on a mission to die. One of them came back, but she stopped leading. She could barely move without him." Here, Natalie's voice goes high, and she has to pause. It's the first sincere emotion I've ever seen from her.

A MASTERY OF MONSTERS

"Then one day, that horrible man died. And every single person he wronged rose up. The woman was reborn. She would never love like that again, and the man she hated was dead, but make no mistake, she would have her revenge."

I lick my lips. "I won't let you use Jules for whatever you have planned."

Natalie laughs. "Oh, honey. You don't have to use anyone when you have the same goals."

"Goals of setting Monsters free and letting them kill people?"

The good humor drains from her face. "With everything you have seen and learned about the society this semester, you still believe whatever it is they feed you. I thought you were smarter than that." I swallow under her stare. She's standing across from me, but it feels like she's looming over me. Pressing down on me with her eyes. "Do you know what the difference is between my faction and the Progressives?"

I shake my head.

"The Progressives want equality for Monsters within an inherently unequal system. Dr. Weiss never intended for Monsters to be equal like the Progressives believe he did. Otherwise, we would know the name of the man they call Patient Zero, would we not? It was Francis McLaughlin, if you care. My predecessors fundamentally disagreed with the Progressives' approach, though I admit the theories they threw around didn't help our reputations. But I can assure you that since my ascension to the role, we have been focused on one thing and one thing only, and that is the complete and utter destruction of the Learners' Society." She does lean toward me now. "You cannot achieve liberation within a system of bondage. And I'll tell you a fun tidbit: your Progressive leaders understand this exactly.

They don't want your partner to be free. They just want to give him enough shiny things to distract him from the fact that he's in chains."

I fight not to brush down the goose pimples that have risen on my arms. Everything in me is screaming to deny what she's said, but I can't. It was perhaps the worst mistake I've ever made to think that this woman was just some unhinged leader of a failed faction. She's not. Natalie Soer is a powerful woman with a vision and the people to make it happen.

And now my brother is bonded to her.

Jules spots us and starts walking over. A beatific smile graces Natalie's face again. She raises her glass to me. "Congratulations, again, Ms. Black. I'll leave you with one final question to ponder: Who brings the apocalypse?"

"I'm so fucking tired of riddles."

"Aren't we all?" As Jules reaches us, Natalie grins. "Perfect timing. There's someone I want you to meet."

My brother gets whisked away, though he throws me an apologetic look over his shoulder. Meanwhile, Virgil returns to my side. "Got some great tips about Monster evolut—" He stares at me. "What?"

"Who brings the apocalypse?"

"The God of Monsters," Virgil says automatically, then frowns. "Where did you hear that?"

"How did *you* know that answer?"

"It's from old lectures that Dr. Weiss would give. Some were transcribed. I used to read them for fun."

"On brand in the worst possible way."

"Some of us like reading!"

"What does it mean?"

A MASTERY OF MONSTERS

He shrugs. "People want to know why tragedy happens to them. Dr. Weiss never discovered what caused Monsters to be born into this world or why the spontaneous birth rate started rising, so it was more of a placeholder. I don't think he believed in a real God of Monsters. He was as close to an atheist as you could come in his time. And even he said in later lectures that it was only a concept. Why?"

"Natalie just asked me that."

Now it's Virgil's turn to roll his eyes. "Ah yes, the Pro-Libs believe there's a real God of Monsters. And that what they're doing is serving Them. But they believe in a lot of bullshit that's been disproven. Though you can never disprove a God."

"Unless they die," I say.

"If they die, I think it's far more likely that they were just human."

What I actually care about is if Natalie and Bernie are talking about the same God. And if this God exists, whether it's a real entity or a person, should They be killed or saved from those who wish Them harm?

I pick up my plate and load my desserts onto it, including the mini Basque cheesecake.

It's none of my business.

I'm invested in keeping the people I care about safe.

The Gods can die if they want. It's not my job to protect them.

# CHAPTER FIFTY-FIVE

I look out the car window at the other people alongside us in the ferry. Virgil borrowed Margot's SUV to take me to Bailey's place, where I'll spend the winter holidays. I thought Jules would come today, but he ominously said that he had affairs to get in order. I cross my arms over my chest. We just got him out of one bad situation. I hope he hasn't found himself in another one. People died in Natalie's rebellion. I won't let Jules become a casualty. I plan to keep a very close eye on him and his new partner.

Now it's just me, Virgil, and the radio, which is, predictably, playing Christmas songs.

After last night's ceremony, we're back to being dressed down. Or I am, anyway, in my jeans and puffy jacket. Virgil is in slacks, a dress shirt, and a peacoat.

"What are you going to do during the break?" he asks, tipping his seat back.

"Not study."

"Of course." Virgil stares out as the island gets closer. There's something at ease in him now. It's more noticeable, the ways he held himself tight, fearing what was to come. Though it still isn't over. The Monster's Ball is next semester. But at least I have three tries at the Master title, and three tries to defend. Better odds than the Bachelor candidacy.

I don't know if he's thought about the kiss. It's both like it just happened and like it happened years ago.

This is the one rule I know he won't budge on.

Because it's not arbitrary or unfair. It's obvious why it's in place. We're bonded for life. Nothing would make that messier than a relationship.

"What will you do?" I ask him. "Contemplate how deciding to partner with some random girl with a knife actually worked out for you?"

"It wasn't that random. Henry did see you on the security footage and tell me to check things out."

"What?" I have a vague memory of the first time we met, and Virgil saying there was a ping or something on the cameras. "I thought whoever was watching told you to go outside. Like, the people from the Mastery group who watch them."

"Yeah, but it's Henry's system. He gets pings on movement too." He shrugs. "If anything was fate, it was the fact that we'd only recently set it to see that far because of what happened to Samantha."

"So . . . he saw me throw?"

"Yeah, he just didn't think that was enough to choose a partner, but, I mean, we did work well together at Big Sandy Bay. Plus, you needed me to help with your brother, so the bargain cemented us together. It made you devoted in a way I couldn't be sure the others would be."

"Fair enough."

I don't mean to be disappointed. After all, I knew those facts too. Virgil chose me because it happened to work out that way.

Even so, I can't help thinking about Henry's role. That man never does anything by chance. Plus, the guy from the Mastery group, *he* was the one who started that fight. That actively antagonized me. Almost . . . almost as if he was trying to get me to fight with him. To see what I could do.

I shake my head.

That doesn't make sense. If Henry wanted Virgil to see me, to know me, to pick me, why was he such an asshole when we first met? I was the last person he wanted Virgil to pair up with, it seemed.

The ferry docks, and Virgil drives me to the tiny house community and carries my bag to the door. Bailey thanks him and then disappears inside with my backpack, like it's a bunch of luggage instead of the same thing I would have brought to stay for a weekend.

Me and Virgil face each other in the snow. I stare at him as flakes fall onto his head and gather in his lashes.

"Well," I say. "See you next yea—"

"Those weren't the only reasons I picked you," he says looking down at his shoes. They're rubber things that protect his loafers from the snow. I spent at least ten minutes making fun of him for them.

"Okay . . ."

He looks at me then. Properly. "I picked you because you were what I wanted to be. When you wanted to do something, you just did it. When you were angry, you let it out. You weren't afraid to be yourself even if you knew people wouldn't like it. I wanted to be that way, but I was too scared. And at first, I was scared to see that in you. It's why I left like that at Big Sandy Bay. But then, I couldn't stop thinking about you. I met those other people who Henry lined up for me, and every single one I compared to you."

I swallow. I want to look away, but it's like his eyes are trapping me. Keeping me still.

"I wanted *you*. But, well, I guess I'm used to not getting what I want. So I didn't try to approach you again. But then you turned up at McIntosh Castle. I tried to play it cool, but it was like . . . *that moment* felt like fate. I knew I had a chance to hold on to you, and so I took it. I proposed that deal. You are the greatest risk I've taken in my whole life, and I was right to do it."

My bottom lip trembles, and I bite onto it.

*Once, and never again.*

"Despite the many times I'm sure you've regretted it?" I ask with a laugh. I want to cut the tension of the moment. To ruin it, because living in it is too hard.

"I never regretted choosing you. Even when you pissed me off. Even when I wanted to quit. I still knew I had only gotten this far because I was with you." He reaches out and adjusts one of my braids, tucking it behind my ear. "That girl from my mom's story . . ."

"What about her?"

He doesn't move his hand, keeping a hold of that single braid, the tips of his fingers resting on the side of my neck. "She should have let the bird sing whatever it wanted exactly as it chose. She should have asked for its story and learned why it pecked and fought the others. Maybe then she would have realized that it was beautiful and strong and special just as it was. Maybe then they could have had more between them than obligation."

"Didn't you say they were friends?"

"I thought so. I needed to, I think. So I wouldn't feel bad for the bird. And I suppose it never occurred to me that she could have loved it as it was." He drops his hand and smiles. "Have a good holiday, August."

"You too," is all I can manage.

It's several more moments before he finally walks away.

*Once, and never again.*

Bailey insists on hosting us for Christmas because her tiny home is actually larger than Dad's small, shared apartment. She was aghast that he didn't remember the Trini dishes their mom taught them. We're all given a crash course in making paratha roti from scratch, the secret to a good curry, and John Legend's (Bailey adjusted) macaroni pie recipe. The latter of which she waited until Grandma died to admit is better than hers.

We bring it out to the barn for the shared holiday dinner. We do it on Christmas Day, though it's technically nondenominational, so me and Mia just do snow-themed decorations.

Last Christmas, we were out in the cold, crying and handing out missing posters. Eating warmed-up casseroles dropped off by my parents' coworkers.

Now we're just living without Mom.

I sit between Jules and Bailey with a loaded plate. Dad is on Jules's side and keeps clapping him on the back or shoulder, making excuses to touch him, as if to remind himself that his son is there. He doesn't know how close he was to losing him. Bailey has her camera beside her. She's been taking pictures nonstop the whole holiday. I think she doesn't only want to look back on her memories with Mom. She wants new ones with us, too.

A MASTERY OF MONSTERS

After dinner, Dad and Bailey get involved in an Uno game with some of the other community members.

Jules stands and says to me, "Let's go for a walk."

I have basically become macaroni pie after several helpings, and the last thing I want to do is walk around in the cold, but I grumble and stand, shrugging on my jacket.

The two of us venture out into the snow. The area is surrounded by multicolored lights. They're part decoration and part functional, according to Mia.

My brother leads us toward the back end of the land. The whole space is flat, and so even though we're far away from the community, we can still see the twinkling lights.

"I lied," Jules says.

I look back at him.

My brother is staring at the ground with his hands in his pockets.

"You lied? About what?" I ask.

He swallows so hard, I see it going down. "I needed to talk to you away from all of them."

"Jules . . ."

"I was with Mom the night I got bit. But . . ." He swallows again. "But I already knew I was a Monster. I was born that way. Mom told me what I was a couple of days before because she saw the signs. We were supposed to meet someone that night. I think that's why she was so tense and got pissed at you about training."

I freeze in place, eyes glued to my brother.

Mom knew Jules was a Monster, and she'd been training me, training us *both*, because she knew. Was she training me . . . for Jules? For the candidacy? Like Corey's parents had? "What happened?" I ask, because I know something must have.

"After you left that night, we went to meet that person. Mom didn't want Dad to get suspicious, so she went by herself, and I snuck out after. She picked me up, and we drove to the Scarborough Bluffs. Except the person didn't come, and we were attacked." Jules clenches his hands at his sides. "It looked like a blur, but it went after her, except then it saw me and came after me instead." He sucks in a breath. "It bit me, and she was begging it to let me live, that she would die if it would just let me live."

I don't like this story. I don't want to hear this. I want to bury my head in the snow and pretend this isn't happening.

"It backed off like it was listening to her. Mom told me to join QBSS and to keep everything a secret to protect the family, and then she threw herself over a cliff," Jules finally chokes out. "And it left me alone."

No. That can't . . . Mom can't . . . I shake my head and back away from Jules like physical distance between us will change his story. He's wrong. Mom would have found a way out of that. She always had an exit plan. *Always.* "Did you see her body? Maybe—"

"She's gone! I saw . . . she's gone. The Monster only left because it got what it wanted." He shakes his head. "I couldn't see it properly. I didn't lie about that. If I'd seen its form, if I knew who it could have been . . ."

There's a roaring in my ears so loud that I can barely hear what Jules is saying.

Mom isn't missing. She was never missing.

Mom is dead.

And she knew about QBSS. Knew about Monsters.

Jules lied about everything because she told him to.

My brother keeps speaking, though I'm struggling to listen to him. I slump to the ground. He says, "But no one in QBSS knew her. And they—I mean, the way they talked, they hated the society and Monsters. That's why I thought Bernie was the better shot. He said he knew her, but now I know he lied. I decided to cut my losses and bonded with Bernie, and I thought everything was fine, but then Davy killed that girl and shit hit the fan."

I hide my face in my hands. It's too much. All of this.

She can't be dead.

She can't be.

I stopped looking, but I never stopped believing that Mom was alive.

"Do you know what this means?!" Jules asks.

I peel my hands away from my face to meet his eyes. "I . . . I . . ."

"Someone came after her! They wanted her dead for some reason. The amount of times we moved, you think that was a coincidence? Training us the way she did? She was running. Someone with control of a Monster killed her."

"Or a Wild." My voice is detached from my body.

"A what?"

I scrub my hands over my face because I don't want to be doing this right now. I don't want to be learning this, and I don't want to be teaching about the society either.

Jules says, "I thought I could handle this myself. I wanted you to stay out of it, but you have a direct connection to some of the highest-ranking people in the society. Henry and his Mastery group, and Adam, who is now the Doctorate. If anyone would know what happened, one of those two must."

What would that mean if Henry or Adam knew Mom? She

must have been in that dossier Henry put together, but did they actually *know* her? They must have known something about her if she and Carrigan were friends. Why would he hide that from me? Did he set that fight up at the park? Set *me* up? What for?

Mom is dead.

She's gone.

We won't ever get to move beyond that moment. She was so mad at me for wanting to stop training that night. I thought she was just pushing another expectation on me when really, she was scared. She was trying to prepare me for whatever she thought was coming. She was trying to protect me. Protect Jules. And in exchange, I yelled at her and ignored her call.

I scream just to get it out. Scream and scream and scream. Tears running down my face.

She should have told us! So many things would be different if she'd just told us!

I'm choking, gasping; it's like I can't breathe.

Mom is dead.

She's not coming back.

Our family is never going to be back to what it was. Not ever.

Somehow, I'm curled up on the ground in the snow, and Jules is sitting next to me. I don't know how long I've been like this. My tears are frozen to my face.

Mom isn't just dead.

She was murdered.

They hunted her down, and even if she chose death, they forced it on her.

Jules is muttering about how it's his fault. I see it from my brother's perspective. He felt guilty, and at the same time, he was slowly becoming a Monster. He kept everything inside, trying to do it all himself, the way Jules always does.

And I hadn't exactly been in a position to help with the way I was acting. I left my brother alone.

I raise my head and look at Jules.

I still have him. He's still here.

This time, he won't be alone.

"There's more," Jules says. My muscles clench. I don't know how much more I can take. "Mom said to go to QBSS, to join them, but then she also said that once this person saw me, he'd help. That once he knew she was dead, he'd come find me. But he never showed up."

"Who?"

"She said it was too dangerous to give a name, but . . . she said . . . she said he's the Doctorate's son. I didn't understand it because I didn't know what a Doctorate was. I asked Bernie, playing it cool so he wouldn't know why I was interested, and learned there were three sons. But I don't know. I looked them over when they questioned me at Summerhill, and none of them reacted."

*Carrigan.*

That motherfucker lied to me. Played it off like Mom was no one to him. But she knew enough about the society to be targeted by them.

And worse, he'd abandoned her. She'd been counting on him to help Jules, and he looked my brother in the eye at Summerhill and didn't do shit even when Jules's life was on the line.

*Go forth and cut those strings, Ms. Black.*

*Cutting and cutting and cutting until you get to the puppet master.*

I don't know who to blame for her death, but I will find someone.

Something needs to go in the gaping hole where finding Mom used to be. That hope I always held on to.

I need the person who did this.

Next semester, I'll enter the society with a new goal.

I'm going to find whoever killed Mom, and I'm going to have my Monster rip their fucking throat out.

# EPILOGUE

They gather in Henry's office because they always do. The fire in the elaborate brick fireplace is roaring, and Henry pokes at the wood, rearranging it to better stoke the flames. His guests are both overheated, but neither of them says anything to discourage his actions. They rarely do.

Henry releases the poker and joins them in the armchair opposite the sofa where they've settled. The pieces are older than all three of them, and his mother used to keep them covered in plastic and stored away. She was too afraid of them being ruined to use them. Henry, however, feels differently. And she's dead, isn't she? His whole family's dead. Mother, father, and little sister. He may as well do as he pleases. And he wants to sit on the same furniture that his ancestor sat on. It's worth the risk.

Not everything is, however, which is what they've come to discuss today.

"Well, last year was rather eventful, wasn't it?" Henry says, reaching for the tray of coffee on the low table between them. "I'm glad to see that we're all still here and could get together at the beginning of this new year."

The guests do not much care to dabble in pleasantries, but it's Henry, so they do. They discuss how happy they are to see Adam take on the role of Doctorate, and how fortunate it is that Virgil didn't lose his humanity and become sentenced to live underground, and even a small note of sadness for Bernie, who was a pawn in a bigger game.

Yes, a much bigger game is to be played.

Unfortunately, someone else is playing their own game too.

Though the guests don't think of it like that. As a game. But Henry has to think of it that way. He's played a game of hide-and-seek with his family for years. They're great at the hiding part— cozied up under earth and worms where he can't find them. What he likes is that when you lose a game, it doesn't matter. It can't, or you're a spoilsport. If it goes wrong, you simply start over again. You give yourself another chance to win.

Henry likes to win.

And August Black has the potential to become an integral piece of his winning strategy.

He's always known that. It's why he arranged things that way. Though he admits that he hadn't anticipated her personality, nor how the others would react to her. That had made things difficult. He's still deciding if it was worth it.

"What do we think of her?" Henry says, and both guests straighten, because this is what they want to discuss. Henry knows this too.

"What exactly do you want her to do?" Margot asks. She refused

A MASTERY OF MONSTERS                573

both coffee and tea. Henry found her somewhat difficult last year, but in a way that's interesting. She is evolving beyond him. He enjoys that. Appreciates when his students strive to outdo him.

Of course, she figured out what he'd done months ago. She was astute like that. She didn't know what he'd chosen August for, but she was aware that he had chosen the young Ms. Black and arranged to make it seem like Virgil was the one choosing. And Margot hadn't liked it. She wanted to be let in on his plans, but it wasn't time yet. And in Henry's opinion, Virgil *had* been involved in the choice. He was the most important part of it.

Virgil is the most important part of all this.

Before, he'd just had promise, but now, he's evolved into producing real results. Those bent prison bars are proof.

What Henry cares about is if August is to be given some credit for that. If she can be counted on to help Virgil evolve even more. And after . . . well, can she be counted on for what comes after, too?

Henry leans back in his chair. "I want from August what I want from all of you. Though I admit that she's quite a bit more remarkable than anticipated. Rough around the edges but effective. I want to know if she can be made to care about this cause. She has her brother now. Her goal is achieved. Will she want to push for more?"

"She will," Virgil says. "She cares." August has a viciousness to her that Virgil lacks. And something has been building in the girl lately, Henry has noticed. A burning ember sparking into a flame. It's righteous, indignant, and ferocious. Henry would like it very much if they could use it.

Henry turns to Margot. This is her chance. She could expose what he's done. The play he set up to bring August into this game. Or could reject involving the girl outright.

"She cares about Virgil," Margot says. "That will be enough."

Henry lets a slow smile spread on his face. That's his girl. She doesn't trust. No, Margot's been burned too many times for anything as fragile as trust, but she can see the cards laid out, and plays accordingly. Even when she disapproves.

He'll have to watch her. He can't have her switching sides in the middle. It's best if they're all on the same team.

"Well then," Henry says, folding his hands together. "Let the real games begin."

Revolution, Henry thinks, is on its way.

# ACKNOWLEDGMENTS

I finished the first draft of my first novel in my first year at Queen's University. It was also my first time having my heart broken, as I sent my werewolf book to literary agents and got no response. I wasn't cut out for writing, I thought. I needed to grow up and concentrate on schooling and pursue a "real" career. I was an overachieving student unaccustomed to failure. It wasn't until my third year of university when I decided to give writing another try. I read aloud from my failed novel to my creative writing course peers only to stun them into an awkward silence. *Oh,* I thought, *This story is just bad. It will never work.*

Years later, I looked at it again. In it, amongst the cliché phrases and meandering plot, I saw a young Black girl who, despite growing up in predominately white spaces, had chosen to draft a novel starring a Black woman. When I attended university, I didn't feel Black enough and simultaneously felt hypervisible because I was Black. I avoided Black community spaces on campus, convinced that I didn't belong. But I had found belonging in fiction. And as an adult, I found it in the writing community once I had unpacked enough to understand that there is no right way to be Black. I made the decision to rewrite and reimagine my first novel, and to follow a girl who felt abandoned discovering community for the first time, while also examining what it means to be critical of the spaces you occupy and the way you occupy them.

I hope that following August's journey helps you learn to be kinder to yourself, and give yourself more grace, even if you're a young overachiever like I was. I failed, yes, but I didn't fail forever. And I'm still learning to love myself, but I love myself now more than I ever have.

Thank you to my amazing agent, Kristy Hunter, who is always such a champion of my works, even when half of the time I'm like, "Here's something random I wrote," and drop it in her inbox. And thank you to my editor, Sarah McCabe, who I feel so privileged to continue to work with. I trust her to understand my stories and vision and enhance them with her thoughtful and thorough feedback. Five years into my career, I am so appreciative of having such a fantastic agent and editor who not only help with my work but also advocate for me in the publishing industry.

Thank you to Cassie Spires, who is always so enthusiastic about my work and was so supportive of this project. Fun fact—we met and became friends in university! It feels poetic somehow that she was the first reader of the edited first draft of this book. And thank you to the wonderful friends who listened to my lengthy rants and panic texts and also celebrated with me when I was screaming and joyful: Laura Fussell, Kevin Savoie, Lindsay Puckett, Lainey Kress, and Ashley Shuttleworth.

A huge thank-you to the Canada Council for the Arts, whose generous grant helped support me during the research phase and writing of the first draft. It also allowed me to travel to Kingston, Ontario, to do the setting and on-location research that was very necessary after years away from the city and campus. Having been a peer reviewer myself, I understand how competitive this granting process is, and appreciate the immense privilege of being selected to receive funding.

Thank you to Lune Dube, Kendra Herber, and Dani Moran for their invaluable character consultation and feedback. And thank you to the Tyendinaga Mohawk Territory Language and Cultural Centre for their translation services.

And thank you so much to Tom Roberts for the gorgeous cover illustration and to Greg Stadnyk for his continued fantastic work with the cover design. Thank you to Anum Shafqat for all the communication and hard work you do behind the scenes, and to Maryam Ahmad for all your publicity efforts and championing of the book. Another thank-you to Cayley Brightside for continuing to be such a joy to work with and the entire Simon & Schuster Canada team.

Thank you to the rest of the Simon & Schuster team who put in the work needed to make my words into the finished novel you read: Justin Chanda, Karen Wojtyla, Anne Zafian, Jen Strada, Elizabeth Blake-Linn, Chrissy Noh, Caitlin Sweeny, Bezi Yohannes, Perla Gil, Remi Moon, Amelia Johnson, James Akinaka, Saleena Nival, Elizabeth Huang, Trey Glickman, Shannon Pender, Amy Lavigne, Julia Ashley Romero, Lisa Moraleda, Nicole Russo, Christina Pecorale and her sales team, and Michelle Leo and her education/library team.

And finally, thank you as always to my wonderful partner, who has always been so supportive of me and my career, and to my adorable beagle coworker for keeping me company as I put this story together.

# LISELLE SAMBURY

is a Trinidadian Canadian author and Governor General's Literary Awards finalist. She has a love for stories with dark themes, complicated families, and edges of hope. In her free time, she shares helpful tips for upcoming writers and details of her publishing journey through a YouTube channel dedicated to demystifying the sometimes complicated business of being an author.